Dear Reader,

Welcome to the American West. A land of unspeakable beauty and undeniable harshness. Even in modern times, the West is still a symbol for the freedom and promise of America, a land of growth and opportunity.

This untamed wilderness has become an integral part of our cultural mythology, and it is here that we have set our unique collection of historical short stories. Here is a collection that captures the spirit of America's last frontier.

Award-winning authors Heather Graham Pozzessere, Patricia Potter and Joan Johnston have created three unforgettable heroines. Women with the courage to leave their pasts behind them and head out in search of a new life. Women with the strength to follow their dreams and forge their own destinies.

We are delighted by this opportunity to bring you these three stories and hope you will enjoy them.

Sincerely,

Tracy Farrell
Senior Editor
Harlequin Historicals

Untamed

MAVERICK HEARTS

HEATHER GRAHAM POZZESSERE
PATRICIA POTTER
JOAN JOHNSTON

Harlequin Books

TORONTO • NEW YORK • LONDON
AMSTERDAM • PARIS • SYDNEY • HAMBURG
STOCKHOLM • ATHENS • TOKYO • MILAN
MADRID • WARSAW • BUDAPEST • AUCKLAND

HARLEQUIN BOOKS
300 East 42nd St., New York, N.Y. 10017

UNTAMED!
Maverick Hearts
Copyright © 1993 Harlequin Enterprises B. V.

All rights reserved. Except for use in any review, the
reproduction or utilization of this work in whole or in part
in any form by any electronic, mechanical or other means,
now known or hereafter invented, including xerography,
photocopying and recording, or in any information storage or
retrieval system, is forbidden without the permission of the
publisher, Harlequin Books, 225 Duncan Mill Road, Don Mills,
Ontario, Canada M3B 3K9

ISBN 0-373-83259-1

LONESOME RIDER
Copyright © 1993 by Heather Graham Pozzessere.
AGAINST THE WIND
Copyright © 1993 by Patricia Potter.
ONE SIMPLE WISH
Copyright © 1993 by Joan Johnston.

Published Harlequin Enterprises B. V.

Printed in the U.S.A.

CONTENTS

Lonesome Rider

Heather Graham Pozzessere

Chapter One

Indian Territory, 1867

He had only been standing at the bar at the stage-coach stop a few minutes when she first arrived.

And from the moment she arrived, he should have known there was bound to be trouble.

Even with the war long over now, and hordes of Easterners and, in particular, displaced Southerners traveling west by wagon loads now, such women were rare.

In fact, he didn't think he'd ever seen a more beautiful woman—white, black or Indian.

Something drew his eyes to her the moment she walked through the door. He'd heard the stage arriving, of course, and that was surely why he, ever wary, had allowed his gaze to slide toward the door. And then he had seen her.

The setting sun was behind her and she stood silhouetted for a moment in the door frame, trying to pierce the misty environs of the inn, he imagined. But while her eyes adjusted, his were free to drink her in.

She had chosen her clothing well for her westward journey: a simple cotton gingham day dress with a bodice that buttoned all the way to the neck. She couldn't possibly be wearing more than one petticoat. Yet the very simplicity of her dress seemed to enhance all that was so very elegant about the woman. She was tall and slim, but beautifully, gracefully curved at the right places. Her throat was long and white and regal. Her face belonged on a statue—one of those ancient Greek ones—it was so exquisitely shaped and molded with fine cheekbones, a straight nose, perfect lips, wide-set eyes and femininely arched brows. Her hair, drawn into a net, knot at her nape, shone beautifully despite its severe restriction there. It was a fascinating color, not red, not gold. Soft tendrils escaped the knot to wisp gently over her forehead and delicately frame the edges of her perfect face.

She stepped farther into the room, her expression giving nothing away. It was an all right place, such as stage stops went, Blade reckoned. Neat enough, with a number of wrought wood tables strewn here and there, a big cast-iron stove squarely in the center and a long bar stretching the length of the room. There were rooms upstairs for overnight guests, intended for the more gentle types of clientele traveling west these days. There were no handsome carpets about as might grace the floors of many such an establishment back East, and there were certainly no pretty paintings to decorate the walls. But Jeeter and Molly Dickinson, the sprightly old couple who ran the place, kept it up, kept it nice, kept it clean. Poker games went on some evenings, and some evenings, Molly was as likely as not to sit back in her old rocker and grace all her guests with a little Bible reading.

There was no reason that the woman with the beautiful face and fiery hair shouldn't have come here, Blade decided.

But from the moment she approached the bar and old Jeeter assured her she could have a lemonade, Blade felt certain that there might be trouble.

Since he stood at the end of the bar, it was natural that her eyes should fall his way when Jeeter went off to call Molly from the kitchen for the lemonade. She studied him with a certain fascination, then seemed to realize that she was staring. She blushed to a rosy hue and quickly turned away from him, focusing her eyes on the bottles on the shelves behind the bar.

What had she seen? he wondered. Anything more than a tall man with nape-length ebony-dark hair, black eyes and hard features? Anything more than a half-breed?

The stagecoach driver had come in now, a gray-beard with a full face of whiskers and a little jerk to his walk. His guard, the man riding in front with him, followed behind him.

His beard was grayer, but he was skinnier, smaller and had a more pronounced limp. Maybe he was exceptionally good with the rifle he carried. Blade hoped so. Blade picked up his whiskey and left the bar area free to them, striding across the room to a table in the rear. He sat with his back to the wall—he never exposed it, never.

He was barely seated before it began. The door burst open again and another group came in, surveying the place from the door. Men. Three of them.

All three were dressed in long, dirty dusters as if they'd been out on the trail some time, sleeping in their coats and wearing them through whatever. They wore old slouch hats pulled low over their brows. They had a look about them that indicated they were brothers. All were of the same medium to tall height, had the same sandy colored hair, and the same rough and craggy features.

The tallest of the three—perhaps the oldest or the leader—strode straight toward the bar. Jeeter had just come back with the lemonade. "Whiskey, a bottle of it, and good stuff, not watered-down slop," the man said to Jeeter. Jeeter looked uncomfortable right off, glancing toward the stagecoach driver as if he might find some assistance there.

Jeeter turned to the bar, found a bottle and set it on the bar. "Glasses," the man growled. "What do we look like, a herd of animals?" He started to laugh and turned to one of the men behind him. "A herd of animals, eh, Petey? Is that what he thinks we look like?"

Blade could have answered that question quickly and easily, but for the moment, he was determined to hold his peace. He didn't want trouble himself. Not here, not today. There was still too much that he just had to get done.

After that nothing much would matter.

"It's the best whiskey in the house," Jeeter said.

But the man wasn't listening anymore. He had turned his attention to the woman standing at the bar and he exhaled in a long, slow breath, then finished the sound with the touch of a whistle. "She's the best in the bar, I dare say!" he exclaimed, ignoring the whiskey bottle and walking toward the woman. "Hello there!" he said.

She turned to him, refusing to slink away. Her eyes slid over him in a scathing fashion. "Hello," she said in reply, the sound of her voice as cold as ice. In all of his life, Blade didn't think he'd ever heard anyone say a single word with such ice-cold distaste.

The man at the bar tried to ignore the sound of it, but the tick at his throat and the blotchy color that came to his face belied the look of calm he tried to give her. "What are you doing in these parts? Traveling by stage, eh? I'll get you wherever you want to go much faster, honey. And I'll make the trip a hell of a lot more interesting."

From his rear table, Blade could see her eyes now as she stared at the man. They were green. Sharp, sparkling, bright, beautiful green. They held a startling sizzle of cool anger.

"No, thank you," she said, once again her words unerringly polite, and yet her tone...

Enough to freeze the flames in hell, Blade thought.

"Now, wait a minute," the man murmured, inching closer still.

The old stage guard stepped forward. "Now you wait a minute there, sonny—" he began.

The man spun around. "Petey! Jed!"

Petey snatched the rifle from the guard's hand. Then Jed spun him around so that he started to go flying against the wall.

"See here!" Jeeter spat in outrage, but Jed had leapt over the bar by then, and before Jeeter could pluck up his old dusty Colt—one that had seen some good service in the Mexican War—Jed had seized the weapon and pointed it at old Jeeter.

Now the fellow at the bar touched her, reaching out dirty fingers to stroke one of those tendrils of her gold-and fire-colored hair. "My name's Matt, lady, and I like to hear it. I like to hear it screamed out real good and it don't matter none whether the scream comes from pain or pleasure."

It didn't seem that there was any way to avoid trouble. Blade was deftly, silently on his feet. But the woman wasn't going down without a fight, either. Even as Blade approached the pair, her hand was connecting with the fellow's face, nails clawing it apparently, because Matt-who-liked-to-hear-his-name was crying out himself.

"Bitch!" he swore, and, grasping her, started to slam her down on one of the rough wood tables.

That was Blade's opening. He gripped Matt by the shoulders, wrenching him up. He spun him around to face him, and when he made sure that Matt saw him he gave him a sound punch to the jaw.

Matt went down, clutching his chin, eyes on fire, furious.

"Shoot the breed!" he roared.

Blade spun, the knife from his calf flying. He caught Jed in the hand before the man could begin to fire Jeeter's old Colt.

Petey was aiming the guard's rifle at him. Blade drew his own Colt, leveling it right at Petey's eyes.

Petey dropped the rifle.

Blade stepped over Matt, reaching a hand down to the woman. She accepted it, meeting his eyes, and leapt up from the table. Then she cried out a warning.

He swung around. Matt was up, reaching for his gun. Blade swung out with his fist again, determined he wasn't going to leave any dead men lying around for the law to find, not if he didn't have to.

He caught Matt, and saw that Jed was leaping across the bar, coming for him. He started to turn, then saw that the woman was both quick and opportunistic. She had grabbed the whiskey bottle and cracked it over Jed's head. Glass cracked, whiskey sprayed, and Jed went down. That left Petey, who was rocketing toward Blade again.

Petey was wild—all brawn, no brain. Blade stepped aside, let Petey shoot by, then brought both hands clubbing down upon his back.

Petey fell to the floor with a soft sigh.

Blade met her eyes again. Over Petey's prone body. She was studying him anew. Carefully, with no apology. And no blush now.

What was she seeing?

A half-breed still. Maybe she was glad that he was a half-breed, thinking his speed and skill must have come from the years he had spent killing and scalping the white men who had first come to tame this land.

Maybe she was even wondering if he spoke her language.

"Good going, young fellow!"

It was the stage driver, hurrying to him, reaching out to shake his hand. "I can tell you, son, the company will have a fine commendation for you!"

Blade shook his head. "No, no commendations. Thanks. I just think you should get on your way."

"There could be a reward!" the stage driver said. "A monetary reward! You can't just let—"

"No commendation!" Blade repeated, unaware that his voice was every bit as cold as hers had been earlier. "You need to get under way here, before another group like this shows up."

The driver seemed to have sized him up quickly and was ready to obey. "Mrs. Dylan, he's right. Seems our best move now is to get going on, before more riffraff shows up." He spat on Matt's downed body and stepped over it.

But Mrs. Dylan didn't seem to be in any kind of hurry. Her green eyes were set on Blade. A rush of heat swept through him suddenly. She wasn't just the most beautiful woman he had ever seen, she was the most desirable. She brought tension and hunger to his loins, and a raw, savage pain to his heart.

He'd been alone for years now. He'd known whores and ladies in that time. This was different, because she was different, and he didn't want to feel this. He was suddenly furious. She had caused this, surely. With her cool voice, her emerald eyes and her lithe, so elegantly curved figure.

"Lady, you need to get going! You should be hightailing your pretty rear right back East—"

"I'm not going back East!" she snapped coolly.

"Then you need to get going!"

"Will you excuse me just a moment, gentlemen," she said to the driver and the guard. "I'd like to speak to this man."

"Watch out for the ones on the floor, Mrs. Dylan!"

"I will," she promised.

The two left the bar. Jeeter was busy mopping up behind it. Blade surveyed the woman, his eyes narrowing as they swept over her.

"What?" he demanded.

"I'd like to employ you."

"What?"

She spoke quickly and earnestly. Her voice, as cool as it could be, was wonderful and melodic to him. "I might have been in serious trouble here if you hadn't come along. I realize that this is a dangerous and raw place. You seem to be at loose ends—perhaps in danger of having your face flattened yourself," she said, indicating the unconscious men at their feet. "I can pay you very well. Very well indeed."

"I'm not for hire."

"But I really need you—"

"You really need to go home!"

"I can pay you well."

He was startled when he suddenly grasped her arms, drawing her against him. "You can pay me well? Well enough? Well, let me tell you how I'd want to be paid. You. I'd want you, Mrs. Dylan, just the same way old Matt here wanted you."

She jerked away from him, her emerald eyes liquid as she stared at him. She should be sufficiently outraged, furious, he thought. And she'd walk away, thinking about her beautiful, marble flesh being mauled by a . . . half-breed.

"And what if I were willing to pay?" she whispered.

"What?"

"What if I were willing to pay?" she demanded defiantly.

"We're not talking about a one-shot deal here, lady!" he said roughly. "We're talking about whenever and wherever I choose. Think about it—I may not be worth my price!"

Her eyes, emerald ice, surveyed him once again. "It's damned sure you're not worth that price," she assured him. She started for the door at last. She swung around to face him. "You're good, but not that good!" she told him, that same ice in her eyes, the challenge more than he could resist.

"Oh, lady," he said softly, "you just don't know how good."

He felt the green fire of her eyes warming him, awakening him, and—damn her—exciting him.

No, he wouldn't fall for this kind of woman, not now. There was still a raw, gaping, bleeding hole inside of him where his heart should have been. There were things he had to do, and he could not—would not—get involved. . . .

"Good day, sir!" Mrs. Dylan said, then turned and left as regally as she had come.

The dying sun touched her hair. And she seemed to leave in a blaze of fire, Blade thought, resisting the urge to smile.

Chapter Two

There were two reasons Blade determined to follow the stagecoach. He'd set the trash brothers—Matt, Jed and Petey—on their horses and promised them dire consequences if they were ever to meet up with him again, but there was still the possibility that the men would go after the stage, for revenge if nothing else. He'd had to get them out of the saloon, though, since he couldn't rightly leave them for old Jeeter.

But even if the outlaws didn't follow the stagecoach, it was heading right through a corner of Apache territory. Mescalero Apaches were a people fed up with the land already taken from them and determined to give little quarter to the white populace, which had often dealt mercilessly with them. If the whites called them savage, so much the better to the Mescaleros.

He stayed behind, though, at a good distance. And for the first few hours, he began to wonder what he was doing. The stagecoach was going to go through the wilderness just fine. The brothers from the inn wouldn't have been patient enough to follow prey this long. His only fear now was the Mescaleros, and so far, it seemed, they were being quiet. With the war over, forts were popping up all over the place, and all the trails were being heavily traveled by the military, sometimes hundreds of men in U.S. cavalry blue. Perhaps the Mescaleros were keeping their distance because of the increasing number of reinforcements. At any time now, the military bugle could be heard, calling fighting men into action.

He was being a fool. He should turn around and head back. One look at this woman was enough to know that she was pulling him along by nether parts of his body, and, in truth, he wanted no part of it.

Yet he kept riding.... At least, Blade justified, she was going in the same direction he wanted to go.

By nightfall, they would be coming up on Jackson Prairie, one of the small towns that had sprung up in the past ten years. It was thriving nicely enough. It had come under Indian attack once in that time, but a cavalry fort was only a twenty minute ride away, which had given the residents courage to hold their own. They had repelled the Indians before the bugler and the cavalry had arrived, tenaciously shooting their rifles from their bedroom windows. Jackson Prairie, it seemed, was new and wild and reckless, but here to stay. There were good wells, which tapped into a fine water supply, and against the dry dust bowl of much of the land around it, it was a welcome haven. Even before the war, the land around Jackson Prairie had begun going for fair prices. It was good, wide open space, perfect for cattle grazing.

Once the stagecoach reached Jackson Prairie, there wouldn't be any need for him to follow. Jackson

Prairie wouldn't be a bad place to spend the night, Blade thought. A little whiskey, a good bath at the boardinghouse and a game of cards. And women to be had for the asking.

Strange, but the thought suddenly didn't seem to do too much for Blade, unless the woman was a tall, slim, elegantly dressed Easterner....

Mrs. Dylan had already offered herself, more or less, he recalled. But somehow, with her, that just made him angry. It wasn't her vocation, and she hadn't suddenly been smitten with him.... So what would make her so determined to make it in the West that she would so quickly make such an offer to him?

The answer eluded Blade. And even as he sought it, he realized that he had ceased to pay attention to the stage, now just a speck on the horizon.

There were buttes surrounding the valley. And looking up, to his right and left, Blade could see horsemen on those buttes.

Apaches. Mescaleros. Five riders to the south, another three to the north. His only hope was that their weapons might be old and outdated, that what rifles they had weren't repeating ones. He spurred his horse, leaning now, pulling out his Colt. If he could reach the stage before the Indians could...

But he couldn't. The driver saw the threat coming and set his whip to his team. The stage began to race wildly, careening down the rutted trail through the wilderness. The guard was up on one knee from his position on the box, firing at the Indians, who were converging on the stage.

The Indians were nearly naked. Some were in leather leggings and vests, their bronze arms gleaming, ink black hair waving, bare flesh covered with paint. Some wore only breechclouts, and more of their muscled, gleaming flesh was apparent.

As Blade raced in behind the war party, one Apache fell from his horse, caught by a shot from the stage guard's rifle. Blade fired with his Colt, bringing down a lagging rider. Then, as he spurred his bay gelding to greater speed, he saw another rifle appear, from the window of the stage.

She was firing. The very elegant and beautiful Mrs. Dylan was firing from the stage window. She hit one of the Apaches in the shoulder and the man shrieked out in pain and fury, flying from his mount onto the dirt of the trail. Within seconds, Blade's fine bay was leaping over the fallen man.

He could hear the stage driver shouting to the horses. "Get up, get up!" The whip cracked in the air. The remaining five Apaches were closing in, Blade close on their heels. He aimed and fired again. Missed. Fired, and took one of the men from the rear.

He felt a bullet whiz by his ear and he ducked lower against the bay.

Suddenly, Blade heard a grinding sound. He was just taking aim again when he realized that the treacherous trail and reckless speed were causing the stagecoach to capsize. The vehicle was wavering, rocking... crashing down hard upon its side. The horses, jerked back in the fall, screamed and whinnied, tripping over the harness and themselves. The driver flew wide, the guard flew farther. The Apaches,

four now, ignored them, converging on the compartment.

On the woman.

No fire rang out from the compartment. Was she
dead? Blade wondered, and his heart seemed to slam
hard against his chest. Damn her, she should never
have been here!

Another bullet seemed to chip at the flesh on
Blade's cheek, it came so close. He instantly returned
the fire. An Apache made a clean fall into the dust.
His three companions hurried on, one wrenching at
the door to the passenger compartment, the other
pausing upon the downed structure to aim his rifle at
Blade.

Blade leapt from his horse, diving into the dirt just
in time to miss the shot. The Apache stalked, his knife
gleaming. The muscled warrior slammed against him
like a living wall of brick, and they tumbled in the dirt.
Blade found himself on his back, the Apache straddled over him, hatred in his black eyes, cold fury con-
stricting his hard features. The Apache's knife
glittered right over his eyes, coming closer and closer.

Blade gripped the Apache's wrist, knowing that he
fought for his life, that the Mescalero would offer him
no mercy. Their eyes met. For aeons, it seemed, they
were suspended in time and space, neither able to best
the other. From the corner of Blade's eye, he could see
that the other survivor of the attacking war party had
wrenched open the door.

And found the woman. The one the driver had
called Mrs. Dylan.

She was unconscious, and that was why she had stopped fighting. Unconscious, or dead.

Her hair had come free from the knot at her nape. It hung down from her lolling head like a waving sheet of pure golden fire. The Apache was about to take her with him.

And she would disappear forever....

He gritted his teeth, straining harder against his enemy. Black eyes met black eyes. Then, with a tremendous burst of energy, Blade shoved against the man, flipping him. Their positions were changed, but the Apache still held the knife, wickedly long, sharp silver, flashing in the afternoon sunlight. Blade stared at it, tightening his grip upon the Apache's wrist. The warrior suddenly cried out. The knife fell.

Blade used his fist then, hard against the Apache's chin. His enemy went limp. Blade leapt up, catching the last Indian just as he was about to mount his horse.

Mrs. Dylan came to just then. Immense emerald eyes opening to see the painted man carrying her away. She let out a wild shriek, her arms flying, nails raking. The Apache threw her down as she drew his blood, then the flat of his hand connected hard with her cheek. She cried out and started to rise again, true alarm blazing in her eyes.

But Blade caught the man's shoulder just then, swinging him around.

The Apache was good. He caught Blade in the jaw before Blade could duck. For a moment, Blade saw stars. Then he saw that the Apache meant to take the advantage, and he quickly countered with a fierce blow to the Apache's gut. The man started to double.

Blade joined his fists together and brought them down on the Apache's nape. The Indian fell with a whish of air and a grunt. Blade rubbed his knuckle for a minute, looking at the fallen brave. Then he stared over to where she lay, arms pushing up against the dirt. Breathing hard, she stared at him.

What was she thinking? One bronzed savage for another? he wondered. She was the one who had propositioned *him*.

He reached out a hand to her. She accepted it, rising gracefully. "I told you to go home," he said.

Her chin was high. "And if you had accepted my offer, you could have been making some gain for what you just did for free."

"Go home."

"I'm trying to go home."

"Go back East."

"I have nothing back East."

"Well, what do you have here? You nearly had yourself a whole tribe of Mescalero Apaches! What good would that have done you?"

Her emerald eyes surveyed him with a level cool. "But it didn't happen. You came back."

"Yes, that's right. And you've already agreed that you might be a fitting payment for me, so maybe it wouldn't make much difference to you if a dozen or so Apaches were to demand their own payment."

Her hand lashed out to strike him. But he was quick, ready for anything she might do, and his fingers were winding around her wrist before she could touch his flesh. He wanted to shake her. Shake her until she understood what an idiot she was; she was a rose on a barren landscape, a delicate flower trying to root in stone.

He wanted her to know just what she was willing to offer. No, he wanted her, period. Right then and there, on the dust of the plain, hard and fast. He would show her how raw and wild the world could be. How savage. How damned cruel, and savage. . . .

"Thank the Lord above us!" The dry cackle sounded before Blade could say or do a thing. It was the stage driver, picking his way over the shivering, frightened horses and harness to reach him and Mrs. Dylan. "It's you again. I'm telling you, young fellow, you deserve some kind of commendation! Gold, my man, gold! Something to set you up fine in the West. The investors in this company will surely be willing to pay something, I'm right damned sure of it—oh, pardon for the language, Mrs. Dylan, I do beg your pardon."

"Oh, I imagine Mrs. Dylan can deal with a little rough language, old-timer," Blade said dryly. "She seems to deal well enough with just about everything else."

Her emerald eyes were locked with Blade's black ones. She didn't say a word for the longest time, just stared at him. Then she turned to the driver. "Shorty, what will we do now? Can the stage be righted? What about the horses?"

"We'll have to get them up and see how they fared," Shorty said.

The guard, his broken rifle dangling uselessly from his hands, was standing by the lead horses. He threw his rifle aside with disgust and reached down, running his hands over the haunches of the first horse. "This fellow seems to be in one piece. We just need to get them up carefully. They're sure to be all bruised up and frightened. Can't let them panic again or they'll strangle us and themselves in the harness. You've done us fair and fine so far, sir," he said, tipping his hat to Blade, "if you wouldn't mind giving us a few more minutes of your time . . ."

Shorty snorted. "What about these fellows?" He indicated the Apaches. "Some of them just might come to—madder than a hive of bees!"

"You deal with them, Shorty. Tie 'em up if'n you don't want to shoot them. I need this young buck—" The guard broke off, wincing at the term he had used for Blade. Buck. Indian. Like the Apaches on the ground.

Blade smiled, walking toward the guard and the horses. "Sioux," he said briefly. "My mother is Oglala. She's gone now, but I still miss the family. I go back whenever I can. There's nothing like a good scalping raid to get the juices flowing, you know?"

He stepped past the man, placed one hand on the lead horse's nose and one on the harness. He whispered softly to the horse. "Easy. . . ."

With a simple pull, the animal was up. The other horses followed suit, one screaming with pain. Blade walked around to the animal, running his hand over the sweating flank.

"Broken," he told the guard. "You're going to have to put this one down, and reharness the others."

By that time, Shorty—with the elite Mrs. Dylan's help—had tied up the Apaches. Blade was surprised they hadn't just shot the Indians. The white men seemed to find the Apaches and Comanches the most savage of the Plains Indians—well, along with Paiutes, maybe, since they believed in human sacrifice, with or without white men around. Many white people didn't think that they were shooting people, they just acted as though they were putting down animals—just the way they were going to have to put down the horse.

But Shorty didn't seem to be that kind. He was still grinning. Blade might have given the stage guard a turn with his talk about scalping parties, but he could see that Shorty knew it had just been talk. Shorty seemed to know that whether or not Blade was dressed like a white man, he had no intention of ever pretending to be anything but what he was—a half-breed, one damned proud of the breed part of the term. Blade admired his mother's people, loved his grandfather and loved their way of life—the hunting, the fishing, the warmth in the tepee in the cold of the night....

But he couldn't go back right now. He had lived in the white man's world with his father, and had seen too much. He had seen his father killed, along with the others. His Sioux grandfather would understand, as other men might not, that there were things he had to do. Or he could *never* go back.

"It's going to take some time to get this harness back in shape," Shorty said, scratching his head. He looked at Blade. "Think you could take Mrs. Dylan on in for us, sir?"

Blade smiled, lowering his head, conscious of the fact that Shorty was an all right old fellow. "I—"

"I don't mind waiting," Mrs. Dylan said flatly, chin high. She was oblivious to the trail dust on her cheeks and gown and unaware of the elegant mantle her hair created, streaming down her back. "There's a rock over there—"

"And every Indian in the territory might be out in two minutes, once they see the gleam of your hair," Blade warned her coolly. "They're enterprising fellows. Even if they're not interested themselves, they do a lot of trading with the Comancheros. White slavery. It's a booming business."

She gritted her teeth and flashed him a heated gaze. "I've come this far—"

"Mrs. Dylan, ma'am, it would be a fine favor to both Sam and myself if you would be so good as to ride on into town with this gentleman," Shorty said.

"This gentleman?" she inquired sweetly, staring at Blade.

Blade grinned, staring in turn. "Renegade, half-breed. Do them the favor, Mrs. Dylan. You're dangerous. You're going to get these nice old men killed."

She inhaled, blinking briefly, then she turned to Shorty. "I'll ride on in with—" she broke off, arching a brow at Blade. "With—?"

"McKenna, Mrs. Dylan," Blade chimed in. "My name is McKenna."

Her brow remained arched, as if she wasn't convinced he could really have a name like McKenna. "I'll ride in with Mr. McKenna," she told Shorty.

"We'll have your things in just as soon as can be, Mrs. Dylan," Shorty assured her. "Just go on into the Jackson Prairie boardinghouse. Mrs. Peabody will see to your needs. And we'll be there mighty soon, I swear it.''

''Thank you, gentlemen,'' she said. She turned to Blade. He strode over to his bay and waited for her to join him. She hesitated at the horse. He wondered if she wouldn't leap right up, but if she was going to do so, she was certainly taking her time. Without further ado, he set his hands on her waist and hiked her up on his bay.

It felt good to hold her so, Blade thought. Good to feel her beneath his touch. She was elegantly slim, but he could feel the curves of her hips and the heat that burned through her.... He leapt up behind her, arms encircling her as he took the reins.

Her back went very stiff against his chest. She could feel him, too. He was damned sure of it. She was so very much aware of him behind her, touching her.

''Is this a long ride, McKenna?'' she demanded.

''You want it to be a short one, is that it, Mrs. Dylan?''

''Well, it seems that the sooner we are out of one another's company—''

''What happened to 'thank you'?''

''What?''

''What happened to 'thank you'?'' Blade repeated. ''I did just save your life. Or, at the very least, your freedom and virtue. The last doesn't seem to mean a great deal to you, but surely the first of those does!''

She twisted in the saddle. For a moment he saw the green fire in her eyes. She was itching to slap him. Hard. Gouge into his eyes, probably.

"Don't even think about it," he warned her softly, and leaned very close to her earlobe, breathing in the sweet scent of her, feeling again the miraculous warmth of her. "You want a fast ride, Mrs. Dylan? You've got one!"

And he spurred his bay.

The fine, faithful horse took off in a staggering leap, and the three of them began to race against the plain, against the dying day, for Jackson Prairie.

Chapter Three

Blade's horse barely slowed its gait as they came into Jackson Prairie, racing through the roads on the outskirts, slowing to a trot only when they reached the one big street that slashed through the town—Main Street by name. Most everything was right there. There was a bank—the First Savings and Loan of Jackson Prairie—and there were numerous shops, including Harvey's Barber and Mercantile Shop, and Mrs. Havover's Domestications. There was a dentist's shop, Dr. Weatherly Dayton, M.D., a tailor, a cooper, and more. There were two blacksmiths, and there was plenty of trade for both of them, and their shops were in either direction off Main Street, one being on South Street, and one being on North Street.

Mrs. Peabody's boardinghouse was dead center on Main Street, directly across from the Jackson Prairie Bar and Saloon. Blade reined in on Mallory, his big bay, right in front of the boardinghouse, slipping off the horse's back quickly and reaching up for Mrs. Dylan.

Her hair was exquisitely windblown, completely freed from its dignified knot, a wild mane of fire and gold all around her. Her eyes seemed brighter still against it, furious with the recklessness of his wild ride, he imagined, and yet meeting his eyes with that challenge that never faltered. He had his hands around her waist so there was little she could do but set hers upon his shoulders as he lifted her down. She was close, so close, sliding against the length of his body. His jaw locked and then his whole damned body seemed to lock. And since she wasn't wearing more than one thin petticoat, she must have felt the rock hardness of his body, just as he felt each sweet curve and nuance of hers. He suddenly wanted to throw her from him—simply because he was so very loath to let her go.

She opened her mouth as if she were about to say something to him, but just then the door to the establishment, which was up two steps to the wooden sidewalk, suddenly opened, and they swung around together.

Mrs. Peabody stood there, surely having heard them ride up. She was a portly lady with very round blue eyes and silver hair and a quick, easy smile. "Good evening," she told them pleasantly, looking them both up and down. "Why, it's Mr. McKenna," she murmured, smiling.

Blade didn't come into many towns, and he didn't give his name out often. But if there was any place he'd managed to feel that he belonged in the last few harsh years, it had been here. It was the closest thing he'd known to home—since his own had been burned to the ground. There were few people he really liked, fewer still he really trusted. Mrs. Peabody was one of the even fewer still that he liked *and* trusted.

"Evening, ma'am," he told her, then realized that he was still holding the golden-haired Mrs. Dylan by the waist.

And Mrs. Dylan was still holding him by the shoulders.

Her hands snatched suddenly free from him.

"Is this Mrs. McKenna, sir?" Mrs. Peabody asked. "Will there be one room needed for the night, or two?"

"Two!" Mrs. Dylan said swiftly, smoothing down her crumpled blouse, then the wild mane of her hair. She took two steps away from Blade, meeting Mrs. Peabody's kindly gaze. "I'm Jessica Dylan, Mrs. Peabody. I'll be staying a few days, if you've got room."

"Why of course, Miss Dylan—"

"Mrs. Dylan," Blade corrected politely. He decided to enlighten Mrs. Peabody. "There was some trouble with Mrs. Dylan's stage."

"Apaches!" Mrs. Peabody exclaimed, holding her heart.

"Yes, but it turned out all right."

"Mr. McKenna is very resourceful," Jessica Dylan said, and it sounded as though she were trying to speak while grating her teeth all the while.

"Mrs. Dylan isn't bad herself—with her fists or a rifle," Blade said pleasantly.

"Well, that's wonderful, young woman, just wonderful!" Mrs. Peabody applauded. "You come right on up here, Mrs. Dylan, and we'll get you squared away. I'll put you in the blue room and have a tub of hot water brought in right away so that you can bathe off the prairie dust and tension!" She came down the steps and slipped a matronly arm around the younger woman's shoulders, sniffing over her shoulder to Blade as if he was somehow responsible for the things that men did in general. He lowered his head, grinning, and followed as Mrs. Peabody led Jessica Dylan up the steps and into the foyer.

They entered a narrow hallway with a set of stairs that led to the second floor. The sitting room and dining room were to the left, both furnished with richly upholstered chairs and handsome settees, with pretty lamps and frill work. The men's rooms were to the right, including a library with leather armchairs and sofas and brass spittoons. Blade had spent many an evening in the library. Tapestried carpets covered the polished wooden floors, and the curtains were just right for all the windows in each room—the ladies' rooms having frilly adornments, the men's rooms having draperies of a plainer style.

They didn't pause downstairs, but hurried up the long stairway, Mrs. Peabody calling out as they did so. "Jane! Jane, get the boys moving if you will. We need the tub and lots of water up here! Quickly now!"

"Yes, Mrs. Peabody!" the maid called from below. Then the maid was yelling to someone else to get a move on.

There was a small landing at the top of the stairs, then there were hallways stretching out in both directions. Blade followed the women until they stopped before a door. Mrs. Peabody pressed it open, a firm hand on Mrs. Dylan's back pushing her on through.

She turned her stout body about like a barrier, facing Blade. "You'll have the green room, right next door, Mr. McKenna. And you just go on down and help yourself to a brandy in the library and relax a spell. I know you'll be wanting a bath before dinner, but you'll just have to wait a bit. I've got more tubs, but I haven't got more help to fill them up. If you don't mind now, the lady goes first!"

Blade smiled. "Why, that's just fine, Mrs. Peabody. I don't mind waiting in the least. And the green room is here, next door, right?"

"Right as rain."

The door closed on Blade. He grinned, then stepped out of the way as he saw two of Mrs. Peabody's boys, one a black lad of about sixteen, his blond-haired companion a year or so younger, both strong and with clean-scrubbed faces that attested to Mrs. Peabody's insistence on cleanliness in her house.

Someone had told him once over at the saloon—some old geezer who looked as if he might have been allergic to water, both drinking it and bathing in it—that Mrs. Peabody was so insistent on danged blasted bathing that she had one tub for lady guests, one for gentlemen, and one for her hired help, and that all three had to be replaced just about once a year.

Blade nodded to the boys with their heavy load, then hurried down the stairs and outside. He slipped his saddlebags from his bay's shoulders and walked the horse around to the stables where a slim Chinese lad was brushing down one of Mrs. Peabody's carriage horses. He left Mallory with the boy and went into the house, leaving his saddlebags with his clean clothing, shaving equipment and all on the hardwood dresser with the wavery mirror in the green room, so called, of course, as it had been painted green.

He noted that there was a door against the wall near the dresser. One that must lead into the blue room.

Mrs. Peabody was an interesting lady, he mused.

And then he wondered if he was glad or dismayed about the door. Irritated, he told himself that the damned thing didn't matter either way. He'd stay tonight, and he'd spend his evening at the saloon. Maybe he'd even spend a few hours with one of the perfumed ladies there.

No. One of the whores, not ladies. It was the "lady" part he didn't like about Jessica Dylan. That and more—much, much more. The way she fascinated him. The way she was just so damned beautiful and beguiling. The way she made him forget too damned much.

He left his room, hurrying down the stairs again, to pour a brandy and sit back in one of the handsome leather chairs in the library. He closed his eyes, savoring the fine brandy as it rolled over his tongue then burned slowly down his throat.

The whiskey over at the saloon wasn't nearly as fine as Mrs. Peabody's. But nothing about the saloon was as fine as anything at Mrs. Peabody's—even though Mrs. Peabody and Henry Larkin, the saloon's owner, were very good friends. Blade had a feeling that although the two of them were running very different establishments, they both had similar, shrewd heads for business. The saloon offered everything that Mrs. Peabody's didn't, and vice versa. Mrs. Peabody's was elegant and refined—the saloon was far from it. But then, there were some damned good poker games to join over at the saloon, while there sure as hell—heck—were no poker games to join at Mrs. Peabody's.

Both Henry Larkin and Mrs. Peabody were making very good money. Stagecoaches were a miserable way to ride west. They were small, cramped and crowded. Most stops were poor indeed, with mud-chink guesthouses in which the mud sometimes fell on guests as they slept at night, especially during the dry season. There were other miserable places, establishments run by men who wiped the dinner plates clean instead of washing them for the next set of travelers. In such a world, both the saloon and Mrs. Peabody's place were just a small step from heaven.

He sipped more brandy and leaned his head back. He'd seen a hell of a lot of the West in the last few years.

Ever since the war had ended. Looking. Always looking. Because he couldn't stop now, not until he found the men who had destroyed everything and everyone he had ever loved.

Not until they were avenged.

He leaned back in his chair relishing the warm burn of the brandy in his throat. He closed his eyes. Sometimes, because of the memories, he hated to do so. Sometimes, he would see a spring day, with a few white clouds drifting across the sky. Then he would see Mara waving from the well, and his father standing on the porch, smiling at him and Mara, so damned proud that he was about to become a grandfather. Then Mara would be running toward him. He would wave at her to stop, because she shouldn't be running then, it was too close to her time.

Then ...

The men. Three of them would be on their horses, clad in red leggings. They would be coming out of Kansas, onto the Missouri side. Coming because John McKenna had damned John Brown for being a heinous murderer and not God's instrument against the inhumanities of man....

He could hear it still. Dear God, he could hear it still. The first blast of the shotgun. He could see it all, again and again, as if the world had slowed, as if he watched it all take place again in the black recesses of his mind and heart.

He could see the first bullet hit his father right in the chest. He could see the handsome old man fly back, snapped against the logs of the farmhouse. He could see the crimson stain spill across his white cotton shirt.... He could hear his own scream. His cry, his warning, and he knew exactly where he was—again.

He had started to run, and felt the agony in his chest, burning his lungs. He never had a chance of reaching Mara. There had been another burst of fire. God, he could hear it explode, too. Then he could see Mara, flying backward, falling, falling to the ground.

And she, too, had been stained in crimson, a massive hole in her chest, and he had been running and screaming. He had seen men—had seen their faces. He had thrown himself upon the first of them, the blue-eyed one, still mounted, and had dragged him down, his bare fingers around his throat, throttling him.

Then there had been the pain. Blinding, searing, like a flash of fire and light before him. Then there had been darkness. Blackness, a terrible void.

Blade didn't want to awaken from it, he didn't want to survive. He was afraid to awaken, he wanted it to be a dream, never the truth, dear God, he didn't want to awaken....

"Mr. McKenna!"

Startled, he jerked his head up. He'd dozed. Resting there on the fine leather chair in Mrs. Peabody's library, he'd done what he hadn't done for a long, long time.

He'd let down his guard.

It was her fault. The woman's. Jessica Dylan's.

But it was Mrs. Peabody standing in the doorway, smiling benignly. "I didn't need to waken you, Mr. McKenna—"

"Blade, Mrs. Peabody. We've been friends some time now."

"Well, then, that's fine, Blade, but you'll have to remember that my Christian name is Rose."

He smiled. "That's fine, Rose."

"I wouldn't have interrupted you—you were really resting so nicely—except that I know how you love a good steaming bath when you come off the trail. It's all ready for you upstairs. I've gotten that nice Mrs. Dylan all taken care of, and now it's your turn! I'll be seeing to my dinner now. I haven't had a guest in a day or two, and now you and Mrs. Dylan in one night. I'm anxious to whip up a fine meal for you both. It's so nice to have the company.'' She cleared her throat delicately. ''I know how you like a game of poker, too, *Blade,* but I do hope you'll be having dinner here before adjourning over to Henry Larkin's place.''

He stood, setting down his brandy glass. ''Rose, your meals are always the finest in town, and you know that quite well. Of course I'll be having dinner with you.''

''And Mrs. Dylan.''

''And Mrs. Dylan. And then I will be spending the remainder of the evening over at the saloon.''

''Fine,'' Rose said, her chubby little hands folded before her, her lips set in a sweet smile. ''Get on to your bath now, before the water cools.''

She left to walk toward the kitchen, which was a separate building reached via an enclosed walkway, because she wasn't about to have her nicely furnished house burned down by a cooking fire. Blade hurried up the stairs.

He paused outside Jessica Dylan's room. He couldn't hear anything. Shorty hadn't come in with the stagecoach yet, and Blade found himself just standing there, wondering what she was wearing after her bath.

He swore at himself and moved on.

The tub in his room was wonderfully inviting, steam rising in great swaths from it. He stripped down quickly, careless of where he cast his boots and pants, shirt and jacket. He started to sink into the water, wincing when the burning heat first touched his flesh, then slowly sinking all the way in. There was a holder with soap and a cloth, and he picked up both, scrubbing his face first, then his arms, then the rest of his body. He ducked his head beneath the water and scrubbed his black hair. Finally, he sat back, rinsed the cloth, and set it over his face. It felt so damned good just to lie there. He could doze easily again.

Damn! He didn't want to doze again, didn't want to dream, didn't want to remember.

He froze suddenly, curling his fingers around the tub, aware of motion and movement in the room. There was a clicking sound.

Her.

She had come through the connecting door. He could follow her movements exactly. He had been living too long in a state of constant awareness—chasing and on the run—not to have his senses keenly attuned to sound and movement.

And smell. Mmm, he could smell her. The clean, fresh scent of her porcelain flesh....

She was standing above him. Hesitating.

He ripped the cloth from his face, staring at her heatedly in return.

"Yes?" he demanded icily.

She stared and jumped back, but then stood her ground.

Her hair was free, all about her shoulders, just washed and fire dried and radiantly beautiful. He ached to reach out and touch it. Gold and copper. It glittered, it beckoned, it beguiled. No more so than her perfect face, her emerald eyes. Her...person.

He no longer had to wonder what she was wearing. Mrs. Peabody had provided her with a dressing gown. It was far too short, and he could plainly see her long, slim bare feet and her slender ankles, hinting of very shapely, long legs. The gown was a pink frilly thing, with a V bodice that didn't quite close well at her throat and breast, being far too large for her. Her flesh was beautiful. Her throat, long and extremely elegant. The hint of the rise of her breasts...

His fingers clenched very tightly around the rim of the wooden tub and he barked at her, "What?"

"Don't scream at me," she said.

"Don't sneak in on me. You do that at the wrong time, and you'll find yourself getting shot."

"I wasn't sneaking—"

"You don't even come in on a man quietly in the West, Mrs. Dylan. You will get shot."

"Only an outlaw would be so wary—"

"And I never did tell you that I wasn't an outlaw, did I now, Mrs. Dylan? I just might be one. The worst kind of an outlaw."

Her chin lifted. "There's only one thing I do know about you, Mr. McKenna," she said flatly.

He arched a brow.

"You are one hell of a rude bastard!"

He grinned, sliding deeper into the water, eyeing her warily. "What?" he said again.

"Dammit, I need you to work for me," she said, aggravated.

"I'm busy. You need to go home."

"Who the hell do you think you are to decide who can and who can't make it in your precious West, Mr. McKenna?" she demanded coolly. "I'm not going back East. I've told you. I am home. I have land near here. My husband bought it when he was stationed at the fort. Before—he died. It's mine now. It was important to him, and I'm staying.''

''You might find yourself dead within a week,'' Blade said coldly. He needed her out of here. He was staring at her pale throat, at the fascinating rise of her breasts, at the way one of the pink frills rose and fell with her every breath. He could feel the heat of her stare on him, warming him, entering him. His flesh was afire, so much hotter than the water.

''Not if I have you—'' she began.

He stood, heedless of whether he shocked her or not with the bronze length of his body.

She was, after all, in his room.

''I'm not for hire, Mrs. Dylan. I've got my own way to go, and I need to keep moving.''

''Maybe I'm moving the same way.''

She was trying to keep her eyes level with his. They slipped now and then. Maybe she was heading the same way. He'd heard he might find just who he was looking for at the fort. They were damned near it now.

The beautiful white marble of her throat and face was swiftly turning crimson. He realized he was naked, returning her stare.

''I'm not going away, and I need help, and I can pay you very well—'' she began, then broke off.

He had stepped out of the tub. Wet and bronzed from head to toe, he was suddenly against her, heedless of soaking Mrs. Peabody's dressing gown, sweeping her hard against him, into his arms. He couldn't resist. He couldn't resist the urge to touch her, the anguish to hold her. He had to feel her flesh, had to know if it was really as soft as silk, as perfect as it appeared. He had to grind his lips down upon hers, to taste them, to find out if they were as sweet as the promise they seemed to give....

Her heart thundered against his. He formed his mouth to hers, forcing her lips to part. He ravaged her mouth, hungrily kissing her, tasting her.... Oh, God, the taste of her was sweet. Mint and lilac. Her lips were perfect, unwilling, ungiving, and suddenly parting to the onslaught of his as her fingers dug into the muscles of his arms.

Surely she felt him. All of him. The fire and the hardness, the burning and hungry demand. He lifted his lips from hers, afraid of what he'd do if he couldn't get her away. His fingers bit into her upper arms. His eyes blazed hotly into hers.

"I think I've told you my price," he said hoarsely.

She was shaking, her emerald eyes blazing. "If I have to—" she began miserably.

"Oh, you'd have to. And I'd have to have a hell of a lot more than you've just given to find out whether or not you're good enough to meet the price."

Her flushed skin went white. Her hand was about to fly, her fingers just itching to get to his face once again.

"No, Mrs. Dylan, not on your life!" Blade yelled, and swept her up into his arms. She gasped startledly, her arms around him to keep from falling.

He strode across the room, swinging open the adjoining door with his bare foot. He set her down on her bed. "Go home!" he roared. And he slammed the door between them.

He heard a cry. A very soft, quickly stifled cry of pain and dismay. He grated down hard on his teeth, swearing silently. Why did it seem to tear at him that he had hurt her, that he had been so brutal? It was better than what he might have done.... So much better than just taking her. Having her then and there. Sating the hunger, the longing, the anguish....

He swore and turned to his bath. Henry Larkin's Jackson Prairie Bar and Saloon was just across the way. And he was going there just as damned fast as he could.

Chapter Four

There was one thing definite about Jessica Dylan—the woman was tenacious.

It was amazing. Blade had murmured an excuse to Mrs. Peabody after all, and had taken his meal over at the saloon. Soon after, he had found himself in the midst of a pretty good poker game, the stakes rising swiftly, the play running smooth and fast. Roxy Niemes, one of Larkin's girls, resplendent in a short black and crimson affair that left more of her legs bared than covered, was perched right behind him, keeping his whiskey glass filled and occasionally draping long painted fingernails idly upon his shoulders. She was discreet, quietly watching the play, patiently waiting.

He was doing well. Damned well. He already had taken a fair amount of gold from the men at the table, one of them a middle-aged, sandy-haired cattle herder, one a young blond miner and one a tall, dark and lean Easterner in a fancy dress frock with an extravagant red cravat.

A hand of five-card stud had just been dealt. One down, three up, the last down. The miner had two kings showing. Blade had a pair of tens. There was a third beneath his hand. The miner threw in his bet, waiting for Blade to call him or raise him.

And that was when he saw her.

She walked into the saloon with supreme confidence—and arrogance, he determined. Her hair was neatly knotted again at her nape with very soft tendrils escaping to frame her elegant face. She was dressed in a beautiful gown in shades of blue, with rows of black and white lace at the sleeves and hem and bodice, which dipped low upon her breast. She paused just inside the doorway, her emerald eyes sweeping the many tables where men sat about gambling or propositioning the girls or just swilling down their whiskey. She stared at the long bar, the stunned, mustachioed barkeep, the stairway that led to the rooms above, and then to him. He had forgotten to throw his coin down. The miner cleared his throat, and Blade dropped his gold.

Her emerald eyes blazed into his.

She turned to the barkeep. "A whiskey, please."

The bartender coughed softly. "Ma'am, I don't rightly know if you've seen what kind of place this is—"

"Are you refusing to serve me, sir?"

"Why, no, of course not, ma'am. A, er, whiskey, coming right up."

It was Blade's deal. He was moving the cards through his fingers too slowly. It didn't matter, though. The rest of the players had seen Mrs. Jessica Dylan, and they had forgotten the game.

They all stared at her, gaping. Then they regained their manners and closed their mouths. The Easterner stood first, tipping his hat to her. The cattle herder leapt up next, and then the miner close behind.

Blade gritted his teeth, black eyes locked with hers, and stood. Roxy made some small noise behind him. If Jessica Dylan gave any notice to Roxy at all, she gave no sign.

"Gentlemen," she murmured softly.

"Ma'am!" It came in a chorus from the lot of them, only Blade remaining silent.

"May I join you?"

The cattle herder cleared his throat softly. "Why, ma'am, we aren't playing parlor cards."

"It can be a rough game," the miner added.

She smiled very sweetly. "Nevertheless, gentlemen, I'd love to join you. It is an honest game, I believe."

"Dead honest," Blade promised her. He had sat down at last, and stared into her emerald eyes once more. What was her game?

"Then, if you all don't mind..."

The miner hurried to the next table to draw a chair for her. The cattle herder cleared room for her whiskey. She sat and looked at the table. "Someone has called someone, so it seems."

Blade flipped over his cards, showing three tens. The pot was his. The deal passed to his left.

To Mrs. Dylan.

She picked up the cards and shuffled them like a professional cardsharp. They flew around the table. "Let's make it five-card draw, gentlemen. Jacks or better to open. Dollar ante.'' She was swift, and she was all business.

The men at the table were suddenly moving very fast.

Roxy made another of her *tsking* sounds in the background. ''Need another, hon?'' she whispered huskily to Blade, pointing at his glass.

Another? He needed the whole damned bottle. He nodded. Roxy filled his glass. He gulped down the amber liquid, staring at Jessica Dylan. ''How many cards, Mr. McKenna?''

He slid one across the table. ''One.''

Luck was with Blade. One card completed his straight. She had bet against him and lost.

The next hand, the miner's deal, Mrs. Dylan took with a full house.

The game progressed. Mrs. Dylan proved that she was a good player, never showing her cards when she didn't have to, seeming to know when to fold, when to hold, when to cut her losses, and how to win.

The cattle herder fell out first, the well-dressed man next, then the miner. That left only Blade and Mrs. Dylan.

The hour had grown incredibly late. Even Roxy sighed in a pique and joined the few remaining men in the room at the bar. It didn't matter. Blade hadn't even managed to look at Roxy in hours. He'd barely heard her voice. She had paled away, faded like an old photograph.

Perhaps that would happen to any other woman with Jessica Dylan in the room.

Blade kept his black-eyed stare hard on her.

She kept her emerald gaze equally strongly upon him. She was playing way more than a card game here, and he knew it. She had tried to do a lot of gambling with him already. What was she after with this? Trying to make him lose all his money so that he would be forced to enter her employ? He didn't know. He was suddenly determined to win the game.

She was capable of a good bluff, he had seen that already. He began to call her bluff, time and time again. At first, between the two of them, the wins and losses still seemed about even. But then he managed to get her to keep up with his raises on a pat hand— three aces, two kings. She couldn't beat it, and she didn't. Next hand he was amazed to see his cards fall in every bit as nicely. Draw poker. He held two queens. She opened. And then she dealt him another queen and two aces, and asked for three cards.

"You opened," he reminded her.

"So I did." She shoved her coins on the table. "Fifty dollars."

"A hundred."

"I see your hundred. I raise you a hundred."

"I see your hundred—and I'll raise you two."

She started to push in the coins, then bit her lower lip in irritation. She seemed to be a few short.

"I can write you a promissory note—"

He shook his head. "Whatever we're gambling for needs to be on the table. Right now."

She looked at her cards. They must have been good. As good as his? He didn't know.

But he was a gambler. Was she? he wondered.

"I have my earrings," she said, reaching for them. But her ears were bare. "Oh!" she murmured, lashes sweeping downward. "I left them right across the street in my room. If you'll just—"

"No."

"What kind of a gentleman are you?" she demanded irritably. "I can make good on any of my bets! If you'll—"

"No," he said flatly, leaning forward. "All bets on the table. Here and now."

She stiffened. "And just what is it you want on the table?" she inquired coolly.

He shrugged. "I'll take—you."

Her eyes flashed with anger. "I've offered you myself before, if you recall."

He shook his head again. "Not for any business deal, Mrs. Dylan. Just for the night."

Her eyes burned. Her fingers were itching again, he knew. She'd love to slap him. She'd really love to whack him across the face. She was so determined, and so desperate, it seemed, at times.

"And what do I get in return?" she asked.

"Might I remind you, my money is all on the table."

"It's not enough," she insisted.

He lifted his hands, palms up. "You can fold," he reminded her politely.

Her teeth gnashed together. "I want more!" she insisted.

She was a fighter, he thought, and he was startled by the sudden emotion he felt for her. She didn't quit.

And she hated like hell to lose.

He leaned forward. "All right, let's lay it all on the table. If I win, I get you for the night. No strings attached. If you win, you get me. In your employ. For free. For, let's say... maybe a month. How's that?"

She was breathing very hard, he could see. Her breasts were rising and falling swiftly.

"Is it a deal?"

"Deal," she said very softly. He started to turn his cards. Her fingers fell over the back of his hand. "How do I know you won't renege?"

"You'll have to trust me."

But she stopped him again. "How do you know I won't renege?"

He smiled. "Because I won't let you," he assured her confidently. "I collect on all debts owed me."

His black eyes met her emerald ones. And once again, he began to turn his cards. He started with an ace, another ace, a queen.

"Two pairs!" she exclaimed, her triumph sliding into her voice. She laid down her hand.

It was a good hand. Three jacks, two kings. A damned good hand.

But not good enough.

She started to reach for the pile of coins on the table. He cleared his throat loudly. "Ahem, Mrs. Dylan."

She stopped, freezing with her palms around the coins, staring at him.

He laid out his last two cards. "I've a full house, too, Mrs. Dylan. And mine is queens high."

"Oh!" The sound escaped her. And once again, those elegant, blazing green eyes were on him. His fingers fell upon hers, curling hard when she would have wrenched her hand away. "You're mine, Mrs. Dylan—for the night. And thank the good lord! The night is still young!"

He let her snatch her hand free. She started to rise.

"Reneging, Mrs. Dylan? Don't forget, I collect on all debts owed me."

"No! I'm not reneging!" she snapped back. "I pay all my debts," she assured him. And her voice was suddenly husky, he thought. Feminine. Vulnerable. Enticing him to a new hunger. "Just not here!" she whispered. Her eyes were on his. Unblinking. "I'll be waiting to pay. The—the doors connect," she reminded him.

Then she turned. And, head held high, she fled gracefully from the Jackson Prairie Bar and Saloon.

Chapter Five

Mrs. Peabody's was very quiet when Blade returned. He heard a clock strike. It was one a.m.

He came into his room and leaned against the door. Inhaling, exhaling. What did he think he was doing? Taunting her, trying to torture her into going home? Why the hell did he care what happened to her?

He gritted his teeth. He did care. Maybe it was the first time he'd cared in a long time, and maybe it was damned hard to have to feel again instead of move on, seeking nothing but a vengeance that had now turned ice cold, but all the more determined. Why her?

There were no answers. Hell, maybe there were, he thought again. All he had to do was look at her, watch her, hear her voice. He'd cared when he'd followed her to begin with. He'd cared because he hadn't wanted to see blood running against her marble flesh, because he hadn't wanted to hear her scream…. Because once he had seen her, he hadn't wanted to imagine another man touching her, hurting her, having her.

He pushed away from the door. He wasn't going to demand anything from her. The poker game had been his bluff. She needed to go home, whether she saw it or not. It was his last chance to convince her. He could never really touch her. She would be like a taste of honey, sweet, beguiling. She would make him hungry, again and again.

The door between the rooms was closed. He stared at it for a long moment, then angrily crossed to it. He threw it open, certain that he'd find her still defiant— or gone.

But she was not gone.

She was there. She stood before the window with the curtains in her fingers, drawn back slightly. Her lower lip was caught between her teeth. She was in a silky gown of soft, sheer blue. It molded over her breasts, fluttering against the length of her. Her flesh was just visible beneath the sheer fabric. She had stood there, watching the road, waiting for him. Miserably, from the look in her eyes and the way she chewed on her lip. But determinedly. He had told her that he collected on debts.

She had told him that she paid them.

She spun around, staring at him, her fingers falling uneasily over the fabric of her very sheer gown as if she just realized how translucent the gown was, how very much she had given away.... And longed to cover once again.

He closed the door between the rooms, narrowing the space between them. He leaned against it, crossed his arms over his chest and stared at her, eyeing her slowly, from the tip of her golden head to her bare toes. He tried to still the thunder that suddenly began to beat within him.

"Go home," he told her softly. "Go home."

"I cannot go home," she insisted.

"Go home, and we'll call off this stupid wager."

There was moisture in her eyes. It made them dazzle like gems against a night sky. She seemed very vulnerable then, and he didn't want her hurt. He'd put her on some kind of damned pedestal, and he'd be happy if she'd just go home. East. Where the world wasn't great, he thought, but where the dangers weren't quite so many, quite so fierce, quite so constant, either. Away from warring Comanches, Apaches, Comancheros. Away from bitter halfbreeds, longing for a touch of paradise against the anguish and emptiness. . . .

"Do whatever you want," she told him. "I cannot go home."

With an impatient sound he was across the room. He gripped her soft smooth arms tightly in his hands, shaking her hard. "Don't you understand what you're going to find here? I'm not invincible! I'm flesh and blood. Even if I stayed with you, I'd probably die with a bullet or an arrow in my heart."

Her chin was high, her head back. She hadn't made a sound, not a single protest against the rough way he held her. "You told me you were good," she reminded him. "So damned good."

"But I can still die—and leave you alone, don't you see? And if you think I can be a bastard, lady, you haven't seen anything yet."

"I have to stay!"

"Can you really pay the price to do it?" he lashed out.

"Yes."

No, damn her! She didn't know what she was saying, what she was offering.

"All right," he whispered fiercely. "All right, have it all your way. And pay up, lady, pay up!"

His fingers moved over the soft, sheer fabric that so barely covered the beauty of her body. With a narrowly controlled burst of violence, he grabbed the fabric, ripping it from throat to floor with a soft hissing sound that seemed as loud as a gunshot in the night. She gasped, her fingers reaching for the split sides.

"No," he warned her, shaking his head. "You want to pay your debts, time to pay them. You want to take chances with savages, well, Mrs. Dylan, fine. Start with me."

He still never meant to hurt her.... Never meant to touch her.... Not just for her, for himself. Because he dared not take that first sip of honey....

But at the moment, none of it mattered. His hands were upon her, he was drawing her to him, sliding away the last of the silky blue fabric, finding her naked flesh. It was smoother than any touch of silk. Jesus. He crushed her against him, feeling the rise of her breasts, stroking his palms and fingertips down her back, seizing her lips with his own. He felt her trembling beneath him. Her hands fell upon his chest....

Her lips parted beneath his. Sweet. A taste of honey, he thought. He plundered her mouth deeply, ravished it. She clung to him, accepting the onslaught, her heart thundering as his lips came from hers at last, touched upon her throat, her shoulder, down to her naked breast. She was beautiful, perfect, her breasts hard and firm, the nipples an exquisite rose shade, puckered now, and hardening against the harsh lave of his tongue. Her breath caught. Another gasp escaped her. Her fingers curled into his dark hair, into his shoulders. She stood trembling still, damn her, not fighting him yet. He pushed himself against her, touching her flesh, savoring it with his fingertips, with his lips, with his tongue.

His heart hammered. His loins ached, his desire soared, and the hunger, the thunder, the beat within him was unbearable. Fight me, damn you! he longed to cry to her.

But she just stood, trembling, her fingertips on him seemed so erotic, her scent filling him, her incredible ivory-skinned body an aphrodisiac that threatened to engulf him. He saw the darkness of his hands against the pale cream of her body. Fight me, he thought again. Dammit, make me stop this before I find myself damned....

But she didn't fight him. And from that point, it didn't matter. He bent down until his face lay against the warm silk of her belly, his lips touched and tasted, and his hands curled around her buttocks. Then he was rising, sweeping her into his arms and striding across the room. He laid her on the bed, the blue bed, with its clean sheets and soft plump comforter and feather pillows. Her hair spread across the sheets like gold against a blue sky, pure fire and elegant softness. Her eyes had fallen, but they didn't meet his. Still, she didn't move, and the beat of her heart seemed to thunder within her chest, her frantic pulse visible at her throat.

The length of her stretched before him. She didn't reach for the covers, didn't turn, just lay there as his eyes raked over her, her elegantly slim throat, the fine bones of her shoulders and collarbones, her breasts, firm and erect, the slimness of her waist, the curve of her hip, the long, shapely length of her legs, the soft, blazing gold enticement between them. . . .

His boots hit the floor first. His shirt and pants quickly followed. She heard him strip, heard his clothing hit the floor, and still her eyes didn't open. But she knew what she was getting. She had seen him before.

Naked, he came down beside her. He felt the heat of her body with the length of his own. Desire erupted, hard and searing within him. Longing, aching. He straddled her, found her lips, and kissed her with a strength that was far more hunger than force. He found her tongue and filled her mouth. Dropping his head lower, Blade caressed and tasted her breasts once more, stroking her belly with the flat of his palm, threading his fingers into the down of her triangle, lower, touching her, stroking her . . .

A sound emitted from her. She moved, just shifting, gasps catching in her throat, her body trembling against his touch. She seemed exquisite. He eased himself down the length of her, forcing her thighs apart with the weight of his body. He touched her with the wet heat of his tongue, stroked, delved.

Another sound escaped her, one that caused her to twist violently, burying her face in the pillow lest her cry be heard. She trembled wildly as he held her, stroked her, caressed her.

He rose above her, cooling the fire that swept through him with a soaring need. Her eyes remained closed. She trembled wildly, but when he took her lips they parted swiftly at his touch, answering the hunger within them. He stroked down the length of her body with his thumb, parting her. Then he entered her, taking her with a hard, swift movement.

She uttered a cry that she could not swallow quickly enough, a ragged sound of pain. And, of course, he knew why, even as it was too late to possibly erase it, for he had already torn through the barriers of her innocence. He went dead still, cursing himself, cursing the hunger and drive and anguish that still pulsed through him.

The one cry was all that had left her. She lay silent, unmoving. She was pale, and her eyes were closed. He remained impaled within her. Words, harshly spoken, tore from his lips.

"Open your eyes!"

She did so, their emerald depths glittering, defiant.

"You can't be any Mrs. Dylan."

"I am Mrs. Dylan," she whispered. There was a film of wetness on her eyes. Tears. She wasn't going to let them fall. "I swear to you, I am a Mrs."

"Mr. Dylan was an abstainer?" he asked mockingly. He was still furious with her, furious for what she had allowed him to do, furious with himself for having done it. Furious for wanting her so desperately even now....

"Mr. Dylan died," she said flatly.

"Damn you, Jessica!" he swore at her suddenly. "We could have stopped this at any time. Now the damage is done—"

"There is no damage!" she cried. "I did what I chose—"

"Because you will not go home where you should be?" he asked.

"I—"

"Have it your way, Mrs. Dylan!"

Indeed, the damage was done, and he was as explosive as gunpowder, fevered, in agony. He cupped her chin in his hand and found her lips once again. He kissed her hard, deeply—near savagely—and began to move inside her. What cry she might have emitted was swallowed by his lips. His hands roamed freely over her body, cupping her buttocks, holding her, guiding her, stroking her soft flesh. Her hands fell upon his flesh, nails biting into his shoulders. Her lips soothed his wounds. She seemed to sheathe him with warmth and wetness, her body a sweet glove, her warmth a golden fire. His hunger built, the speed of his thrusts multiplied. No matter that he had tried to take care, and perhaps it mattered no longer. Her gasped breaths were escaping sweetly by his ear, coming faster and faster. She moved beneath him, body held too tightly to his by the force of his hand upon her buttocks, yet melding so sensually to his, naturally finding his rhythm, his hunger. He whispered to her, assured her, led her, lifted her. The fire exploded inside of him and he knifed even more deeply into her, shaking with the force of the climax that had seized him. He eased himself again and again into her and from her, watching her face, but her eyes were closed again. Before he would move from her, take himself from her, he needed to *see* her.

"Look at me."

She did so. Eyes still liquid. Her face still pale. Her lips trembling just slightly.

"Damn you, I never meant to hurt you—"

"You didn't hurt me. Well," she murmured, her eyes falling, "perhaps—a little. But—"

He groaned, falling to her side at last. She was struggling for the covers. He kept the weight of his body hard upon them.

It was too late for her to cover up now. Too late, because he was so damned aggravated, so furious. And more.

He was entrapped. Just as if she had cast some gold-and-fire net around him, a fragile web that, nonetheless, held him powerless. He couldn't leave her.

Blade had touched her, had her, held her. He wanted her again and again. He wanted to teach her that there could be so much more. He wanted to feel the movement, the heat of her kiss upon him, the liquid movement of her limbs. He wanted to know her— what went on in her mind, what gave her reckless courage and raw determination....

"It was my choice!" Jessica said angrily. He could hear the pain in her words, and he winced.

He came up on an elbow, staring at her. "I wouldn't have been in here if I had known!" he nearly roared.

"Shh!" she whispered as wild alarm filled her eyes.

He gritted his teeth. "So you don't mind sleeping with a half-breed, you just don't want the world knowing about it?"

She inhaled sharply between her teeth. Then, she tried to leap away. He dragged her back, the weight of his body pinning her to the bed when she struggled.

"Damn you—" Blade said again. He could feel her lie still, rigidly still, her emerald eyes staring into his, her face so very beautiful, so very proud.

"How dare you!" she said angrily. "Don't blame me for whatever chips you carry on your shoulders!"

He started. He had never really known that he carried a chip on his shoulder. He'd spent his life being proud of being Sioux. But his father had been a fine man, too, a good man, a strong one, a fair one. And he'd lived in his white father's world for a long time. He'd learned that there were many men and women who considered any Indian a savage, a different breed, untamed, uncivilized. And so he'd spent most of his life making damned sure that everything he did, he did the best it could be done.

Once, his fastidiousness had made him invaluable to Quantrill, and when he walked away from Quantrill's white man's savagery, he had used his running, shooting and fighting abilities to fight with Mosby in the East, in the Shenandoah. He'd known all along that the Union generals were determined to hang Mosby's men when they caught them, and so he had been determined never to get caught. It hadn't mattered. If they'd known him from before, he'd have had a price on his head. He hadn't planned on staying with

Quantrill long, it was just that Quantrill had been the one after the Red Legs, the Kansas Jayhawkers.

He had learned early a certain stoicism. That had helped him on the day. His Rebel troops had lain down their arms. Surrendered. Surrender had meant that it was time to go after those men again. The men who had stripped him of his life.

Blade rolled his weight from her once again, stepping to the floor. Naked, he padded to the window in the silence of the night. Jessica went for her sheets, instinctively. He could see her movement from the corner of his eye.

From somewhere near, a wolf howled. He saw Jessica shiver, yet he didn't think it was from the strange cry of the wolf. How could she be such a damned strong-willed woman and yet seem so achingly vulnerable and beautiful, binding slender ribbons inexorably around his soul? She made him want her again. Made feelings beat within him once again, just looking at her there. He knew that if he touched her...

"Damn you!" he said softly, to the night.

"Why!" she cried, a note of passion in her voice. "You can turn now and walk away. You won, I lost, remember? I always pay my debts. You're free. You can leave whenever you want. I've paid—"

He swung on her. "Paid? I think I said for the *night*. It's only half over, the best that I can see!"

Jessica fell silent, a blush staining her cheeks. Blade strode to the bed, newly aroused, and not giving a damn that she would see his hardness. She had nothing against half-breeds and she was willing to sell her soul to stay. She wanted to play the game no matter how rough it became.

He wrenched the sheets from her and straddled her. She clenched her jaw, her eyes flashing, her hands coming up against his chest. But he caught them.

"One month," he told her. "You wanted me, you've got me. One month. So you manage to do whatever it is you have to do out here in that amount of time."

"But—"

"What is it that you're so determined to do?" he demanded.

Emerald eyes locked with his. "Land," she said softly. Her lashes swept over her eyes, then her gaze met his once again. "I want to claim the land. It was my husband's."

She was lying—or at least, she wasn't telling him everything, Blade thought. "One month," he said. "Then you're on your own."

"I'll pay you well—"

"Damned right," he said very softly. "Here's the deal. You get me. And, Mrs. Dylan, I get you."

"You've had—"

"A taste," he murmured, and bent down. Slowly, slowly he captured her lips. Teased them, played with them. He waited for her mouth to part, to accept his sensual invasion, to return the touch, sweet motion by sweet motion....

Her arms wound around him, and he made love to her again.

So slowly. So sensually, teaching, exploring, discovering. Touching, laving, still tasting, whispering, having.... Becoming one with her. Bronze flesh against ivory, slick, fluid. Hungry. Creating a storm, a sweet tempest, bringing her with him until she writhed so erotically beneath him.

And when he finished, he captured her lips to keep silent the cry he had wrung from her being. She lay beside him, dazed, panting, flushed. Then she turned away.

"No!" she whispered.

"A month," he reminded her. His arms around her then, he pulled her to him gently. She was so warm, silken still. It seemed just as sweet to hold her. And she did not pull away. She paid her debts—

And kept her bargains, so it seemed.

Golden strands of hair softly entangled him. He lay awake, staring at the ceiling, wondering what he had done. A month. Had he cast them both into the fiery pits of hell . . . ? Or the sweetest heights of heaven?

Chapter Six

Jessica woke early, as she was accustomed to doing, yet it seemed that her eyelids were heavy, that it was hard to open them. Her lashes fluttered. The first thing she saw was his hand. Large, powerful, long-fingered, bronzed, nails clipped, not manicured, but clean. It lay around her waist, holding her close against his body.

She closed her eyes tightly again, recalling the night, assuring herself that she must be absolutely horrible, yet not feeling that she was in the least. She had to get to the land, she reminded herself. She was determined to get to the land, and maybe she had been willing to pay almost any price to get there.

But . . . this price hadn't quite occurred to her until she had first seen McKenna. And no matter what she tried to tell herself, a certain fire had stirred and burned deep within her from that moment. He was beyond a doubt the most intriguing man she had ever seen. He was perhaps an inch or two over six feet, lithe, graceful, silent, his every movement one of perfect ease—startling in a man with such broad shoulders, such fine, taut muscle structure, she thought. He was straight as oak and hard as stone, his face something handsomely chiseled from granite. His sleek, thick, pitch-black hair and ebony eyes were a striking giveaway to his Indian heritage, while the hard planes of his face somehow combined white and Indian characteristics into a visage that was arresting, strikingly handsome, and still so very rugged. He had fascinated her from the first seconds she had seen him. When she heard him speak, she felt tremors steal down her spine. When he looked directly at her, she felt fire seep into her bones.

She'd never felt anything quite like it before in her life. Ever. She'd been in love, or, rather, she had loved, and perhaps there was a difference. Charlie had been a part of her life forever. She had known him so very well. It was circumstance that had come between them, war that had split them apart.

And yet... As much as she had loved Charlie, as much as she was here on his behalf, she had never begun to feel for Charlie what she did for this man.

A hard throbbing suddenly began within her heart. Well, she had won. She had lost...and then won. He'd told her that he'd come with her for a month. That was all she would need. But then, in a month...

She swallowed hard, not wanting to waken him. She wanted to rise and dress, to hide herself. Morning's light could be so harsh. She started trembling each time she remembered just how he had made her feel. Turning crimson, Jessica prayed that no one else in Mrs. Peabody's boardinghouse had heard how he had made her feel.

One month. She had him. He had her. Could he really want her so much? she wondered. He had been so damned furious with her innocence, or perhaps it had been her lack of expertise or—

No. He hadn't wanted an involvement, she reasoned, and men always seemed to think that any inexperienced woman had to be after more than she was willing to say.

He would never understand. She owed Charlie, she had to get to the land and stay there long enough to find his papers. And she would have done anything...with *this* man. She couldn't explain it. Couldn't explain what Blade had touched within her.

She drew away, easing from the bed. She winced somewhat as she tried to walk, hurrying across the room to the washbowl to drench and cool her face. She shivered in the brisk morning air, washing her throat, breasts, arms. She dropped the cloth at last, turning to open her trunk, which Shorty had brought by at dinnertime last night. She withdrew a corset, pantalets, a petticoat and a cool calico dress. Although it was cool now, she was certain the afternoon would be warm. She had just stepped into the pantalets when her eyes fell upon him. He hadn't made a sound or a motion, but his black eyes were on her and she flushed, suddenly certain that he had been awake, watching her, since she first had risen. They were enigmatic eyes, so Stygian dark, so piercing and demanding. She lowered her lashes quickly, trying to draw the dress over her head before she had tied the pantalets.

He laughed and came swiftly to his feet. She could feel him at her back, pulling up her dress, finding the lace on her pantalets and pulling it into a sturdy tie. She quickly smoothed the calico down, her cheeks still flushed. Eyes downcast, she murmured swiftly, "I have to pick up a few things I had ordered last night. My land isn't far from here. I'd like to start out right after breakfast, if that's all right. If—"

She hesitated. He was still at her back. She swung around and felt tremors all over again because he simply had such a beautiful body. Tall, bronzed, his chest devoid of hair, glistening even by daylight with taut muscle. She swallowed hard. "You, er, need to get dressed."

He nodded, offering her a dry smile that caused her to blush all over again. She had started all this by bursting into his bath. She shouldn't be dismayed by his nakedness.

"That is," she murmured softly, "if you haven't changed your mind. You—you did say that you'd come."

"Hmm. You've got me. I've got you."

She exhaled, a shaky sound of relief. Then she spun around quickly. "I'm just going to go downstairs—" She broke off, her eyes going wide. "The—"

"Bed next door," Blade finished for her. "Don't worry, I'll go mess it up. I'm not too sure what we can do about this one."

"Do?" she murmured, then glanced at the sheets that gave away everything. "Oh..."

"I can just steal them," he offered politely.

"Oh, yes, that should go unnoticed!"

He grinned and laughed. "We'll put a bandage on your hand. You can say that you cut it opening a letter last night or something."

"Will it—work?"

"Better than nothing, I imagine," he assured her. He turned and left her, crossing through the door that connected their rooms, returning to hers with a swatch of clean, white linen cloth. She stood still while he wrapped her hand. She was painfully aware of his very natural nakedness once again, and she stiffened as she breathed in the sensual scent of him. His eyes were suddenly on hers. "What's wrong?"

"You—you really need to get dressed. You—"

"Look ready?" he suggested, laughing. She bit her lip, lashes sweeping over her eyes.

"There you go again, just dying to give me a good right to the jaw," he said.

She sighed. "I didn't say that you look ready to—"

"But I am—always," he assured her huskily.

Her eyes flew open. "Braggart!" she accused him, and he started to laugh again. He finished wrapping her hand, then suddenly drew her into his arms.

"Want to test me?"

"No!" she exclaimed. But, God, his touch... What was the magic? How could he be so fierce and so tender? Jessica pondered.

Such a stranger... while she was beginning to feel that she knew him so very well.

His lips touched upon hers. She struggled against him. "There's business—"

"Debts to be paid!" he agreed.

"Here—I mean, now?"

He laughed softly again, releasing her. She saw in his black eyes that he had been teasing her, taunting her all along. He didn't need to force anything. He had lots of time. That was the agreement. And she did always pay her debts.

"Go on down," he told her. "Do what you have to do. I'll be ready when you are."

Jessica spun around and hurriedly left the room. She met Mrs. Peabody on the landing at the foot of the stairs. "Good morning, Jessica, dear. Oh, no! Your hand, dear! What did you do?"

"Oh, it's just a scratch. I cut it with my letter opener. I'm fine. I'm afraid I was on the bed, though, and there are a few spots of blood." And she had to be the color of blood by now, too. Would such a lame story fly? What was Mrs. Peabody going to do, accuse her of lying? Of misconduct beneath her roof?

"Don't you worry about that at all," Mrs. Peabody said. "Jane will get them out with lemon juice. I'm just so concerned about your hand."

"It's nothing, really. I swear it." It *was* nothing— that was honest enough, Jessica reasoned.

"All right, dear, I won't press it. How did you sleep?"

"Wonderfully. I wish I could stay longer," Jessica said. Well, it wasn't a lie. Once she had fallen asleep, she had slept like the dead. And she did wish that she could stay longer. Mrs. Peabody had made a beautiful home out here in the wilderness. It was comfortable, warm. So incredible after what she had been through traveling.

"Why don't you stay another night before moving on, dear? I'm sure you'll hit problems and hard work aplenty once you leave. One day of rest might be just the thing you need."

One more night in this proper place with Mc-Kenna? She didn't think so. Just the thought made fresh color seem to fly to her cheeks. And she only had McKenna for a month. One month.

She shook her head. "I—I really can't, Mrs. Peabody, though I would love to."

"I understand, dear. You want to get going to your own home."

"Yes. But it's not even a full day's ride from here. I'll be back often enough. In fact, I'll be back next week for a few days to buy cattle."

"That's wonderful. I'll be expecting you."

"And Mr. McKenna," Jessica said softly.

Mrs. Peabody had begun to move her portly body when she turned back, smiling. "Pardon, dear?"

"Mr. McKenna has graciously consented to work for me for the next few weeks." Mrs. Peabody was staring at her. "I—I've had a great deal of trouble ever since I started on my way here. He bailed me out twice, so... well, I seem to need someone."

"But Mr. McKenna is working for you?" Mrs. Peabody repeated, astonished.

Jessica nodded. "What's wrong with that?"

"Nothing, nothing. It's just that, well, he's so much his own man, dear. I would have never believed that he would have consented to work for anyone else. And then again... Well, dear, surely, if ever there was someone in need... Oh! Here I go babbling. You just run around to the stables, right around the corner. Your wagon should be loaded, your horses ready. Everyone in this town was just pleased pink at the orders you gave. And," Mrs. Peabody added, "the gold you had to pay for them all!"

Jessica grinned. She liked it out here. She liked the honesty. She hadn't come West intending to stay. Now she began to wonder what it would be like.

"Thank you, Mrs. Peabody, I will just run around and check on the wagon."

"Coffee and breakfast will be on when you come back," Mrs. Peabody called to her.

Jessy stepped outside and walked around the corner to the stables. Her wagon was waiting right in front. It was exactly what she had wanted, a big, flat wagon with a high box seat, the kind of conveyance fit for a ranch that was starting out. There were two roan horses harnessed to it already. The horses looked fine and strong, the harness well made and nicely polished. A man came out of the stables when she approached, a crinkled older fellow named Delaney. His eyes were bright Irish blue and his smile was broad. "Morning, Mrs. Dylan. We've got it all, every last speck of stuff you wanted! There's coffee in that bag, flour there, salt right over here. Let's see, there's the fabric you wanted, the grain, the jarred jellies and fruits, and Mrs. Shrewesbury even had some canned tomatoes, beans and turnip greens. She threw in a few of her fresh vegetables and fruits for you—she started out here herself from back East, and says she knows getting started is hard. I think you're just about all set, at least to get started."

"That's fine, Mr. Delaney. Thank you so much. What about the lamps?"

"In the back of the wagon. You've got some oil there, too, and a big box of candles. You should be just as right as rain. You've done ordered and paid for just about everything. Except one thing that's darned important," Delaney told her.

"Oh?" Jessica asked. "What did I forget?"

"You forgot that you're going out a day's ride from town. A woman alone out there might plum be a target for any no-account outlaw in the territory!"

"I'm not going alone," Jessica assured him quickly. "Mr. McKenna is coming with me."

"McKenna!"

Mr. Delaney seemed as startled as Mrs. Peabody had been. "McKenna has agreed to come with you?"

She nodded. "From what I've seen, he can probably outgun any no-account outlaw."

Delaney nodded. "Yes, well, damned right you'll be safe. Just—" He hesitated.

"What is it?"

"You watch out for him, too, Mrs. Dylan. There's some out there that believe he's a no-account outlaw, but there's some truths out here in the West, and one of them is that a man's got to do what a man's got to do... and Mr. McKenna, he only went after a vengeance that was rightfully his! But you be careful where you bandy his name about, Mrs. Dylan. You don't want to be the downfall of a damned fine man!"

Jessica stared at him, stunned by his vehemence. She didn't know what he was talking about.

I never said that I wasn't an outlaw . . . Jessica suddenly remembered Blade's words. Wasn't that what he had told her? Something very much like that?

"I'll be careful, Mr. Delaney," she promised. "He won't be with me that long. Only a month."

"Then you look hard and find yourself good help, and get yourself established in that time, young woman, you hear me? We're willing to do all we can from town here, you know."

She smiled. "Thank you."

"You go on and have your breakfast at Mrs. Peabody's. I'll have McKenna's horse saddled and ready when you are. Smart girl. I couldn't imagine how you could have forgotten how wild and lawless this land can be."

"No, I was really good, Mr. Delaney," she said wryly. "I was careful. I've bought—and paid for—everything." Including McKenna, she added silently. She offered Mr. Delaney her hand. "Thank you. Thank you for everything."

"Thank you. It's not often we're paid in gold by such beautiful young women out here," Delaney told her with a wink.

She smiled. "Thanks again." She turned and walked around the dusty corner to the wooden sidewalk, then hurried into Mrs. Peabody's. She found Blade already seated at the dining room table. There was a huge plate of ham and eggs and sausages and biscuits set before him, and he seemed to be enjoying them tremendously. Jessica sat across the table from him while Mrs. Peabody served her some coffee.

"Thank you," Jessica said.

"Everything all set?" Mrs. Peabody asked cheerfully.

"Yes, Mr. Delaney was wonderful, he pulled everything together."

Blade chewed on his biscuit, arching a black brow as he stared at her.

"Mr. Delaney said I ordered very well, and that I have everything I need."

"I hope so," Blade told her.

"This pot is empty," Mrs. Peabody said with a tsk. "Let me run out to the back, I'll be back shortly." She exited the room with a bustle.

"You're damned sure you've got everything?" Blade asked Jessica.

"Well, I had been," she murmured, "but now that I see how you eat..."

He grinned at her, unperturbed. "Spent a lot of energy last night. Made me really hungry this morning."

She blushed, picking up a biscuit.

"Don't you dare throw one of those!" he warned her.

She couldn't resist the temptation. She gritted her teeth and threw.

He caught it. Mrs. Peabody walked in. He started to butter the biscuit.

"Here's more coffee—" she began, but Blade was up, smiling, taking the pot from her.

"You sit down, Mrs. Peabody. I'm going to the buffet to get Mrs. Dylan a plate. She's going to have to learn to have a hearty breakfast like a Westerner, right? If she didn't acquire a good appetite last night,

I'll just have to see that she does in the future. Of course, we'll have to hope that she can learn to be as good a cook as you, my dear *Rose!*"

He was at the buffet, heaping her plate with eggs and ham. She could never eat it all, even though she was starving. He set the plate before her.

She met his black eyes. "Thank you!"

"Grits! I'll get you a bowl."

"No, that's fine. Really, I've never eaten them—"

"This may be Indian territory, but it's damned close to Texas. Grits are a staple, you'd best get used to them. Easterners!" he said, black eyes on her. Then he added very softly, *"Northeasterners!"* He turned away from her suddenly, his tone changing. "Mrs. Peabody, this was delightful, as usual."

"Have more coffee, Mr. McK—er, Blade."

He picked up his cup, walking with it to the rear window of the room, from where he could see Mr. Delaney's stables.

"Things look about ready," he said.

Jessica sat back, sipping her coffee, studying him. She felt warm tremors assailing her once again. There was so much she liked about him. He was exceedingly handsome this morning in fitted dark trousers, a black cavalry-styled shirt and riding boots. His dark hair, cut to his nape, seemed exceptionally sleek, his face clean shaven but rugged.

Outlaw? He couldn't be. His manners were perfect. He could taunt her easily enough, but he was kind and courteous to Mrs. Peabody, the perfect gentleman. He was so obviously Indian, yet so obviously white. He had been well educated somewhere, but he seemed to live nowhere, with nothing but his beautiful bay and his saddlebags. And vengeance. The whole idea gave her goose bumps. And yet, he had his right to it, that was what Mr. Delaney had said....

He turned, his coffee cup cradled in his hand. "Eat up," he told her.

"If you're in a hurry, I don't have to eat—"

"Yes, you do," he said with amusement. "You're definitely going to need your strength."

For the ranch? For herself? For him?

She lowered her face quickly. Damn him, she had to stop blushing. She wasn't going to let him spend endless days and nights doing this to her!

Her hunger had been real; she ate everything. When she was finished, they rose, and she discovered that Mrs. Peabody already had asked her boys to bring Jessica's trunk out to the wagon. They were all set to go. Moments later, they both had said their goodbyes. She crawled up on the wagon, taking the reins. But Blade leapt up beside her, taking them from her.

"You're welcome to ride your horse—" she began.

"He's tethered to the back," he assured her curtly. Then his gaze was upon her for a long moment. "I've got to make sure I earn my keep, eh, Mrs. Dylan?"

She gritted her teeth, swiftly looking downward, aware that Mrs. Peabody and Mr. Delaney were still waving, watching them start their ride out of town.

"I do wish that you'd stop that!" she whispered.

"Why? You were the one doing the bargaining, the one who suggested the price."

"Because I would have paid anything—"

"For this land? I am dying to see it!"

"My husband left it to me!" she said icily.

"Your husband—the chaste Yank?" he said.

"The dead one," she murmured, looking away. Then she stared at him suddenly. "Does that bother you? That he was a Union soldier?"

"That *you're* a Yank?" he inquired, his gaze upon her again, a black brow arched. "No," he said after a moment. "Hell, no, the war's over, isn't it? Long over."

But there was a note of bitterness to his voice. The war wasn't really over. Not for him.

"I don't give a damn what he was, or what you are, Mrs. Dylan. Not so long as it doesn't affect our bargain."

She stiffened her shoulders and looked ahead. "If you're going to earn your keep, McKenna, start getting us there!"

He, too, looked ahead, and they rode in silence for a long while.

Morning turned into afternoon. They stopped at a stream, watered the horses, drank deeply themselves and moved onward again. Blade rode his bay for awhile, and Jessica took the reins. She soon learned why he had been helping her. In an hour, her hands were blistering.

"The trail is steep here!" he yelled at her suddenly. "You've got to control those horses!"

"I'm trying!" Damn the blisters. She took firm hold, and they moved through the trees. And then, with the sun setting and casting an incredible golden glow upon the valley below, she saw it.

Charlie's land. There was the house, a log structure, big and sprawling in an L-shape. There were corrals and paddocks before it, long stables and a huge barn. Even from this distance, she could see they were all in need of repair. Still, the spread below her was impressive.

"How much is yours?" Blade asked.

"Five hundred acres," she told him.

He sniffed. "Cattle land, trees, a stream passing through there..." He shrugged. "Maybe you're right. Maybe this place is worth fighting for. I haven't seen ranch land quite so fine since—"

"Since?" she asked softly.

"A different life," he murmured. "Let's get down there."

Twilight was with them even as they reached the house. They worked together in silence, getting the candles and lamps first so that they could see what they were up to. Blade cared for the horses, taking them into the stables he had swept out to give them water and grain.

Jessica began to sweep the house. It was filthy, years of grime and dust having accumulated on the furnishing. Nonetheless, it was a fine house. There was a kitchen with a sink and a pump that drew fresh water from the well.

Charlie had furnished the place. There was a big leather sofa that sat before the fireplace, two rockers at its sides. There was a knit rug on the wooden floor, and a dining table with six well-carved seats. Down the hallway there were four bedrooms, two of them fully furnished with cherrywood bed frames and dressers, and one even had a beautiful washstand with a marble top. The largest bedroom also had a screen that surrounded a big wooden tub, and Jessica promised herself that it would be one of the first things she cleaned in the morning. That night, she swept and scrubbed the floors and countertops, stripped the bed, plumped up the mattress, and put new sheets on it. When she turned, he was there. He stood tall and strikingly handsome in the lamplight.

"Horses are all taken care of," Blade said. "A hinge was off the front door so I took care of that, too." He smiled suddenly, watching her with a new interest. "Then I smelled something good from inside. Can you actually cook?"

"You didn't think I could?"

He strode to her, picking up her hand. His fingertip traced the bubblelike blisters, and she winced. "You've had servants your whole life," he said softly.

She wrenched her hand back. "Fine. Don't eat."

"I'm a gambling man," he reminded her.

She strode by him quickly. She'd set the ham and beans in a pot above the fire as she wasn't too sure about her stove yet. The mixture was bubbling, and she found two of the plates she had cleaned and filled them, bringing them to the table.

"I'll get some water," she said, eyeing him nervously. "The glasses are right there. They're washed. Or—I suppose you might want whiskey. The coffee is on now, but it will take a minute—"

"Never mind," he told her, "I bought something from Mrs. Peabody this morning myself." His saddlebags lay near the door. He pulled out a bottle of red wine and brought it to the table. "Will you join me, Mrs. Dylan?"

She nodded. He poured the wine. She sat down and sipped it quickly. Then, sliding a napkin onto her lap, she dipped into her food. Across the table, Blade joined her.

Warm, flushed and exhausted, Jessica quickly drank a glass of the wine. She could feel his eyes on her. He took a spoonful of the ham and beans, still watching her.

"Will it do?" she whispered.

"It's excellent."

"Thank you."

"What are you really doing here, Jessica Dylan?" he asked suddenly.

"You just said that it was good land. You said—"

"Good land. But you're rich. You must have had some decent life back East."

"I want to be here. Is that so difficult to understand?"

"Just difficult to believe," he told her dryly.

"And what about you?" she demanded. "Are you some kind of outlaw?"

"You tell me," he replied.

She drained a second glass of wine. It was getting to her tonight. Perhaps because she was so very tired. She set the glass down and stood uneasily. "I'll get the coffee," she murmured.

But he was beside her, a subtle grin on his lips, sweeping her into his arms. "I'll take care of the coffee. You—we don't need any."

He carried her into the bedroom, laid her upon the bed and started to take her clothing off.

"I can manage."

"You can't manage anything else tonight," he told her curtly.

Ah, yes! She owed him. The days were when he worked. The nights were when she paid.

Instead, she found the covers pulled up over her nakedness and felt his palm upon her brow.

"Good night, Mrs. Dylan."

He left her then. Alone. Untouched. She bit her lip, wondering if she hadn't been a disappointment to him, if he didn't want her with the same fire he once had. She should be relieved, she thought. Surely, she was. She was so exhausted. So she slept.

Not alone. In the morning, she awakened with the first rays of sunlight. They fell softly into the room. She started to rise, again realizing she was naked. And then she felt his touch, his fingers sliding down the length of her spine, curving over her buttocks. Her breath caught. His hand circled persistently on her hip, drawing her around to him to meet his eyes.

"Good morning, Mrs. Dylan."

She started to tremble. She was amazed. She wasn't afraid. She wanted him.

His lips found hers. He touched her, guiding her hands upon him. He kissed her mouth, her cheeks. He spent long moments laving her breasts, then, moving lower, creating hot fires between her thighs. He stroked her there, kissed her there and made love to her until she was crying out softly, arching, straining to meet his thunderous beat. She needed him, ached for him, longed for the sweet surcease she had so recently learned was within the magic of the world. Suddenly, it was hers. The sweet heat and lightning shot through her. She clung to him, screaming out. And there was no reason for him to still the sound with his kiss, for there was no one to hear them in their wilderness.

Later, the sun streaked in more fully. She turned to him suddenly, biting her lower lip. He groaned softly, caressing her side as he held her to him. "What now?" he asked. "No more modesty, no turning away? No distress over what comes between us?"

She met his eyes, shook her head, and turned bright red.

He laughed out loud, as he stroked her cheek with his knuckles, then leapt from the bed. "Up, Mrs. Dylan! It's going to be a damned long day!"

Chapter Seven

To Blade, it wasn't so incredibly amazing that Jessica began to rise in the middle of the night, saddle and bridle her horse and begin to ride out. It was amazing that she really believed she did so without waking him!

Actually, it all began after they had been in the house about five days. They had been long, productive days. He'd forgotten how good it felt to work on the land. The satisfaction of repairing broken fences, fixing a house. A home. Jessica—who had seemed such a hothouse flower from the East—proved to be anything but. Maybe she'd just never blistered her hands before.

She had a knack for making a house a home, and in those first few days it seemed that he was living in some kind of dream of paradise. He'd work through the day, and at night, she'd always manage to make something tempting. There were warm, clean drapes up all over now, fresh hot coffee always ready—and even flowers on the table. At night, after dinner, they would spend a few hours before the fire, and he would tell her his opinion of the best cattle to buy, or how to judge a ranch hand once she was ready to start hiring on men.... It was downright homey.

Sometimes they even went a little further. They were two closed people, opening up just a little to give one another personal glimpses. He learned that she had been born in New York State, that her family had been in the country since the first Pilgrims had landed, that her father had made his money in steel and that she had been his only heir. Blade had been curious that anyone so wealthy and comfortable in the East would brave such hazards in the West. "Money is only worth the things that can be bought with it," she had said softly, staring into the fire.

"You could have bought a lot back East."

"Things only have value if you really want them. I really wanted this land."

That was as far as she had gone. On his part, he had told her that he had gone to school back East himself, to a Virginia military academy, and he even conceded that he had ridden with Mosby until the bitter end of the war. She'd heard plenty about Mosby's men, even in upstate New York, and he knew she was curious, staring at him, wondering why a half-breed Sioux would risk his neck so for the Confederate cause.

He didn't tell her about Quantrill. And though he easily described life with his mother's people—the warmth, the harmony that could exist within the tribe—he never mentioned the Sioux wife he had brought home to his father. He tried to explain to Jessica that some of the Plains Indians had formed deep friendships, while others were natural enemies, fighting one another since tales and memory could recall.

They both gave. They both held back. And still, the domesticity of their situation seemed to be swiftly entangling him. The days, the evenings, and the nights.

It was wrong. Wrong to have such a hunger for her, to hold her through the dark hours, needing her, demanding her. Wrong for her, wrong for him. But he couldn't let her go. He couldn't let this beauty slip though his fingers, couldn't fight the fascination of being with her and seeing her flower with each night....

She seemed to need him in turn, even hunger for him. Her delicate ivory fingers were so sensual upon his dark, bronzed flesh. It was wrong, perhaps. But it was a part of this strange paradise, and so the early days passed with a touch of magic.

Then it began. And perhaps what was most amazing of all was that she didn't realize he followed her.

Actually, the first night, she didn't ride. She rose, slipped on a robe, and went out to the barn. The first time she had started to rise he had asked her what was wrong and she had gone stiff, saying nothing and pretending to sleep once again. The second time, he had let her go. But he had followed her. And in the barn she had paced over the entire space, stomping in each stall. It went on at length, until she grew tired and frustrated and returned to the house.

He had slipped into bed just two seconds before her. He had almost demanded an explanation, but then he had decided to wait. *She* would tell *him* what she was doing.

She didn't.

The next night, she rose and dressed silently, slipped from the room, and headed for the stables. He followed her as swiftly as he could.

The moon was full. She could see easily enough, and she seemed to have an abstract idea of where she was going. They rode south along the corral and over a small hill to a clump of large, scattered rocks. The stream ran just behind them; he could hear the bubble of water even as he carefully lagged behind her.

She dismounted, looked about with dismay, then began to try to push the rocks. They were good-sized, to say the least, each weighing well over two hundred pounds. He might have pitched in and helped her. He watched her with astonishment instead.

When a rock or boulder seemed set in the ground, she gave up and started on a new one. In all, she managed to move perhaps two or three before she paused, looked at the moon, then looked around herself, shivering. She didn't see him because he'd been very careful to take a stance behind the grove of trees to the extreme south of her.

She was going for her horse, he realized. He swiftly mounted his bay bareback, and easily beat her to the ranch and back into bed.

She joined him within a matter of minutes, anxiously watching his face to assure herself that he slept, crawling in very carefully beside him.

He waited, aware that she lay there, still as a candlestick, waiting for him. He kept his eyes closed, and at last, it seemed, she sighed and slept. Baffled, he lay awake.

They made plans the next day for a trip into Jackson Prairie for more supplies, for cattle and hopefully, a few hired hands. They would go at the end of the week.

That night, she rose again. And he followed her. And she tried to push stones. Once again, he beat her back to the house. And she slipped in beside him. And he lay awake, absolutely confused. What in God's name was she doing? And why the hell didn't she trust him?

When she slept, he came up on an elbow and studied her. She had curved against him already—naturally. Her hair was a golden sweep around the two of them, her delicate features so perfect and serene against her pillow. Her vision caught upon something in his heart. Even the touch of her flesh against his was newly evocative.

He was tempted suddenly to pinch her awake. To demand an explanation. Instead, he lay watching her. He didn't pinch her. He swept his arms around her and held her closely to him.

But the next night, he determined, was going to be it.

It started the same. Stew for dinner, coffee before the fire. They were both rather silent. When her eyes touched his, he didn't say a word, just set down his mug, swept her up, and made love to her. Hard, passionate love, created by his anger with her silence. He drew from her a fiery response that evoked his ultimate tenderness in the end, and when she was captured gently within his arms again, he knew that he was in love with her.

The past still hurt. It was a huge void in his heart. He owed Mara, he owed his father, he owed his unborn child. But when that debt was paid, he would love the golden blond Yankee beauty, who might well be maddened by moonlight.

She rose again, just as she had the past two nights. He waited. He followed her. And she went back to shaking those damned rocks. He wasn't going to ride back ahead of her, he decided. Tonight, when she finished, he'd be here. Right here, in her path, waiting.

But even as he stood there, watching her, he heard a noise from the east, just past the spring, and was instantly wary. He blended against the trees and watched.

There was another man watching Jessica that night. He had a scar across his face, starting below his eyes, continuing to his jaw. A big-brimmed hat hid his eyes. He was atop a charcoal gray horse, waiting silently, watching.

Then suddenly, he was moving toward Jessica.

He spurred his horse to gallop close, then suddenly leapt from the animal. Jessica had, at the last moment, seen him coming. She had drawn a small pistol from the pocket of the simple gingham skirt she was wearing, but the man had flown upon her before she could begin to fire the weapon. Blade heard her gasp and hit the ground, hard. Then he heard her scream, and suddenly fall silent, even as he was on his way to her. The man was talking to her. Heatedly. "I'll have those papers, Mrs. Dylan. The captain ain't coming back to haunt me now! I'll have his papers, and I'll have his wife, by God!"

She could fight. Jessica could fight. She was wild beneath the man—biting, clawing, scratching.

But he was stronger. And infinitely pleased to discover she was naked beneath her simple blouse and skirt. As he wrenched up the latter, Blade was upon him, silent as the night behind him, striking like lightning. Maybe he'd meant to kill from the beginning. Maybe he'd been so furious to see the man's brutality toward Jessica. Maybe it had just been that he was touching Jessica. Maybe it was just happenstance...

Blade pried the man from her. The stranger turned, snarling, reaching for the knife at his calf. Blade belted him in the jaw and the man spun around. He fell on his knife, dead even as he hit the ground.

Jessica cried out softly, trembling. She looked up, meeting Blade's eyes, swallowing hard. "Thank God—" she began.

"What the hell is going on here?" he demanded furiously, reaching for her, jerking her to her feet. She was still trembling. Maybe he should have given her a little sympathy, he chided himself. After all, she had come so close to rape, perhaps worse.

But Jessica had been in trouble since she had come here. This man had known who she was. She had needed a bodyguard. She had wanted protection from this man. She wanted more. And Blade was willing to give it. She was forcing the game, and she wasn't letting Blade play with a full deck. He couldn't give her the least bit of sympathy. Not one iota of tenderness. She'd just get herself into worse trouble.

"Blade, damn you, you have no right—"

"Oh, madam, you are wrong! You've given me every right—"

"You're paid for your services!" she cried wretchedly.

He was amazed at just how cutting the words seemed to be, how they tore into his heart. He grabbed her shoulders suddenly, wrenched her against him and shook her. "I'm not paid to be a fool, Mrs. Dylan, and maybe I'm just not paid well enough for your lies!"

"I've never lied to you!"

"You've never told me the truth!"

She fell silent, pulling away from him. She was still shaking. He gritted his teeth, then came behind her, shoving her along.

"What—?"

"Go back. Now. I'm going to bury this fellow, and then I'll be right behind you. And then you can tell me who I just killed and why. And I want the truth, Jessy. Damn you, I want the truth!"

She didn't seem to move very well on her own, so he picked her up bodily and set her on her horse. When she was gone, he looked around, then picked a spot in the grove and buried the man. Dirty, sweating and exhausted, he returned to the house. She was sitting before the fire in the rocker, staring at the flames. The whiskey bottle was at her side. She'd poured a shot for him. And one for herself.

She heard him enter. It was a moment before her eyes slid to his, then back to the fire again. He walked over to stand behind her, picked up the whiskey, swallowed it down. His hands fell on her shoulders.

"Let's have it, shall we, Mrs. Dylan?" he said softly. "No lies."

"I never lied to you. My name is Jessica Dylan, my money came from my father, and I was married to a Captain Charles Dylan who was..." She hesitated a moment, clenching her jaw. "He was my best friend all of my life. I loved him with all my heart."

Blade moved to the fire, staring at her from a position at the mantel. "You loved him so much. You married him. But you never made love with him?"

Her eyes rose to his. "You don't understand, maybe you can't understand."

"Try me."

She lifted her hands. "I was an only child. My mother was dead, my father was always away. Charles lived near me. He was older. He came to my schoolroom, he made snowmen for me. He read me stories. He gave me the world. At the beginning of the war, he finally asked to marry me. Things moved too quickly. We had a wedding, at which he was burning with fever. I sat with him through the night. Before he really recovered, they had ordered his troops to move, and he was sent West in an army ambulance. I would have come. He wouldn't let me."

"And in all that time, he didn't come back?"

"There was a war on. And it wasn't *all that time*," she added softly. "He was killed at the end of 1863."

Blade lifted his hands. "All right, Mrs. Dylan, you've still got me, I'll admit. What does all this have to do with the man I killed tonight?"

She shivered, drawing her feet up on the chair, hugging her knees to her chest. She started to speak, but fell silent.

"Jessica, now!"

"Charles was worried. He was third in command of the fort out here, and, due to conditions back East, he was being sent a number of Confederate prisoners. They kept escaping, and Charles was being blamed. But he knew that there were two men, at least, who were aiding and abetting the escapes. One was an enlisted man, Manson Jenks—"

"The fellow I just killed?"

Jessica nodded, swallowing hard. "I imagine. I never met the men, either of them, I just received letters from Charles about them. The other man was the commanding officer of the camp, Lieutenant Harding."

"Harding!" Blade exclaimed.

"You've heard of him?"

He shrugged. He'd heard of Harding. He'd outrun him once. "He's a colonel now, I believe. He's still stationed at the fort. Still running it, I believe. But I don't understand. Why are these men after you?"

"Charles found some correspondence between them that proved they were taking bribes from the Confederates to release them. Charles didn't dare mail the letters to me, but he did let me know he had buried the proof on the property he bought. He—he loved it out here. He was fascinated by the different Indian tribes, even the Apaches. He loved the landscape, the vistas. He thought that I might, too. And so he bought this property."

"And then?"

She shrugged. "There was a major uprising among tne prisoners. Someone had given them weapons and had helped them escape. Charles was killed. And even then, well, he was blamed for the whole episode. It's on his military records. I just couldn't leave it that way."

"But you little fool! You were willing to risk your own life—"

"Don't you see?" Jessica asked. "He was my life. For years. And he was a good man. He deserved so much more. There was no one left to fight for him— just me. I had to come here, and I still have to find those damned letters and prove the truth!"

'Harding might well be after you now," Blade warned her.

She nodded. "I know. I have to find the letters fast."

"Why didn't you tell me? Why the hell didn't you just tell me the truth and let me help you?"

"Well, you're not fond of Yankees," she reminded him. "And I was afraid that you—"

"That I would what?"

"That you might try to stop me. I have to do this. I can never go forward, never really live anywhere, until it's done."

You're a fool, he wanted to tell her. Charles is dead and gone, and none of us can do anything for him. He turned away from her, facing the fire. "Go to bed," he told her briefly. She didn't move. He swung around on her. "We'll find the damned letters tomorrow night. I assume you have some idea of where you're looking and that you weren't trying to lift rocks for the hell of it?''

She nodded, her face pale. "He had a cache in the stables once, he had written to me. But he mentioned the stream and rocks in another letter, so he must have grown worried that he might have been seen around the barn and moved whatever he had. I—I didn't just come out here blindly."

"No, you just walked into outlaws and Apaches by blind fool chance!"

She stood then. "And you!" she reminded him softly.

He was silent a minute. "And me," he agreed, turning to the fire. A moment later Blade heard her rising, approaching him. "Go to bed!" he repeated.

She turned and did so. He stared at the flames a while. He wondered why he was so damned mad when he understood.

Because he couldn't bear to see her in danger, hurt. He sighed and rose and went into the darkened bedroom. He splashed water from the pitcher into the bowl and scrubbed his face and hands, stripped off his shirt and scrubbed his chest.

He felt her delicate fingers on his back. He felt them touching his shoulders. He heard her voice, soft, entreating.

"Blade..."

He stiffened. "Go to sleep, Jessica. Just go to sleep."

Her delicate fingers withdrew as if his flesh had burned them. She was gone.

He finished scrubbing, grabbed a towel and dried himself, roughly. He threw down his towel at last, and crawled onto his side of the bed. He couldn't bear it any longer. She'd used him because she'd loved another man so deeply. Maybe that was what hurt, too. He really didn't know.

And it didn't matter anymore.

He groaned softly and drew her into his arms. He tasted her tears on her cheeks. "Love me, Jessy, love me!" he told her. His lips found hers. She responded sweetly, erotically, hungrily. She gave in to his demand...never knowing that what he demanded was emotion, and not just surrender.

Chapter Eight

They found the documents the next night.

Blade had been tempted to start looking first thing in the morning, but though they so often seemed to be alone at the ranch, he couldn't forget that Jessy had been accosted last night, and that it was amazing how quickly people could sometimes appear from a vista of apparent emptiness. They were both anxious now, but Blade decided they would wait.

It wasn't a long search. The night was light, with a full moon rising above them. Midnight approached. They could hear the calls of owls, the occasional howl of a wolf.

Blade had the strength Jessy lacked to lift the big stones, and after his fourth try, he found the leather satchel buried just beneath the surface. He wouldn't let her open it there. They hurried to the house, then searched through it. Letters and notes fell from it, and he and Jessy scanned them quickly. He found one from Harding ordering Manson Jenks to see that the prisoners were freed from any shackles, and another stating that Friday would be the right night to taste fresh air. There was a letter from Jenks, assuring

Harding that "everything was in order, and should
move as smooth as silk," and that there were things in
this war that could "beat bootlegging."

He wondered how Charles Dylan had managed to
get this correspondence, and realized he must have
done so very carefully—and with great courage and
determination.

The last of the letters he discovered was to Jessy. It
wasn't sealed in any way, just folded over, and he
opened it, having no idea of what it might say.

Jessy, if you are the one finding this stash, it will
mean that I am gone, and that you have braved
tremendous rigors to come here. Bless you, Jessy.
Take care of yourself. Your life is far more precious than my honor, so don't do anything at all
dangerous. I'm very afraid these days. I don't
know who to trust. I love you with all my heart,
and pray for your happiness. Death holds no fear
for me, only the pain of leaving you.

Ever,
your Charles

Blade hesitated a moment.

"What is it?" Jessica asked worriedly.

He handed her the letter. She read it. He saw her
fingers begin to tremble and he turned away. He knew
that there would be tears in her eyes, that she would be
furiously trying to blink them away.

She had loved Charles. An emotion pure, sweet and
beautiful, and based on years of companionship.
While what she felt for him . . .

Well, hell. He was a hired hand. One she had needed desperately. One she had been willing to pay well to keep. He'd been the damned fool to fall in love with her. Even when he had thought that his own heart had been broken and had turned to stone he was here helping her exonerate a man. Forgetting his own quest.... No, it was never forgotten.

She folded the letter, put it away in the pocket of her skirt. The others she stuffed into the satchel.

"I'll have to do something with these, now that we've found them," she said. She stood. "I guess—"

"Don't guess!" he warned her, aware that there was a harsh edge to his voice. "What you're holding now is dangerous evidence against a powerful man. Manson Jenks was here last night. He surely told Harding that he knew you had come, and just as surely, Harding is going to realize that your husband had evidence against him, and he's going to be wanting to make sure that you don't get your hands on it, either. When Jenks doesn't appear, Harding is going to be very worried. He's going to have to come after you."

"But I'll just see that someone else gets the letters!" she exclaimed.

"He's a colonel now, Jessy! We've got to go above him, we've got to find a general." He paused for a moment. "Sherman has been riding out here. After the Indians," he added wryly. "We'll go into town first thing in the morning, and you'll go in with Mrs. Peabody, and don't you even think of moving out of her place until you hear from me again, do you understand?"

"But what—"

"I'm going to find Sherman," he told her.

"You want me to just sit and wait?" Jessica asked.

"No. I want you to order more supplies and wait. But I don't want you away from Mrs. Peabody for a minute, do you understand?"

"I—"

"Jessy, damn you, you paid a high price for me to protect you, remember? Let me do it."

Her chin set and her face paled. She stood up and walked across the room to the bedroom door. "Good night," she said icily.

He nodded and watched her go. He stared at the fire, and at the leather satchel. He shoved the satchel under the sofa and stretched out upon it.

It suddenly occurred to him that, if he were caught, this might be his last night with her. He couldn't be caught. But there were still a lot of Yanks out there who knew him. It wouldn't matter he tried to tell himself. Not if he could take a few of them down with him.

No, if he were going to take anyone down, he wanted it to be the right men now. The war was over. He was tired of the fighting. He was even ready to make peace with an army ready to decimate his mother's people, he realized. He just wanted revenge on a few.

To help Jessica, he might never get that chance.

He rolled over. He couldn't hold on to the letters. Once they were delivered into the right hands, Jessica would be out of danger. He tossed on the sofa again, onto his back. He heard a sound in the night. His eyes flew open instantly.

Jessica. He half-closed his eyes and waited. She was wearing a soft, sheer gown. Her hair was free, newly brushed, cascading all around her in a rich golden fall. She hesitated by his side, and must have seen his eyes closed, he thought, because she started to turn.

He reached out for her, caught her arm, pulled her back. He swept her down beside him, held her, kissed her. He enwrapped her in his arms. He held her close and stared at the ceiling, praying. Please, God. Please, God. He wasn't even sure what he prayed for.

Just a life with which to hold her again.

Mrs. Peabody was delighted to see them. She was startled when Blade said that he couldn't stay to supper. "You're headed over to the saloon, I'll wager!" she chastised him immediately. But he smiled, and assured her that he was not, his eyes touching Jessica's.

"I'm not, Mrs. Peabody, I mean, Rose. I've got a ride ahead of me tonight." Jessica was standing next to Mrs. Peabody. Tall, slim, shapely, her eyes steadily upon his, so anxious while she tried so hard not to give away the emotion.

Blade tipped his hat to them both and turned, starting down the two steps to reach his big bay in the street. "I'll be back as soon as I can," he promised.

He mounted quickly and started to turn his bay for the westward course he needed to take. Sherman was traveling along the Washita, he had been assured by Mr. Delaney. The general was moving very slowly because he was visiting officers stationed at forts deep into Indian territory.

"Wait!" Jessica cried suddenly. She picked up her skirts and hurried down the steps, running to him. She came to a halt as he quickly reined in, and stood looking up at him, concern in her eyes. Liquid, shimmering, so beguiling. "You shouldn't be doing this! It's not your fight, not your problem, and I'm so afraid...."

"Afraid of what?" he asked her.

She moistened her lips. "You never said that you weren't an outlaw!" she reminded him softly.

He smiled. "I'm going to be all right," he told her. "Now let me move on while there's still a little bit of daylight left."

She stepped back. He started to ride. She ran after him once again. "Blade!"

He reined in. "Jessica—"

"I love you," she said swiftly. "Please, please, take care of yourself. I—I love you."

He nearly fell off his horse. He wanted to. Wanted to forget the damned letters, forget revenge, forget everything in life. He just wanted to hold her, and live with her, and know that he could wake with her every morning of his life. He wanted to grow old with her.

But it wouldn't be any good. They could never run from Harding. They couldn't run from his past, either. He reached out and touched her cheek and felt the dampness of her tears there. "I love you, too," he told her softly.

Then he spurred his bay. He dared not wait any longer.

He rode through the night. Thankfully, the moon was still nearly full and there was plenty of light. It was easy enough to follow Sherman's route along the river—remnants of camp fires along the way, broken branches on the foliage, heavy footprints along the trail. Blade could tell that there was a fairly large encampment moving west, for there were marks from many tents, little things that people lost along the way. A rag doll lay in the trail, a broken pipe, a strip of calico that had tied back some pioneering woman's hair. Army officers often brought their wives with them. Women cast into a hard lot, but an intriguing and adventurous lot, too.

He picked up the little rag doll and carried it with him. Maybe he could return it.

It was just at dawn when he came upon the camp. He saw the sentry by the river before the sentry saw him, and he called out quickly. Men had a habit of shooting first and asking questions later when a man looked as much like a Sioux as he did.

"Ho, there!" he called out, raising both hands in a peaceful gesture to the very young soldier by the river. The man took a look at him and began seeking his gun—where he had lain it by a rock by the river—too late. "I'm looking for General Sherman!" Blade called out irritably. "And don't pick up that weapon because I don't want to shoot your damned fool head off!"

Maybe it was the warning. Maybe it had just been his very natural use of the English language—with a little bit of Missouri thrown into it—that advised the young sentry that Blade was not his enemy. Maybe the sentry realized he still had his scalp.

"The general is in camp, sir!" the sentry called out quickly. He had gained some dignity. He held his army-issue rifle, but did not aim it at Blade. "I'll call for an escort, sir!"

The sentry whistled, and a second man in cavalry blue appeared, this one an old-timer, one who quickly eyed Blade. He saw that the half-breed was alone and presumed he might be a scout. "I'll bring you into camp," the older man said, still watching him curiously.

"Thank you. I've letters with information I think he'll find exceptionally interesting," Blade said.

"Come with me."

Blade dismounted from his bay and followed the old man. They passed through the wakening camp, men rising, dressing, shaving, washing. They all paused to watch.

Blade felt their eyes. Felt them roam down his back. Did any of them know him?

They reached one tent with a middle-aged officer just pouring coffee in front. He paused the second he saw Blade. He had a haggard look about him.

Blade knew that look well. Most men had worn it after the war. Many men still did.

"Lieutenant Gray, this man has come to see General Sherman. Says he has important correspondence."

"It's an old matter," Blade said. "But an important one."

Lieutenant Gray looked at him, scratching his chin. "What's your tribe, Blackfeet?"

"Oglala," Blade replied.

"I heard about a fellow like you once," he said. "A half-breed with Mosby. Faster than lightning."

"Had to be," Blade said.

The lieutenant grinned. "The war is over," he said. He hesitated. "Though they did say this particular fellow had once been with Quantrill."

"Briefly, so I heard," Blade agreed.

The lieutenant turned, still grinning. Blade realized that he hadn't quite been breathing. He gulped in some air, then let it out.

"I'll find out if the general can see you," Lieutenant Gray said. "Help yourself to some coffee in the meantime."

Blade did so. It was hot and strong and black, and helped a little against the exhaustion he had begun to feel. But he felt something else, too—eyes upon him. Union army eyes. These were the men he had been fighting not so long ago. Now they were men with faces.

Lieutenant Gray returned. "This way, sir. General Sherman is quite curious."

Blade followed Gray into Sherman's big field tent. The general was behind his desk. He was a man of medium height and medium build, with a ragged face, helped somewhat by his beard and mustache. A little man, Blade thought, for one who had ravaged so much of a countryside.

A smart one—a brutal one, in a way. Hell, Sherman had sure helped to bring it all to a close. And now he was bringing his talents and energies against the Indians in the West. There was just no way he could ever be a man Blade would like, he decided wryly.

But at least he hated Indians openly, and he had made no bones about his plan to bring the South to her knees. He was the right man to bring Harding to his knees, as well.

Sherman stood, eyeing Blade curiously. "All right, so what is it that sends a half-breed ex-Reb into my camp?" he demanded flatly.

Blade didn't say a word. He handed the leather satchel of letters over to the man.

"What's this?" Sherman demanded.

"Letters, sir," Blade responded. "Read them, General."

Sherman sat at his desk. Blade realized that Lieutenant Gray was still behind him. Maybe they had been afraid that he intended to knife Sherman the moment he had been alone with him.

Sherman glanced through every letter. He looked at Lieutenant Gray. "We just met with a Colonel Harding at the fort, eh, Lieutenant?"

"That's right, General."

Sherman drummed his fingers on the desk. He stared at Blade. "What's your name? Who are you? What's your involvement in this?"

"My name's McKenna. I'm working for Dylan's widow. I've left her back in Jackson Prairie, at the boardinghouse there. I came as quickly as I could. I'm sure Harding will come after her if he even suspects she might have found the letters."

"Mrs. Dylan knew about these letters?"

"She came West to find them."

Sherman nodded. "Lieutenant, arrange a party to travel back to Jackson Prairie. See that Mrs. Dylan is safe, then move on to the fort and relieve Colonel Harding of duty. He'll be placed under arrest to face a court-martial.'' He studied Blade. ''I'll assume you'll be accompanying my men.''

Blade nodded. Lieutenant Gray hurried out.

''I heard tell of a half-breed Sioux with Mosby. Was that you?''

Blade hesitated. This was it. Mosby had been a legitimate member of Lee's army—not like Quantrill, who had been an embarrassment to the entire Southern command. Still... ''Yes, sir, that was me,'' Blade said.

Sherman drummed his fingers on his desk. ''Custer used to hate Mosby with a passion. Used to hang any of his men he could get his hands on.''

''Yes, sir. Colonel Mosby was careful to hang only Custer's men in return.''

''Sad state of affairs, eh, among civilized men? He was one hell of a raider, your commander.''

''Yes, yes he was.'' Blade hesitated. ''If you're going to put me under arrest—''

''Hell, sir! The war is over. I admire the man, and I bemoan our losses to him. That's all.''

Blade started to turn. Sherman's words stopped him once again. ''Though I must say, there was some rumor that Mosby's half-breed rode with Quantrill first. With boys like Bloody Bill Anderson. Men who dragged Union officers out of trains, stripped them, and shot them right in the back.''

Blade felt his spine begin to freeze. ''If you're going to hold me, General—''

"Oh, there was lots to the story. It was my understanding some Red Legs bushwhacking out of Kansas had mown down the half-breed's whole family. Father, pregnant wife."

Blade turned to him. "I didn't stay with Quantrill," he said softly. "Even after what I'd seen, I couldn't."

"There may be worse ahead out here," Sherman warned him. "The West is going to be a rough place with the war over. Custer didn't like Mosby. A lot of men don't like Indians."

Blade shrugged. "A lot of Indians don't like white men, but being a mix, General, I find that I really have to try to like myself. And if I'm not under arrest, I'm staying out here. No matter what."

Sherman leaned forward, studying him. "There's a lot of bushwhackers straight out from Kansas in the army here. There were a number of them at that fort I just left."

"So I'd heard, General."

"You might have been looking for a few men out here right from the start, mightn't you?"

"I might."

Sherman wagged a finger at him. "You'd best be damned careful, McKenna. Harding needs to face a court-martial. You can't just ride in and shoot up all my men."

"I have to—"

"Yes, Mr. McKenna. You go. Ride with my troops. They move quickly. They must be about ready to ride. Take care, McKenna. I like you, and I'll be damned if I know why. I hated Quantrill and I'm not all that damned fond of Indians, sir, but I admit, I do wish you the best.''

So Blade turned and walked out of the tent. The warmth of the sun struck him, and he smiled suddenly. A massive weight seemed to fall from his shoulders.

''Mr. McKenna!'' Lieutenant Gray called out from atop a handsome roan. ''Are you ready, sir?''

''Indeed, Lieutenant!'' Blade mounted his bay. And in the morning's light, they started to ride hard, back to Jackson Prairie.

The night seemed to last forever.

Jessica tried to sit still with Mrs. Peabody, sipping her sassafras tea. She tried to answer the woman's questions intelligently, tried to forget that Blade was running after the army.

At nine she jumped up and said that she was exhausted and needed to sleep. She never slept.

She paced the blue room for hours. She worried endlessly. Each time she closed her eyes, she saw him. He was so tall, dark and completely fascinating. She remembered his eyes, the way they could pin her to the wall, the way they could touch her with warmth and fire. I love you.... The words had just tumbled from her. Maybe she hadn't even realized it until then. Maybe she had known that he had given her something she had never imagined. But until she had seen him riding away, she hadn't known that she had really fallen in love with him, that their lives together now meant more than anything else. I love you, too, he had told her.

But though he now knew all about her life, she still knew very little about his. And she was so afraid. He had been taking chances to ride into a Union army camp. And if anything happened to him . . .

It wasn't even dawn when she rose and dressed. She slipped out of Mrs. Peabody's and hurried around back to see Mr. Delaney. He was already up and busy, brushing down someone's carriage horse. He arched a brow when he saw her. "Morning, Mrs. Dylan. Aren't you supposed to be waiting in the boarding-house for McKenna to come back?"

"Yes," Jessica said, looking at him intensely. "I've got to know what I'm watching out for, Mr. Delaney. I've got to know something about him."

Mr. Delaney lowered his head. "Seems like you've got to ask him, now, Mrs. Dylan—"

"Mr. Delaney, please! I need help. Blade is gone, and now I'm terrified that he might not come back. You've got to help me, please, Mr. Delaney. I—I swear to you, I'd never hurt him. I'm in love with him."

Delaney's eyes shot swiftly to hers. Then he shrugged. "Well, I guess there's lots of people who know the truth. I wouldn't really be telling tales out of school."

"So help me, please!"

Delaney shrugged again. "He was ranching with his father back in Missouri, back before the beginning of the war. His father took an active stance against the bushwhacking goin' on, and anyway, some Red Legs come down and killed the elder McKenna and Blade's wife.

"Wife, yes, ma'am," Mr. Delaney said in response to Jessica's gaping mouth. "She was expecting a little one at the time. Anyway, Blade done joined up with Quantrill and his men—until he seen what they did in a raid. That kind of brutal violence wasn't what he was after. He just wanted to kill the men involved. He couldn't find them what with the war beginning and all. He traveled east and joined up with Mosby. Fought out the war. And then came back."

"To find the men?" Jessica whispered.

Mr. Delaney hesitated a minute. "We'd heard tell that a lot of the men had joined on with the Union, and that they'd be in one of the forts in this vicinity. I imagine that's why he was coming this way when he ran into you." He hesitated again, then said very softly, "Yes'm, Mrs. Dylan. That's why he'd ridden out here—to find the men."

"Thank you," she said softly. "Thank you." Jessica started to walk back to the boardinghouse, her mind reeling. He was an outlaw.... No, he wasn't an outlaw. He'd ridden with outlaws. And he'd had a wife killed. A pregnant wife. Jessica fought a sudden rise of tears. He'd never told her. He'd said that he loved her, too....

But not enough. And that was why he had ridden on. Sure, he wanted to make sure that she was safe—his end of the bargain. But then he was going to ride away again. After those men. She was so immersed in her own thoughts that she didn't hear the riders at first. And then ...

Then it was too late. When she looked up, she saw a cloud of dust coming down the street. Then the men.

Ten of them, armed, wearing blue, atop cavalry mounts. The first of them, a grim-looking man with dark eyes and mustache, leapt down and came toward her. "Jessica Dylan?"

"What do you want?" she demanded. She knew. Her heart was beating a thousand miles an hour. He'd told her to stay in the boardinghouse! Mrs. Peabody would have lied for her, found her a place to hide. The men could have ripped the place apart, but now...

"You're under arrest," the man told her, reaching for her.

She snatched her hand away, taking a swift step backward. "Arrest! We are not in a state of military control here!" she cried angrily. "You can't arrest me. I haven't done anything—"

"We have reason to believe that you were engaged in traitorous activity with your late husband, a conspiracy that cost many lives during the recent War of Rebellion," the man said.

"You've no authority with which to arrest me. Don't touch me. I'll scream so damned loudly it will be heard all the way to Washington!" she cried.

His hands were on her. He wrenched her toward him. "I'm Colonel Harding, Mrs. Dylan. *Harding*. I want what you've got from your late husband, and I'll do what I have to in order to get it from you. Do you understand?"

"I don't have anything—" Jessica began.

"Lady, you're a liar!" Colonel Harding fired back.

She wasn't lying, she didn't have the damned letters, they were in Blade's hands as he crossed the plains. Right into the hands of the Union army. A man who had been with Mosby. With Quantrill.

Her mind raced. She didn't dare give Harding the least hint that someone else was holding the damning evidence against him. She had to let Harding believe it was still buried on her property somewhere.

She lifted her chin. "You're the lying, murderous traitor, Harding. You killed Charles, I'm sure. You probably shot him in the back once you found it was the only way to frame him. They say a Reb did it, but you and I both know. You killed him."

Harding lowered his head, his eyes burning into hers. "All I can assure you, ma'am, is that I will kill his widow, slowly, if I don't get what I want."

"And how will you explain that?"

"I'll find a way. Come willingly now, or it will be the worse for you."

She stared at him, gritting her teeth. Then she began to scream. "This man is taking me unlawfully! He's a murderer, he was a traitor to his cause—"

Harding's hand slammed across her cheek. Stunned, she nearly fell. He lifted her. She gathered what strength she could muster and began beating him, fighting him. She found herself thrown, stomach down, over a horse, then gagged and tied there, like a beast ready for the slaughter.

Harding caught her hair, lifting her eyes to his. "We'll have time to talk, Mrs. Dylan. Lots of time."

He dropped her hair and hurried to his mount.

"See here!" someone cried. It was Mr. Delaney. "What do you think you're doing? You can't do that to a lady. What kind of officer are you—"

"She's part of a conspiracy, dangerous as a rattler!" Harding told Delaney.

"Bull crap!" Mr. Delaney announced indignantly. There was a crowd gathering around him. Jessica couldn't see the people because her hair was blinding her, but she could hear them. She heard Mrs. Peabody's voice.

"Don't you dare think to take that young woman, you barbarian! We'll have the law on you! We'll—" Mrs. Peabody shouted.

"Good day!" Harding roared. "Men, ride!"

And beneath her, Jessica's horse began to move. To walk, trot and gallop. Racing her out of town.

And far, far away from Blade McKenna....

Chapter Nine

The sun was high, and it seemed as though they had been riding forever. Jessica had been barely conscious, but now she was suddenly aware of one of Harding's men speaking to him.

"We ain't taking her to the fort, right?" she heard him ask. "Colonel Harding, we're your men to the last breath, but if you take her back to the fort, some of the guys there just might not think it's right, they might feel some sympathy for her, they might just...well, sir, they might just protest!"

"Dooley," Harding said with a trace of exasperation. "I am not taking her to the fort."

"Then—?"

"We're heading back for her place."

"Her place?"

"The land Charles Dylan bought when he was out here and left her, Dooley. Where the hell else would he have left anything of value to him!"

Dooley fell silent.

Harding chuckled softly and continued. "No one will see or hear her there. She can scream until the sun sets and rises again, and no one will hear her."

They kept riding.

When they reached her property, Jessica was so stiff from being in such an awkward position during the ride that she couldn't stand when Dooley came to lift her from the horse. She fell against the creature, her feet and ankles numb.

Harding didn't care. He quickly had a hand on her elbow and started to drag her to the house, calling orders to his men. "Tear apart the barn, the stables. See what you can find."

Jessica longed to tell him that he could dig from here to Kingdom Come and he wouldn't find anything. But she didn't want him to know or even suspect that someone might be riding away with his evidence. If he did start suspecting, he'd probably begin asking questions in town. God forbid if he found out Blade had the evidence . . . and that he had also killed the man who had never come back. But . . . but if Blade had found Sherman and managed to walk into the army camp, then maybe . . .

Then what? He'd come back to town. She wouldn't be there. Mr. Delaney and Mrs. Peabody would tell him what happened, and he would come for her.

Except that he wouldn't know where to come. . . .

Yes, yes, he might! This was the logical place for Harding to have brought her. To the ranch Charles Dylan had loved so much, the place that was his, the place he had come whenever he'd had a few spare minutes away from the fort.

Could he come in time? Jessica wondered.

She stumbled up the steps to the front door. Harding wrenched her to her feet. He kicked the door, still dragging her.

The house seemed so strange. No fire burned in the hearth. There was no aromatic scent of coffee in the air, no feel of life today. Yet it was still different from when they had first come, Jessica realized. It was neat, it was clean, it had little touches of home in the drapes, in the afghan over the sofa, in the cloth on the table, the vase there. It was a house that waited. Empty, and a little cold because of that, but waiting for them. For her and Blade.

Because they had, strangely enough, made it a home.

Harding shoved her into the chair before the cold hearth, then gripped the edges of the hearth and stared into her eyes. "Where are they, Mrs. Dylan?"

She lifted her chin. "Where are who, Colonel Harding?"

"Don't get wise with me, Mrs. Dylan. They. The letters. My property. Stolen by your husband."

"I haven't the faintest idea of what you're talking about."

"No? Yet in Jackson Prairie, you called out to everyone that I was a murderer!"

"Charles wrote home, of course, Colonel. He told me that you were a vile traitor and murderer, and that some of the Confederates had the money to buy that break they made. That is why I know that you are a traitor and a murderer."

"Colonel!" Dooley called impatiently.

Harding forgot Jessica for a moment. He turned to Dooley—who had apparently been sticking his nose around the house.

Dooley threw a shirt across the room. One of Blade's. Harding caught it, and stared at Dooley.

"My husband's—" she began in exasperation.

"I don't think so. I think she's living here with someone," Dooley said. "There's a shaving mirror and a razor in that bedroom. Looks all nice and cozy and domestic. Seems the widow here is into a little bit of entertainment."

Harding looked down at her with a sardonic smile. "That's good. Why, I won't have to feel half so guilty now. Raping old Dylan's widow might be kind of a cruel thing. But since she's just some cattle herder's whore, well, then it won't be quite so bad. We can have lots of fun until she decides to talk, or before we get to the real violence. Dooley, you go ahead and start a fire. I'm going to question my prisoner a little further in the comfort of her bedroom. I do want her to feel at home. But I need some good hot pokers. If I can't gently persuade her to turn over the letters, she'll have to lose one eye, and then the other. Dear me, Mrs. Dylan! You are going to be a mess before I leave you. And such a beautiful woman! What a pity."

He reached for her. Jessica struck out, slapping him hard, her nails raking across his face. Harding swore, wrenched her up, and threw her. She stumbled for balance and turned to flee. He caught her around the waist, lifting her. She clawed at his hands, but he didn't seem to care. "Get the damned fire going!" he ordered Dooley.

She fought. She fought even as Harding dragged her toward her bedroom. She gripped the frame to the door and flung her weight wildly around.

Harding shouted for Dooley again. "Get over here! Leave the damned fire for a minute and help me get this witch in here!"

Dooley obliged, prying her fingers away from the doorframe. She was a fighter. Blade had told her that. But she couldn't fight them forever. Her heart seemed to constrict within her breast. No, this was her home, her place. It was where she lived and loved with Blade. Where she had discovered hope and desire and happiness once again. Where she had even dared to dream of a future, here, in this wilderness. She'd fight for it even if it killed her.

"No!" she shrieked. She heard her skirt rip and saw Dooley reaching for her bodice. "No!" she shrieked again. And then, amazingly and suddenly, Dooley was gone. Plucked from her, thrown across the room. She followed the motion of his body, saw him crash against the far wall, eyes go wide, then close, all consciousness stolen from him in one swift second.

She looked above her. Blade. He had come for her. In time.

She stared at him, into his dark, passionate eyes. She touched his cheek, bronzed, handsome, so rugged, so very appealing and arresting. She ran her thumb over the tight pad of his lower lip, and thought his was the most noble face she had ever seen. "You made it," she whispered softly.

"The army made it, too. A troop is right behind me."

"And—"

She broke off as she suddenly heard gunfire from outside, and then a bullet whizzed by them both, making a very strange sound as it sank into the bedding.

"Roll!" Blade shouted to her. He was on top of her, rolling with her. They both crashed down to the floor on the side of the bed. "Stay!" he commanded.

Well, she would stay, all right, but she had to see what was going on. She inched up, gazing across the bed, watching as Blade leapt up, jumping, spinning, avoiding the next bullet Harding sent flying his way, then pitting himself against the man. The gun went flying. Blade lit into Harding, his knuckles crunching into his cheek. He raised his fist to slam it down again. Then he paused. "He's out," he said, and rubbed his fist. "Out cold."

Blade lifted him up, hiking him over his shoulder. He turned to Jessy. "I wanted to kill him," he said huskily. "I wanted to kill him for touching you. I should turn him over to Lieutenant Gray. Gray is a good man, and Sherman wants Harding to stand trial. It is best—it will clear Charles Dylan."

"Yes, yes! Turn him over to Lieutenant Gray!" Jessica cried.

Blade nodded, and left her. There had been a skirmish outside, too, Blade realized. Yet, by the look of it, it had ended as quickly as it had begun. The Union troops who had followed Harding had been quick to surrender to Lieutenant Gray.

Jessica rose stiffly and walked to the window. She could see Blade handing the man over to a good-looking man. Gray. He was in control. It was over, she thought. At last. All over.

And Blade was alive and safe, and she was alive and safe, and there was nothing left except—

"Don't make a move, Mrs. Dylan."

She had forgotten Dooley. Forgotten that Blade had thrown him across the room, that he had seemed to be as out cold as Harding.

"Listen to me. All that I want to do is get away, and fast. I didn't have anything to do with your husband's frame-up, lady, honest. I never wanted to hurt you, but I've got to get out of here. I can't let that crazy half-breed get a good look at me. Wave! Wave quickly. Let them see that you're all right. Then you've got to find some way to get me out back. I've got a knife against your spine. Feel it? I can slice right into you in a matter of seconds. You'll be dead before you fall. Do you hear me?"

She nodded. She heard him. She heard the death of hope, of life, of love.

Outside, Blade finished saying something to Lieutenant Gray. He turned to her. She tried to smile. She lifted a hand.

"I'll kill him," Dooley whispered suddenly. "I'll hurtle this knife at him the second he steps through the door. Then I'll throttle you. I won't go down alone, I won't let him get me, I won't let him get me!"

It was Blade! The man was terrified of Blade. She swallowed hard. Blade had come here, Mr. Delaney had told her, because he had heard that some of the men out of Kansas were at the fort.

And Blade was staring at her. She was trying so hard to smile, to look normal! But he knew her, knew her so very well. He looked at Gray again. "I've a few things in the barn, Lieutenant, that I need for the general. If you'll wait here for just a moment..."

His voice seemed to fade away. Lieutenant Gray was obviously confused, but he was also quick, and he acknowledged Blade's request with a nod. Dooley, behind her, exhaled a sigh of relief. "Get me out of here now!" he commanded Jessica.

She nodded. She turned away from the window. "There's no back door. There's a window—"

"Get me there!"

She turned from the window and started to walk. She had barely taken two steps before she screamed, spinning at the sound of shattering glass.

Blade. Crashing through the window, his hands around Dooley's throat, was Blade. He wrenched Dooley from her, throwing him to the ground. He straddled the man, his knife drawn, a savage look upon his face.

"God!" he raged suddenly. "You!" He grasped hard at Dooley's hair, wrenching it up. He raised his knife. He was preparing to scalp the man. And then... kill him, in cold blood.

Jessica watched, frozen. The bastard probably deserved it. But somehow, that didn't matter. What mattered was Blade. "Blade, no! No!" Jessica cried.

Blade paused, his knife held high, hatred burning darkly in his eyes. "You don't understand, Jessy," he cried out. "He was with them. Three of them. They came on my property. They shot down my father. And they came after Mara. They killed her—and our baby. She was running and running and they just shot her down. And they thought they'd killed me.''

"Blade! I *do* understand what happened, Mr. Delaney told me. But Lieutenant Gray will take care of him, the army will take care of him. The war is over, I swear, we can see to it that he's prosecuted, I know they'll see justice done. He's down, it's all right, we're safe. Blade, I know how you were hurt, but Lieutenant Gray is outside, right? Let's give this man to the army, let him face the law. Please, God, Blade!''

"This is him," Blade said softly. "Frank Dooley, worked for Lane back in Kansas, so long ago now, eh, Dooley? This is him. I saw his face. Saw him shoot down Mara, then he came for me. Lord, I've waited forever for this moment. I swore that I'd kill him slow. That I'd take his scalp before he was even dead.''

"Blade!" Jessy cried, rushing to him, falling down by his side where he straddled Dooley so tightly. She gripped his arm. The arm with the knife. It was like holding steel.

"Blade, you can't! You can't. You've got to turn him over to Lieutenant Gray. You have to! Please! If you don't, you'll have to run again. They can't let you take your vengeance, even if they think you're right. Gray will be obliged to come after you. And more men will die. Let him go to trial. Let Lieutenant Gray take him. Blade, I love you more than I've ever hated anyone in my life, you've got to feel the same way! It's the only chance that we've got!''

"Listen to her!" Dooley cried out. "Listen to her! I didn't want to kill anyone. Lane sent us out. He said we had to clear your place, that too many men were listening to old man McKenna. And sometimes, we were threatened, too. If we didn't follow orders, we'd be killed ourselves. McKenna, please! The others are dead!'' he said in a sudden rush. ''Jake Morgan died out here in that Confederate break that killed Dylan. Quantrill killed Yancy Thomas not a year after your— after your place was raided. It's over, McKenna, it's over! Please, lady, don't let him scalp me alive, do something, please—''

''You shot down a pregnant woman!'' Blade raged.

Jessica realized that she hadn't gotten through to him. He was standing so rigidly, so tensely. He didn't even seem to feel her touch upon him. Tears stung her eyes. She didn't mean anything to him, not at this moment. He had waited all these years to find and kill the men who had slain his family. Jessica was certain that Dooley was telling the truth. The others were dead.

Dooley was broken. And it was almost damned certain that the Union army would deal with him. He'd hang. They had to leave it the way it was! Dooley, grateful to die by the rope rather than inch by inch at Blade's hands. And Blade, for his own sake, had to let him go.

And Jessy... had to have Blade. She had to gamble. It was her only chance. ''Blade!''

He couldn't feel her touch, so she dropped her hand from his arm, standing, stepping back. ''Blade, I love you, I want you to marry me, I want to stay out here and build a life with you, I want us both to let go of our pasts. Can you hear me, Blade? Please, give him over to Lieutenant Gray. I beg you. There's so much out here that's lawless, let us be part of the law. Worse will come, there will be more injustices. There will be battles ahead, but Blade, let us have peace together. I beg you, give him over to Gray. I—I can't stop you from anything, I understand your hatred and your heartbreak, I just pray that the love we can have in the future can be stronger than all the hatreds of the past. I'll—I'll be outside.''

"Lady!" Dooley screamed. "Don't leave me!"

She had to leave him. She was almost blinded by her tears. She was so afraid. If Blade killed Dooley now, Gray would have to bring Blade in.

She opened the door and stumbled outside. It was cool, clean and crisp.

They were standing before her. Gray and all his men, with their prisoners—and the dead—thrown like cargo over their horses.

She could see Harding. He'd killed Charles. And she had thought that she'd wanted him dead, but now it didn't matter. He was going to face trial. The name of Charles Dylan had been cleared.

Yet that didn't matter so much to her now. What really mattered was Blade. She had fallen in love with him. She had lived blindly for a long time, getting the deed to her property, managing to ride out to claim it. Wanting only to prove Charles innocent. Then Blade had somehow forced her to see that there was so much more to life.

"Mrs. Dylan?" Lieutenant Gray was coming to her, his eyes anxious. "What—?"

She shook her head. "I—I don't—"

"Here's another one for you, Lieutenant!"

Jessica heard Blade's voice and spun around. He was standing there, holding Dooley before him like a rag doll. He lifted the man and threw him down at Gray's feet. "Lieutenant, take him, please! Get him away from me. Far, far away."

Gray nodded and two of his men rushed forward. Dooley was taken quickly away and mounted on a horse. He stared at Jessy and she shivered. She felt Blade's hands on her shoulders.

Lieutenant Gray saluted them both. He lifted his hat to Jessica. "It's fine land, Mrs. Dylan. Mighty fine land."

"Thank you."

"Thank you, Mrs. Dylan. And McKenna, thank you. You've our most sincere appreciation. And—" He hesitated. "And I think you might find this a peaceful place in the future. A place where you might raise a herd of cattle, do a little farming...settle down for a spell."

Jessy felt Blade's smile. "Maybe," he told Lieutenant Gray.

Gray's troops moved then, their horses riding out of the yard, slowly disappearing into the setting sun. A cool breeze brushed Jessy's hair about her face. She felt Blade's chin on her head. "When's the wedding?" he asked softly.

"Tomorrow? At Mrs. Peabody's! She and Mr. Delaney can be there that way. That is, assuming we can get our hands on a minister."

"I'll find one," he promised her. "I'll get my hands on one. Even if I have to ride back to the Union army to do so!"

Jessy laughed. "Seems to me like you never really were any kind of an outlaw. And if you were, you've been fully pardoned."

"That's how it seems," he agreed.

Then, shaking, he swept her into his arms. "If the wedding's at Mrs. Peabody's tomorrow..."

"Yes?" she whispered huskily.

"Think we could start the honeymoon at home tonight?"

Laughing, she ran her fingers through his ink black hair and fell in love with his ruggedly handsome features all over again. "I think so!" she whispered, and he carried her into the house. "I love you," she whispered.

"I love you. I never knew just how much until I nearly lost you."

She didn't know what to say, and so she kissed him.

"And to think!" he said softly. "I won you in a poker game. On a gamble."

Jessy smiled, stroking her fingers through his ink dark hair. "And to think! I kept you on a gamble!" she replied. She arched a brow and smiled again. "I love the West," she murmured. "I love the wild, wild West—and the wild, wild things you can find in it!"

"Oh?" Blade asked.

"Mmm. And I love you."

"Oh?"

"Want me to prove it?"

"Mmm."

They walked through the house. They both knew that they'd made it. Out of the fire, into life. And their future loomed there before them, wondrously in their Western frontier. They had slept together in the wilderness.

And then love had made it a home.

* * * * *

A Note from Heather Graham Pozzessere

There's just nothing like the Wild West: the beautiful vistas, the plains, the mountains. To many, the West promised a new life. Hardships were inevitable, but hope always rode ahead. The stories that have come down to us from our courageous ancestors who blazed the trail are wonderful in themselves. Tears, laughter, adventure and tragedy awaited folks on the great frontier.

Even as a child I loved Westerns and the actors who brought them to life: Jimmy Stewart in *The Man Who Shot Liberty Valance*; Errol Flynn in *Santa Fe Trail*; John Wayne, who rode to the rescue so many times! Then came Clint Eastwood in *The Good, the Bad and the Ugly* and *Hang 'Em High*. I was one of the first people in the theater to see *Unforgiven* when it opened.

Maybe the horses have something to do with it. That and the romantic tradition of riding off into the sunset. Perhaps it's the people who have inspired such fascination with that time gone by: gunslingers, lawmen, dance-hall girls and the noble Native Americans, whose lessons we are still striving to learn today. They all had a story to tell.

I live in Coral Gables, Florida—about as far away from the Old West as a person can get—but I think that once you get a taste of anything Western, you develop a fondness that lasts a lifetime. I also live with five children, ages two to sixteen, and I can honestly say that every day is certainly an adventure. Then there is my husband, Dennis, who is always willing to prowl unlikely sites with me, likes old graveyards and out-of-the-way museums, has shown me how a Colt works and will dig into his own library for information when I'm at a loss.

I'm delighted to be a part of this collection and I hope you enjoy my story as much as I enjoyed going back to that frontier.

Heather Graham Pozzessere

Against the Wind

Patricia Potter

Chapter One

Independence, Missouri
June, 1866

The woman's eyes opened wide, suspicion clouding their soft hazel color, when she heard Seth Hampton's drawl. The hopeful, even eager look on her face froze.

With a sinking heart, Seth Hampton waited for the condemnation he sensed was coming. God knew he'd heard it all the way to Independence. General Lee had surrendered, the Confederacy had collapsed, but he wondered now whether the war would ever truly be over. He had traveled several thousand miles to escape it, but now he saw something close to hatred reflected in eyes that were much too wary, much too weary, for a young woman.

And much too familiar. They were part of what he'd hoped to escape: the years of pain and violence and grief. And the memories. And the nightmares.

Kate MacAllister. That was her name, according to the wagon master. It fitted her. No-nonsense. No frills. Although with those lovely eyes she probably could be quite pretty, her hair was drawn back and well covered by a sunbonnet that did little for the oval shape of her face. And her dress, though clean, was so faded he could barely tell what color it might once have been. But it fitted slender curves, and she moved with a grace that was appealing.

So was the inherent strength in her face. It was written all over the determined jaw and the strong, firm line of her mouth. But now, a hostile expression had spread across her face, and a sense of sad futility swept through him. Nothing had changed in the past year, nothing at all.

"Is that a Southern accent, Dr. Hampton?"

He nodded once, keeping his eyes as expressionless as he could. He needed her. She needed him. It should have been that simple, but nothing was simple these days. "Does that make a difference, Miss Mac-Allister?"

Her eyes grew even more frosty. "Did you fight for the Rebels?"

Seth's jaw set. "I doctored for the Confederacy."

Her chin jutted out. "Did you fire a gun?"

He had. Several times, in fact, when a wounded man on the ground was being threatened. He didn't know whether he had killed. He'd prayed to God he hadn't. Seth nodded.

"We don't need you, Doctor," she said abruptly. "We don't need a traitor." She turned her back to him and started to walk away.

Seth reached out a hand to stop her. He felt her tense as she stilled and turned back to him, and he tried to measure his words. "The war is over, Miss MacAllister. We've all suffered, but now it's over."

"Not for me," she said, in a voice that was obviously just barely under control, as her hazel eyes flashed with anger. "Nearly my whole family is dead. Two brothers dead, a third brother dying. My parents dead of broken hearts. My fiancé lies somewhere in Pennsylvania. All because you Southerners wanted to keep slaves." Her voice broke. "And you think it's over? Forgive and forget? Oh, no, Doctor. Not ever! We don't need help from the likes of you. We'll find another way to get to California."

"There is no other way," he said quietly. "Not for you. Or me. Not this year."

"Then we'll stay here." There was the slightest sheen in her eyes, as if she were fighting back tears, and for the first time she looked vulnerable, despite her anger. Seth didn't even try to stop her when she turned again, not until she stumbled slightly, and then he took two long steps to steady her with his hand. Her head swung toward him, and he saw the tears, no longer hovering, but splashing down a face filled with despair. She made a futile effort to wipe them away with her hand, then jerked from his grasp and almost ran toward a group of covered wagons clustered in the shade of a grove of trees.

Seth felt as if a fist had plowed deep in his stomach. But the wagon master had warned him. No one wanted a Southerner on this trek west. But he'd had to try.

"I'm sorry, Doc. I really hoped it would work." The wagon master's voice was sympathetic. He had been hovering nearby, hopeful and anxious over the out-come of the meeting.

Seth turned to see Cliff Edwards. He shrugged. "Maybe I'll try it on my own."

"I wouldn't advise it," Edwards said. "There's been numerous war parties—Arapaho, Cheyenne, even Sioux out there. Indians think too many folks are coming onto their lands, and there was a massacre of Indians last year at Sand Creek. Didn't make them feel too kindly toward us. And even if there weren't Indi-ans, you'd need some kind of guide to get you through the mountains and deserts. Why don't you just go back home?"

Home. Seth smiled crookedly. How could he tell him there was no longer a home, just a house where his brother and his brother's wife, the woman Seth had loved for years, lived?

"Guess I'll just wait around and see whether any-one else needs a hand," he said instead.

"Doc, I'd give almost anything I have to take you along with us. These folks don't know how badly we'll need a doctor before we reach California, but rules are rules. You have to have the required wagon and sup-plies. You being a Reb doesn't make them amenable to changing that, nor to any family taking you on."

"You don't feel that way?"

"Hell, it wasn't my war. I didn't lose anyone. But most of these people did."

"I did, too," Seth said. "A brother. Another brother fought for the North."

"Hell, maybe I should tell her that."

"I don't think it would do any good," Seth said wearily. "I've seen that look too many times."

"Her brother needs you. I wish I could make her see that."

Seth's interest was immediately piqued. "What's wrong with him?"

"Lungs, I was told. Got real sick in a prison camp. Andersonville. God-awful cough. Miss MacAllister said the army doctors claimed he wouldn't survive another winter in Illinois. But I just can't take them without another man along. He can't pull his weight. It takes a lot of strength to drive one of those wagons across this country. That's why I suggested you. God knows she's going to need you. Or someone like you."

Familiar pain coursed through Seth. He had thought he was escaping from the constant ache at the waste and destruction of war. At one time, he had even thought he might become immune to it, and he'd known many army doctors who had, who had even become callous about it. But he had realized back then that he didn't want that, for he couldn't accept the opium of indifference. He wanted to care. He wanted to keep his soul. No matter the price. And the price was high. So damnably high. The nightmares never stopped, and neither did the aching sense of loss. And now there was the rejection, even hatred, that he constantly faced.

But after the war, after his duty ended, he'd known he couldn't stay in Virginia. There were too many shadows there among the hills he had once loved, too many memories of shattered men and screaming horses. The once-joyful innocence of his life had been mutilated beyond repair.

The West. It had beckoned to him as the North Star had once beckoned slaves to freedom. An untouched land in need of doctors. A promised land without reminders of sweet, beautiful Blythe, or the time when he and his brother might have killed one another in the name of duty. A healing place.

He wished he could help Kate MacAllister. He wished he could help her brother. He wished he could heal just a few bitter wounds, both in himself and in the raw, agonizing aftermath of war. Fool's thoughts. His brother had called him a Don Quixote. Perhaps Rafe was right. Perhaps he was running from all the wrong things, rather than, as he'd thought, to the right things. But then Rafe had always said he had been running against the wind all his life.

Seth turned his attention back to the wagon master, who was looking at him oddly. Had so much time gone by while he was wool-gathering? "Do you think she might let me look at her brother?"

"I don't know," Edwards said. "You might ask her."

Seth figured he already knew the answer. He tried again on his own behalf. "You can't use a scout—?"

Edwards shook his head. "We have our two. And you have no experience. Even if I did, some of these people would be mad as hell if I used their money to hire on a Reb. A private party, like the MacAllisters, taking you on...now that would be different."

"You're leaving in four days?"

"Yep," Edwards said. "We're already late. Won't be any more trains this year, not unless they want to winter in the mountains. I hated delaying this long but we needed the time to get the wagons in top shape."

Seth hesitated. The thought of the MacAllisters nagged at him. "The doctor said Miss MacAllister's brother can't stay here another winter?"

"That's what she told me."

"You can't . . . take her anyway? Even without me, or someone else?"

"The MacAllisters can't pay much. Few men are willing to take on that kind of responsibility and hard work without a damned good reason. Now you—you look responsible. I was willing to take a chance on you, but not some of the others she talked to. Got fifty families depending on me. A weak link can get people killed. You break your rules once, you might as well not have any at all. Sorry, Doc."

"Which wagon is she?"

Edwards paused. "You sure you want to do that? Try again?"

Seth shrugged. "I've spent four years getting through a war. I suppose I can survive another one. In any event, maybe I can help the brother."

Edwards searched his face. "I hope you can—if they will let you. I feel damned bad about this. They've already bought the wagon and supplies, but then Jeremy got sick real bad. I just can't risk it, Doc. I can't."

Kate had nearly beaten the material to oblivion. She had meant only to wash it, but now, as she looked at

Jeremy's shirt, she noted with dismay that she had nearly ruined it. There were new rips in the cotton cloth, which was already threadbare.

She couldn't quite make herself wish it was the Reb, rather than the shirt, that she was thrashing. She had never physically struck any living thing in her life. But she felt totally justified in striking out at this innocent piece of cotton cloth. For a moment, it represented her loathing for anything—and anyone—Southern.

She was particularly bitter at the thought of showing the Reb her disappointment moments ago, of showing even a hint of frustration. She hated the thought of tears, much less exposing them to a—a hateful Reb. She hadn't really cried since the disasters started, the disasters, one after another, that had caused her to leave the only home she'd ever known, the place where she had once felt safe, so long ago.

She'd had to be strong for her brothers, eleven-year-old Nick and nineteen-year-old Jeremy. She couldn't show any weakness, because she feared that if she did she might shatter into a million pieces, like a collapsing dam. She often felt like that these days, full of cracks and on the verge of breaking. And if she did, what would they do?

So she had armed herself with whatever weapons she could find—mostly anger against the Rebels who had caused all this. They were the target to blunt all the sorrow and grief and anguish of the past four years. Anger had helped her survive and had given her the strength to keep the farm going for Jeremy—even if it meant working twelve hours a day in the fields.

And then Jeremy had come home so wounded in body and soul that even that goal was gone.

She had learned to block away other emotions, bottling them so tightly that they couldn't get out. This way nothing would weaken her purpose in saving what was left of the MacAllisters. There was no longer any laughter, tears, or even smiles. She knew deep inside that her stoicism was not good for Nick or Jeremy, yet she didn't know how to undo it without coming apart altogether.

She nurtured harsh thoughts toward Cliff Edwards for even suggesting the Reb to her, for building hope that perhaps she had finally found a hired man he would accept. Mr. Edwards knew what had happened to her family, knew that Jeremy had almost died in a Reb prison. How dare he suggest she hire a—a traitor? Even Jeremy had agreed with her decision when she told him minutes ago, though he couldn't hide his own disappointment.

Kate needed some relief from the anger and frustration she felt. She had to get Jeremy to California. She had to. But not through the help of a man who'd helped destroy him. She took a pair of pants and started to pound on those.

Taking a Reb with them to California! She'd rather take the devil.

But, dear God in heaven, what would they do now?

If they will let you. Cliff Edwards's last words. If the MacAllisters would let him help. After meeting Miss MacAllister and watching the anger boiling in

those expressive eyes of hers, he knew it was a very big
if.

Seth returned to the rooming house where he'd left
his medical bag. The room was cheaper and cleaner
than those in the hotels, which had sprouted everywhere, it seemed. And the cost included meals such as
he hadn't had in a very long time. Here he had found
little hostility, at least once he'd said he was a doctor.
The proprietress, Mrs. Rose, had had no kin in the
war, and the city of Independence had leaned toward
the south in its sympathies. He'd soon discovered,
though, that Mrs. Rose didn't have much use for either side, after surviving both the Jayhawkers and the
Bushwhackers.

Her husband had died years earlier in a mining
camp where he had gone to make their fortune. He
had sent her enough money to join him. The money
and the news of his death had come on the same stage
coach. So she had invested the money in a house in
which she could establish a livelihood. Hence, she'd
begun to mother her boarders, as well as her two children. One had just survived measles through the help
of a doctor, and she would hear no wrong said about
any of them. She had taken Seth to her quite ample
bosom with the express intention of coddling him and
fattening him up.

She greeted him now as he came in, her face beaming as she told him she had, just this minute, taken an
apple pie from the oven. Seth, as usual, didn't have the
heart to argue. Hers was one of the very few friendly
faces he had seen since Kentucky, and her pies were
very, very good.

He gave her his most engaging grin. "Do you suppose I can buy half that pie from you?"

"No," she said. "Absolutely not. But you can take it as a gift."

"Mrs. Rose," he said, thinking the name fitted her perfectly, with her plump cheeks and happy disposition, "that just isn't right."

She puffed herself up, obviously used to controlling her boarders. "And who are you, Doctor, to tell me what's right?"

He backed down quickly from her indignation. "Then I thank you." He rose and went to the sink, pumping some water into his hands. "I'll be back a little later."

"Is that wagon train working out?" she said. "You know, this town needs another doctor."

"I know," he said, "but . . ."

"I know." She sighed. "The call of the West. I know it well."

"You're wonderful, Mrs. Rose," he said.

"Aye, and you remember that, Doctor."

Seth got together his medical bag and the half pie and rode his horse back to where the wagon train was camped, hesitating only a moment before dismounting and approaching the MacAllister wagon with his peace offering. He would probably end up with more pie than he wanted, and not exactly in the the place it belonged.

A boy was whittling outside the wagon. Seth guessed he was twelve or so and, upon noticing that he had the same hazel eyes as Kate MacAllister, decided he was probably her brother. The boy's eyes opened wide as he watched Seth approach, and then his nose wiggled as he sniffed the delicious smell that came from the pie. He glanced suspiciously, however, at the doctor's bag in Seth's other hand.

Greed was obviously battling with personal loyalty. "You that Reb my sis talked to?"

"I'm afraid so. I brought a peace offering, and hoped I could take a look at your brother."

The boy gave him a dubious look, but his eyes remained on the pie. "Kate's down at the river washing clothes."

"May I see your brother, then? And you could watch the pie for me."

"I don't know if I should do that. Kate said you was a Reb. She doesn't like Rebs."

"What about you?"

"I don't like 'em, either. Killed my two brothers."

"My brother was killed, too."

"He was?" Morbid interest shone in his eyes, although his back was stiff.

"Yep. And I have another brother who fought with the Yanks. Doctored a bunch of them myself. Mr. Edwards said maybe I could look at your brother." Seth offered a brief prayer for forgiveness for his lie.

"He did?" The boy obviously had made Cliff Edwards a hero. "I guess it would be all right, then. Jeremy's not feeling so good. He's inside."

Seth nodded and handed the boy the pie. He looked at the piece of wood the boy was working on. "That's a fine-looking dog."

"That's Blacky," the boy said. "He died." It was said in the same singularly blank voice that Seth had heard too many times before, a voice that spoke of a kind of numbness to death. He felt the same pain he'd experienced earlier. No boy should have to take the fact of death so... naturally.

"I'm sorry," Seth said, but the boy only nodded, as if it didn't matter. "And who should I tell your brother gave me permission to enter?"

"I'm Nick. For Nicholas," the boy explained solemnly.

"Well, Nick, you take care of that pie for your brother, all right?"

The boy nodded and watched as Seth moved up to the wagon flap and rapped against the wood before pulling the canvas back and entering.

It was dark inside. And hot. A man was asleep on the one visible bed. His breathing was raspy and his color, even in the filtered, dim light, pale and unhealthy. Seth drew in his breath. The man on the bed looked so young—probably not more than twenty.

He stooped down next to the poster bed that rested along one side of the wagon. He noticed two additional mattresses rolled neatly underneath the bed, along with several boxes. Every square foot of space was utilized.

With a slight sigh, he listened carefully to the young man's breathing, and he knew the other doctor had been right. The lungs were damaged, probably by pneumonia or some other lung disease.

The young man moved slightly, his foot brushing a broom, which fell, and he woke up, slowly focusing his eyes on Seth. His eyes were brown, not the hazel of his siblings'. Seth recognized the wary look in them. Eyes that had seen too much.

"Who are you?"

"A doctor."

The man coughed—it was a hacking, painful cough—and reached for a cup next to him, sipping its contents slowly. His face showed his struggle to contain the cough.

Seth leaned down and opened the bag and took out a powder. "Here, add this."

The man looked at him suspiciously. "What is it?"

"Snakeroot. It might help. If not, we can try quinine."

The man was obviously going to refuse, but then he started coughing again, this time nearly gagging. He didn't seem to notice as Seth took the cup from his hand and mixed in the powder. He held the patient's head and guided the concoction down his throat. The coughing slowed, and the man looked up at him, his forehead beaded with sweat. "You're that Reb Kate told me about?"

Seth nodded.

"I thought she told you nothing doing."

"She did, but the wagon master said you were sick, and I thought I would see if I could help. Just temporarily. Unless you have a doctor?"

The man, Jeremy MacAllister, as Seth recalled, glared at him. "You're not wanted."

Seth smiled grimly. "So I've been told."

"Then get the hell out of here."

Seth ignored the anger. God knew he'd done it before, especially when he'd had to perform amputations. "Cliff Edwards said you were at Andersonville. Pneumonia?"

MacAllister coughed again, but it did not have the force of the previous episode. "Yeah, I was in that hellhole of yours."

"Was it pneumonia?" Seth insisted.

"How in the hell do I know? No doctors . . . at least none worth a damn. Even if there was, there was no medicine, no shelter, no food. I just know I was damned sick the whole time." His words came in short breaths, as if each came only with difficulty, and his voice was deepened by the constant coughing.

"When did this last spell start?"

MacAllister turned away from him without answering.

"When?" Seth's voice was sharp, authoritative, and the man—more a boy, Seth thought sadly—turned back to him.

"Two weeks ago," he finally said reluctantly.

"The cough's been getting worse?"

MacAllister nodded.

Seth could almost guess what had happened. The MacAllisters had arrived three weeks ago from Illinois. The strain of the trip and then the work involved in preparing for the trek west had probably sapped what little resistance and strength Jeremy MacAllister had had.

He went back into his bag. Nearly every penny he had was invested in that bag, and in a larger one in the rooming house. He pulled out another bottle of the powder he had just given MacAllister, and a bottle of liquid. "I'll leave this with you—it's snakeroot. And this is quinine. Use the latter sparingly. And rest." He straightened up. "I'll be in town a few more days. Cliff Edwards knows where. If you need anything—"

Seth didn't wait for parting words. He didn't want to give Jeremy MacAllister time to refuse his offerings, and that was exactly what he expected. He quickly stepped out of the wagon, noting the young boy still hovering nearby. The half pie was next to him, but there was a big thumb mark where he'd apparently tasted. Seth smiled to himself. At least there was enough boy left in him to do that.

He found his mount contentedly munching grass. Sundance had seen him through the last two years of the war; he was one of the few surviving thoroughbreds from the Hampton farm, which had once raised some of the finest horseflesh in Virginia. Sundance, a bay whose coat had once fairly shimmered in the sun, was still too thin. Even a year after the war's end, the stallion had never reclaimed the sleek beauty that had once been his. Instead, there was a muscular gauntness that spoke of too many lean years.

Seth took just a moment to run his hand down the animal's neck, receiving a reassuring whinny in response as Sundance moved his head to nuzzle him for a brief moment. Seth tied down his medical bag and swung into the saddle. "We still have a long way to go, boy," he whispered. "Just maybe we'll do it by ourselves. What do you think of that?"

Sundance flicked his tail in seeming agreement.

Seth sighed. It was pretty damn bad when your only friend was a horse. Well, it had been worse.

"Let's go see if there's more pie," he said, and Sundance willingly trotted down the road back to Independence. Seth just wished he really cared about that pie but he suspected that he wouldn't be able to eat any, and if he did it would taste like ashes.

Balancing her wash in one hand and a bucket of water in the other, Kate MacAllister emerged from the woods along the river to see the Reb emerge from her wagon. Anger, hot and violent, seized her, and she started to increase her pace, disregarding the water slopping out of the bucket. But before she reached the clearing, she suddenly stopped as she saw him run a hand down his horse's neck. There was something about the way he did it that made her watch, a sort of wistful communion with the animal, which responded in kind.

And then he swung up into the saddle, and she thought—reluctantly—that she had seldom seen a more natural horseman. There was so much grace between the two, a continual flow of movement that she couldn't contain a certain admiration and even envy.

He was bareheaded, she noticed, his blond hair glinting gold in the sun. She suddenly thought of his eyes, vivid blue-green eyes that had viewed her earlier with something close to compassion.

She shook her head. She didn't want to think of him in any favorable way. He was a Reb, part of the catastrophe that had destroyed most of her family and ruined the few remnants. Jeremy, Nick and herself. So much of their beings had been stolen away by the war: Jeremy's health, her future with the man she loved,

Nick's childhood. Sometimes she thought the only thing that sustained her was hatred. Yet how could it be otherwise, when her mother and father and two brothers lay buried? How else could she not succumb to loneliness and fear?

Kate moved again, noticing that Nick was no longer outside. He must have stepped into the wagon, she thought. He had been wonderful with Jeremy—patient and uncomplaining, always turning down invitations to play with boys from the other wagons to sit with Jeremy or try patiently to tempt him with food.

Dear heaven, he was only eleven, so young to have lost so many. At least she and Jeremy had had their chance to be young. *Don't cry. You can't let Jeremy see you cry.* Kate forced down the threatening tears and pasted a smile on her face.

She stepped up on the short ladder into the covered wagon, wishing with all her might that they had not bought it. They had spent so much of their small hoard of money on the wagon and supplies, and now...

Kate had consumed most of the morning going to the suppliers, hoping they would repurchase the wagon and the other goods, but none were interested. A deal was a deal. And she knew there would be no more takers, not this year. She hated to think Jeremy and Nick would have to spend the winter in this wagon, but they could not afford to rent even the meanest of rooms now, not and have enough money left to make a new start in California, if they ever arrived. Choices. All of them equally harsh. She felt so completely helpless.

There *was* the Reb. But that was no choice at all, no matter what the wagon master thought. She couldn't stand being so close to someone who had been in any way involved with what had happened to those she loved. She couldn't put her family in the hands of someone like that. She couldn't.

He's a *doctor*, a traitorous part of her mind said.

But he said he'd fired a gun. He was as bad as any of them.

A doctor. A doctor for Jeremy.

She couldn't. She'd already discussed it with Jeremy. He'd agreed with her. His one experience with a Reb doctor had been horrible; the prison doctor had been an incompetent and a drunk, and had probably killed more Union soldiers than disease had.

Jeremy was sitting up, which was an improvement, and he and Nick were arguing about something. Kate's eyes rested on an object in Nick's lap.

"What is that?"

Jeremy gave her a sullen look. "That Reb doctor came by here. Tried to bribe Nick with that damned pie and me with some medicine. Probably just flour, or something."

But Jeremy did look a little better. Not quite as flushed as he had hours ago. Kate looked at Nick's hopeful face. Perhaps she shouldn't have been so tight with the money. It had been so long since he'd had any kind of treat. Part of her wanted to take the pie and throw it in the Reb's face; another part looked at Nick's too-thin face and anxious eyes and wanted him to have everything in the world.

Her voice softened. "I think we can keep it. There's no sense wasting good food out of spite. I don't see any obligation. We've already told him no."

That was all Nick needed. He quickly found a knife and cut three pieces, offering the first to Jeremy, and the second to Kate. But Kate was afraid she might choke on it, no matter what she'd told Nick. "I'm going to save mine for tomorrow. You go ahead and eat while I hang up these clothes."

"You sure, Kate?" Nick said.

"I'm absolutely sure," she assured him as Jeremy looked at her warily. He, too, had looked a little longingly at the slice, sniffing it with more enthusiasm than she had seen him show toward food in days. She ducked out before either of her brothers could say any more and moved toward a rope stretched between two trees. She stretched upward, wishing she were a bit taller, and hung their clothes up.

She heard eager talk coming from the direction of the other wagons, and she tried to close her ears to it. She had depended so much on this trip—on the chance to take Jeremy to a warm, dry climate where he could improve. She hadn't realized how much she'd been depending on it until Cliff Edwards reluctantly refused them a place in the train. She had argued. She and Nick could manage. They had managed the farm alone these past two years. She'd done everything a man could there—plowed, harvested, even repaired fences.

But she hadn't controlled a team of four oxen, Mr. Edwards had retorted, not up mountain trails and across rivers. If only she could hire a man...

She had tried. Dear God, how she had tried. She had put up notices all over town. But they were going to California, and available single men were heading to the gold and silver finds in Colorado. No one was willing to take on the responsibility of a woman, boy and invalid for months.

No one but a Southerner, an ex-Reb, a lean man with hair of gold and a wistful smile. A dangerous smile, she was already discovering, since she couldn't seem to dismiss it from her mind. There had been something lonely about it, something that touched her in a peculiarly poignant way.

Her brothers would turn over in their graves. So would her mother and father, who, she was convinced, had died of grief as they lost one son after another. The doctor said it was her mother's fever, and her father's heart, but Kate knew the real culprit.

How could she even think of hiring him? It would be a betrayal of everything she'd loved. Her chin set. They would make do. She'd try to talk to Mr. Edwards again. Reason with him. Even beg if she had to.

But she just couldn't force herself to hire the Rebel.

Chapter Two

In the end, Kate had to swallow her pride. It did not endear Seth Hampton to her that he made it easy. She didn't want it to be easy.

She wanted it to be hard, so that she could hate him.

But after a talk with Cliff Edwards and then a conference with Jeremy and Nick, she'd known she didn't have any choice but to approach the Reb. Time had made her see reason, but it hadn't made her like it.

Another factor had prompted her surrender. Jeremy had improved the next day, after another dose of the medicine and the mixture of quinine. But she did not fool herself. If they ran out of medicine, which they would, and they stayed in the wagon during Missouri's cold winter, she could lose her brother.

Pride and dislike weren't as important as Jeremy. She'd thought of the word *hate,* but she'd eventually had to dismiss it. It had such an ugly sound, and, she'd been taught, hate was unworthy of the MacAllisters, who were—always had been—God-fearing people. Still, she couldn't help considering that particularly unwholesome emotion, and she didn't like Seth

Hampton one bit for being so darn nice about her surrender.

She went to him the next afternoon. She had gotten nowhere with Cliff Edwards, not with pleas or with tears. He was even less sympathetic than before, now that he knew she had an option—an option he very much favored.

"Give the Doc a chance," he'd said. "If he doesn't work out, well, then we can leave him at one of the forts along the way."

Clenching her teeth together, she'd said she would talk to her brothers about it. Nick, strangely enough, had been in favor. Jeremy...well, Jeremy had argued and then understood the necessity behind it. It was either accept the Reb's offer or stay here, and Jeremy didn't want Kate to have to live in this wagon all winter. They didn't have time to try to find anyone else.

So Kate finally asked Cliff Edwards where Seth was staying and made the long walk into Independence. His landlady said Dr. Hampton was in the stable, and Kate, feeling dusty and sweaty and reluctant, went inside.

He was currying his horse, talking to it all the while, and she tried to listen, since he obviously didn't see her. "Miss Virginia, do you?" he was saying. "So do I, but just wait until you see California. They say it's the promised land for fine fellows like you. The richest grass you'll find anyplace. You'll get all prime and frisky again—" His words stopped, as if he had sensed something, and he turned around slowly, his eyes becoming wary when he saw her.

"Do you always talk to your horse?" She couldn't stop the question. She never heard anyone do that before. Horses were for working.

"We've come a long way together," he said noncommittally.

She hesitated. "I talked to Mr. Edwards."

He waited, he green-blue eyes steady and patient.

"I—we—don't have any choice but to hire you, if you still want to come."

"Accepted," he said. His eyes remained on her, but it was clear that he was demanding nothing more.

"We don't have much money to spare...."

"I don't need any," he told her. "I just needed a place on the train."

"No," she said abruptly. "We have to pay you."

"Food will be enough," he said, turning back to the horse.

"Mr.—Dr. Hampton?"

He turned back to face her.

"Thank you for the medicine you left. It did seem to help."

"I'm glad," he replied simply.

"But—"

"But you're still not happy that I'm going along with you?"

"No."

He sighed, and the sound was resigned, sad. "At least we have honesty between us."

"Neither is Jeremy pleased," she added, a little desperately. She was suddenly feeling addlepated in his presence, strangely susceptible to his easy charm. *Southern charm.*

"I know." Again Kate heard his resignation.

Kate wished he wasn't so reasonable, so infernally understanding. Resentment grew, but so did something else as she discovered that her gaze didn't want to leave his solemn one. She found herself studying his face and finding it difficult to dislike. His sandy eyebrows were thick, and arched in such a way that they gave him a relaxed, even lazy look. His features were regular, except for a cleft in his chin that made him look sensuous and vulnerable. He had a mouth that she suspected usually smiled easily. It had, the first time she had seen him, but now, while not grim, it had firmed into a straight line. His striking sea-colored eyes appeared depthless, as if they contained a hundred secrets.

"Why do you want to go west, Dr. Hampton?"

"Is that important?"

"Yes, to me it is. We have to trust you."

"Do you, Miss MacAllister? Trust me?"

"No," she said flatly. "I feel like I'm being blackmailed by Mr. Edwards."

"I think we both are, Miss MacAllister. We'll just have to live with it."

"You'll have to sleep outside. You understand that?"

"That's fine," he said easily. "I've been doing little else during the past few years."

It was the wrong thing to say, and he knew it almost immediately. She didn't need reminders of the side he had taken during the war.

"Miss MacAllister. Please understand one thing. I could just as well have served on the Union side. My only concern was saving lives."

"But you weren't on the Union side, were you, Doctor?"

"It didn't make any difference to me. I doctored the wounded from both sides."

"So our boys could go into your prison camps." Her words were bitter.

He shrugged. There was obviously no use arguing. "Did Edwards say when you're leaving?"

"Sunrise, day after tomorrow."

"I'll be there."

She hesitated. "There's not much room left in the wagon for your belongings."

"I don't need much. I came all the way from Virginia on horseback. Two bags, that's all. Mostly medicines."

She looked at him curiously. "All the way to California?"

He looked amused. "I don't need much, Miss MacAllister."

"Why are you going?" she asked again.

"There was no reason to stay in Virginia," he said. The amusement had left his eyes.

"No family?" She didn't know why she asked that. She didn't want to know. She didn't want to know anything about him. She didn't want anything to do with him but what was absolutely necessary.

"Two brothers, two sisters," he said. "Three in Virginia, one in the New Mexico Territory."

"You're lucky," she said, the bitterness creeping into her voice again as she turned around. "I'll tell Mr. Edwards he has his doctor."

"If your brother needs anything before then," Seth said, "send for me."

He received only a curt nod for his trouble.

Ten days passed on the journey, and speech between Seth and Kate and Jeremy MacAllister remained at a minimum. Only Nick seemed willing to give Seth a chance.

Each morning, Seth tied Sundance behind the wagon and drove the team and wagon over heavily rutted roads, his backside feeling every one of the ten to twelve miles they made each day. He longed, instead, for the saddle and the easy gait of Sundance.

He rode Sundance each night after the wagon train stopped for the night. Kate MacAllister had made it very clear that she wished to spend no more time with him than necessary, so he usually disappeared with one of the scouts, picking up tales about the trip west, about Indians, or about the buffalo that were being slaughtered by white hunters. It was usually very late when he returned to find a plate of food on the driver's seat of the wagon. Usually his bedroll had been placed next to the wagon and Kate had disappeared for the night.

Each family prepared its own food, although after a few days several families started to join together in the cooking duties. The MacAllister wagon, however, was usually avoided. The guides said it was because

Kate was a single woman and he was a Reb. Neither were welcome additions to the train.

Jeremy continued to improve from the snakeroot and quinine. And, Seth thought, rest. At Seth's insistence, the MacAllister wagon led the train, so that the dust wouldn't irritate Jeremy's damaged lungs. It had caused some grumbling among the other families, but Cliff Edwards's orders were law.

This part of the journey was flat and dry. The only scenery was a few farms, including some that had been burned by either Confederate or Union sympathizers. The scars of war were still with them and did nothing to reduce the lingering bitterness in the MacAllister wagon.

Seth drove himself physically, never going to his bedroll until he was so exhausted he knew he could sleep. The nightmares that had haunted him since the war stayed at bay, however, and each morning he murmured his thanks for that fact.

He welcomed young Nick's company. Restless and bored with the slow pace, the boy often sat up on the seat with him, while Kate MacAllister stayed stonily inside the wagon with the older brother. There were endless questions, which Seth enjoyed. He had always liked children for their innocence and curiosity and open-mindedness. And that was particularly true now.

"What is Virginia like?"

"Green and lush, with rolling hills and wide rivers."

"Did you have slaves?"

"Nope. My family didn't believe in slavery."

"Then how come you were a Reb?"

Seth hesitated. Slavery hadn't been the issue to him. Loyalty to Virginia had. Loyalty to friends. But if he'd actually had to fight, he might well have chosen the North, as his brother had, because he, too, believed in the Union. As a doctor, though, he didn't see that sides made any difference. Just saving lives. Blue or gray. But he didn't know whether he wanted to explain that. His pride prevented him from saying anything that would even sound like an excuse.

"Doctors have no sides," he said.

"That's not what Kate believes."

"What do you think?"

"I don't know," Nick admitted. "I think I like you, even if Kate doesn't."

The honesty of childhood. Seth felt both pleasure at the boy's reluctant acceptance and a kind of aching hurt at Kate's continuing rejection. It was going to be a long, long trip. It already had been, in fact.

That night, Jeremy was well enough to help gather wood for the fire. Seth stayed at the campfire to keep an eye on him, rather than take his usual ride out. Some color was coming back into the young man's face, and his light brown eyes had life in them again.

Kate had taken off the sunbonnet she wore almost constantly, whether to keep the dust from her hair or for some other reason Seth could only guess at. He immediately thought someone should burn the damn thing, for her hair was her best feature, light brown and seemingly touched with gold. It softened her features, and she looked pretty and young, especially when she looked at Jeremy with something close to pleasure. She even spared Seth a look without the usual censure.

Scattered fires lit the dark night sky, and the haunting sound of a harmonica from one of the wagons drifted over the various campsites. Kate had made beans and biscuits, which had become their staple diet at night. Cliff Edwards said that once they left the farming country the men could start hunting and fresh meat should be available. But compared to the meals Seth had had during the war, the dinner, which tonight was hot, was a feast indeed.

Conversation remained stilted, however, as if a fence had been erected and the MacAllister side posted against a trespasser named Seth Hampton.

Yet there was a softness to the evening. A half-moon reigned overhead amid a sea of stars, and a soft breeze had brushed away the bruising heat of the day. Talk from the various wagons had stilled as the travelers listened to the sweet, sad strains of "Lorena," a song sung by both the Reb and the Yank sides during the war.

Kate sat still, her head tipped back, her eyes gazing into the distance, and Seth remembered her words that first day. A fiancé lost in the war. Jeremy, too, looked lost in time, in memories, and Seth felt an aching sadness of his own. He thought of Blythe and his brother, Rafe, and their child. But the hurt was not as strong as it once had been, the loss not quite as bitter. But the loneliness was still there. Deep and painful. He felt as if part of him were missing—the strongest, most giving part.

Kate looked up at him, and for the brief moment their eyes met, a sudden acknowledgment of loss and pain was exchanged—a second of understanding. But then, with a will Seth couldn't help but admire, Kate almost visibly pulled away, her face suddenly confused.

She almost leapt to her feet. "I'm going for a walk," she said.

"I'll go with you," Nick said eagerly.

She shook her head. "Not now. Why don't you go play with some of the other boys?"

Nick hesitated a moment, as if weighing the currents in the air, currents obvious even to him. But the boy's reluctance to join the other boys was clear. Seth realized then that he'd never seen Nick join boys his age.

"How about helping me find some wood for the fire tomorrow morning?" Seth asked. "Maybe we can find something for you to carve with."

Kate threw him an angry look, as if Seth were stealing something from her, and Seth merely shrugged, his own anger beginning to rise. Nick was still a boy, but he had been caring for his brother as if he were an adult, and no one seemed to notice. He suspected that Kate had so much on her hands herself that she had forgotten what it was to be young, to need some security and pleasure.

"He can go with me," Kate said ungraciously.

"Why don't we all go?" Nick asked.

Jeremy, who was leaning against the wagon wheel, looked interested. He had been barely civil to Seth in the beginning, but had now progressed to a wary acceptance.

"Miss Kate?" Seth inquired politely.

It was clear to him, and probably Jeremy, if not Nick, that Kate's whole reason for a walk was to avoid his presence. Yet this time he was not ready to let her off lightly.

Kate looked at her two brothers, one mildly curious and the other eager. It was Nick's face that helped her decide. He asked for so little and had gone through so much. She supposed she could tolerate the Southerner's company for a brief while. A very brief while!

She didn't understand, however, why the prospect wasn't as distasteful as it should be. She had watched him in the past ten days as he'd befriended Nick and even eased Jeremy's resentment. Both facts had stiffened her own resistance. And yet...

Seth Hampton had one of the most striking faces she'd ever seen. Though not classically handsome, as her betrothed's had been, it had a kind of integrity that she'd tried not to notice and a kindness that was difficult to ignore.

But he was still a Rebel. A traitor. One of those who had robbed her of everything, and part of her couldn't let go of that fact. She had stayed as far away from him as possible in the small area they inhabited, and she had even been a little grateful for the way he disappeared each night. She had also felt an odd disappointment. That made her even angrier. And more confused.

And tonight, when he had looked at her with pain in his eyes, with a loneliness that she instinctively knew matched her own, she was flooded with unfamiliar feelings—a rush of warmth and even empathy. Worse, she felt a flooding confusion she hadn't experienced since the war had started and so much had fallen on her shoulders. She'd been so sure she was right in disliking and resenting Southerners. In some way, it had made things easier to have an object to blame.

But Nick looked so expectant. Kate decided to tuck away her own feelings for the moment—just for the moment. "All right," she said as she put her arm around Nick's shoulder, effectively closing out Seth Hampton. If he noticed, he didn't show it. He just fell into step alongside them as the harmonica music changed from a ballad to a merry jig.

Nick, catching the mood, twisted loose of Kate's arm and darted ahead toward the stream. There were no woods here, only plains that bordered a narrow, shallow waterway still thick with mud stirred up by the many animals that drank from it.

The sky stretched to infinity, with a million stars sprinkled across its rug of blue velvet. For a moment, Kate felt a kind of peace she hadn't known in a long time, since the news arrived that her two brothers had been killed, along with her betrothed, and Jeremy, at sixteen, had run away to avenge them.

Now, however, as she looked at her brother skipping stones, she felt a little tranquillity seep back into her soul. Jeremy was unquestionably better. They were bound for a town called Sacramento, a place of unusual beauty and opportunity, she'd been told.

Perhaps it was time to stop thinking of the past and start thinking of the future. It would be better for both

Nick and Jeremy, and for her, too. She heard another splash, and looked up. Dr. Hampton had moved away from her and was stooping next to Nick, his hand returning to his side after evidently skipping a stone of his own.

A Reb skipping stones like her brothers had? But he wasn't like them. He didn't believe in the same things. The old anger refused to surface, though, and again a peculiar warmth curled unexpectedly through her. She saw the side of the Reb's face, its expression intent and serious as he searched the ground, like her eleven-year-old brother, for the perfect stone to make the perfect skip. There was something terribly endearing about the act—a wistful return to childhood that touched her in ways she didn't want to be touched.

He apparently found what he sought and picked it up, turning to her with a tentative grin. "Would you like to try?"

She surprised herself by taking it. One of her older brothers had taught her to skip a stone, but that had been a long time ago. She pulled her arm back and tossed, but the stone fell into the stream like a . . . like a stone. Nick tossed her a disgusted look and Kate felt a moment of chagrin before another stone was dropped into her hand and her arm was drawn back. The touch on her arm was gentle but firm, and it seemed to burn a hole in her skin.

"It's in the twist of the wrist," the Reb said solemnly, as if he were discussing a matter of the greatest importance. The gravity of his deep voice sent tremors through her. He had no right to be disarming. No right at all, she thought as she followed his instructions. She saw Nick's eyes on her, widening slightly at her apparent willingness, and she wondered whether she had been that much of an ogre these past months. She moved her wrist as instructed, and the stone still sank, just like a stone.

"You need a lot of practice, Miss Kate," Dr. Hampton said chidingly, his soft, drawling words curling around in the air like molasses dripping from a bottle. Dr. Hampton, she warned herself. Dr. Reb Hampton. She refused to think of him as Seth, even after these past ten days. She turned around and found herself inches from his face, from a sensuous mouth that was smiling slightly and eyes so bright that even in the night she felt they could light the sky by their own power. She had the worst urge to move ever so slightly so that their lips would meet. . . .

The sound of the harmonica was still drifting through the air. Now, the notes were more plaintive, sad and filled with longing. Kate felt the sadness to the tips of her toes. She felt the whisper of Dr. Hampton's breath, warm and clean, and the tingling along her spine grew in intensity.

Dear God, was she that lonely, that foolish? She suddenly jerked away from his hand. She was as much a traitor to her family as he was to his country.

"I have to go back," she said, hating the trembling in her voice. "We'll be leaving at sunrise."

"Ah, Kate . . ." Nick said, his voice so normal that Kate envied him desperately.

Kate turned away from the eyes that looked into hers so steadily. She didn't want to look at Dr.

Hampton. She didn't want to betray herself, and that, at the moment, was exactly what was happening.

"Come on, Nick. We have to check on Jeremy."

"No, we don't. He's doing fine."

"Nick!"

This time, her brother didn't protest, but Kate saw the shadows return to his face, and once again she felt guilty. She transferred that guilt into her anger, which she directed toward this man who stirred feelings she didn't want. Or understand. "Leave us alone, Doctor. Stay away from me and Nick."

He stepped back, and his lips, which had been smiling, turned grim. "As you wish," he said. For a contrite moment, she watched him stride quickly along the stream, his stiff back counterpointing the usual easy grace of his walk. She felt something new throbbing inside her, not the sharp sword of loss, but rather an inexplicable poignancy. Was it for something that could never be?

She wished with all her might that they didn't need Seth Hampton. Perhaps by the time they reached Fort Walker they wouldn't. Perhaps then she could tell Cliff Edwards the arrangement just wasn't working. Hopefully, it would be too late then for Mr. Edwards to abandon them. It was a plan, at least. A plan that might help her keep her sanity.

For the briefest slice of time, Seth had felt whole. He'd felt real again, like someone who could accept pleasure. He had thought he had lost that simple feeling.

He had gone home after the war, to what had once been home. The farm that the Hamptons had built back in 1816 had been destroyed, and although his brother had asked him to join him in rebuilding it, he simply hadn't had the heart left. He had tried. Dear God, how he had tried, because it was so important to Rafe and Blythe. They'd wanted him as a partner to rebuild the family's reputation for breeding fine horses, and Seth had considered it. But he, too, had once loved Blythe, and he knew he would never really be comfortable with them. There would always be an ache in his heart if he stayed, a reminder of what he had lost. He loved his brother too much to be jealous of him, but neither would their house ever be his home.

His brother had wanted to give him money for his share of the land, but he had demurred. It would take Rafe a great deal of money to rebuild, and Seth didn't need much. When Rafe felt financially comfortable, he could then send Seth what he felt fair. Rafe had tried to change Seth's mind, but Seth had simply left one morning, leaving only a note bchind. He didn't like goodbyes. There had just been too many of them in the past years.

Since then, he had molded his hopes and dreams and steered them in one direction: west. They didn't include anyone else, or even much expectation of happiness. Too much had been extracted from his soul after four years of bloody war.

And then, tonight, he had opened himself up again, only to have someone else slam closed the door of light. The shadows were back, clouding his mind with familiar images. He knew as well as he knew death always followed life that the nightmares would return tonight.

Seth would walk several miles, and then perhaps take a ride. Maybe he could wear himself out tonight, passing the dark hours awake. He didn't wish to wake up screaming, not with Kate MacAllister nearby. He had gone through that once with Blythe and had seen the pity on her face.

Seth didn't think he could stand that again. Even if Kate MacAllister had any pity left to give.

Chapter Three

The sound of moaning woke Kate. Her mind felt dense, and it took her a moment to clear it. Sleep had not come easily last night. She had found herself lying awake, listening for sounds under the wagon. She had been tense and confused, still bewildered by those womanly feelings of hours ago. Feelings she shouldn't have for an enemy.

It was growing increasingly difficult to think of him that way, and yet she must. She could never reconcile her bitterness toward the Confederacy and anyone who had been a willing part of it.

But still she'd wondered about him. He had looked so alone when she had torn herself from his grasp. She had heard him telling Nick he had family and she wondered why someone with relatives would leave them? He had spoken of his brothers with affection. But then, there was so much she didn't know, because she hadn't wanted to ask. She had told herself she knew everything she'd needed to know. He was a Southerner. But that argument wasn't working as well as it once had.

It had been very late when she finally fell asleep, and now she had to shake the heavy cobwebs from her mind to fathom the low cries she was hearing. Her first thought was Jeremy, but as she adjusted her sight in the dark wagon, she saw the he was breathing better than he had in weeks. Nick, too, was peacefully asleep.

The noise, almost a sobbing, was coming from below. Kate hurriedly pulled on a dressing gown. It was a worn, almost shapeless garment she'd had for years, but at least it covered her. She quietly moved to the opening of the wagon and lifted the flap.

The approach of dawn had lightened the sky to a dull gray, brightened only by a splash of light to the east. There was some movement near the horses and oxen, but she didn't know whether the disturbance was merely the early wakening of the beasts or the men already tending them. She jumped from the wagon and stooped to where she knew Dr. Hampton had been sleeping since they had left Independence. He had chosen a place nearby in case Jeremy needed him. As she watched him in the dim light of dawn, Kate felt an aching sense of shame. She had offered him nothing, not an extra blanket or pillow or anything to provide more comfort. He was thrashing now, and she saw the glint of something wet on his face. He was muttering— No, it was a moan. "No more," he was rasping out. "Please, God, no more."

And then: "Morphine!" It was almost a shout. "Got to have morphine!" His body shuddered, as if preparing for unbearable pain, and Kate thought her heart might break at watching such personal agony, such hopelessness. Even her own losses seemed less terrible at the sight of his racking grief. She swallowed the lump in her throat and reached out, touching his arm lightly.

He woke immediately, his eyes wide open and perceptive. He was so much quicker than she in reaching the same level of alertness minutes ago, and she realized he must have been aroused this way many times before. Necessity? Training? He looked toward her, and then his hand went to his face, and she knew he was searching for the wetness there, as if this nightmare had occurred before. She turned away, instinctively knowing he didn't want sympathy, or even acknowledgment of what had happened.

"I'm sorry," he said in the deep Southern drawl that had so infuriated her the first time she'd heard it. But now it had the slightest hesitation in it, and the unexpected vulnerability it implied was appealing. "I didn't mean to waken you."

"Of course you didn't," she said. "I was just going to start a fire."

Dressed in nightclothes? The unspoken question hovered between them.

He turned his face away from her, and she moved away to give him privacy, but not before she saw his arm go up and his sleeve brush against the dampness on his cheek.

Kate leaned against the wagon and looked up into the sky. The stars were fading now, and the moon looked nearly transparent as the first thin line of light started to spread over the horizon. She was hearing more noise now, as people were beginning to stir. Soon, one of Mr. Edwards's men would be knocking at each wagon, telling the occupants they had only a short time before departure. There would be the smell of coffee, perhaps some bacon, or even eggs that some of the women had purchased from farms along the road.

She sensed, more than saw, Dr. Hampton standing beside her. "I'll start the fire," he said, his voice firm again, with no trace of the previous hesitation. She turned. He was tall, about six inches taller than her own height, which was greater than most women's. She seldom had to look up at a man, but now she did, as she studied his lips, which twisted into a small, abashed smile, much like Nick's when he had been discovered doing something he shouldn't.

At the same time, though, Kate sensed he didn't want any questions. His usually clear eyes were clouded and strained, and lines that shouldn't frame the eyes of one his age had etched trails in his face. His usually clean-shaven face was slightly bristled now, which, instead of making him look slovenly, had the opposite affect. She wanted to reach up and touch them, to feel those bristles across her cheek. . . .

Good heavens above, what was happening to her? She was standing in her nightclothes before a man she detested and imagining the most absurd things.

"I'd better get dressed," she said, and turned, fleeing from him. Fleeing from herself.

Seth took up his former habit of riding Sundance at night and keeping a certain protective distance, in attitude if not always in geography, from Kate MacAllister and her family.

He had felt exposed that night when the nightmare returned. He had hoped, when he'd finally lain down in the wee hours of that morning, that he had exhausted himself enough to keep it from recurring. But, perhaps because he had allowed his emotions free rein that night, the nightmare had attacked even worse than usual.

The dream took him back to the medical tent during the last battle for Richmond. They had run out of chloroform, the most popular anesthetic, and morphine. There was only whiskey for amputations, and nothing for stomach wounds. The cries were haunting, and there was so little he could do without medicine. He could only try to save a few lives, often in such agonizing ways that he often wondered whether it was worth it. And then there were more wounded. Always more.

Seth didn't want to surrender to the nightmare, but sometimes even during a hot day he broke out into a cold sweat and memories bombarded him like the shells that had once rained on so much of Virginia.

Jeremy was growing stronger day by day, taking over some of the tasks Seth had performed. He unhitched the oxen at night, watered and fed them, and usually started the fire. Seth didn't protest. The boy— and Seth couldn't think of Jeremy in any other way— needed a certain amount of exercise or he would turn into an invalid for the rest of his life.

And this assumption of chores meant that Seth could spend more time away from the wagon. He started taking his evening meals with Cliff Edwards, listening to him talk about the trail and California.

Seth was also being called upon now for his medical skills by others in the wagon train. The first mishap occurred three weeks out of Independence, when one of the children was bitten by a water moccasin along a river. Two days later, a woman's arm was broken. And then there was a foot cut that went unreported and unattended until the foot had swelled to nearly twice its usual size.

Reluctance to call "the doc" disappeared gradually. He first charmed the children with his patience, and then the women as their children succumbed, and finally some of the men, one by one. His opinion was asked about stomach aches, gout, rashes, sunburn. But the thaw didn't quite reach Kate MacAllister's wagon, except for Nick. If anything, the atmosphere became more tense.

Seth understood what was happening. He recognized the attraction between him and Kate, no matter how hard she tried to fight it. Because she *did* fight it, he did, also. He was through with lost causes. God knew he'd had enough of them in his life. He was tired of fighting the wind—much less the tornadoes—that swirled around him with fury. He wanted peace. Dear God, how he wanted peace.

He also wished he could stop wanting Kate MacAllister. Although she looked nothing like Blythe Somers, his first love, the two women had many similarities. Strength. Stubbornness. Total commitment to those they loved. And Kate could be damnably pretty when she took off her sunbonnet and allowed that sun-tipped hair to fall around her face, framing the hazel eyes that flashed and glowed.

Her eyes had been soft that morning after his nightmare. Even compassionate. But he didn't want her compassion. He wanted her acceptance. If she was unwilling to give him even the slightest chance to prove himself, then to hell with even trying.

Still, he wished his body didn't react as it did when she was around. It didn't do the same thing with the other marriageable young ladies on the train; in fact, more than one had signaled interest once he seemed to become socially acceptable and no longer just the "damned Reb."

But with Kate, it was always "Dr. Hampton," that stiff title combined with a deliberate coldness that conversely seared even more scars on his heart. Jeremy, on the other hand, while not burning up with gratitude, was at least following his suggestions without the glaring hostility that had accompanied their first days on the trail.

Over the next few days, the pace of the train quickened as much as possible; the wagons left before sunrise and didn't stop until sunset. Tempers grew short, but Cliff Edwards repeated the same litany over and over again. "We have to get across the mountains before the first snowfall."

They were nearly across "Bleeding Kansas," where they often passed burned-out farms and roving bands of men. Renegades, according to Mr. Edwards. The wagons were ordered to move closer together, and the dust was as thick as in a sandstorm, even at the front wagon. Earlier wagon trains had stirred and pounded the land into fine powder, and the slightest wind sent it sailing in swirling clouds that set everyone to coughing.

Jeremy's cough worsened again, and Seth fashioned him a face mask from a gunny sack and took back all his old duties, driving the oxen each morning after tying the canvas over the wagon to keep out as much of the dust as possible. The resumption of duties meant he couldn't go for his usual long rides, but those were now frowned upon by Edwards, in any event. Many of the guerrillas from both sides had taken up open banditry after the war, and the wagon master didn't want anyone wandering far from the main group.

Kate often took over the reins as Seth sat in back with Jeremy, spooning him various mixtures he hoped would help. But even the snakeroot didn't help much now. He gave him brandy to help him sleep and applied mustard-seed oil to the chest, as well as mixtures of stramonium and hickory leaves.

Kate's overt hostility softened at night as they worked together to get Jeremy to eat some broth, while Nick whittled silently in the corner, his hazel eyes shuttered, his usual questions silenced. Nick worried Seth as much as his brother.

Seth would lean back against the bags of flour and cornmeal and listen to Jeremy's breathing, trying to take the boy's mind off the effort. He discovered that Jeremy had enlisted at sixteen and that he was now only nineteen. He looked years older—except when he slept. But then, Seth knew he looked years older than his age, too. So did a lot of men now. He also knew why the boy sometimes fought sleep, because he did the same thing.

"What are you going to do in California?" Seth asked Jeremy one evening, as Kate sat in a corner mending a shirt in the light of a lantern.

"If I get there," Jeremy said.

"Oh, you'll get there," Seth said. "You're going to be my best advertisement."

Jeremy gave him a faint grin. "Not looking for any patients, huh?"

"Are you decrying my skills?" Pleased at the boy's banter, Seth gave him a devilish smile and continued, "I propose to parade you up and down the streets of Sacramento as evidence of superior ability. I wouldn't take it kindly if you interfered with that plan by not getting thoroughly well."

Jeremy's grin widened. "I'll do what I can, Doc."

Pleasure sifted through Seth at Jeremy's grin. It was the first time the boy had been more than civil to him. It also showed a new attitude, a hopeful one. "You'll have to see to that." He hesitated, then repeated his earlier question. "What do you plan to do when you get to Sacramento?"

"Become a storekeeper, if my sister has anything to do with it." Some of the light left Jeremy's eyes.

"And if she doesn't?" Seth felt Kate's eyes boring into his back. But he knew Jeremy needed his own dream to survive.

"A farm. That's all I ever wanted to do—farm," he said slowly. "But Kate thinks..." His words trailed off.

"You might be surprised how much better you'll feel, when you get out of this dust," Seth said. "I think you might be able to do a lot more than you think."

Jeremy turned away, as if unable even to think of such a miracle. And Seth leaned back against a lumpy sack of something and wished he could make the boy believe.

When Jeremy finally fell asleep, Seth nodded to Kate and stepped down out of the wagon. He needed a walk, to exercise the stiffness in his legs from sitting all day. He was surprised when he heard a voice behind him. "Dr. Hampton..."

He turned. Kate was behind him, her hair in one long braid in back. The embers from the fire on which she'd cooked a meal flared up, and he saw the anger in her eyes.

"Why are you giving him false hope?"

"It's not false hope."

"He'll never be able to plow and..."

"Miss MacAllister," Seth said patiently. "Don't ever tell him what he can't do."

"You want to kill another Yank?" she asked, her voice suddenly harsh and unforgiving. She knew she was being unreasonable, but she couldn't stop herself. He had trespassed on her life, and her brothers' lives as well. She didn't know whether her anger was directed at him or at herself for allowing him to make such an impact on them. On her.

"Don't be a fool," he said, venting the anger that he hadn't known was building up inside. "You'll kill him yourself if you coddle him. You'll drain the life from him."

"What do you know about his life, or our life?" she asked bitterly, "or what it was like before the war." They were beyond the wagons now, walking along a small bluff that overlooked the dry camp. "It's my family, not yours, damn you."

It was the first time she had ever cursed in her life, and she heard herself with horror. This was his fault.

"Is that it?" he asked softly. "Do you think I'm trying to take your family away?"

It was entirely dark now. They were beyond the campfires, and the sky was cloudy, hiding the moon and the stars and blocking out their light.

He heard a small sob. "I don't know what I think," Kate said, sounding like an abandoned child. His anger melted under the sound, replaced by tenderness.

He couldn't see her eyes. He could barely make out her features. The air was already tense, signaling a coming storm, and he felt the heated air vibrating with energy. His body was radiating the same heat, the same energy, the same tension.

"Ah, Kate," he said, his fingers reaching up and touching her chin, rubbing it ever so lightly. "You don't always *have* to know. Confusion is sometimes healthy."

"Someone *has* to. . . ."

"Give Jeremy a chance. He's a man who's been at war. He's no longer a boy."

"But I want him to be." The cry was plaintive. "He should be. And Nick . . ." Her voice trailed off.

"Is much too old for his age," Seth interrupted, "but there are so many children like that now. My sister-in-law took in ten children during the war." He hesitated, knowing what she thought of Southerners. She had said it often enough. "Black and white, all of them had been abused one way or another, and by one side or another. Some renegade Southerners had killed the parents of one, Yanks had raped a runaway slave girl of thirteen. There was a boy, Jaime—he still lives with her—who reminds me of Nick. So much had happened to him, he tried to shut out the world. But he couldn't. None of us could."

"Why did you leave?"

He was silent for a long time. "Remember that nightmare I had?" he asked.

"Yes," she said.

"Virginia is beautiful. God's country. But after the war, whenever I looked at it, I saw death and destruction. It was everyone's battleground. Southern troops destroyed the homes of those loyal to the North, and Northern troops those homes that sheltered Confederates. I could never look at it and see the peace I once knew there."

There was such infinite sadness in his voice that Kate found herself hurting with him. She didn't want to. The South had brought on its own misery. But now she saw what he saw, and she found herself aching at the uselessness of it.

His fingers had moved now to trace her cheek, and again she felt the gentleness in his touch. So sensitive, so light. Her head tipped up toward him, her eyes seeking the face she now envisioned nightly in her own dreams. She hadn't wanted to admit that, and had told herself it was an aberration. So was this. So was this need to comfort.

His lips came down and touched hers, searchingly at first. And then more firmly, as if finding what he was seeking. Kate found herself surrendering in a way she had never surrendered before, not even to the man she had planned to marry. She hadn't had this need then, nor this sudden hunger to right things that were so very wrong, not only for her, but also for him. She wanted to ease him as much as she wanted to ease herself.

All thought escaped her mind completely as she lost herself in his kiss—in the heat that envcloped them as if they had fallen into the heart of a volcano. The attraction between them exploded into flames so greedy they consumed everything in their path except their unexpectedly desperate need for one another.

Seth deepened the kiss, and what had started as a natural extension of those empathetic moments between them became something else altogether.

He felt her body respond as it unconsciously leaned against his and flamed a desire that was entirely unique in its depth and complexity. He hadn't thought he would—could—love again, not after Blythe, but what he was feeling came close to that. Very close. The physical feelings were even stronger than they had been with Blythe, perhaps because when he had kissed Blythe so many years ago she had been so young and innocent, and he had been careful not to go beyond the bounds of propriety. After that, he had loved her from a distance, because she was engaged to his brother.

But Kate MacAllister was not seventeen, and she responded in all the ways of a woman, although he knew it was not entirely willingly. He didn't want to think of that. He didn't want to think that once more he was pursuing something that was totally elusive.

He couldn't stop, however, not with her body yielding to his, just as her lips were, even though he knew that this was a mistake, that it was too soon. Her resentment and grief were still raw. But it had been so long since he had held a woman this way, so very long, and she was life and hope and pleasure. He needed all three to the core of his soul.

He knew she felt the same magic he did, the same momentary sense of something being essentially right. As his tongue nuzzled her lips, her mouth opened to his and her body melded itself into his masculine one. His arms went around her and his fingers played with her braid and then moved up to her neck, massaging with tender, sensuous strokes.

Kate had thoroughly confounded herself by opening her mouth to his, and now she found the taste and feel of his tongue dizzying. She felt her body quivering in the oddest way. She needed his steadiness and strength to keep on her feet, and she therefore, quite sensibly, leaned farther into him.

Nothing else, though, was sensible. The world was swirling with sensations she'd never known existed. She felt the strength of his arms and the movement of his muscles against her, which did things to her body that made her blood feel like liquid fire.

He took his mouth from hers long enough to whisper, "Pretty Kate," and the two words were immediately locked forever in her memory. They had been said so warmly, as if he really meant them. She had never really felt pretty before, and had never been told so. Not even by the man she was to marry.

Somewhere in the back of her mind, she tried to remember he was the enemy, that what she was doing was a betrayal of her family, but her mind, her heart and her body were not listening to each other. For this moment, nothing mattered but this wonderfully rich awareness that washed away all the worry and grief. She was so alive. So incredibly alive. His hands were so gentle, and yet each touch was deliciously painful.

His mouth settled easily on hers again, and she found her lips—her tongue—responding instinctively, seeking to explore every one of these extraordinary feelings. She craved more, and wondered at sensations that kept increasing in intensity, one feeding on another until her body trembled with expectancy, with the need to know how much more there was. Thomas Beck, her fiancé, had never aroused these kind of feelings.

The thought was invasive—and destructive. Thomas was dead, lying near her brothers, in Southern earth. Guilt, the most terrible kind of guilt, washed over her, making her feel unworthy, damned. She stiffened, and she felt the same reaction in him.

His mouth left hers. "Kate?"

Why did her name have to sound so pleasant on his lips, the quite ordinary word transformed into something lovely? That Southern drawl. Music. Deadly music.

She pulled away. "I'm sorry. I can't."

She felt his body still, as if he'd turned into a statue, and she couldn't move, either. They were locked together in a battle of wills.

"Because I'm from the South?" His voice was softly angry, and that was more intimidating than if he'd shouted.

"Because you *fought* for the South." She tried to make her voice steady. She didn't know if she succeeded, because her heart was still quaking.

All Seth's feelings of hope died. *Damn. It would never be over. Never.* But he tried. One more time, he tried. "The war's been over for a year, Kate."

"It will never be over for Jeremy—for a lot of men."

"Let Jeremy decide that, damn it."

"My older brothers, then," she said desperately.

"And your fiancé," Seth added bitterly. "Well, lady, keep fighting your war. But don't make Jeremy and Nick fight it, too. I'll take you back."

He turned around, taking her arm with none of the tenderness of moments before, merely determination. Kate held back a moment. "Dr. Hampton—? Seth—?"

Seth stopped, hesitated.

"I'm sorry," she said. She wanted to say more. She wanted to say it wasn't the war, not now, but her own guilt, guilt at acknowledging all these forbidden feelings and the sense of betrayal they created in her. How could she care for him and still be true to the memory of her brothers, her parents, and Thomas? Perhaps that was the worst guilt of all. Thomas. She'd thought she loved him, but she'd never had these kinds of swirling, dancing, aching feelings with him. Never.

He sighed, and Kate could sense the regret in the sound. "I'm sorry, too. I should have—" Just then thunder roared across the sky, followed immediately by a streak of lightning. "I'd better get you back to the wagon," he said abruptly. "At least rain will settle the dust. It should help Jeremy." His voice sounded professional, impersonal, and Kate felt a devastating loss.

She wanted to reach out to him, and her fingers flexed with that need—but she couldn't. Especially now, when his voice was curiously cool after having been so warm only moments ago.

So she tried to make her legs move in an ordinary fashion. They objected, and she stumbled just as another roll of thunder seemed to shake the earth, and rain came, suddenly and in torrents.

Kate felt his arms steady her and then gather her up as if she weighed next to nothing. She started to object, but one look at his face now lit by a flash of lightning dissuaded her. His face was set in hard, unyielding lines, his mouth grim and his jaw rigid. He seemed not to notice the rain that plastered the thick hair around his face.

Her head was next to his heart, and she heard its steady beating, a sound that made her feel safe and warm. Even now. Even with the bitterness still alive between them. But soon that safety would be gone, and in a moment of honesty she realized how much she, and her brothers, had come to depend on him, how they all had come alive again in their own ways.

Why couldn't she accept her own feelings?

They reached the wagon and he helped her inside and then assisted her and her brothers in securely tying down the canvas to shut out the rain. He worked silently, his hands deft. As he tied the cords in one corner, Kate thought that his hands had a peculiarly masculine beauty of their own, his long, sure fingers capable of both strength and gentleness.

When he finished, he quickly examined Jeremy and told him he wouldn't need the mask tonight. Seth mixed the now-familiar snakeroot in water and handed it to the younger man. Then he gave Nick an irresistible smile that Kate wanted for herself. But when he turned back to her, it was gone. His face was grave and his eyes were hooded. "I'll be leaving."

"You can't sleep outside." She didn't want him to go. But she couldn't bear to have him stay, either.

"I don't plan to," he said simply. "I'll be bunking with Edwards, if you need anything." He paused. "I think I'll be leaving the train at Fort Kelly, in Colorado. I've been talking to young David Cochran. He's learned a lot in the past month. He'll help you out."

"Mr. Edwards—?" Kate started to protest, but something in his face stopped the words. There was a harshness she hadn't seen there before, an unbending firmness.

"But, Seth—" This protest came from Nick, whose expression was disconsolate. Kate wondered when Dr. Hampton had become Seth to Nick.

Even Jeremy looked dismayed, and Seth almost re-thought his decision. But he couldn't. He would only end up hurting them all the more.

"Fort Kelly's a few more weeks away," Seth said. "By then, we'll be out of the dust, and the weather should be dry. I'll leave enough medicine. You'll be fine."

"But you were going to Sacramento with us," Nick persisted. "You said you were."

Seth smiled ruefully, but the usual warmth didn't reach his eyes. "Things change, Nick. I thought I might try Denver. The scouts say it's a booming place that needs someone like me, and I think your broth-er's going to be just fine after getting to the moun-tains." He hesitated. "I—well, I think it's time to find my own way. Might even go gold-hunting."

Kate was too shocked to say anything. When had he made this decision? Why? Because of tonight? Or be-cause of the way she had treated him throughout this journey?

What would they do without him?

He had become a member of her family. Without any of them actually realizing it, he had carved him-self an important place in their lives. A Southerner. A Rebel. And she didn't want him to go. And yet she couldn't ask him to stay. She knew what would hap-pen if she did, and she also knew she would hate her-self if she allowed it to happen. So, apparently, did he.

As he stepped out of the tent and she retied the flap, she looked back. The crowded interior of the wagon was suddenly very, very empty.

Chapter Four

As Seth made his way through the driving rain, he knew he had made the right decision in leaving. He had been thinking about it for the past few days, although he had continued to hope that things might change. There had been changes, a lessening of hostility with Jeremy, and even, at times, with Kate. But, after tonight, he knew nothing had really changed, at least not with Kate.

Part of him balked at making that decision, the decision to leave, to give up. He had never been a quitter. But, God, he was tired of fighting wars. He didn't need another in his life. And he wasn't going to torture himself again by wanting someone who loved another, or who didn't want him.

For a while, he had allowed himself to think about the valley Nick and Jeremy talked about, the Sacramento Valley, which was supposed to be so fertile and beautiful. But it had been a fool's dream.

Kate MacAllister had made it very clear that she would never accept what he was. And he couldn't change that attitude. He had tried. He had thought time might help, but it had been more than a month now, and despite the obvious attraction between them, he couldn't pierce the wall she'd constructed against him.

He didn't think he could stay in such close proximity to her and resist doing what he had done tonight. When he was around her, his fingers ached to touch her, to make the look in those eyes soften, to bring much-needed laughter to them. And that, he'd discovered, was disastrous for both of them. He had not missed the pain in her eyes tonight. Whether it had been for him, or for the man who had been killed in the war, he didn't know. He didn't think he wanted to know. He only knew that if he stayed, the pain would probably grow deeper, and he wanted no part of making it so. It was not easy to be torn by loyalties; no one knew that better than he.

The mood in the Edwards wagon, occupied by Cliff Edwards, the man who cooked for him, and the scouts, was gloomy. The rain was hard and steady, and probably long-lasting. They would miss valuable travel time.

Seth gratefully agreed to a game of poker. The stakes were low, which was fortunate, since he couldn't concentrate.

He was down five dollars when Edwards threw in his cards. "Time to turn in," he said. "What about you, Doc?"

Seth shrugged. The last thing he wanted now was sleep. The nightmares came when his mind was in turmoil. And God knew it was roiling now, as much as the storm outside.

"How's the MacAllister boy?"

"This rain will help settle the dust. That should help."

"Hmm . . . I hope so," Edwards said. "He seemed so much better for a while."

"Once we leave this dust behind . . ."

"I'm sure glad you're around, Doc. So are the other folks, now."

Seth hesitated. "Not all of them."

"I ain't heard any grumblings lately."

"I'm thinking about leaving, taking off toward Denver."

Edwards looked at him sharply. "Not you, too. Gold-hunting don't seem your style."

Seth grinned. "It's not. But doctoring is. You have, what, a hundred people? Most of them fit. I hear the gold camps are crowded, and they don't have any doctors." It was a plain, bald-faced lie. He didn't know whether they did or not, but it seemed logical.

"What about the MacAllisters?" Edwards watched him closely, and Seth kept any emotion from his eyes.

"Once in the mountains, Jeremy should be fine. And David Cochran could help them out. I've been keeping an eye on him. He seems willing and competent."

"You made a bargain," Edwards said.

"Predicated on things working out," Seth reminded him. "They are not."

"Miss Kate, you mean?"

Seth shrugged. "Her resentment is natural enough."

"I don't think that's all of it," Edwards said shrewdly. He had seen the way his two most interesting passengers looked at one another when they thought they were unobserved. He hadn't missed the need in their eyes, a need that they seemed bound and determined not to allow each other to see. Pride was a terrible thing, he thought. So was obstinacy. They had three more months to go on this trail. At least three months, and time could do a lot for obstinacy. If he could only tempt Seth Hampton into staying. But, looking into those determined eyes, he wondered if he could.

And he sensed that now was not the time to argue. So he only nodded. "I can't hog-tie you and make you stay, but I sure would be sorry to lose you." He rose, then added, "I'm going to take one last look around camp. Check on the sentries. Make sure none of them have ducked into wagons."

Seth felt his usual restlessness. "I'll go with you."

Cliff Edwards threw him a poncho. "Damned if I want *you* to get sick."

Seth smiled wryly. "I never get sick. Four years of war, sleeping in snow sometimes, riding in icy rain. Never even a fever. Sometimes..." The smile disappeared, and Seth's face looked bleak.

Edwards winced inwardly. He liked Seth Hampton. He liked the dogged persistence with which the soft-spoken doctor convinced former enemies to trust him, to let him help them. Hampton had an unusual compassion that drew people to him, regardless of their prejudices. Edwards also liked Kate MacAllister and her dedication to what was left of her family. Both of them had gone through a crucible of fire, and both had been made strong by it. Now they needed tempering. Maybe by a third party.

He had three weeks to do it.

"Come on, Doc," he said. "Let's go."

The rain continued for three days without cessation. The road became impassable, and the heavy wagons bogged down in mud. The wagon train made a total of only eight miles in those three days. The only good news was Jeremy, who, as Seth had predicted, improved dramatically. Despite his protests, he was still ordered to stay inside the wagon. A cold would be catastrophic for him.

Seth drove the wagon the few miles before Edwards disgustedly called for an early stop. Nick rode in front with him, despite the rain. He didn't say anything—didn't even ask any of the usual questions—but silently worked at his carving, glancing over occasionally at Seth's face.

When Seth checked on Jeremy, he didn't stay long, just measured out the medicine and kept his conversation to a minimum, asking only whether the boy had passed a good night. He was always aware of Kate's presence—too aware. Tension radiated between them, as neither of them was willing to risk even the slightest overture.

The rain was lessening at the end of the third day. Tempers throughout the wagon train were short as a result of the enforced confinement in too-small wagons. There was no hot food, nothing for children to do, no way to stretch stiff limbs. Men had to go out into the pouring rain and feed and water the miserable oxen and other livestock or stand for hours at sentry duty. Cases of dysentery broke out, and Seth believed it came from a stream where some of the travelers had refilled their water kegs. Previous wagon trains—there were so many of them—had used the streams carelessly and left them polluted.

He had made sure the MacAllisters filled their kegs well upriver of the main trail, and had advised others to do the same, but apparently some had paid no attention. Cliff Edwards had ordered, henceforth, that all families were to follow Dr. Hampton's orders, or they would be asked to leave the train at the next fort or town.

In the meantime, Seth prescribed calomel for the worse cases of dysentery, and arrowroot and other indigenous astringents for the milder cases. By the fourth day, nearly everyone was well again.

The rain finally stopped, and the train moved on slowly. The road was still muddy, which made it difficult for even the oxen to pull their loads, and streams were hard to ford because of high water. They were now approaching Big Sandy Creek, and Edwards feared the heavy rains might make the usually placid creek difficult to cross.

It was. They camped overnight along the rushing waterway, hoping it would go down during the night. By evening, it had dropped a little, but was still chest high at the fording place, and the current was strong.

But Cliff Edwards felt they couldn't delay any longer. The skies were cloudy again, and there might well be more rain, pushing the water level even higher.

Loads were exchanged; the stronger teams and higher wagons took goods from other wagons. Wagon boxes were raised from the bolsters to keep provisions from getting wet. Ropes were attached to the riggings of each wagon to steady it as it crossed the creek.

Although the MacAllister wagon had been first in line, it was now moved back so that heavier wagons could go across first. One wagon overturned in the water, and everything not tied down went floating downstream. Kate, who had been watching from the bank, went back inside her wagon and tied everything down that she could. Flour, cornmeal and bacon had already been transferred to wagons with higher beds.

When she finished, she rejoined Jeremy and Nick, who sat on the bank watching as the wagons moved slowly across the river. Seth was across the river, helping with the ropes balancing the wagons. Kate could see him perfectly from where she was. He was helping pull ropes stretched taut around trees for leverage. He and several other men had taken off their shirts in the humid heat, and the sun hit the glistening beads of sweat on his chest like tiny fragments of gold. His blond hair, so like the golden corn her family had once grown, was tousled as if he'd been running his hand through the curling tendrils that fell over his forehead.

He was magnificent in his concentration, in the way his muscles moved and in the manner in which he grinned at something someone said to him. Need seethed within her, need so potent that she clenched her fist into a ball so tight she felt she might break her own fingers. No matter how hard she tried to dismiss that craving, she couldn't. She just couldn't. It was there, something so sweet and wild and impossible that she ached in every feeling part of her. How could she let it go so easily? Let *him* go?

One of the wagons started to tip, and she heard a scream and then the terrified bark of a dog as it fell from the wagon. The current caught it and started to sweep the animal toward where they were sitting. Before Kate could do anything, Nick was up and running for the edge of the stream, apparently in an attempt to grab the animal. But he fell into the water, and then he, too, was tumbling over in the heavy current.

Kate heard her own scream as she got to her feet. "He can't swim!" she screamed as she ran down to the edge. Neither could she, and though every instinct pushed her to go into the water, she knew she would only make things worse.

Then Jeremy was there, ready to go in, but Seth, on the other side, yelled at him, "Stay there, I'll get him!" With movements so fast Kate could barely follow them, Seth was in the water, his strokes strong and fast. Kate felt Jeremy's hands on her.

"He'll get Nick," he said, and there was such confidence in his face that Kate believed him. She had to. Dear God, she couldn't lose Nick, too.

Two other men were in the water now, but Seth had been the first and was the swiftest swimmer. Kate saw him grab something and shove it toward one of the other men and then swim on. In another moment, she saw two heads, a small one with brown hair and a larger one with gold. A few strokes, and Seth stood up in the water and moved rapidly toward the bank. One of the other men held the drenched dog.

When Seth reached the bank, he put the boy down. Nick was coughing up water, nearly doubled over. Seth turned him over so that the boy lay on his stomach, and he pounded on the boy's back as Kate and Jeremy reached them.

Seth, water dripping down his face and naked chest, looked up. "He'll be fine," he said, with that disarming grin of his. "I'm going to have to teach him to swim, though, particularly if he's dead-set on jumping in first and thinking later."

Nick groaned, coughed again and then tried to sit up. "The dog?"

"Probably a damn sight better than you," Seth said. "Mr. Cochran's got him." His hand moved up to the boy's shoulder and lingered there. "Promise me you won't do something like that again."

Nick looked sheepish—sheepish and pale—but still his eyes lit at Seth's offer. "You'll really teach me how to swim?"

"Promise," Seth said.

"Then you'll stay with us?"

Seth hesitated. "Let's just say I'll make sure you know how to swim."

Nick grinned, and Kate knew it would probably take him a very long time to learn how to swim.

She found herself hoping so. Really hoping so.

Seth stood, pulling Nick up as he did. "I'd better take you across myself. I don't think I want to try that again."

"On your horse?"

"On my horse, Nicholas," he confirmed. "If your sister approves." He looked over at Kate.

"His sister approves," Kate said. "Thank you." She hesitated a moment, and then added, "Seth."

Water was still running down from his hair, over his bare skin, and her gaze was drawn to where golden, curly hair made an arrow pattern down to his waist. Reluctantly her gaze moved upward again, to sea-colored eyes that were suddenly blazing with challenge.

A self-conscious tremor rumbled through her body. So did something else. Waves of desire that went way beyond gratitude. *It's just that he saved Nick,* she argued to herself, and saw him grin, as if he knew exactly what she was thinking and knew she didn't believe it for a second.

"I'll take you, too," he offered quite easily, but there was a teasing note in his drawl, the drawl that no longer offended her.

The thought was terribly tempting. Holding on to him, her arms around that hard body, those cabled muscles. But, as tempting as the image was, it was also unnerving—too unnerving.

She shook her head, unable to utter the refusal. "I'd better stay with the wagon."

Kate saw his eyes cloud, and she knew instantly that he had taken it as another rejection, when it wasn't that at all. She simply no longer trusted herself with him.

But before she could say anything he turned away, and she knew he was going to get his horse, which he had tied on a long rope to graze as they took the wagons over. She saw Nick tag along with him, and she wished with all her heart she could be as easy with him, that the tension wasn't so thick between them. But she had made it that way, and now she didn't know how to change it.

The campfires burned merrily that night. They had made it across with only a few goods lost, and no lives—thanks, they all knew, to the quick action of Seth Hampton.

The family who had lost some of its supplies had them replenished through contributions. The Cochrans, who owned the dog that had fallen from the wagon, brought the animal to see Nick.

"This is Betsy," Edie Cochran said, shyly introducing the dog to Nick. "She's going to have puppies. Would you like one of them?" The young girl looked at Nick as if he were the next thing to God.

Nick swallowed deep. "Would I!"

"You can have your pick," Edie offered graciously. Nick's eleven-year-old face went three shades of red, but his eyes glowed.

Kate wanted to cry. It had been so long since she'd seen real pleasure on her brother's face. And now twice in one day. A miracle. Seth Hampton's miracle.

One of several, she realized. Not only Nick's rescue today and the smile now, but Jeremy, who looked on contentedly and who hadn't coughed the whole day.

And herself. She hadn't realized how much she had locked her heart away, her feelings. When she had watched so many die, she'd had to, or she couldn't have gone on. But then, she realized, it had become a habit. She didn't know now when she had looked at a sunset or a sunrise and seen beauty instead of a long day of work ahead. Even this trip. Years ago, it would have started as a wonderful adventure, but when they had actually left, she had felt almost dead inside, because she was leaving everything she knew and loved behind.

And she hadn't realized how much her own attitude had affected her brothers, how bitterness had replaced the innate sense of joy she'd once had.

But now it was coming back into her, day by day. That sweet appreciation of everyday things. There was a pleasure in living again, in hearing the sad strains of a harmonica, in watching Seth Hampton simply ride a horse, or now, particularly, in seeing a smile transform Nick's face.

She only wished Seth were here to see it. She felt a poignant sadness that he was not. But, as he had done so often recently, he had chosen to eat with Cliff Edwards and his hands. He was quite deliberately and consciously separating himself from the Mac-Allisters, and she was responsible.

Kate had not even thanked him properly for saving Nick or helping Jeremy. She swallowed the thick gob of remorse threatening to block her throat.

She looked at Nick, who was now absorbed with Edie Cochran. Jeremy was talking to Daniel and David Cochran. She realized how isolated they all had been. She had been so concerned with Jeremy or so wrapped up in her own mixed emotions that she had made little effort to make friends, and again it was her brothers who had suffered. Nick had taken on so much responsibility and had become so withdrawn.

She had constructed a shield of grief and loss and bitterness so thick that she hadn't even noticed.

Fighting back tears, Kate slipped off and walked down the wooded bank of Big Sandy Creek. The water was still high, rushing to join some other ribbon of water. Night had fallen, and the earlier threatening clouds had dispersed, leaving the sky cleansed and clear. Stars blinked lazily, and a three-quarter moon sat benevolently overhead, its image reflected in the water, which now appeared equally benign. It was difficult to think she'd almost lost her brother to it hours ago.

If not for Seth Hampton. Seth Hampton. The name was like him. It had a warm sound to it.

"Miss MacAllister?"

Her last name sounded odd now, too formal after so many weeks. When had she started thinking of him as Seth? This afternoon? Weeks ago?

She swung around to look at him. It was almost as if her thoughts had summoned him.

His eyes were quizzical, but his lips smiled, a wonderful sensuous smile that seemed to light the world— at least her world. She shivered under its impact, warning herself.

"I . . . came for a walk," Kate explained sheepishly.

"Nick?" Seth inquired.

She couldn't stop a smile of her own. "He has a disciple now, a nice young lady, and the promise of a puppy. I would say he is very well—thanks to you."

He looked uncomfortable. "There were others who helped."

"But not as quickly as you."

He shrugged off her gratitude. "I'm just glad he's all right."

"I think he'll be much better now."

He raised a questioning eyebrow.

"I'm beginning to realize a few things . . . namely, that I haven't been fair, not to Nick or Jeremy. Or you."

His eyes, which were wary, softened. "You had reasons."

"I thought I did," she said slowly.

He moved closer to her, his hand touching her chin softly. "Don't," he said. "Don't feel guilty."

"It's just—"

"Just what?"

"I don't like myself very much at the moment."

"I do," he said simply, his hand moving to the side of her cheek before dropping and taking hers. "Go for a walk with me, Miss MacAllister."

"Kate," she told him softly, and she matched her steps to his as they walked beyond the campfire and the voices. He found a fallen log and gestured to her to sit down. She nodded, and he helped her down, then gracefully settled next to her.

Kate looked out over the creek, then at the sky overhead. "It seems so peaceful now." She chewed on her lip. "I don't think I could have survived losing someone else."

Seth pulled her against him, holding her lightly, but with a warmth that seeped through to her soul, a soul that was increasingly hungry for that kind of touch.

"Tell me about your home," he said.

Kate didn't know if she could. The silence stretched between them, but, strangely enough, it wasn't an uncomfortable silence.

He prompted her. "Is your name really Kate, or is it Kathryn?"

How had she ever thought his drawl offensive? It lingered in the air now, fine and comforting.

"Kathryn Mary," she said, "after my grandmothers."

"Kathryn Mary," he repeated. "I like that."

She shrugged. "Everyone called me Kate. My brothers started it when I was small."

"How many were there?"

"Four. The two oldest were twins. John and Jacob. They were four years older than I, and they always looked after me. Jeremy came four years after me, and then, of course, Nick. There was one other girl, born two years before me, but she died of a fever when she was only one. So John and Jacob always felt . . ." Her voice died away.

"Protective?"

She nodded, then added painfully, "They both died at Gettysburg."

"I'm sorry, Kate," he said.

"It nearly killed my mother, and then Jeremy ran off at sixteen to avenge them, and that *did* kill her. She lost her will to live. My father, he just didn't seem to care about the farm anymore. The twins and Jeremy had loved it and had always worked with him. When they were gone, he lost heart. Nick found him dead in the barn one morning."

Pain washed through Seth, pain for her and for young Nick. But there was more. He remembered her mentioning a fiancé. He wanted to know. He had to know.

"You said you were betrothed?"

"He died at Gettysburg, too," she said. "Practically the whole unit from our county died that day. I grew up with Thomas Beck. It was always expected that we would marry. Have children." She hesitated. "But I think a part of me always ached for something else. There seemed so much more to the world than a farm in Illinois. But everyone expected . . ."

She turned and looked up at him. "And then they were all gone, and no one expected anything, and all I felt was loss. I could finally see the world, but all I wanted was my family back, and everything the way it used to be."

The tears she hadn't shed before started coming, and she felt him put his arms around her, pulling her close to him, allowing her to soak his shirt with long, heaving sobs. He didn't try to stop her, or even comfort her with words, but merely let her release all the anguish inside.

She didn't know how long she cried, but she felt his lips against her hair, his hands soothing her in that sure, compassionate way of his. There were no questions, no demands. There was only a haven of acceptance. Somewhere deep inside, she realized for the first time that she had blamed herself in some way for what had happened, feeling that her dream of seeing the world had somehow caused the demise of her family.

She wondered now whether her anger against Seth was really anger against herself.

The tears were finally spent, and for the first time in a very long while she felt a wonderful relief. But she also felt exposed in a way she'd never been before.

She straightened. "I'm sorry," she said, and then gave him a weak smile. "I've said that several times now, haven't I?"

"There's nothing to feel sorry for. I suspect you've needed to do that for a very long time."

"Still—"

His hands played with a tendril of hair that had escaped from her braid. "Still nothing," he said. "You don't know how many times I've wanted to do the same thing."

"You?"

"There's a certain advantage in being a woman, you know."

No matter how hard she tried, she couldn't imagine Seth Hampton breaking down, or even showing the slightest weakness. Her face showed her doubt, and he gave her that easy smile of his, the one that always wriggled its way into places it shouldn't.

"I think I'd better get you back to the camp, or I might do something I shouldn't."

She wanted him to. How much she wanted him to, but despite these moments of tenderness, there was an uneasiness about him now, a quiet reserve that had been there since she'd broken away from him the other night.

She could still feel, however, that compelling, magnetic attraction between them. She knew he wanted to kiss her. She also knew he wasn't going to. The strength of will that was so evident within him wasn't going to allow it. With a desolation that crept through every crevice of her heart, she knew that nothing had changed, that he still planned to leave, that he had offered something before and wasn't going to risk its being refused again.

Kate also knew she couldn't offer anything herself. She wasn't sure yet whether she wouldn't run away from him again—for whatever reasons. Perhaps she was afraid of her own vulnerable emotions, or of losing him as she had lost so many others. She felt racked by so many conflicting feelings.

It was as if he read her mind. He rose with that grace that was always so sensual, pulling her up easily. She wanted him to pull her into his arms, but he didn't.

He did, however, catch her face in his hands and lean down to kiss her lightly. "Don't ever doubt yourself, Miss Kate. You're a very strong lady. And you have a lot to give. Don't run from it. Don't ever be afraid. And don't ever, ever feel guilt for something you can't help."

He walked her back to the wagons and gave her that wry smile of his, the one that always went straight to the core of her being. Then he turned, striding off again. Alone. Always alone. Just like her.

Chapter Five

Seth stayed as far away as he could for the next week and a half, mostly scouting with Dallas Terry, learning as much as he could since he'd soon be on his own.

He had to start weaning himself away from the MacAllisters and the growing feelings he had for all of them. It would be damned difficult to leave them, but he envisioned only pain for himself, and for Kate, if he remained with them. Her beliefs were simply too ingrained, her feelings too deep and her loyalties too strong, for her to ever to give herself freely to him. And that was the only way he would have her.

He'd known since that evening they had walked after Nick's mishap that he could probably bed her. But then she would probably hate him for a lapse she would consider traitorous, and he couldn't stand that. So he found himself wandering out more and more.

Since Jeremy had been feeling so much better and had eagerly assumed most of the duties Seth had once performed, Seth mostly limited his contact with the MacAllisters to teaching Nick to swim when they camped alongside a stream or river. Nick was a quick learner, despite his attempts to pretend otherwise, and

Seth felt confident that he now knew enough basics to never again repeat the mishap at Big Sandy Creek.

After one such lesson, Nick, feeling extremely proud of his growing competence, begged him to stay and take supper with them. Kate, he said, had cooked a particularly tasty stew.

Seth was about to decline when he caught sight of Kate. She was stepping out of the wagon, a shapely ankle revealed as she stepped down and a pretty green dress gracefully swishing around her slender form. Her hair was tied back with a matching green ribbon, and the green in her hazel eyes warmed when she saw him. He felt his intended refusal die on his lips, to be replaced by a certain immediate arousal throughout his body.

But, although she smiled warmly, she seemed flustered, saying little as she dished out a stew that was a great deal tastier than that prepared by Cliff Edwards's cook. Jeremy, too, was quiet, although he was obviously feeling much better, his face now a healthy tanned color.

Seth tried to keep his eyes on the food, but it was more than a little difficult. Whenever he glanced up, his gaze met Kate's, and he had a damnable time moving it. Her face, like Jeremy's, was slightly tanned from the sun and now flushed from the fire. Her eyes were lovely, filled with an uncertainty and vulnerability that moved him immensely. But then, everything about her seemed to affect him in some lunatic way. He wasn't usually speechless, but there was so little to say now.

Now that he planned to leave. He knew how damned difficult it would be. To leave not only her, but also Nick, who had wormed his way into his heart, and even the reticent Jeremy, who watched him with such cautious eyes.

Seth carefully avoided conversation on Fort Walker, or the future, or his planned departure. He also avoided mentioning the recent war. And Kate's family.

But Nick chattered on about the puppy he was to have, and even Seth was caught up in his eagerness and enthusiasm.

"Did you ever have a dog, Seth?"

Seth looked into Nick's eager eyes. "Many of them. Even had a baby fox a friend of mine rescued from a trap."

"What happened to it?"

"Well, I—we doctored it, and I kept it until it was well enough and old enough to be on its own, and then my brother took it deep into the woods and released it. It's probably a pretty old fellow now."

"Your brother?" Kate asked.

Seth looked embarrassed. "I'd gotten attached to it," he said simply and was startled—even a bit stunned—when Kate's lips broke out into the most spontaneous, open smile she had ever given him. It was so incredibly lovely, like a sunrise, full of light and quiet, glowing beauty.

"You doctored a baby fox?" Kate's question was spoken softly, almost wistfully. "And wanted to keep it?"

He winced at the sentimentality of the image. "I was a boy."

Kate smiled. "I think you would probably do the same thing today."

"At least I've progressed enough to turn it loose myself," Seth said with a chagrined smile.

"Have you?" The question came from Jeremy, and his question went far beyond the obvious. Jeremy had the smallest grin on his lips and a kind of searching look in his eyes.

Seth nodded slowly, trying to tear his eyes away from the tender look in Kate's eyes. He liked it...very much. And he wasn't sure how long it would remain there.

"And your brother?" Kate asked, interest shining in her eyes and making them lovelier then ever.

"I had four of them. Rafe and I were the closest, since we were only a year apart. The others were considerably older. I think he was destined to be a lawyer, as I was a doctor. He could argue any point of view."

"And you?"

He found himself trapped by the bright interest in her eyes. He shrugged. "Rafe always said I was single-minded, that once I decided on something, nothing would change it."

"Is that true?" Her eyes had changed. They were no longer tender but intense. And he knew she was asking another question altogether. He knew all the MacAllisters were waiting for an answer. Was he really going to leave them at Fort Walker?

"Yes," he said simply. "Rafe found that out." Seth didn't know why he added that last statement. He knew it invited another question, and perhaps it was time to answer it. Time they knew more about him. About exactly how doggedly stubborn he could be.

There was a silence, a kind of pall that fell over each one of them before Nick broke it. They all sensed there was a Pandora's box here.

"How?" Nick asked.

Seth looked directly at Kate as he answered. He wasn't going to apologize for anything, not for his role in the war, not for his loyalties, not for doing what he'd thought he had to do. "My brother joined the Union army—in the West, so he wouldn't have to fight his friends. But toward the end he was moved back into the Shenandoah Valley, where I was posted. I didn't know it, not then, nor on Christmas Eve, when I and a wounded Confederate general escaped a Union ambush and took refuge on the farm of a friend of mine."

Seth was watching Kate's eyes, saw them widen a little at his choice of words, but he didn't give her time to wonder long.

"Rafe knew the area, and he was ordered to track us down. He didn't know his quarry was me, of course, any more than I knew he was in Virginia."

Seth paused, and the three listeners seemed to move closer, their faces obviously fascinated at the drama of the story. "He found us. I would have shot him before I let him take my patient."

It was Jeremy who fastened on the words *would have* and urged him to continue. "But you didn't—?"

A muscle twitched in Seth's throat and his lips firmed in a tight, narrow line before speaking again. "That's not the point. I would have, and he knew it."

"What happened?" Nick prodded.

"Interference—from two armies. A standoff. I was able to take my patient away." He knew his voice softened as he remembered that remarkable Christmas, when two armies had confronted each other and a ragtag bunch of orphans Blythe had gathered had made both sides remember their humanity. For a few hours, anyway. And then the wedding. The wedding of Rafe and Blythe, his own love, that same day.

"And now?" Kate's soft voice interrupted the bittersweet memory.

"We're friends again. We both did what we had to do, and we knew the other had no choice."

"Would he have shot you?"

Seth shrugged. "He would have taken me prisoner."

"Why didn't you fight for the North, too?" Kate asked, and Seth grimaced as he realized again that his decision five years ago was always going to stand between them.

"It didn't seem to matter much to me what side I chose," he explained once more. "I was a doctor. There's no right or wrong about wounded. I thought the Confederacy needed me more."

He stood. "Thank you for dinner," he said abruptly, and he left before he saw the familiar condemnation in her eyes....

* * *

He left the next morning with Dallas again. Before sunrise. Before he saw her. Before a brief glimpse of hope surfaced again. Before his body started reacting in wanting ways again.

Damn. Loneliness was now a constant ache within him. Less than a week and he would be on his own again. The thought was agonizing. They rode together most of the morning, both in silence. Seth was preoccupied, and Dallas's attention was completely on the trail ahead.

Unfortunately, Dallas's concentration left Seth too much time to think. It was becoming more and more difficult to stay away from Kate MacAllister, especially after that evening when he'd tasted her tears and glimpsed her wistful vulnerability. He had realized then that he loved her, but he also knew he couldn't live with that anger against the South, and Southerners, he sensed was still simmering within her.

It was late afternoon when a squad of blue-coated soldiers approached. A lieutenant introduced himself as Roswell Campbell and reported they were on a mission to alert travelers about a band of Cheyenne that had been attacking army supply wagons and civilian wagon trains. The fort was still eighty miles away, five or six days by wagon train.

"Can you accompany us to Fort Walker?" Dallas asked.

"How large is your party?"

"Fifty wagons—about a hundred and fifty people."

Lieutenant Campbell shook his head. "You should be safe enough if you keep your people together.

They're selecting easy pickings—a lone wagon, perhaps two or three. There's a damned lot of movement, and gold fever has made folks careless. We're urging the smaller parties to join up with outfits your size—at least to the fort. Do you think your wagon master will agree?''

"I can't speak for him," Dallas said. "Why don't you ride on back—they're only about ten miles east—and talk with Cliff Edwards? Take a bit of supper with 'em. We still have to scout out another campsite."

The lieutenant's face brightened. "It will be damned good to have something besides hardtack and beans." He started to turn his horse away, but then he glanced back. "Be careful."

Dallas nodded. "Always am."

Once the soldiers were gone, Seth turned to Dallas and asked about the Cheyenne. He soon wished he hadn't.

"There's been trouble for years," Dallas said, "and it came to a head two years ago. The Cheyenne believed too many whites were coming through their territory, and some young hotheads started raiding. Stage lines, stations, wagon trains. The Colorado militia, under the command of a man named Chivington, went after them. Instead of finding those who were guilty, he attacked a peaceful camp, slaughtering men, women and children. Even mutilatin' them. Some Cheyenne ain't forgotten that. I don't blame them none," he added. "Despite a treaty last year, some ain't ever forgiven the white man for that day. Don't suppose they ever will. So keep your eyes open, Doc."

With that, he spurred his horse ahead, and Seth followed, wondering whether there was peace any place in this country.

Kate helped prepare the meal for the soldiers who arrived just as the train stopped for the evening. She was grateful for the distraction, for a few new faces, for something to do. She'd missed Seth terribly since he'd left so abruptly last night.

Her body had felt tense all night, hungry in a way it had never been before. Her mind was muddled and bemused by the man, who was both so stubbornly gentle and so maddeningly resolute. She had so wanted to touch him last night, especially when he had talked about his brother with such sad affection.

She had wanted to comfort him as he had comforted her, to feel his arms around her as they had been the other night. But she didn't know how to tell him. He had made it clear that he didn't want to stay with them, that he preferred to strike out on his own.

She felt an emptiness that grew in intensity each day they came closer to Fort Walker.

She wished she had the right to ask him to stay. But he had made it clear that he wouldn't, and she couldn't find it in herself to beg. Not to a Southerner. She still couldn't quite get over that obstacle. No matter how much she tried, it kept returning to haunt her. It seemed such an utter betrayal to those she had loved.

Kate used some of the dried apples she'd been hoarding and made two pies, one for the soldiers and one for her family. They all needed a lift—including

Seth, whom she hoped would join them again to-night.

But he didn't appear, not for supper, or even later, when an impromptu dance was held. Members of the train brought out their instruments: harmonicas, fiddles, even a flute. The soldiers were very gallant, paying attention to all the single women in the party, and particularly to Kate. She had brushed her hair and tied it back with a ribbon and put on her one good dress—the green dress that had so obviously met Seth Hampton's approval the night before. She tried to enjoy herself as she danced with the young lieutenant and then a sergeant, but she found herself looking for the gracefully tall man with the golden hair and the sea-green eyes.

Others were, too. All the young women of marriageable age, and even some who weren't, were asking where "the doc" was? For the first time in her life, she knew the terribly bitter taste of jealousy, though she realized she had no right to do so.

When a large number of the men also asked, Kate realized how many friends Seth had made on this trip, despite the hostility he'd braved during the first few days and weeks. He was no longer seen as "the Reb," but simply as "the doc."

"Miss MacAllister, will you honor me with another dance?" The lieutenant had an eager look on his face, one difficult to refuse. She nodded her head, took his proffered hand and found herself twirling around to the music.

When they slowed just a bit, the lieutenant gave her a disarming grin. "There will be another dance at Fort

Walker. There always is when a wagon train comes in. I hope you will save me several dances then."

Kate hesitated. She could not even think of Fort Walker now. They would lose Seth there. "I'm not sure, Lieutenant...." She went red as she realized she'd completely forgotten the man's name. She'd never done that before, and especially not when someone had been kind enough to ask for a dance. But all her thoughts had been of Seth, for Seth. *Where was he?*

But the lieutenant didn't seem to mind. "Campbell, Roswell Campbell. My friends call me Ross."

"Lieutenant Campbell," she acknowledged.

"Ross, please."

She smiled at his eagerness, wondering whether she could have appreciated it more weeks ago. Before Seth. Now, everyone paled beside him.

"It'll depend on my brothers, whether Jeremy's well," she said, "but thank you for asking."

"That was wonderful pie tonight."

Kate wished someone else thought so, and then she scolded herself for thinking so. Why? Why, for dear Heaven, could she not erase the Southern doctor from her mind?

She looked up at the young officer and saw admiration reflected in his eyes. He was a handsome man, handsomer than Dr. Hampton, but he didn't have the charisma that Seth Hampton had, nor the lines of character carved into a face molded by adversity.

"Thank you," she said. She thought again of Seth Hampton out riding alone, or with only one or two scouts. "Are there really hostile Indians out there?"

The laughter left his face. "I'm afraid so. But you don't have anything to worry about here, not on a train this size."

"Have—have you seen any?"

His expression sobered. "Aye," he said, with a trace of a Scottish accent. "There's been a few skirmishes. We were sent out to escort a supply train and came upon some Cheyenne attacking it. But when they saw us, they galloped off."

"Is there danger . . . for the scouts?"

"I wouldn't worry if I were you, miss. I heard that Cliff Edwards hires only the best. They know what they're doing."

But Seth Hampton wasn't the best, not as a scout. He wasn't a scout at all. He was a doctor. She swallowed hard, and tried to lose herself in the dance steps.

The soldiers were gone in the morning. Despite the revelry of last night, Cliff Edwards had everyone up before dawn. He wanted to make at least sixteen miles today, he said. Because of the roving Indian raids, he felt it more important than ever to get under the protection of Fort Walker as quickly as possible.

Everyone was now ordered to stay with their wagons, and Cliff Edwards kept the wagons as close to each other as possible. Nick sat up on the wagon seat along with Jeremy, and was told to watch for any cloud of dust, for any large group of horsemen.

Kate walked alongside the wagon for a while. She was terribly restless and apprehensive, although she didn't really understand why. She only knew she'd felt like this before—once about the time she'd learned that her brothers had been killed, another time just before her father's death.

She felt that same sick dread now, and found she couldn't sit inside the wagon. Nor could she sit patiently beside Jeremy and Nick. Particularly Nick, who had grown quiet again. He, like her, kept looking for a horseman on a bay horse.

Keep him safe, she found herself praying. Please keep him safe.

Dallas Terry slowed his horse, and Seth followed suit. After a day and night on the trail, there were almost back to the train, according to Dallas. No more than a couple of miles at the most, especially if Cliff Edwards had made the time he'd intended.

In the past thirty hours, they had traveled probably a total of forty-five, fifty miles, looking first for a good campsite for the next two nights and second for any sign of the Indians the army had told them about. So far, there had been none.

They were riding back to the wagon train from the north, making a sweeping movement. It was something with which Seth, after years in the army, was familiar.

But now it seemed that Dallas sensed something odd. He had been unusually tense during the past few minutes, almost as if he sensed danger. He was leaning over the side of the saddle, scrutinizing marks in the ground. Suddenly he dismounted and dropped to the ground, looking more closely at a scattering of tracks. "Unshod ponies," he said. "Not long passed."

"Cheyenne?"

Dallas shrugged. "I don't know. Could be Arapaho. Even Sioux, though they don't usually come this far south."

"How many?"

"'Bout ten ponies here, but that don't mean anything. Could be more around. Goddamned Chivington. Doc, you go back and warn Cliff. I'll scout on ahead, see if I can find any more tracks."

Seth hesitated, not liking the idea of Dallas going on alone. "I know how to use a rifle, if you're worried about that."

Dallas looked at him with amusement. "Doc, I didn't doubt that for a moment, or you wouldn't be with me. Cliff sizes up a man real well. I just think he should be warned. May be nothing at all. But then again..."

Still Seth hesitated, and then his attention turned to the left, to low hills dotted by grass. A flock of birds was rising, almost as one, up into the air.

"Christ," Dallas said, and swung back up on his horse just as a group of horsemen suddenly appeared on the hill. No more words were necessary as they spurred their horses into a gallop and rode for their lives.

Seth soon realized they would not outrun their pursuers. They both had been riding most of the day, and their horses were tired. Sundance no longer had the speed and endurance he'd had before the war. He glanced around, and the riders behind were closing. His glance went to Dallas, just as his companion's horse stumbled and went down.

He whirled his own horse around and saw that Dallas had managed to jump free as the horse fell, an arrow in its side. Seth raced back and leaned down, offering a hand to Dallas, who swung up behind him. Seth made for a small hill to the right. He had his rifle out now, and as they reached the hill, both he and Dallas jumped down. Seth regretfully slapped the haunch of his horse, sending it racing away as he and Dallas fell down lengthwise on the ground.

Dallas had lost his rifle, but he had his pistol, and ammunition in his gun belt. Seth had a repeating rifle, his prize possession from the war, but the additional shells were in his saddlebags. Confederate General John Mosby himself had given him the rifle after Seth had rescued a wounded general. He hadn't used it in war, but he had hunted with it, and, like most Southerners, he was an excellent shot.

The Indians were almost on them when Seth and Dallas started firing. There were eleven of them, and Seth took aim at the leader. "I'll take the one in front," he said to Dallas. "He looks like the leader."

The scout nodded. "I'll try for him, too."

"Thought you trusted me," Seth said wryly.

Dallas grinned. "I do, but sometimes *I* miss. One of us might take him. Then you fire to the left, and I'll fire right."

Their guns exploded almost simultaneously, and the Indian fell as Seth found another target to the left and squeezed the trigger. The Indians were still coming—just a few feet away now—and both Seth and Dallas brought down the two riders directly in front of them. They hugged the side of the hill as the hoofs went around them, and then they turned, each taking aim at the back of one of the attackers.

The riders also turned, and a hail of arrows fell around them, along with a lance. Seth felt a burning sensation in his shoulder, and another in his side. He knew the gun was slipping from now-numb hands, and he felt a terrible sense of sad irony. Four years of war, and then, when he thought he was fleeing it at last....

"I'm sorry," he heard himself whisper to Dallas. I— Tell Kate..." But then waves of pain wiped away every conscious thought, and the earth went spinning around. He tried to keep his eyes open, but the sun was disappearing, and the light. And then the blackness was total, and he sank into oblivion.

Chapter Six

The sound of gunfire reached the wagon train, and Cliff immediately stopped the long line of wagons and told the men to prepare to circle the wagons.

There were too many shots, too close together, for anything but trouble. And Dallas and the doc were late. Edwards's instincts were all tingling.

He went from wagon to wagon, asking for a few volunteers and emphasizing that they were to be under his scout's command. They were not, under any circumstances, to instigate an attack unless it was necessary to save themselves or someone else.

Kate listened silently, her heart freezing with fear. She knew. She knew to the depth of her soul that something had happened to Seth Hampton. Dr. Hampton. The Rebel. She knew, and she was sick with the knowledge. She felt everything inside her clench into a hard knot.

"Sis?" Nick had moved next to her and was looking up anxiously at her. Kate couldn't answer; the words were locked in her throat.

Jeremy, who had been driving the wagon, looked toward her. "Can you handle things here? I want to go with the volunteers."

The Kate of several weeks ago would have objected. Not Jeremy. Not Jeremy, who had struggled so desperately to get well, who had already seen too much war.

But this Kate couldn't. Let them live their own lives, Seth had said. *You have to let go.*

And she knew that she herself would volunteer if she thought she could be of any help. But she couldn't. She was a terrible rider and a worse shot, although she had tried to learn before they left Illinois. She would have to wait, and she knew it would be as hard as anything she had done in her life, as hard as the times when she had waited for others to return. She didn't know whether she could survive another loss.

So, her heart in her throat, she merely nodded at Jeremy, refraining even from saying "Be careful." He was a man who had fought a man's war.

"Do you suppose it's Seth?" Nick asked tensely.

"I don't know," she finally managed to say. For Nick. Only for Nick could she present a brave front, when inside she was trembling. "I hope not."

"But you don't even like him," Nick said, looking defiant and angry, his eyes tragically large and lost-looking.

"Yes, I do," she said, putting her hand on his shoulder. "In the beginning, perhaps I didn't. I didn't really know him then."

"I liked him even then," Nick said. "Even if he was a Rebel."

"I know," Kate said. "Sometimes you're very wise, you know?"

"I want to go with them."

"I do, too, Nick, but we would just slow them up."

"I want to do something."

"Why don't you carve him something?" she suggested. "He thinks you're very good, you know. He told me so. I think he would like to have something of yours."

If he comes back, and if he does, for when he leaves. A remembrance when he leaves. The trembling inside turned to sickness, a sickness that churned in an expanding pit of loss, of emptiness, of fear. *Oh, Seth. Stay alive. Go if you must, but please stay alive.*

Nick's face brightened slightly, and he disappeared inside the wagon to find a proper piece of wood.

As she started to guide the team of oxen into a circle, she watched as the volunteers rode off on horses provided by Cliff Edwards's remuda, the extra mounts brought along for the scouts and for hunting parties. Jeremy looked good in the saddle. Sure and strong and healthy. So different from when they had started this journey. Was it the trip? The dry weather? Or Dr. Seth Hampton, who had provided not only medicine, but hope, as well? She whispered a quiet prayer as they rode off.

Kate finished guiding the oxen into the circle, as they had already practiced doing several times. When she braked the wagon, she scrambled down from the seat and walked over to where Cliff Edwards stood, a growing group of travelers around him. Every man had a weapon at his side. So did some of the women.

Edwards was giving instructions to those who held guns. To the others, to the children and the other women, he gave alternate directions. His practical, unemotional voice was soothing.

"You, Miss MacAllister, can you take some of the children?"

Kate nodded.

"Play a game with them—keep them busy?"

Kate wondered whether he was also trying to keep her busy, to keep her from screaming, from running after Jeremy and Seth. She wondered whether her face showed all those things. But she only nodded and took six children whose parents held guns.

A story. That's what they need, she thought. She tried to remember back to her own childhood, to the cozy nights in the farmhouse when the family had gathered together, when her brothers had teased and played. As the only girl—the only sister—she had been spoiled shamefully by them, and by her mother and father, too. She had been wrapped in a cocoon of safety. When it was torn away, she had been so utterly naked and exposed.

So she had constructed a new barrier, so that the hurt wouldn't be so vulnerable to new wounds, one of resentment and anger. *Please come back, Seth. Please come back.*

A story! Think of a story. Don't think of Seth. You can't bear that now. She blinked back tears. Fairy tales. Fantasy. Happy endings. She needed all three now. She needed to believe in them. She had believed in so little for so long now.

She settled the children around her. "Once upon a time," she began, "there was a girl named Snow White...."

There was the sound of gunfire again in the distance. Kate's hand tightened around that of a small girl next to her as she continued the tale of the seven dwarfs.

She tried to keep her eyes from the plains, from the direction of the gunfire. She tried to keep them on the fidgeting children, who, despite the story, wore fear on their faces.

"And the prince leaned down and kissed Snow White, and slowly, so slowly, she opened her eyes...."

As she had. Seth had slowly brought her back to life again. Don't destroy it now, she prayed silently to God as her voice droned on with the remembered words of the fairy tale while her mind was someplace else. *Please keep him safe.*

Her head snapped up as she heard some shouts and looked out again. Horsemen were coming in, moving rapidly toward them. She tried to pick out a bay stallion, a golden head, among them, but she couldn't. And then she saw Seth's horse. It was running alongside the others, its saddle empty.

"No!" she found herself screaming, and she was up, ignoring the children for the moment as she ran toward the opening between the wagons.

And then she saw him. He was being held by Dallas Terry in front of the scout's saddle. He was slumped over, his head bent, and she knew he was unconscious. Or dead.

The horsemen came straight to Cliff. Dallas helped lift Seth down to a group of standing men. Kate saw the broken ends of two arrows sticking from Seth's body.

Terry's jaw was tight. "Saved my life. He could have gotten away, but he came back for me when my horse went down. Damn fool."

Cliff looked over him. "He's still alive."

"Bleeding like a stuck pig, though," Dallas said.

"Indians?"

"A small band. What was left of them went ske-daddling when they saw reinforcements. The doc here did pretty good with his gun."

As they were speaking, Cliff was checking the wounds. "Got to get those damned arrows out. Wish to God we had another doctor. I'll have to do it. Dallas, you heat a knife, make it two knives. We'll have to cauterize it. I can't sew like the doc here."

Kate stood frozen, looking at Seth's white face, then at the blood thickening and drying on his shirt and pants. She'd never noticed what long lashes he had, or how much he looked like a boy with his hair tousled and his eyes closed. But then, how would she have? She had banished him, over and over again. Her heart swelled with an anguish she thought she would drown in.

She knelt and took his motionless hand, the one that had such gentleness in it, and she tried to give to him some of her own strength. Live, she demanded silently. *Live!*

She sensed, rather than felt, Jeremy hovering next to her. And Nick. But then some men moved in and picked Seth up, carrying him over to the cook wagon, where a fire had already been started.

She wanted to do something. She had to do something.

"Mr. Edwards, please, is there anything I can do?"

"Get his medical bag. We'll need chloroform. Thank God we have that."

Kate hurried off to do his bidding. She knew exactly where he kept it, along with the larger bag with additional medicines. She found it quickly and returned at a run.

His shirt was gone now, cut off, apparently so as not to disturb the arrow. His pants had also been lowered to show the second arrow. Blood seeped from both wounds.

She looked at Cliff. "Should I wash it?"

He nodded. "Pour whiskey around it, too. Dallas will get you some."

Someone handed her a bucket of water, someone else a cloth. Everyone was gathered around, concern written on their faces. Everyone was praying for him. She knew that as she looked from face to face. He had made himself a member of her family, but he had also apparently made himself a member of everyone's family.

Dallas, grief written all over his hard face, was also kneeling now as he handed Kate a bottle of whiskey. "Come on, Doc," Kate heard him saying. "Ain't no one died for me yet. Don't want that on my ledger, you hear me?"

But Seth didn't seem to be hearing anyone. Wake up, she wanted to scream at him. Don't do this to me.

And then she realized what she had silently said. To me? Everything had been to her. Everyone had taken from him, herself most of all. No one, she thought, had reached out to him. Her hand took a cloth and gently, so very gently, cleaned the blood from around the two arrows. They were so ugly, those protruding pieces of wood that were draining the life away from Seth Hampton.

When the old blood was cleaned away, fresh blood continued to leak from the wounds. She took the bottle of whiskey and looked at Cliff Edwards. He nodded, encouraging her.

She hoped Seth would remain unconscious. She had seen alcohol poured on wounds before, knew the extreme pain involved, but she did it anyway, reluctantly. He didn't move, and she'd wished he had. He was so unfamiliarly still, all that restless energy quieted.

"Miss Kate?"

She looked up at Edwards in question. His expression was compassionate.

"You better move now."

"I want to stay."

"It won't be pleasant. I don't want a fainting woman on my hands."

"I won't faint," she said firmly, "and I've helped with calving."

"This ain't nothing like calving, Miss Kate," he warned.

"I'll stay," she insisted.

"Okay. I guess you're as much family as anyone. You think you can handle the chloroform?"

Kate nodded.

Cliff found the small bottle in the bag and handed it to her. "Do you have a handkerchief?"

Kate looked up, and Nick nodded, starting at a run for the wagon and returning in minutes with a white, lacy piece of cloth.

Cliff Edwards looked at her. "I don't know how much we'll need. But if he starts moving at all, pour a little more on the cloth. We can't afford him moving when I'm taking out the arrows."

"I understand," Kate said.

"You sure you want to do this? Dallas could do it."

"I'm sure," she said softly, her hand resting gently on Seth's shoulder. She owed him this, at least.

At Edwards's nod, she placed the handkerchief over Seth's nose and slowly poured chloroform on it. Cliff waited several moments, and then put his hands on the remaining shaft of the arrow, tugging it as gently as possible from Seth's shoulder. His face tightened with the effort as he tried to maneuver the arrow and the wound widened, pouring more blood across Seth's skin. If only the damned thing had gone through, then he could cut off the shaft and pull it out the back, but it hadn't, and he was afraid to push it through. God help him, he just didn't know enough to risk it.

Kate felt herself tense all over, and she struggled to keep her hand steady on his face, to keep from trembling and being banished from his side. For some reason, she thought Seth might want her there. She hoped so.

The arrow finally came out, along with a new rush of blood, and Cliff called for the knife. Clutching the hot handle in a piece of cloth, Dallas handed it to him.

Cliff looked at Kate. "Don't go soft on me now."

"I won't," she said. She steeled herself as Cliff touched the white-hot blade to the wound and she heard the sizzle of skin and smelled the sickening odor of burning flesh. The patient flinched without opening his eyes, and moaned.

"More chloroform."

Kate obeyed, pouring more of the precious liquid onto the cloth, hoping it wasn't too much. Her other hand was balled in a fist so tight she felt her short nails drawing blood as they dug into skin. She welcomed it. She wanted to hurt.

Cliff's hands were now moving to the arrow embedded in Seth's side. The wagon master's fingers were again carefully trying to withdraw the arrow head. Kate saw the worry on his face, and the care.

"Damn," Cliff muttered. "It doesn't want to come." He handed the knife he'd used to cauterize the wound to Dallas. "Try to hold the wound open," he ordered as he continued to twist and pull the shaft from Seth's body.

Kate was not even breathing now, as if by holding her breath she could pass on life to the man lying beneath her hands.

Cliff pulled again, the time roughly, and the arrow finally came out, accompanied by a river of blood.

Another knife was ready now, and Kate stiffened against the repeat of such an ugly sound and such a devastating smell. She poured another drop of chloroform on the cloth and found herself holding her breath again, her heart caught in her throat. "Please, please, please," she heard herself saying in a soft, crooning voice. She didn't know who she was saying it to.

The blood finally slowed. Her hands dropped from the chloroform and grabbed the towel, soaking it in the bucket still beside her and washing the blood away again. The skin around both wounds was black and raw and blistered, but the bleeding had stopped.

She looked at Cliff. His hands were trembling slightly now as he dropped the knife. He looked up, directly at her. "That, Miss Kate, is why I wanted a doctor along. Christ, I hate this. The doc could have done this so much better."

He stood. "We'll have to wait here a couple of days, anyway. We can't move him on one of those wagons, and I'm not going to leave him, not with those Indians around."

Everyone standing around knew what that meant. Cliff Edwards had said repeatedly they couldn't stop for any one person, yet that was exactly what he was saying now. And there was not a word of disagreement.

"I'll take care of him," Kate said. "Put him in our wagon."

"You'll need respite, Miss Kate. I'll help." Kate looked up at a woman she'd spoken to only briefly. "He helped my man when he broke his arm. Anything you need, you call, hear?"

"You send your brothers over to our tent to eat. We'll take good care of them," another woman said.

"You don't worry none 'bout fixing meals, Miss Kate. We'll bring them over," a third chimed in.

The offers kept coming, even as Dallas and several other men picked Seth up and carried him to the wagon, laying him down on the bed that Jeremy had occupied. She suddenly thought of Jeremy and looked up. He was standing there, nodding his approval.

"I'll sleep under the wagon."

"Me too," Nick said.

If Kate wasn't so preoccupied with Seth, she knew, she would question Nick's sudden generosity. He had been wanting to sleep under the wagon with Seth almost from the first day the Reb had joined them. But now she just nodded. "Get me some water, Nick," she said.

Kate spent the remainder of the day next to Seth, washing away the sweat that beaded on his forehead, her hands calming him when he started thrashing against what must be excruciating pain. Cliff had said to leave the wounds exposed, but every time she looked at the raw, ugly wounds she wanted to cry. It was evening before he really woke. She had been watching for any movement, and there was the slightest flutter of eyelashes, and then his eyes, his beautiful green-blue eyes, opened slowly, their depths fogged with pain.

She leaned down. "Seth," she whispered. "Can you hear me?"

His eyes opened slowly, fixing on her. "Kate?"

"Yes."

"Pretty Kate," he whispered, and closed his eyes again. A muscle throbbed in his cheek, and Kate saw his fists clench against the side of the bed.

She wanted to do something for him, something more than she had, but all she could think of was taking his hand and holding it, letting his fingers press against hers until she thought the bones would break. Just when she thought she could no longer bear it, his fingers relaxed and his breathing softened.

As it grew dark, she lit a lantern. Cliff came by occasionally and spoke softly, taking a brief look at the patient. So did Dallas, his hat in hand. "Damned good man," he muttered as he stared at the patient, who was now turning restlessly in his sleep. "But a damn fool," he said, echoing his earlier words.

Kate felt something poignant surge through her. "He'll always be a damned fool," she said, cussing for the second time in her life, but in a voice that was almost a caress.

Jeremy brought her a plate of food and asked if she needed to leave for a few moments to stretch her legs or something, but she couldn't even bear to do that. Not now. Not when he might wake again.

She leaned back against the barrels, as she had seen Seth do when he looked after Jeremy, and she thought of the hours he had spent with her brother, asking for nothing in return. How patiently he had borne her hostility.

She replenished her cloth with water and brushed it along his face, tracing the fine crinkles along his eyes, and laugh lines around his face, the tiniest suggestion of a dimple in one cheek. Now that she thought about it, she knew she hadn't seen him laugh, not really, in all the weeks she had known him. Yet she instinctively knew that that mouth had once laughed often and richly. She wanted to hear it now. She wanted it more than she'd ever wanted anything in her life.

She brushed the blond hair back, remembering how rich it looked in the sun. Now it was damp and darkened by dirt and sweat. The usual sheen, the usual life, was gone from it.

Kate suddenly realized she didn't even know how to reach his family if anything happened. Someplace in Virginia. A brother. No one else. She remembered the terrible sense of aloneness she'd felt in him.

If anything happened? It couldn't happen. She wouldn't let it. She entwined her fingers with his, entwining her life with his. He might not want that. He probably wouldn't. Not now. But she would give him what she could. She didn't realize she was crying until she felt the wetness on her arm.

"Live, Rebel mine. Live." She heard her own harsh, insistent whisper. She heard it, and she felt the painful tightness behind her eyes, that denseness of immense grief as tears welled at a greater speed than could be released.

She heard herself whisper the same litany again, and the tears fell unrelieved. She had cried for her family and for herself the other night; he had helped her wash away so much of the loss and guilt. But now she was crying for him, for his losses, for everything he had borne so steadfastly, for the loneliness she had seen in him and ignored. She cried for all of it. But now there was no comfort. None at all.

Chapter Seven

The night passed agonizingly slowly. Kate left Seth's side for only a few minutes to relieve herself. By dawn, he was alternately clammy and burning up with fever. She frantically searched his two bags for books on what to do. She finally found one that suggested, in the event of inflammation, the use of warm water or wet dressings "to encourage suppuration."

But she didn't know whether those treatments were right for a case like Seth's. Any touch resulted in his body reacting violently, even when he was unconscious. And he didn't regain consciousness for her to ask.

She sent Nick for Cliff Edwards, and together she and the wagon master huddled over the patient. The immediate area around the shoulder wound was reddish-purple, surrounded by a wider ring of red than earlier.

Seth was muttering, thrashing, much as he had during his nightmare weeks ago, and Kate knew that once more he was reliving horrors she could only imagine. But this time she wasn't able to wake him.

She told Cliff about that night and watched as his eyes clouded.

"He drove himself too hard. These wounds shouldn't ordinarily kill someone, but I suspect he's worn out. Damn, he has to fight, and from what you told me, maybe he won't—maybe he doesn't want to."

"He does," Kate argued fiercely. "He never gives up. He told me that." But he had, she knew. He had given up on her. She knew that was why he'd kept disappearing, why he'd gone with Dallas, why he had planned on leaving the wagon train, because he had never received anything from her but distrust.

Maybe Cliff was right. Maybe Seth Hampton was tired of fighting so many wars. His brother. Her. How many others? So much death. Hostility. Hate. He had fought them all with that same determinedly decent stubbornness of his. She had seen it that night he'd had the nightmare, had glimpsed the hell he was still carrying with him. And she had done nothing to help him, to even try to understand. She'd been too concerned with her own ghosts.

"Anyway," she said, "I'm not going to let him give up." She shook him gently, calling to him insistently. "Seth. Seth, you have to wake up. Seth."

She washed his face, then started calling him again. "Seth." The name sounded fine on her lips, as if it belonged there. Why hadn't she realized it earlier?

"Seth . . ."

He quieted, then opened his eyes. Their usual deep green-blue was hazy with pain. His gaze moved around, obviously trying to focus. He moved slightly, groaning as the pain struck him with renewed fury. Then his gaze found Kate.

"You're . . . still here?"

"Seth, listen to me. I have to know what to do. You have to help us, Cliff and I."

"Cliff . . ."

"He took the arrows out, cauterized the wounds—"

"That's why—" He didn't finish the sentence, and the words disintegrated into a sound that was almost a whistle, a sound that would have been a moan coming from anyone else. His eyes closed.

"Seth, there seems to be infection. Tell us what to do. Don't go away again. Don't go away."

His eyes opened again. He gave her a twisted effort at a smile. It nearly broke her heart, or what was left of it.

"Take more than an arrow to . . . kill me. Poultices. Warm water with tannic acid."

"Acid?"

He nodded.

"But—"

"But it will hurt like hell," he said in answer to her unspoken question, before he closed his eyes against the pain again. "Opium. Hypodermic syringe. In small bag . . . marked. Better than chloroform. I'll stay awake."

"How much?"

He tried a weak grin again, but it came out as more of a grimace. His eyes found Cliff. "We're not moving?"

"We've stopped overnight."

Seth looked around at the light flooding the wagon. "You're a liar, Cliff."

Cliff looked uncomfortable. "We took a vote."

"Damn, you need . . . to keep moving. Winter. Snow." He tried to move. "Oh, Christ," he muttered hoarsely, his eyes closing again. It was obvious that even that small effort had renewed the agony.

Kate had already moved away, peering into the bag and finding what he'd described. She had to keep him awake long enough to help her.

"Seth? Seth?" She knew the will it must have taken for him to surface again. His eyes opened.

"How much of the acid . . . and the opium? Where do I use the—" she looked at the needle "—this?" How could she ever do it, knowing so little?

"In arm . . . muscle," he whispered. "Just fill until I . . . shake my head."

She did as he ordered, looking doubtfully at the needle when he nodded. And then his body started shivering, almost convulsing, and his eyes closed as he slipped back into unconsciousness. She looked at Cliff.

"I don't think we have any choice, Miss Kate. You want me to do it?"

She did. She did with all her heart. Yet Seth had showed her, had trusted her. She owed him this. Hadn't she just told herself she would keep him alive? She shook her head and stuck the needle in a muscle in his elbow, concentrating with all her might.

In minutes, his breathing seemed to come easier, more regular. Cliff had ordered some hot water, and together they prepared the solution and dabbed it on the cloth, making a poultice and applying it to the shoulder wound. She winced as she did so, afraid, so afraid, that she would deepen his pain. If not now, then later.

But she wouldn't let him die.

Aided by the opium, Seth slept during the early hours of the day, while Jeremy kept watch, demanding that Kate get some rest. She wouldn't be good for anyone if she didn't, he argued, and he would wake her if there was any change.

The horses and oxen were fed. Scouts roamed the area, but there was no sign of the Indians. Cliff Edwards used the time to require everyone, including women, to do some practice shooting. They could replenish their ammunition at Fort Walker. It was already August now, and they needed to get through the mountains by the first of October.

But he wasn't going to leave a man who had saved the life of one of his scouts.

If he wasn't feeling so damnably pushed, he would have been bemused by Miss Kate and the doc. He should have known from the beginning that part of her hostility was due to her attraction to the Southerner. She had visibly softened during the trip, had dropped some of the reserve that distinguished her in the beginning. And yet, when everyone else had succumbed to the Southerner, she had seemed to cling to her prejudices.

But he knew love when he saw it, even if he personally had never suffered from that particular disease. And he had certainly witnessed it in the past several hours in the way Kate MacAllister had touched the patient, the way she had looked at him. If the doc survived these wounds...

He had seen enough of Kate MacAllister to know not to underestimate her unbending determination.

He grinned. The doc wouldn't dare die. He just wouldn't. And Cliff Edwards would bet his last bag of beans that Dr. Seth Hampton would accompany them all the way to the Sacramento Valley.

The path to that decision should be most interesting. He would also bet his last pouch of tobacco on that.

Seth woke to a sea of pain. He felt as if he were drowning in it. It was all he remembered—the pain. Pain and shadows. So many shadows. His head felt full of oatmeal, or something else much less benign. Like the devil's pitchforks.

He tried to move, but pain racked him. His shoulder was on fire, and another kind of pain, a sharp thrust that seemed to go through him, tormented the whole left side of his body. His mouth felt as if it were stuffed with cotton. His general condition, he thought, diagnosing himself, was something less than miserable.

He barely remembered an insistent voice calling his name when all he wanted was blackness. Sweet oblivion. Oblivion from the agonizing pain that burned through him, from the nightmares, from the certainty that there was no such thing as peace for him.

And then he had felt her hands, gentle yet unsure. He recalled the look in her eyes as she demanded from him his own cure, the intensity of her expression as she insisted he get well. Or was it his own imagination, the lunatic delusion of a sick man?

He tried to focus his eyes. Kate MacAllister was slumped beside him, her eyes closed, her face exhausted, her dress wrinkled. Her cheeks were smudged, as if a child's fist had rubbed tears away. But if there had been tears, they couldn't have been for him. She wouldn't cry for a man she called a Rebel, for a man she partly blamed for the destruction of her family.

She was so pretty, even with that smudged face. Maybe even prettier than when her hair was so neatly tied at her neck and her face was scrubbed clean. Tenderness crept into his soul, pushing away some of the pain. She looked this way because of him, because she must . . . care, or she would have given him over to someone else.

If anyone else had wanted him.

Maybe that was it. Maybe no one else would take the Rebel, and she felt responsible. That infernal responsibility of hers, that core of strength that kept her going, that had kept what was left of her family going. Jeremy! How was Jeremy? He was in Jeremy's bed.

But he couldn't wake her to ask. She looked so exhausted. How long had it been? Opium. He remembered that. He remembered the acid. That was why he burned the way he did, while the pain in his side was more like scissors slicing through him. Jeremy. Where was Jeremy? And Nick? He moved, and waves of new agony swept over him as he tried fruitlessly to reason.

Indians. Dallas. What had happened to Dallas? But Dallas was alive. He remembered seeing him, far away through a haze. Or was that a dream? The Indians were coming at them. The wagon was swirling again, just as it had before. And he was hot. So hot. But the Indians were still coming. "Kate," he cried out frantically. And then, "I'm sorry," he said through clenched teeth as he was slung back into the maelstrom of his nightmares.

"I'm sorry." The low words woke Kate, pierced her consciousness with their anguish. She wasn't even sure she'd heard the words, or understood. She just had the impression of infinite sadness. How long had she been asleep?

He had moved. She saw that much. He was still hot—but not as hot, perhaps, as this morning, though she wasn't sure—and the splash of red on his shoulder had not spread.

She pushed back some ringlets of hair that had escaped the convenient braid and glanced down at her dress. It was stained with blood and the tannic-acid solution. But she didn't dare stir for fear of waking him. Twenty-four hours. It had been more than twenty-four hours.

A knock came at the back of the wagon, and she said softly, "Yes?"

It was Nick, a pot in his hand. He glanced down at Seth. "Still asleep?" He was whispering now as he handed the pot to Kate. "Some broth Mrs. Cochran sent over. How is he?"

"I don't know," she said softly, hearing her own desperation and wanting to control it. God knew Nick had enough heartaches in his young life. He didn't need another.

But her own desperation was impossible to control. She had feared she couldn't bear loss again, so she had built a shell of iron around herself. But it had split open. Seth Hampton had split it open, and she no longer had any protection.

She reached out and touched him, the heat of his body flowing into hers, and she suddenly realized she was glad that shell had split open. Whatever happened now, she had been awakened. It was like the story of Snow White. She was feeling again, just as deeply as she knew Seth Hampton had felt. She had known it from the evening he'd had that nightmare, and again that evening he'd comforted her when she had cried. She'd even known it before that, the way he cared for Jeremy and saved Nick's life. He cared about everyone. Not about the color of their uniforms or their politics or their prejudices, but about the person inside.

And she was learning to do the same, as he had forced her to do. She swallowed, cherishing the simple connection of her skin to his.

He moved slightly, as if, in some way, he felt that connection, too. His eyes opened, focused slowly and settled on her, a slow smile appearing that went straight to the core of her heart. It was so tentative, so strained, as if he were forcing it for her sake rather than his own.

"You...look tired," he said. "Have you been here—"

"Since you were wounded," Nick broke in, and he grinned as Seth's gaze moved to him. "I brought you some soup. Mrs. Cochran made it."

Seth had never felt less like eating—less able to eat—but he forced his smile to widen. "Thank you." And then he remembered his last thoughts, which were still wandering disjointedly in his head. "Jeremy?"

Kate frowned. "Jeremy is much better than you."

A small particle of light came into his eyes. "I don't think that's... much of a recommendation for my doctoring skills."

"Or mine," Kate said wryly. "How do you feel, or is that a ridiculous question?"

He moved again, and she saw him wince, his smile disappearing. She picked up the cloth and wet it, then wiped his face. When she finished, her hand fell naturally to his and he took it, his fingers almost crushing hers as he seemed to fight a wave of pain. Then his fingers slowly relaxed.

"Dallas?"

"He escaped without any injury—except guilt."

His brow furrowed in an unspoken question.

"He feels responsible. Says 'nobody ain't never died for me before,'" she said with a smile as she tried to imitate the scout. "'Don't want it on my ledger.'" *Or mine, either.*

"I'll try not to be the first," Seth said.

"He'll appreciate that." She hesitated. "So will I."

He moved his left hand—the one unhampered by injury—up to her face, and trailed a smudge where a tear had fallen. "Tears?"

"I was worried about you."

"I'm indestructible. My brother told me that once."

"I wish he, or you, had told *me*." She allowed his fingers to continue their path before his hand fell to his side. "Do you think you can eat? Everyone in the wagon train wants to cook something for you."

Seth looked surprised.

"You've made a lot of friends," she said, a little shyly. "I had to fight to keep you."

Seth raised an eyebrow. At least that answered one question, and the answer was a surprise. "A Rebel?"

"A Rebel," she confirmed. "Now, about that food..."

He didn't eat much, just a few mouthfuls of broth, before he sank back, exhausted. He closed his eyes, and she started to back away. "Don't go," he said.

She didn't. Instead, she gave him her hand and held it until once more he fell asleep, this time peacefully.

Chapter Eight

The wagon train resumed its pace the next afternoon. Seth insisted, claiming he knew how much his body could stand. His face had regained some color, and the swelling and redness were receding. The wounds, which he said should remain open to the air, looked ugly and raw, and Kate knew he was still in a great deal of pain and would suffer even more in the jolting wagon.

Their wagon took the lead again so that dust wouldn't get into his wounds. Kate stayed next to him, feeling every jolt, hurting herself as she watched him trying to hide the pain she knew he felt. To try to take his mind from it, she asked him questions, about Virginia and his family.

He gave her a weak grin when he said he came from "a long line of divided families." He and his brother had been nothing new.

"My grandmother's father was a Tory," he said, "and my grandfather a patriot. Her father killed his father's brother and burned his home and sent him to a prison ship. My grandmother didn't approve, and ran off to join Francis Marion, the Swamp Fox, in protest." He grinned. "I hear there were some fiery times.

"And then her daughter, my mother, who was a fervent American, fell in love with a British raider who captured her brother's ship during the War of 1812."

"But..."

He looked at her, that wry, twisted smile on his face. "You don't understand how that can happen, do you? How hearts have loyalties all of their own?" There was no question in his tone, only a resigned statement.

Seth continued slowly. "They each had a very strong love for each other, a stronger commitment than most. And fierce loyalty to each other. Perhaps because they went through so much together—and apart. I envied them that commitment, that love, that loyalty that surpassed everything else."

But as he spoke, the light seem to fade from his vivid sea-colored eyes, and Kate felt as if it had gone from her soul, too. She knew what he wanted, what he demanded: unreserved, unqualified acceptance.

She had thought she was giving it, yet he'd obviously sensed something in her that she hadn't even realized. How do you suddenly give up five years of anger? Of hate? It was like his wound, it took time to heal, and though she'd thought she had healed, he knew she hadn't. Not completely. And that total healing, she knew, was the only thing he would, could, accept.

They arrived at Fort Walker six days later. Seth was walking a little now. He had pulled on a shirt for their arrival, even though Kate knew it hurt him to feel anything close to his skin.

But nothing could hurt as much as the emptiness that filled her. He would be leaving now. He'd told her last night.

It had been after Nick so tentatively handed him the carving of Sundance, the horse's head held so proudly. Seth had taken it slowly, almost reverently. "It's beautiful, Nick," he said. "Thank you."

Nick had hesitated a moment, then said. "You are going on with us, aren't you?"

Seth had just shook his head. "I think I have a few days of recovery to go. It will be better accomplished at Fort Walker." Kate had known he was protecting her, just as he protected everyone. He hadn't wanted Nick to know she was the reason. But *she* knew.

There was a dance that night on the parade field, under a full moon, with lanterns providing additional light. It was the dance the young lieutenant had promised, and he was there. So was Seth, though he only watched. His arm was strapped to his body to keep it from pulling against the shoulder, and she'd offered to shave him, an act that could have been a disaster, since her hand shook so. Her whole body had gone weak at the intimacy of the act, at touching him, at being so close to him.

Seth looked relaxed as everyone from the wagon train stopped to tell him how much he would be missed, how they wished he would continue with them.

Kate noted the easy way he deflected the requests, even as his eyes warmed at their concern and their obvious affection. He smiled, and Kate knew a rare pleasure that sliced through her like a knife. She had never seen that smile before, and it was breathtaking, like the first sun in the morning.

She knew then that she had to have that sun, that she would do anything to hold on to those rays. And in that moment she felt them replace the last vestige of bitterness that remained in her.

She loved him! The knowledge was sure and shattering. She realized she had loved him for a long time, and now she wondered whether she hadn't fought it so hard not only because of her family, but also because she was afraid of another loss, another death.

Dear heaven, she had come so close to losing him to death, and now she realized how precious any time with him would be, so precious that she could no longer live in the shadows, afraid to love, to care, to live, when he was offering so much light.

She turned down the offer of a dance from the young lieutenant and walked over to Seth, holding out her hand.

"Will you take a walk with me?"

It was almost like the time midway through their journey, when he had asked her on a walk she hadn't wanted to take. And now she sensed *his* reluctance.

"Please," she said.

Seth looked at her searchingly and then took her hand. They walked away from the circle of merrymakers to the edge of the fort, where sentries stood watch. "Best not go beyond this," Seth said.

There simply was no place to be alone. And Kate knew she had to be alone with him. She looked around and finally spied a sign that read Chapel, and she knew that was what she'd been seeking.

The chapel was small and quiet and simple, with only a small cross on a podium. The glow from the moon and lanterns filtered in the windows, sending sprays of pale light dancing along the walls. The music from the dance was dim now, its gaiety a counterpoint to the silent dignity within.

Kate turned to him. "Please come with us to California, Seth."

"Why?" he asked simply.

Kate swallowed. So much was at stake. She had to find the right words. So she chose the only ones. "I love you."

He stilled, his gaze boring into hers. "Because of Jeremy? Nick? I don't want gratitude, Kate."

She bit her lip. "I'm not offering gratitude."

"I'm still a Southerner. I can't, won't, take back, or regret, anything I was or did."

"I know," she said softly. "And I don't want you to change. I want everything you are."

The green-blue of his eyes seemed to deepen, even as a glimmer of light shone there.

"Kate, you have to be sure. You have to be sure you will never look at me and see your brothers, or your father or...the man you almost married. I can't—I won't—live with reservations."

Kate stared into the strong face that she had grown to love so much. "I finally understand," she whispered, "what you meant when you said hearts have a loyalty of their own." And she did. His heart was the truest she'd ever known, so loyal to what he thought was good and right. It was hers that had failed.

"I need you," she said.

"I like want better," he said, a grin beginning to break the severe lines of his face.

"That, too," she said breathlessly.

"Ah, Kate," he said, "I didn't think you would ever say that. If I didn't think we would both go tumbling down, I would carry you away this minute."

She looked at him. Did he mean what she thought he meant? "Does that mean you'll go with us?"

"Only if you'll marry me," he said, his eyes creasing with a pleasure that gave his face even more depth, more distinction. Dear God, how she loved him! How could she have been so blind for so long?

"Yes," she said simply, with a joy that filled every ounce of her, that made her want to sing and dance and shout. How very good it felt. How magnificent. She didn't understand why he loved her, but she was ready now to accept it with every fiber of her being. With all the loyalty in the heart that she was learning to use better.

His smile widened, but there was still a certain hesitancy. "Will your brothers approve?"

"You've already won Nick's soul," she said.

"And Jeremy?"

Kate was honest. "I don't know. Jeremy doesn't say much."

Seth raised an eyebrow, and she knew he was thinking it was a trait that ran in the family.

"And if he doesn't?" He waited patiently.

"I'll be disappointed, but it won't make a difference."

Seth looked down and smiled again. "I love you, Miss MacAllister, my lovely Kathryn Mary," he said in that soft Southern drawl that seeped into her consciousness like warm honey. The same drawl she'd hated at first, and now wanted to hold on to forever. He didn't wait for an answer, but leaned down and kissed her. He had kissed her before. Tentatively. Searchingly. Even tenderly. But this was different.

She felt the difference to the core of her being, where the first tingling of her femininity started doing marvelous things to her whole body. His lips were gentle, but now there was assurance in them, a wonderful assurance, even though only one of his arms circled her body.

Kate was careful of his shoulder even if, for the moment, he seemed to have forgotten it. She thought how amazingly creative one could be when one had a mind to be so. She lifted up on her tiptoes, avoiding touching those raw parts of him, and yet passion made itself felt. It fairly strummed between them, like a telegraph wire strung tight between two poles.

It thrummed and reverberated and sang its own perfect song. Perfect except for the way she wanted all of him close to her, so close that she would never fear to lose him again. The barely restrained passion, out of necessity, turned instead to promise, a promise of things to come. Kate could scarcely wait.

Neither, apparently, could he. With a lightness she'd never seen in him before, he grabbed her hand, holding it tight. "Let's go find a minister," he said, with a grin that reached to his eyes. The dimple she had noticed during his illness deepened, and she wondered how she could ever have denied that face.

She knew only one thing. She would never do it again.

The wedding took place the next day, as final repairs were made on the wagons by the fort blacksmith. Everyone from the wagon train was present, beaming with approval. Several of the women had even provided quickly put-together wedding attire, one offering her own dress, another a veil. An army chaplain said the words, and Jeremy gave away the bride. With pleasure, he had told Seth. With a great deal of pleasure. And relief that Kate had finally come to her senses, he'd added with a grin that broke the usual solemnity of his face.

War, he'd said to her later, and in private, brought out the worst and the best in men. It ruined some. He'd seen that happen in Andersonville to men in both uniforms. He'd also seen the way some, again in both uniforms, rose to nobility. It wasn't the uniform that mattered, but the man inside it.

Nick stood as Seth's best man, and then he ran off to see his puppy, which had been born that morning. Seth had grinned at the abrupt departure, observing with a lustful gleam that he and Kate probably didn't have to worry about Nick being around much during their honeymoon.

As Kate repeated her wedding vows, she felt a peace she'd never known before, a wonderful sense of belonging and rightness. She knew then with certainty that her own wounds were completely healed—even the scars were nearly gone. What was left were good memories, the kind to keep and cherish.

Seth had taught her to cherish the good things. He had taught her so much. She looked at him, her heart swelling with love as he made his vows, his gaze intent on her. His face was relaxed in a way she hadn't seen before, his eyes alight in the way she knew they were meant to be. That craggy face, with its compassion, had always been attractive to her, but now he was incredibly handsome, with that smile that was no longer wistful, but wide and open and happy. His voice was so sure, so deep and rich as he said the words that made him hers forever. Her Rebel. Her stubborn Rebel, who would always go the way of his conscience, whether it was against the wind or not.

She loved him for that now. It had taken her a long time to understand how rare it was, how infinitely precious. She knew it would not always be easy. His conscience would not always coincide with hers, but she also knew how totally empty her life would be without him. She would learn to compromise, although not always to agree. And he, he'd said last night, would not want her to.

When the words were finished, he leaned over. "Mrs. Hampton," he said, "I love you." And then his lips touched hers with a gentleness that turned quickly, as it always did, into something much more violent, until the sound of titters finally penetrated. He gave her a "just wait" look, full of lechery, and she gave him a private but nonetheless promising smile in return.

* * *

Because of his wounds, the consummation of their marriage had to wait, although Kate thought she would die from wanting him so badly. They lay together at night, treasuring the closeness and the marvelous kisses as their bodies grew tense with anticipation.

Ten days after the ceremony, when they stopped for the night, Seth disappeared. He had been driving the wagon, while Jeremy had taken to riding Sundance and hanging out in Cliff Edwards's wagon to give them a little privacy. Nick slept quite happily under the wagon.

They had stopped earlier that night, coming to a halt before crossing another river. Seth had pulled their wagon off a little into the trees, where it stood alone, and then had disappeared on some errands after taking care of the oxen. Jeremy and Nick had also disappeared. She also noticed that everyone was looking at her a bit oddly—a smile here, a smirk there.

A summons came from Mrs. Cochran, and Kate hurried to the Cochrans' wagon, afraid that something had happened to Nick, but he was busy demonstrating his carving skills to young Edie. Kate looked at the carving and smiled; it was a puppy on its back, a bewildered look on its clownish face. Obviously nothing was wrong with Nick. He looked happier than he had in years.

She looked askance at Sally Cochran, who seemed inordinately pleased with herself. "We were hoping Nick could stay with us tonight."

Kate nodded, though she was puzzled. He had stayed there before during the past few days, unwilling to leave the pup. Or was it the little Cochran girl? Even at eleven? Kate understood now.

"Here," Sally Cochran said, thrusting something into her hands. "Something special for dinner tonight. Don't look now," she admonished as Kate started to do just that.

When she returned, Seth was there. So was a table that had mysteriously appeared, covered with a lace tablecloth from someone's store of treasures, a bottle of wine from someone else's, and a number of other delicacies. With a sweep of his arm, Seth seated her as if she were royalty, and from the distance came a lovely, romantic tune from a fiddle.

Except for Seth, everyone had disappeared—almost by magic, she thought with a smile. Or a conspiracy of wonderfully tender proportions.

Seth looked a little embarrassed, his eyes crinkling in the most delightful way. "I asked the Cochrans to invite Nick tonight, and Mrs. Cochran said something to someone, and it seemed everyone thought... well, it might be a special occasion or something." He didn't have to say any more. Gossip always passed up and down the wagons like wildfire.

Kate knew she, too, should feel embarrassed, but she didn't. There was so much affection in the offerings, so much thoughtfulness. She loved the pleasure that shone in his eyes even as he apparently worried about her reaction.

"It's almost like those medieval days—" she giggled "—when they carried the groom up to the bride and tossed him in her bed."

"Hmm . . . I like that picture," he said.

"But without an audience," she chided.

"Just us." His eyes twinkled as Seth and Kate closed out everyone else and wrapped themselves in a world all their own.

Serenaded by an unseen fiddle joined occasionally by a harmonica, they ate slowly, their eyes feasting on another kind of delicacy altogether. Each other. Hands touched, lips smiled, eyes made promises. When they were through, Seth took her hand, and she knew it was finally time. Their time. He had declared himself well, and the entire wagon train population was signaling their approval of this odd match in their own separate, giving ways.

Kate knew that the old Kate would have been embarrassed. Obviously everyone knew what was going to happen this night. But she wasn't. She was profoundly moved that so many people cared so much. She guessed she would get used to it—with Seth as her husband.

Once in the wagon, they undressed slowly. The faint light of a part moon filtered through the canvas, but their silhouettes were visible only to them, thanks to the privacy of the surrounding trees. He helped her first and then she him, her hands touching his scars with tenderness.

But then those memories left as he kissed her, and there was only this moment, this wonderful, glorious moment. He was so beautiful in his lean masculinity.

She gave him her hand, and smiled as he looked at her slowly, and very approvingly. And then they came together. They were still standing, each one's form felt and admired and loved by the other. Her hands ran up and down his side, and then he pulled one hand around to his back and drew her snugly against him, giving her a chance to get used to him, to the now-hard man part of him.

Kate had thought she'd known desire before, especially during those special times with him, but that had been nothing like the hunger rising in her now—the wanting, demanding tingling of every nerve and every sense in her body. She fitted herself closer to him, and their kiss deepened into a maelstrom of yearning.

Seth felt her body tremble with response and it fueled a hunger so strong he couldn't wait any longer. He picked her up and laid her down on the bed, running his hands over her body, memorizing it even though he knew it was his, now and always. So slender. So fragile and yet so strong. His hands met hers once more, and he felt her wondering longing in them, so shyly eager, so unafraid. This was the Kate he'd loved almost from the beginning, the Kate he'd always known existed. He moved his lips down to the hollow of her neck, caressing, exciting, and then farther down, to her breasts. He nuzzled them, licking until the nipples stood stiffly in their own need.

She held both hands out to him, drawing him to her. He felt her trembling turn to a kind of quivering, and he knew it was time. Seth controlled himself as much as possible. Slowly, go slowly. Gently. He was rigid now with his own need, and it took all his will to control it as he lowered himself, teasing her until her whole body arched toward him in instinctive, needy response. He entered her, feeling that fragile barrier, yet holding her tight against the pain he knew would come. But she wouldn't have his hesitancy, he sensed. With the same will and determination that she brought to everything, she arched against him once more, and he lost control, plunging into her with a need he now knew she shared.

There was the smallest cry on her part, and then no more. "Oh, Seth," she whispered in awe as little explosions of ecstasy followed each other like waves in a stormy sea, each tossing her up and then plunging her into depths of emotions and sensations she had never known existed. Her body caught his rhythm and she instinctively moved with him, then against him, as they hurried toward some irresistible beckoning peak, and then *it* happened, the indescribable, unexplainable zenith that exploded the world into spectacular pieces of floating sunbeams and star bursts. Shock waves of rapture rocked her very being as she opened her eyes and met his, eyes that were so bright and warm and loving. "I love you," she whispered. "Dear God, how I love you."

And then neither of them could speak as the sensations continued, their bodies quivering with the incredibly sweet joy of joining, of loving—of sharing the same rumblings of pleasure that kept alive and simmering the past few glorious moments.

He held her then, and she remembered what he had said days ago about his parents and grandparents. *Because they went through so much…they had a very strong love for each other. Hearts have a loyalty of their own.*

She had thought she understood before, but not as much as she did now. And when she looked up at him, she knew he saw everything she was thinking.

His kiss, no longer wistful, but very, very possessive, told her so. Her Rebel would probably always keep going against the wind, but she would always be there with him, fighting it. Joining him in their own mighty storm.

Wind and storm. Sunsets and sunrises. He was all of those. And because of him, she was, too.

* * * * *

A Note from Patricia Potter

I've been worrying about Seth Hampton for three long years. He's been haunting my thoughts, always asking the same question: "Where's my happy ending?"

Seth has been in my imagination for far longer than that, however. He first appeared along with his brother Rafe in another Harlequin Historical collection, the *1990 Harlequin Historical Christmas Stories.* In that story, Seth joined the Confederate army, while Rafe decided to go North. They were both in love with the same girl—and Rafe won.

But not really, for Seth's true love was yet to come.

Untamed! gave me the opportunity to tell Seth Hampton's story, and to joyously end the saga of the O'Neill/Hampton family, which started in my first book, *Swampfire,* and continued with two other Harlequin Historicals and the above mentioned Christmas story.

But Seth's story stands alone. It's a tale of healing—not only of human souls, but of a nation—the slow, painful coming together of individuals divided by a bitter war.

And where else to tell it but in the West, the place of new beginnings. The West has always fascinated me, because it was a proving ground, always testing the strength of those who tried to tame it.

I hope you enjoy reading *Untamed!* as much as I enjoyed participating in it.

Patricia Potter

One Simple Wish

Joan Johnston

Chapter One

"Remember, Harmony, we can't tell anyone. It has to be our secret."

"But why, Momma?"

Alyssa Moreland put an arm around her six-year-old daughter's shoulder and brushed aside the child's shaggy blond bangs. How could she explain to one so innocent how cruel the world could be to a bastard child?

Alyssa felt a sense of desperation. Moving a thousand miles from Philadelphia wasn't going to accomplish a thing if she couldn't convince Harmony of the importance of keeping their past a secret.

The stagecoach was sultry, and everything inside was covered with a layer of fine dust. At least they had the coach to themselves. Alyssa took out her handkerchief, dabbed it on her tongue to wet it, and began wiping Harmony's angelic face clean.

"We're starting a brand-new life in Texas, sweetheart, just you and me. I'll be calling myself Mrs. Moreland, so people will want to know why my husband—your father—isn't with us."

"But I never had a father," Harmony protested.

Alyssa's lips curved in a sad smile. "Everyone has a father, sweetheart." *I just wasn't married to him when you were conceived.*

"Not me," Harmony said with certainty. "Marjorie Rose said I came from the pumpkin patch."

"Nevertheless, if someone asks about your father, what should you say?"

"My poppa got sick with *new-moan-ya* and died."

"And where did we used to live?"

"In a brothel."

Alyssa froze. She stared, stricken, into her daughter's enormous blue eyes. She cupped Harmony's chin and tilted her daughter's face up to hers. "You must never, *never* repeat that to anyone. If someone asks where we used to live, you may tell them *in Philadelphia.*"

The little girl's blue eyes misted with tears. "I'll try to remember, Momma."

Alyssa pulled Harmony close. She rocked the little girl in her arms. "I know this must seem very confusing," she whispered.

"I miss Marjorie Rose, Momma. And I miss Lulu and Sophie and Coralie and Winnie and Olinda and Marybeth and—"

"I know, sweetheart. I do, too."

"Why couldn't we say goodbye to them, Momma?"

"There simply wasn't time." *More lies. Would she ever be able to stop telling lies?* "We can write to them once we get settled in Fredericksburg."

Alyssa had carefully chosen the small Texas town nestled in the hill country west of Austin as the perfect place to start over. It was off the beaten path and had a population that consisted primarily of farmers of German descent. She had heard the hill country was beautiful in the spring, with wildflowers that covered the fields with blankets of color. And there were lots of trees—pecan and cypress and live oak.

"You're going to love living in Fredericksburg," Alyssa promised her daughter.

"But why did we have to leave our home in Philadelphia?" Harmony asked.

I didn't want you to be sold to some man for his pleasure before you were old enough to know a different life was possible. I didn't want you to live the life of a whore. I have only one wish, sweetheart. One simple wish. That you grow up a normal, happy little girl.

Alyssa knew that having her wish come true depended on keeping their secrets. No one must ever find out the truth about Harmony. Or about her mother.

"We left our home in Philadelphia to find a better life, sweetheart." Alyssa clutched her daughter close and whispered, "And we will."

As a widower and an eligible bachelor, Karl Eberhardt had so many invitations to supper that he seldom had to eat at Ellie Cooperman's boardinghouse, where he lived. So he wasn't there when Mrs. Alyssa Moreland and her daughter, Harmony, presented themselves at the dinner table for the first time. Karl would have met them at breakfast the next morning, except Herman Bingaman's mare was having problems foaling. As the town blacksmith, Karl was the closest thing Fredericksburg had to a horse doctor.

He might have met them at the noon meal, only Karl was so far behind in his work at the forge that he decided to send his apprentice, Mrs. Cooperman's fourteen-year-old son Jack, to the boardinghouse for sandwiches and work on through the afternoon. He had plows to sharpen, wheels to repair and hasps, hinges and hammers to make.

Karl checked as soon as he arrived at his shop to make sure Jack had built the kind of fire he needed to do his work. He nodded imperceptibly in approval of the clear, concentrated flame, and the lack of a strong sulphur smell. "A good fire," he pronounced.

Jack grinned. "I cleaned the fire pot first, just like you taught me. And I used wet coal and lots of it."

Karl clapped the gangly youth on the shoulder. "You did well, Jack. You'll make a fine blacksmith someday."

"Have you met Mrs. Moreland and her daughter?" Jack asked as he worked the bellows.

"Not yet," Karl said.

"Ma says she's a real lady."

Karl smiled skeptically. "How can she tell?"

Jack looked surprised that his mother's evaluation of Mrs. Moreland had been questioned. "Why, 'cause of her manners, of course. Delicate, they was. And her daughter's, too."

Karl checked the wheel rim he had stuck into the fire. Color was all-important. If the iron got beyond a red heat while it was being shaped, he would have to cut it off and start again. "How old is the daughter?" Karl asked, more to make conversation than because he was interested.

"Six," Jack said. "But she's as pretty as her ma is beautiful."

"Beautiful, is she?" Karl held the iron over the anvil with tongs and began to drop the bundle as his elbow parted company with his ribs and the flat peen hammer came up over his head in full, regularly spaced strokes.

"Yes, beautiful," Jack insisted. "Blond hair up in a fancy do, and cornflower blue eyes. She's kind of shy, though."

"What makes you say that?" Karl was ready to harden the iron, so he stuck it back into the fire and waited for it to turn a cherry red.

"Her voice, for one thing."

"Oh?"

"It was kinda soft. You had to listen real hard to hear her. And her eyes, for another thing."

"Oh?"

Jack put another scoopful of wet coal on the fire. "She never stares right at you, just kinda peeks up at you from under her lashes."

"And this makes her a lady?" Karl asked, arching a dark brow.

"Well, she was dressed like a lady, too," Jack said. "Ma said she'd never seen the like of it. All them frills and furbelows. Anyhow, Mrs. Moreland plans to open a dress shop here in town. Today she's off hunting herself a place of business to rent."

The iron had reached exactly the desired color. Karl took it out of the fire with his tongs and cooled it in lukewarm water, watching for the moment when the metal was tempered. He pointed it out to Jack so the boy would learn to recognize it for himself.

"The iron must cool slowly," Karl instructed. "That will make it hard."

They worked the rest of the afternoon without a break. Karl insisted his shop be kept neat, so Jack was kept busy returning tools to the worktable near the forge. But there was no way to keep a blacksmith's shop really clean. Karl whitewashed the walls once a year, but the inevitable soot and dust quickly layered everything and everybody.

Even if the soot and dust hadn't been a problem, Karl had burned enough shirts with cinders that now he always worked bare from the waist up. He used a leather apron to protect his pants and his chest from flying sparks. It was hot near the forge, and Karl's body glistened with sweat. His hammer was upraised when he caught sight of a dainty pair of black calf-skin half boots beyond the anvil.

His eyes followed the boots to a pleated hem, then past swags of a very fine blue material to a handspan waist, then up to small breasts and a face that took his breath away. The woman standing before him possessed a firm chin, cupid's-bow lips, and a little bit of a nose and, yes, those eyes were definitely cornflower blue. Unless Karl was very much mistaken, he was staring at Jack's "beautiful lady."

Karl was suddenly very conscious of the soot in the creases of his hands, of the sweat that beaded in the black curls on his chest, of the way his black hair hung lank over his forehead.

"Are you Mr. Eberhardt?"

Karl could barely hear her over the roar of the bellows. "Jack, that's enough now."

"But, Karl—" The boy turned and his jaw dropped at the sight of Mrs. Moreland standing there in front of the anvil.

Karl felt the crimson stain of self-consciousness on his cheekbones as she stared at him, but was helpless to do anything about it. "I'm Karl Eberhardt," he said. His German accent sounded thick to his ears.

She seemed surprised by his size. He couldn't help the way he looked. He had always been tall, and the years with hammer and anvil had broadened his shoulders and strengthened his arms. The meals he missed because he was busy doctoring animals or working at the forge had kept him lean.

He knew his face wasn't much to please the ladies—sharp-boned, blunt features, a straight nose and an even straighter mouth. His eyes kept him from being plain. They were widely spaced, a wintry gray, and accented by ridiculously long lashes and dark, slanting brows.

He stayed clean-shaven because he didn't want a beard catching on fire. But this morning he hadn't shaved, so he knew there must be a rough, dark shadow on his cheeks and chin.

Her small, tentative smile immediately produced two enchanting dimples. "I'm Alyssa Moreland. I just arrived in town yesterday. Ellie Cooperman told me you're a carpenter."

"I work with wood," Karl admitted.

She seemed embarrassed to look upon his naked chest. But he was afraid it would embarrass her even more if he crossed past her for the shirt he had left hanging on a peg near the door. Karl saw her nostrils pinch at the harsh odors in his shop—horse, the slight taint of sulphur, hot iron and hardworking man.

Though she carried a handkerchief in her hand, she didn't cover her face to shut out the smells as another woman might have done. He respected her the more for her tact and her tolerance. She looked up at him, an appeal written in those innocent, cornflower blue eyes. "I need some shelves and a cabinet built for my new shop."

Karl couldn't breathe. He felt like a piece of hot iron under the hammer. "I've got a lot of work to finish here," he managed to say.

She looked disappointed. Straight white teeth clamped worriedly on her lower lip.

"I could get to it tomorrow," Karl found himself saying.

The smile—and the dimples—returned. "That will be fine. I've rented the building next door to Rudy Schmidt's mercantile. I'll see you there first thing tomorrow morning."

Mrs. Moreland turned to leave, but the gravel floor was uneven, and she lost her balance and started to fall. Karl moved with a speed even he had not known he was capable of, and caught her just as her feet flew out from under her.

Alyssa cried out in surprise, then laughed when she realized Karl had caught her a mere six inches from the ground.

For an endless moment, Karl was close enough to smell the lavender in her hair.

"Thank you for saving me. I almost made the most undignified exit of my life," she said with a wry grin.

Karl made sure Mrs. Moreland was steady on her feet before he removed his hands from her shoulders. He felt a red flush creeping up his neck when he realized there were two sooty spots—one on each shoulder—where his hands had been.

"I'm sorry about your dress," Karl said in a voice that sounded nothing at all like his own.

She brushed at the spots with her handkerchief, but Karl knew, even if she didn't yet, that the dress was ruined.

"I'll be glad to pay for the damages," he said in a gruff voice.

She speared him with her wide, cornflower blue eyes. Her hands came up to perch on her hips. "You'll do no such thing! Why, if it hadn't been for your quick thinking, there might be a lot more damage to my person than a couple of spots on my sleeves. No, Mr. Eberhardt—"

"Karl."

"Karl," she said, smiling so the dimples reappeared. "I'm the one in your debt. I'll bid you good day now."

Karl's eyes followed her as she stepped from the dark interior of the shop into the sunlight. Why, Karl wondered, did he have to meet Alyssa Moreland when he was dirty and sweaty and tired? He had been a widower for two years, and in all that time there had never been a woman who had made him feel the way she just had.

He had been shocked by the surge of sexual desire that had thrummed through him when he had held her in his arms. She was so small and delicate! His lips twisted cynically. It was a ludicrous thought—the lady and the blacksmith. He was foolish even to consider such an alliance. And Karl Eberhardt had never been a fool.

He picked up his hammer and tongs and went back to work.

But the idea wouldn't die.

Why couldn't he pursue such a woman? He was as good as the next man. He worked hard, he didn't drink to excess or gamble or have other vices. He had visited the soiled doves in San Antonio, but he figured that was a more responsible way of fulfilling his needs than easing himself upon his neighbors' willing wives and daughters.

Karl was so distracted he missed with the hammer and caught his thumb. "Sonofa—" He cut himself off. He had promised Mrs. Cooperman he wouldn't teach her boy bad habits.

"Gosh, Karl!" Jack said. "You missed!"

"Let that be a lesson to you, boy. Always pay attention to what you're doing. Don't let your mind stray to—" Karl cut himself off again, reluctant to admit he had been thinking about Alyssa Moreland.

But fourteen-year-old boys were surprisingly astute when it came to relationships with females. "It was Mrs. Moreland you were thinking about, wasn't it? She is beautiful, isn't she, Karl?"

Karl took his swollen thumb from his mouth and held it up to peruse it.

"Come on, Karl," the boy insisted. "What did you think of her?"

Karl ruffled the boy's hair. "Yes, Jack, she's beautiful."

Jack grinned. "So, are you gonna court her, Karl?"

"Whoa, boy, hold your horses! I only just met the lady."

Jack's grin broadened. "So you admit she's a lady, too."

Karl laughed. He picked up his hammer and tongs and went back to work. "Yes, she's a lady. And the likes of you and me shouldn't be discussing ladies behind their backs. Mrs. Moreland deserves our respect."

Jack returned to the bellows. "All right, Karl. If you say so."

"I say so." However, even though Karl refused to discuss Alyssa Moreland, she was never far from his mind the rest of the afternoon.

Alyssa had stopped the instant she was beyond Karl Eberhardt's line of sight and put a hand to her heart to stop its pounding. She had the feeling she had just had a narrow escape. But exactly what danger she had escaped from remained a mystery to her.

As a prostitute in one of the most exclusive houses of pleasure in Philadelphia, Alyssa had observed many a naked body. Heavy and lean, hairless and furry, she had seen them all. But she had never allowed herself to look at the man. With Karl, it had been impossible not to see him.

Mrs. Cooperman had waxed poetic about the fine young man—"Widowed, such a tragedy!"—who was teaching her son a trade. When Karl Eberhardt's eyes had caught Alyssa's, she had felt impaled, as helpless as a winged creature trapped by giant hands. But, despite their obvious strength, they had been gentle hands, and she had been released at last to fly away—free.

Only she wasn't free. She was a woman bound by the chains of her past. She could never get involved with a well-respected man like Karl Eberhardt, because she could never tell him the truth. And she had made up her mind that she was done with lying.

Alyssa gathered her composure and marched back across the street to the small shop she had leased. She had great confidence in her ability to make her business a success. If there was one thing she understood, it was ladies' fashions.

When she had first begun planning her escape from the brothel, it was Marjorie Rose who had given her the idea of opening a shop with both ready-made and made-to-order ladies' dresses.

"You know you've got the prettiest wardrobe of any girl here," Marjorie Rose had pointed out. "Anybody needs a seam fixed or a button reattached comes to you. More importantly, you have a sense of style, you know. You're a real lady."

Alyssa had smiled and shaken her head in disbelief. "Good grief, Margie. Think about what you're saying!"

Marjorie Rose was adamant. "You know what I mean. The men seek you out because you look like such a lady out of bed—when you're no such thing behind closed doors."

Alyssa flushed.

"Don't try denyin' it," Marjorie Rose said. "I've heard 'em talkin'. You're the perfect whore."

This time Alyssa's face paled.

Marjorie Rose tapped her chin, oblivious to the cruelty of her compliment. "Which is why they're not going to let you leave this place. You make too much money for them."

"Then I'll have to sneak away," Alyssa said.

That had been easier said than done. It had taken two years for Alyssa to save enough money to pay steamship, train and coach fares not only for herself, but also for Harmony. During that time she had also begun collecting fabric, lace and ribbon that could be shipped west. She had spent every spare moment sewing dresses that would provide the ready-made stock for her store.

In the end, Marjorie Rose had helped Alyssa sneak her luggage out of the house by providing a diversionary fight with another of the girls. The leave-taking from Marjorie Rose hadn't been easy. Alyssa and Marjorie Rose had grown up in the brothel together as girls. As women, they had shared the best and the worst of what their life had to offer.

"Come with me, Margie," Alyssa pleaded the night before she left. "I don't want to leave you here."

Marjorie Rose was typically philosophical. "I don't have the kind of reason you do to leave. Harmony needs a life beyond these walls. It's good you're taking her out of here. But I'd be afraid to face the world having lived all my life here."

"We'll keep each other safe," Alyssa argued. "Please come, Margie."

Marjorie Rose hugged Alyssa hard and said, "Write me when you get settled, care of general delivery. Wouldn't want 'em tracing you through me."

Their eyes were teary when they parted company, but Alyssa forced a smile onto her face. "I'll write. And when I get settled, I'm going to invite you to come live with me."

"You do that," Marjorie Rose said.

The first thing Alyssa had done on her arrival in Fredericksburg was to post a letter to Marjorie Rose.

Alyssa realized now that she had been slightly optimistic about how much money would be needed to get all the way to Fredericksburg, Texas, let alone how much cash it took to set up a shop. She needed a loan from the bank, and she hadn't the vaguest idea of how she was going to get it. All she had for collateral was two huge trunks of fabrics and ready-made fashions she had brought with her. She prayed it would be enough.

Alyssa straightened her shoulders and began her march toward the First National Bank of Fredericksburg. Halfway there she remembered the two black spots the blacksmith had left on her shoulders and stopped short. She smiled and headed back to the boardinghouse to change her dress. It would probably make a better impression on the banker if she arrived sans soot.

Karl made a special effort to be at his best for supper that evening. He took time in his bath to wash his hair. He didn't want to seem like he was dressing up for Mrs. Moreland, so he only wore a clean white shirt and dark trousers with a belt instead of suspenders. He tried buttoning the shirt all the way to the neck, but he couldn't breathe, so he left it open at the top. He gave his boots a quick shine, but they still showed the hard wear they got at the forge.

When he came downstairs at last, his hair was still wet. He had combed it back off his face, but a curl had already slipped down over his brow. He gave Mrs. Cooperman a big smile as he took his regular chair at the dining table. Because he had taken so much time, everyone else was already seated.

"How was business today?" Karl asked Uwe Detmer, the baker.

Uwe nodded his head three or four times. "*Gut. Gut.* I sold all of my bread and most of my pastries."

"And you, Herr Schneider? How is the new roof coming on the bank?"

"Fine, Karl. Got me an eyeful of that pretty little lady, I did, when she passed by today."

"Mrs. Moreland was at the bank?" Karl asked.

"She surely was," Herr Schneider said.

Mrs. Cooperman slapped Jack's hand to keep it out of the biscuits she had just set on the table. "Matter of fact, Mrs. Moreland and her daughter won't be at the table tonight." Mrs. Cooperman smiled slyly. "She got an invitation to dine with the banker, Mr. Bowen."

Karl stared in disbelief at the two empty chairs on the opposite side of the table. "She's having dinner with Max Bowen?"

Mrs. Cooperman chortled. "She sure is! You should have seen how she was dressed when he came to pick her up. My, oh, my! She was wearing a dress—brown velvet, it was—with buttons down the bodice and bows down the skirt. And lace—oh, the most delicate beige French lace at the neck. She was just lovely.

"Mr. Bowen must have thought so, too. 'You look lovely, Mrs. Moreland,' he said. That girl, she blushed so pink, why...she looked like a rose in springtime."

Karl was feeling sick to his stomach, but he took a serving of peas and one of mashed potatoes and pretended he was fine. "What time is Mrs. Moreland due back?"

Mrs. Cooperman winked. "Why, I expect she'll show up 'long about dark."

"Where's her little girl?" Karl asked.

"Oh, didn't I say? Harmony went along with her mother. Mrs. Moreland insisted. Mr. Bowen, he wasn't too pleased about that," Mrs. Cooperman observed with a furrowed brow.

Karl suddenly smiled. "Pass the roast beef," he said. Maxwell Bowen wasn't going to be able to do much courting with a six-year-old tagging along. But it was clear that Karl wasn't going to be able to waste any time. He would have to make his interest in the young widow known to her as soon as possible.

And what better time than when he was working on the shelves for her shop? He would have to take some care dressing himself in the morning. Mrs. Moreland was the kind of lady who would expect her man to have a good appearance. Karl was willing to go the extra mile to get what he wanted.

And he wanted Alyssa Moreland for his wife.

Later that evening, Karl was sitting in a rocker on the front porch taking the night air—or at least that was the excuse he gave himself—while he waited for Mrs. Moreland to return from dinner with the banker. He had moved the rocker into the shadows away from the front door, where there were supposedly fewer mosquitoes, and where he was camouflaged by Mrs. Cooperman's prize forsythia bush.

So he heard Harmony's ceaseless chatter and Max Bowen's impatient replies as they made their way back down the street from the Dollar and Sense Restaurant. Jack had been right on the mark when he said Alyssa spoke softly. Karl knew she was talking to Max, but he had no idea what she was saying to the banker. Not that he would have listened had he been able to hear. Karl would never have stooped to eavesdropping. Could he help it if he just happened to be on the porch?

Karl had a good view of the two of them, so he saw the moment when Max made his move. He had to admire the deft way Mrs. Moreland turned her head so Max's lips met with her cheek instead of her mouth.

Good for you! he cheered silently. Max Bowen was used to his money getting him what he wanted from a woman. Obviously Mrs. Moreland was a lady of superior character. However, Karl was surprised to see that, after Max left her at the porch steps, her shoulders slumped and her chin dropped to her chest. He wondered what could be causing her despair.

All at once he realized that if he didn't leave he was going to get caught. He didn't want her to think he had been spying on her. In several long strides he was inside the boardinghouse. He took the stairs three at a time, and he had just closed his bedroom door behind him when he heard Mrs. Cooperman welcoming Mrs. Moreland back.

"How was your dinner?" Ellie asked.

"We had pork chops," Harmony replied. "I *hate* pork chops."

Karl grinned. With any luck, Max Bowen's dinner with Mrs. Moreland had been a disaster. He pulled off his boots and got himself ready for bed.

Alyssa had her hands full parrying Mrs. Cooperman's nosy questions and getting her still-hungry daughter headed upstairs to bed instead of into the kitchen for the slice of cake Mrs. Cooperman had offered her.

"You can have a big breakfast tomorrow," Alyssa promised the child. "Right now it's time for bed. Please excuse us."

"Why, certainly," Mrs. Cooperman said. "I'll see you bright and early tomorrow morning."

Alyssa shuddered at the thought of waking at the break of day. She had spent her life sleeping until nearly noon. It was going to take some readjustment before she would be able to face the early morning light cheerfully.

As she undressed Harmony and helped her into the brass four-poster they were sharing, Alyssa thought back over the evening with Max Bowen. When should she have made her plea for the loan? There wasn't a moment she could have done it without making Max think that she was offering something more than her yard goods as collateral.

She could only be grateful that she had taken Harmony along. The six-year-old had been a marvelous chaperon. Alyssa giggled when she thought of how Max had reached past Harmony for Alyssa's hand and ended up with a mouthful of half-chewed pork chop in his palm.

"What is this?" He had quickly dropped the masticated mass back on Harmony's plate and wiped his hand clean. But that was clearly the end of any romantic overture for the evening.

Alyssa knew the battle had only begun. She was going to have to keep her wits about her to get a loan from the bank without succumbing to the banker's subtle blackmail.

Alyssa undressed herself and pulled a nightgown on. By the time she slipped beneath the covers to join her daughter, another man had taken Max Bowen's place in her thoughts.

A man with black hair, wide-spaced gray eyes and amazingly strong, yet gentle hands.

If only...if only...

Alyssa fell asleep dreaming of what might have been.

Chapter Two

Karl met Alyssa's daughter the next morning. They were the first people downstairs for breakfast. Harmony Moreland was astonishingly pretty, with big blue eyes that matched her mother's, silky blond hair caught up in braids that swung over her shoulders, a fringe of bangs across her brow and a dash of freckles across her nose. She was wearing a neatly ironed striped pinafore with white bloomers that peeked out below the knees, white stockings and black laced shoes.

She walked right up to him and said, "Hello. My name is Harmony. What's yours?"

"I'm Karl."

Harmony climbed into the chair next to his and pulled a cup and saucer close. "Would you pour me a cup of coffee please, Karl?"

"Wouldn't you rather have a glass of milk?"

Harmony's nose wrinkled. "Milk is for babies."

Karl arched a brow and gave her a look up and down. What did she think *she* was? He made no move toward the coffeepot resting on a trivet in the center of the table. "What does your mother think about your drinking coffee?"

"She thinks at least one of us ought to be awake in the morning." With that enigmatic comment, Harmony started to reach for the pot herself.

"I'll do that." Karl didn't want her to get burned, so he poured the coffee and then watched in amusement as Harmony carefully spooned in sugar and stirred until it dissolved. He watched to see the face he was sure was coming when she tasted the bitter brew.

He was the one surprised when Harmony swallowed, smiled and said, "That's not bad coffee."

Karl chuckled. "You've had better, I suppose."

Harmony nodded vigorously. "At the house where we used to live my friend Marjorie Rose made really good coffee. But she was as bad as Momma about getting up early to fix it. They were always up so late working at night that they slept in every morning."

Karl thought how industrious Alyssa Moreland must have been to sew late into the night.

"How did your father feel about getting up early?"

"Oh, I never had a father." At Karl's startled look, she quickly amended herself. "I mean, my poppa got sick with *new-moan-ya* and died when I was very, very, very small." She looked up from beneath blond lashes to see if Karl believed her, unconsciously mimicking her mother.

The object of Karl's thoughts suddenly appeared in the doorway. He smiled and said, "What a pleasant surprise to see you up so early. From what Harmony tells me, you're used to working late into the night."

Alyssa shot a panicked look at her daughter. What had Harmony been telling the blacksmith?

"All that sewing by candlelight can't be good for your eyes," Karl said.

Alyssa relaxed and barely kept herself from heaving a revealing sigh of relief. "Sewing. Yes. Well, sometimes there's work that has to be finished. You know how it is."

"Yes, I do."

"I guess we've both been so busy we haven't crossed paths at the supper table," Alyssa said with a more natural smile. "Have you lived here long?"

"I moved in two years ago. When my wife died." He wanted her to know he was a widower.

"I'm so sorry." Alyssa put her hands on Harmony's shoulders, which meant she had to stand right next to Karl. What on earth had compelled her daughter to sit down beside the blacksmith? "I hope Harmony hasn't been bothering you."

"Not at all. I hope you won't be upset that I served her a cup of coffee."

Alyssa smiled. "She seems to love the stuff."

"Would you like a cup of coffee?" Karl asked.

"To tell you the truth, I never could stand the taste of it. I'll have milk, if there is some."

Karl poured a glass of milk from the pitcher on the table. "There's eggs and sausage and muffins on the sideboard if you're hungry." He caught Alyssa's gaze and held it as he handed her the glass of milk.

"I'm hungry," Harmony volunteered.

Alyssa turned at the sound of her daughter's voice. "I'll fix a plate for you, sweetheart." She felt Karl's eyes on her as she crossed away from him. Her whole body came alive under his caressing glance.

She fixed plates for both herself and Harmony and took the seat next to her daughter so she wouldn't have to face Karl Eberhardt. But it was foolish to think she could avoid him. Since they both lived in the boardinghouse, they were going to be eating every meal together. Over the next several days they would be spending even more time together while Karl did carpentry work in her shop. Alyssa tried to think of something to say to break the noticeable silence that had fallen between them.

"How long have you lived in Fredericksburg?" Alyssa asked.

"All my life. My parents came here in 1846, when the *Adelsverein* sent German immigrants here to establish a town. I was born a year later."

"And you never left?"

"I fought during the War Between the States—mostly in Tennessee."

"But you were only a boy then!"

"Lots of boys fought. And died. My brother was one of them."

"Do you have more family here?"

Karl shook his head. "My father was killed in the war. My mother died of cholera... nursing my wife. She never recovered."

Alyssa reached across Harmony and put a hand on Karl's sleeve. "I never had family—relatives, I mean—but I imagine that must have been a very hard time for you."

"No more difficult than for you to lose your husband to pneumonia when Harmony was a baby," Karl pointed out.

Alyssa quickly withdrew her hand. "Oh. Harmony told you about that." The lies were always there to catch her. There were pitfalls everywhere. She had better be careful what subjects she discussed. Alyssa busied herself wiping Harmony's face and helping her up from the table. "We'll see you at the shop whenever you're able to come by, Mr. Eberhardt."

"Karl, please."

"What?"

Alyssa looked back at Karl over her shoulder. He could see that she was agitated. "Please call me Karl," he said.

"All right. Karl." She was practically running by the time she reached the back door.

Karl figured Alyssa Moreland must have loved her husband a great deal to still be so upset by the mere mention of him. But he could understand her sorrow. It had taken him a long time to recover from the sadness that had haunted him after his wife's death.

Actually, Alyssa wasn't thinking about her mythical husband. She was too busy explaining again to Harmony the importance of keeping their business private from strangers.

"But Karl isn't a stranger, Momma. He's our neighbor. And our friend."

Alyssa bit her lip to keep from retorting that they didn't know Karl Eberhardt from the bogeyman. Then she reminded herself that her purpose in coming to Fredericksburg was to make sure Harmony had a normal life. Which meant they had to become a part of the community. They would attend church every Sunday, and Harmony would go to school when it started in the fall. They would have friends and neighbors. Like Karl.

She unlocked her shop and ushered Harmony inside. As soon as Alyssa closed the door behind her, she knelt in front of her daughter so they were eye-to-eye. "You're right, sweetheart. I'm sure Karl is a friend you can trust."

"He's your friend, too, Momma."

Alyssa brushed the bangs out of Harmony's eyes. She couldn't allow her own fears to color her daughter's life. Not anymore. She had to take small steps toward the trust that had never been a part of her life in the past. "All right, sweetheart. Karl will be *our* friend."

Karl knocked once on the plate-glass window at the front of the store before stepping inside. A bell clanged over the door to announce his arrival. "Ready to go to work?"

Alyssa rose to her feet with a confident smile on her face. "Sure. I need to decide what I'd like you to do first." She looked around the open space. There was a long counter near one wall. "I'd like shelves on the wall behind that counter." She crossed the room. "And I'd like some cabinets over here, against this wall."

"How many shelves? How big do you want the cabinets?"

Alyssa frowned in concentration. She walked over to the wall behind the counter and reached as high as she could. "No higher than this."

Karl set down his toolbox and walked over to stand behind her.

Alyssa was conscious of being trapped between Karl's body and the wall. She could feel the heat of him along her back.

Karl pulled a pencil from behind his ear and reached up along the length of her arm to mark the distance she could reach. "That ought to do it." Karl was aware of the gentle fragrance of lavender in Alyssa's hair. He closed his eyes and breathed deeply.

"Karl."

Her voice was even softer than usual. When Karl's eyes opened, he realized he had her trapped. She was staring at him warily. He immediately stepped back to free her. "How long would you like the shelves to be?"

"Can you make them run the length of the counter?"

He took another step back, literally and figuratively. "Sure. I can do that."

Over the next several days, Karl and Alyssa were careful never to get too close to one another. However, he twice offered to take Alyssa out for supper, and was twice refused.

"You can see me right across the supper table at the boardinghouse," she had teased. "It would be silly for you to spend your money taking me out to a restaurant."

Karl didn't press the issue. He was afraid to tell her how he felt about her, for fear of scaring her away. It was a very real danger, because Alyssa was having feelings of her own that she didn't understand. Luckily, Harmony was always around to diffuse the tension between them.

Karl completed the shelves first. He was just putting up the brackets when Maxwell Bowen knocked on the glass-paneled front door and stepped inside. He ignored Karl as though the blacksmith weren't there. "Well, well, you certainly are making progress," he said to Alyssa.

"Karl is a wonder, isn't he?" Alyssa said.

Max grimaced. He brushed sawdust off the long counter. "A bit messy, if you ask me."

Karl's lips pressed flat. He and Max Bowen had crossed swords when Karl's wife died. There was no love lost between them.

"I came to ask if you could have lunch with me today," Max said.

"I wish I could," Alyssa replied, "but I'm awfully busy. Besides, I can't leave Harmony alone."

"Karl will be glad to watch the girl. Won't you, Karl?"

Karl turned glacial eyes on the banker. The muscles in his jaw worked. Then he glanced down at Harmony, who had an expectant look on her face. "I'd be pleased to keep an eye on Harmony. The two of us can eat our lunch together at Mrs. Cooperman's."

Alyssa was torn. She still needed to talk Max Bowen into giving her a loan. Maybe she would have better luck over the noon meal. "All right, Max. I'll come. Shall I meet you somewhere?"

"No need for that. I'll come here for you at noon."

When the banker was gone, Alyssa crossed to Karl. He refused to look at her. "I need a loan from the bank," she said. "Max Bowen can make sure I get it."

Karl angled his head over his shoulder and speared her with his glance. "You don't have to sell yourself for money."

Alyssa's face blanched. How on earth had Karl Eberhardt discovered that she had sold herself for money in the past? Harmony must have— Alyssa felt herself growing faint. A dark, swirling tunnel formed in front of her eyes.

Karl realized Alyssa was about to faint. He dropped his hammer and reached out to catch her. He picked her up in his arms and carried her over to the counter, where he laid her down.

"Momma! Momma!" Harmony cried.

"Your mother's going to be fine," Karl soothed the little girl. "She just got a little warm." He unscrewed the jar of iced tea he had brought with him and lifted Alyssa's head, trying to force some liquid between her pale lips. She gasped and choked, and her eyes fluttered open.

Alyssa couldn't figure out what she was doing lying on the counter in her store with Karl Eberhardt's arm around her shoulders. "What happened?"

"You fainted."

Alyssa put a hand to her head. "I never faint."

Karl smiled. "Then that was the best imitation I ever saw." His face sobered. "I'm sorry if what I said distressed you."

Alyssa looked confused.

"About selling yourself for money." Karl saw the panic in her eyes and spoke quickly to assuage her fear. "I only meant I've sold my soul to that devil myself.

"When my wife was alive, I promised to build her a house. I mortgaged my shop to get the money for the house. When my wife died, I didn't work for a long time. Max threatened to take back the house and the land it sits on to cover the note."

"Did he?" Alyssa asked.

Karl's face turned to granite. "I sold everything I had to make sure he didn't." Karl looked off into the street where the citizens of Fredericksburg were going about their daily business. "I couldn't let him have it." He turned and met Alyssa'a blue eyes. "I buried my wife on that land."

Alyssa tried to sit up, but Karl's hold was keeping her half prone. "I'd like to get up now."

"Are you sure you're all right?"

"I'm fine. It must have been the heat."

Karl helped her sit up, then crossed to open a window and let in some air. It wouldn't budge. "I guess I'd better stop long enough to fix this."

"I'll help, Karl," Harmony said.

"All right," Karl said. "You stand right here beside me and tell me when you can feel a breeze."

Alyssa watched the large man and the little girl standing side by side facing the window. She had never known a man like Karl. That is to say, a man who didn't think first of himself. She had never much respected men, always having seen them at their animalistic worst.

Alyssa knew each man was different. At least they had all been different in their sexual preferences. So she supposed they must be different in how they conducted their lives. It was already clear that Max Bowen and Karl Eberhardt weren't at all alike.

Alyssa's eyes settled on Karl. Muscles bulged in his arms as he forced the window up between the painted slats. Alyssa marveled at the size of him. At his strength. Of course, Max Bowen didn't need to be strong to count his money.

"I feel it!" Harmony crowed. "I feel the breeze!"

Karl bent down on one knee, and the two of them stayed beside the window long enough for the wind to ruffle their hair. "We need to get back to work, girl," Karl said.

"What shall we do next, Karl?" Harmony asked.

"I have to finish drilling holes for screws."

"Can I help, Karl?"

Alyssa realized that there was no way the little girl could help Karl drill the holes high in the wall. But she had underestimated the blacksmith's ingenuity.

"I'll tell you what I need you to do," Karl said. He sat Harmony down on the wooden-planked floor, out of the way, and set a large box of screws of mixed sizes in front of her. He took out a screw about two inches long and held it up for her. "I need you to find as many screws this size as you can."

Alyssa realized it was a job her daughter could do but something that was also truly necessary for the work Karl had to accomplish. When Karl passed her, she whispered, "That was a nice thing you did for Harmony."

"She's a nice little girl."

"And I appreciate you volunteering to keep her while I go to lunch with Max. I don't know what I can do to repay you for your kindness today."

There was a slight pause before Karl said, "You can go for a buggy ride with me on Sunday morning."

"What?"

Karl smiled. "I'd like you to see my house. The one I started building for my wife." *The one I'm going to finish for you.*

"I—I—" After all his kindness, how could she refuse him? But Alyssa's eyes flashed with annoyance at the way she had been trapped. "I'll be glad to go."

Karl chuckled. He could tell she wasn't a bit happy about going. All he wanted right now was time alone with her so they could get to know each other better.

"And I know Harmony will enjoy the ride," Alyssa finished.

Karl guffawed. The laugh came up all the way from his belly. It was the same trick she had pulled on Max Bowen, to avoid being alone with him. But Karl didn't mind. If Alyssa was going to be his wife, then Harmony was going to be his daughter. It was never too soon to start becoming a family. "Fine," he said. "We'll go early so we can be back in time for church."

Alyssa might have argued further, but they could both see through the front picture window that Max

Bowen was on his way back to pick her up for lunch. She took one look at herself and began frantically trying to brush off all the sawdust.

Karl stepped up to help her. He was careful not to touch her anywhere the cloth hugged her body, but even so, he was aware of the warmth of her flesh beneath the fabric. And he knew from the sudden tension in her body that she was equally aware of the intimacy of what he was doing. "I think we've gotten it all."

"How does my hair look?" Alyssa asked. "I wish I had a mirror up in here."

"I'll try to get to it this afternoon," Karl said. "And your hair looks lovely." He reached out to tuck an errant strand back into the cluster of curls at her temple, then rearranged a curl at her nape.

Alyssa felt a shiver skitter down her spine as Karl's callused fingertips accidentally brushed her skin. She stared up at him feeling like a doe caught in a hunter's sights. At that moment, the bell over the door clanged and Max entered.

"Are you ready, my dear?"

Karl gritted his teeth. Alyssa Moreland wasn't Max's *dear* and never would be.

"I'm ready, Max." Alyssa hugged Harmony and whispered, "Be good for Karl, sweetheart."

"I will, Momma."

Karl and Harmony had ham sandwiches with boiled eggs for lunch. Mrs. Cooperman agreed to keep an eye on Harmony while she took a nap after lunch and to bring her back over to the shop when she woke up.

Karl was working on the cabinets when Alyssa returned from her luncheon with Max. He watched Max walk her into the alley beside the store. Karl could see them from where he was working but didn't think he could be seen. His mouth flattened as Max grabbed Alyssa's hands and quickly kissed her on the mouth.

Karl jumped up, intending to interrupt them no matter how awful a scene he created. But a moment later Max had left and Alyssa was coming inside. He went back to work and didn't even look up when the bell clanged, just asked, "Did you get the loan?"

Alyssa released a sigh. "Yes."

Karl looked up and saw her rubbing her shoulders. "How much did it cost?"

"Do you mean how much collateral did he ask for?"

Karl nodded curtly.

"All my stock. My fabrics and my ready-made dresses."

"I suppose that's fair," Karl conceded. "After all, it isn't his own money he's loaning. How long did he give you to pay him back?"

"Six months."

Karl rose to his feet like a bear waking from a winter's slumber. "What? I don't think I heard you right."

Alyssa fought the urge to take a step backward. "He gave me six months to pay the bank back."

"How the hell are you going to earn enough selling dresses to pay back a loan like that?" Karl knew he was far angrier than he had a right to be. After all, she wasn't his wife yet. And it didn't matter to him whether her business succeeded. He would marry her even if she had nothing. But he hated the thought that Max Bowen had taken advantage of her. He damn sure wanted to say something about that kiss in the alley! But he didn't have the right.

He watched Alyssa's chin come up. She could be stubborn, no mistake about it.

"You have no way of knowing, of course, but I happen to be an excellent seamstress with an impeccable sense of style. My shop *will* be a success!"

Karl felt the tension ease out of his shoulders. Maybe Max Bowen had met his match. It pleased him to know his future wife wasn't afraid of that pompous ass. "I believe you. I'm glad you got your loan."

"I will pay it back in six months!" she insisted.

"I'm sure you will, *liebling.*"

Alyssa stared at him as he turned his back on her and continued what he was doing. For some reason, Karl's approval meant a great deal. When he'd called her *liebling* it had made her belly do a strange shift sideways. Alyssa put her hand on her stomach. There were so many new experiences. She felt . . . she didn't know what she felt.

Good, she decided at last. With Karl Eberhardt, she felt *good.*

When the day came that Karl began hammering the last of the cabinets into place, Harmony begged to be shown how it was done.

"Don't get in the way, Harmony," Alyssa chastised.

"She's not in the way," Karl said. He helped the little girl hold the hammer. "Steady strokes."

"Look at me, Momma!" Harmony shouted gleefully. "I'm building cabinets!"

Alyssa hadn't seen her daughter so happy in a long time. She thanked Karl with her eyes and was once again caught by a look that she found increasingly disturbing. She quickly turned away and began unloading fabrics onto the shelves Karl had built for her. She had nearly finished and was lifting a bolt of velvet over her head when she felt it being taken out of her hands.

"I'll get that." Karl placed the fabric on the top shelf. "I think maybe I got this an inch too high."

"It's fine. I can reach it if I get on my toes."

Alyssa demonstrated, lifting herself almost even with Karl. She felt his warm breath on the back of her neck and quickly lowered herself and stepped away. A look from beneath lowered lashes told her Karl had been as aware of the intimacy as she was. His cheeks were flushed, and his shoulders seemed tense. But his next words gave no hint of what had passed between them.

"I'll be finished today with everything I have to do in your shop," Karl said. "When do you think you'll be open for business?"

"Bright and early Monday morning," Alyssa replied.

"Then Sunday is liable to be the most carefree day you'll have for a long while." His voice was harsh, his body taut.

"I suppose it will be." Alyssa felt the hairs prickle on her arms as she realized that Karl was far more aroused than she had thought. He turned slightly away from her to hide his condition. But he would have needed blinders to hide the fire of need that burned in his eyes.

"I'll miss seeing you and Harmony during the day," Karl said in a voice too low to be overheard by the child pounding away with a hammer behind him.

"You can always come by and visit."

Karl smiled ruefully. "I'm not usually dressed for visiting during the day."

"I suppose not."

"What time shall we go tomorrow morning?" Karl asked.

"Not too early," Alyssa pleaded.

"How does eight o'clock sound?"

Too early. "Harmony and I will meet you downstairs at the boardinghouse for breakfast a little before eight."

"You'd better," he warned in a teasing voice, "or I'll knock on your door and roust you out of bed."

The thought of what that might be like suddenly occurred to both of them.

"I'd better get back to work," Karl said.

"Me, too," Alyssa said.

"Tomorrow," Karl promised.

"Tomorrow," she agreed.

Chapter Three

Alyssa stared at the one-story clapboard house nestled in a copse of pecan trees. It lacked a coat of paint, the glass windows were opaque with dirt, and it was overgrown with weeds, but it was the kind of house she had always imagined in her dreams. That is, when she had let herself dream. It even had a picket fence surrounding the front yard, though several of the slats were missing and the fence also lacked a coat of paint.

Karl sat beside her on the front seat of the buggy they had driven the two miles from town. She searched his face and asked, "Why aren't you living here?"

"Too many memories, I suppose. My wife and I planned this house together. She helped me build it. When she died . . ." He shrugged, his big shoulders bunching.

"Why didn't you sell it?"

He shook his head, and his lips curled upward on one side. "I can't explain that, either. I couldn't let go of this place, because it would have been like saying goodbye to Karin all over again."

"Karin was your wife?"

Karl nodded.

"May I look inside?" Alyssa asked.

"Sure. Come on." Karl stepped down from the buggy, then reached up to grasp Alyssa by the waist. He could feel her corset beneath the cambric dress she had worn. He almost dropped her when he realized that his body was responding in a blatantly sexual way to the woman in his arms.

Alyssa grabbed Karl's shoulders and found herself with two handfuls of rock-hard muscle. Karl slipped an arm around her waist, and they stood pressed together, breast to thigh. Alyssa lowered her lids to hide the desire that flared deep in her belly. She felt the flush in her chest that quickly skated up to her cheeks. "You can put me down now."

"I want down, too," Harmony said.

Karl welcomed the child's timely interruption. He quickly settled Alyssa on her feet, hoping against hope that she hadn't detected his arousal. Although how she could have missed it, the way they were pressed together, he didn't know.

He turned away from her, picked up Harmony and headed for the house. "Follow me and I'll show you the inside," he said gruffly

Alyssa laid her hands against her cheeks in a vain attempt to cool them. There was no mistaking Karl's reaction to their closeness. He had been polite enough to spare her feelings, but she knew for sure now that he was attracted to her—that way.

For a good man, that sort of attraction, if allowed to continue with a woman he believed his moral equal, would certainly lead to a proposal of marriage. Alyssa knew she could spare them both a great deal of pain if she made it clear to Karl now that they could never be more than friends. She hurried after him, wondering when and how she was going to get that message across.

To Alyssa's surprise, the front door wasn't locked. Another surprise came when she realized the house was furnished. "Why, you must have been nearly ready to move in," she observed.

"It needed a coat of paint," Karl said.

But that was all, Alyssa realized. There were pictures on the walls, doilies on the arms of the horsehair sofa, even a lovely quilt on the big four-poster bed. There was something else beside the bed that stopped Alyssa short.

"Look, Momma, there's a baby's cradle here," Harmony said.

"I see it, sweetheart."

What had happened to the baby? Alyssa wondered. She stared at the beautifully carved cradle, afraid to look Karl in the eye, afraid of what she would see.

"My wife was eight months pregnant when she died," Karl said at last.

Alyssa released a breath of air she hadn't realized she was holding. She didn't say a word, simply turned and put her arms around Karl's waist, laid her head against his chest and held him.

Karl fought the lump in his throat. Alyssa's offer of comfort threatened to unman him. He wasn't sure what to do with his hands. So he wrapped them around her.

Suddenly he realized where he was. In the bedroom where he had planned to sleep with his wife. Karl waited for the haunting memories to arise and force him from Alyssa Moreland's embrace. They didn't come. But before he could act on what had become an urgent need, Harmony tugged on her mother's skirt to get her attention.

"There's a bed in the next room, just the right size for me," she said excitedly. "Come see, Momma."

Harmony grabbed one of Alyssa's hands and started dragging her mother toward the next room. Alyssa turned to Karl and held out her hand to him. He grasped her hand and allowed Harmony to lead them both to the room that had been intended for his unborn child.

Harmony let go of her mother's hand and bounced up and down on the small bed. "See? It's really soft, Momma." She jumped up from the bed and ran to a wooden box along the wall. She shoved it open, and her face broke out in a huge smile. "Toys! Lots and lots of toys! Can I play with them, Karl?"

"Sweetheart, I don't think Karl—"

"Sure you can play with them," Karl said, interrupting her. "Why not?"

Alyssa walked close enough to Karl that she could speak without being heard by her daughter. "Are you sure you don't mind?"

"Someone might as well enjoy them," Karl said.

Harmony was busy dragging out a series of carved wooden toys. A train. A puppet on a stick. A horse and rider. "Look, Momma!" Harmony pulled out a cloth doll with blue button eyes and blond yarn hair.

In an amazed and somewhat reverent voice she said, "It looks just like me!"

"So it does," Alyssa said with a smile.

She jumped up and ran to Karl with the doll clutched to her chest. "Can I have it, Karl? For my very own?"

Karl slipped down on one knee so the two of them would be on the same level. "Will you promise to take good care of her?"

"Oh, yes!" Harmony promised. "What's her name, Karl?"

"She doesn't have a name," Karl said. "You'll have to name her yourself."

Harmony glanced up at her mother and then back at Karl. "Then I'm going to name her Marjorie Rose. After my best friend in Philadelphia."

"Marjorie Rose sounds like a lovely name," Karl said.

Harmony hurried to her mother and held up the doll for her approval. "Isn't she pretty, Momma?"

Alyssa brushed Harmony's bangs out of her eyes. "She does look a lot like a certain little girl I know."

Harmony jerked away from her mother's fussing and headed back toward the box.

"Do you think Harmony will be all right here if we go look at the rest of the house?" Karl asked.

Alyssa turned to him and smiled. "I think we're going to have trouble dragging her away from here when it's time to leave."

This time Karl held out his hand, and Alyssa realized the door she had opened when she had offered the widower comfort. She could keep her hands at her sides and send a message loud and clear. She glanced up at Karl from under lowered lashes and saw the appeal in his eyes. Somehow Alyssa had never learned to be hard enough to reject such an appeal. She reached out and felt her fingers enfolded by his.

His hand was big and warm, and she felt a sense of security that would have surprised her if anyone had suggested such a thing to her mere days ago.

Karl led her into the kitchen. "Karin helped me plan this room."

"How long were you married?" Alyssa asked.

"Six years. Karin was so excited when she finally got pregnant. She—" Karl cut himself off. Some memories were still too painful to be explored.

There was an awkward silence. Neither of them knew what to say. Alyssa resorted to the mundane.

"I see you have an indoor pump. Does it work?"

"It would if it were primed," Karl assured her.

"Did you make the sideboard?" Alyssa ran her fingers over it, admiring the fine workmanship.

"My father did. He made it for my mother. She gave it to Karin and me as a wedding gift."

"Your father was very good at what he did."

"He taught me everything I know about working with wood."

"You made all the toys!" Alyssa realized.

Karl nodded. "Except the doll. Karin made the doll."

Alyssa turned away from the stark look in his eyes and lifted the lids on the stove. "This looks brand-new."

"It is. We never got a chance to light it."

Alyssa whirled and confronted him. "How can you stand to come here? It must be awful—"

Karl put his fingertips against her lips. "When I'm here with you this house feels alive again."

"But your wife—"

"Wished only happiness for me." Karl's big hand slid around to caress Alyssa's nape. He drew her toward him, giving her time to refuse him, if that was her choice. When their mouths were a breath apart, he was the one who hesitated.

Despite all the dinners he had eaten in the homes of lovely widows and daughters, he had not kissed a woman since his wife's death. He had taken advantage of the charms of ladies who sold themselves when he had traveled to San Antonio on business. But he had not kissed them. He had eased his body and found the physical release he needed. But a kiss . . . a kiss fed the soul.

Karl lowered his head and touched his lips to hers.

Alyssa's mouth was soft and tasted of strawberries. Suddenly she was in his arms, and he was kissing her the way he wanted to. His need was urgent, and he let her know with his mouth and his body how much he wanted her, needed her. His tongue teased along the crease of her lips, and when she gasped he slid it inside to taste her.

Alyssa was overwhelmed by feelings that were new and strange. Never had desire come so fast, or been so sharp. She felt herself pressing up against Karl. She rubbed the aching tips of her breasts against his chest and arched her hips up into his. The reactions were instinctive, she must have done them a hundred, hundred times. But the *feelings* were so different with Karl!

She wanted him with a hunger she hadn't imagined possible in a woman. She was ravenous, starving for his touch. She opened her mouth against his and deepened the kiss, sending her tongue searching in his mouth. She found the edges of his teeth and felt him quiver as her tongue slid along the soft underside of his lip.

Her body undulated against his. Karl groaned and lifted her enough to accommodate the difference in their heights. She felt the hard length of him against her belly, as she had with hundreds—thousands?—of other men. Only there was one great, astonishing difference with Karl.

With Karl, the kissing and touching was not a duty. With Karl, it was not necessary to follow through to the culmination of the act in order to earn a generous stipend. With Karl it was purely a matter of wanting and needing him. She felt whole and wholesome and wonderful.

But you can never marry Karl.

The thought came unbidden, and with it the knowledge that letting this go any further was *wrong*.

Alyssa shoved suddenly against Karl's shoulders and jerked her mouth from his. "Karl! No! Stop!"

Karl was ripped from a pleasure greater than any he had ever experienced with a woman. How had she learned to kiss like that, with her tongue driving him wild? How had she known to rock her body against his in just such a way? How had she known to thread her fingers into his hair and tease his nape with her fingernails, driving him to a frenzy of need?

He stared with glazed eyes at the woman in his arms. He wasn't ready to stop. He wanted to carry the act to fruition. One look at her face told him that whatever glory he had found in their touch, she no longer shared. Her face was a pale, almost ghostly white. Her eyes had darkened, and he could see pain and despair and a fervent desire to escape.

Suddenly he was angry. He couldn't have mistaken her desire. She had wanted him as badly as he had wanted her. He was sure of it. So what had caused her to draw back? What was causing her to shrink from him now?

Alyssa's gaze slid from Karl's face to the place where his arms gripped her shoulders, then back up to his face. She might as well have spoken the words. Karl heard them loud and clear.

Get your hands off me.

He abruptly let her go and stepped back. She stared at the fabric on her left shoulder where his hand had been, and he suddenly knew what had caused her to draw back. It made him furious. "Don't worry," he snarled. "I haven't left any soot on your clothes."

She lifted stricken eyes, and he felt sure then that he had been right. He swallowed over the bitter lump in his throat and said, "I won't apologize for the fact I don't wear a fancy suit to work in, with a white collar and cuffs and a string tie." He held out his massive hands in front of her. "These hands do honest labor. If that's not good enough for you, then be damned to you!"

He was halfway out of the kitchen by the time Alyssa caught up to him. She grabbed him by the sleeve, but he was so big she might have been a gnat he was brushing aside as he stormed from the room.

"Karl, wait!" she cried. "It isn't that! I swear it isn't!"

He turned fierce gray eyes on her. "I've seen you with the banker, Alyssa. You didn't turn him away."

Alyssa's startled eyes went wide. "What?"

"I saw you kiss Max Bowen in the alley outside your shop."

"But I didn't kiss Max! He kissed me!"

"You could have fooled me," Karl ranted. "What am I supposed to think, when you let him kiss you but I'm to keep my distance? That I'm not good enough to touch the sleeve of your garment? That I might get it dirty?"

"Karl, please, listen. It's not like that at all."

"What is it like? Explain it to me please, because I don't understand what's going on here."

Alyssa blinked to clear the blur of tears from her eyes. She gritted her teeth in an attempt to stop her chin from quivering. How could she tell him the truth? *How could she not?* Karl deserved an explanation. It wasn't at all true that he wasn't good enough for her. *She wasn't good enough for him!*

Did she dare tell him the truth? Could she trust him with her deepest, darkest secret? There was no question in her mind that he would despise her if he knew what she had done for a living. He would never look at her again with longing in his eyes—at least not with the kind of look a man gave to a woman he wanted for more than the few moments it took to slake his passion.

"It isn't you, Karl. It's me."

Karl's eyes were still wary, but some of the belligerence left them. "I'm listening."

Alyssa's voice was quieter than Karl could remember it ever having been, and he leaned closer to hear her. "Just now, I wanted you. I wanted to go to bed with you," she said baldly.

Karl was stunned. "What? Then why—?"

"That's never happened to me before," she rushed on to say. "That kind of desire, that kind of need." She looked up into his eyes, begging him to understand. "It frightened me, Karl. We hardly know each other. I mean, you don't know me." *You have no idea who I am, what I am.*

"I know I desire you," Karl said. "And if that desire is mutual, I don't understand the problem."

"The problem," Alyssa said in a sharp voice, "is that I can't marry you!"

Karl was stung into retorting, "I haven't asked you yet!" He blushed a fiery red as he realized what he had said. Hadn't asked her *yet*. Which was as good as an admission that he certainly intended to!

Alyssa saw Karl through a veil of tears she couldn't blink away. Here was a good man, a man who deserved an equally good woman. She couldn't let him buy secondhand goods, even if he thought he was getting a bargain. Her hand tightened on his sleeve, and she felt the bunching muscles as he reacted to her touch.

"I've come to Fredericksburg to start a new life for myself and my daughter. There are things you don't know about me—bad things—that I've left behind me."

"It was your husband, wasn't it, who made you leery of marriage? Did he beat you? Was he cruel to you?" He held his hands out again, turned them over and looked at the strength in them. "I can bend horseshoes with these big paws," he said. "But I would never lift my hand to hurt a hair on your head," Karl promised earnestly.

Alyssa shook her head. "Oh, Karl..." One of the tears escaped at last and slid down her cheek.

Karl couldn't bear to see her crying. He scooped her into his arms and cradled her there, rocking her as if she were a small child.

In the comfort of his arms, Alyssa gave vent to the tears she had never shed, tears for a life that had been far more savage and cruel than a good man like Karl Eberhardt could ever imagine. He thought her husband had beat her! He thought she might be afraid of his strength!

Well, she had been hit once or twice before a rowdy customer was ejected. But the truth was, the only brutal beatings she had endured were the constant attacks upon the fragile young woman who hid inside Alyssa's body, determined to survive as her flesh was pounded by sweat-slick, panting customers. Alyssa had learned well the lesson her mother had taught her as a child. She had never let herself feel anything— anything—when she was with a client.

Which was why she had become so frightened when Karl had kissed her. With Karl, she couldn't stop the flood of feelings that surged through her, body and soul. She might have attributed these new feelings to the fact she was in a strange new place, starting a brand-new life. But when Max Bowen kissed her, she had felt nothing. So it had to be something special about Karl himself. Something in him that called to something in her.

Alyssa opened her mouth to tell Karl the truth, but shut it again. She didn't want to lose Karl as a friend. To be perfectly honest, she didn't want to lose him as a lover, either. Why couldn't she have that, at least? She didn't have to ruin his life by marrying him. But there was no reason why she couldn't let him court her. That sort of courtship might go on for years, mightn't it?

Only she wasn't sure he would still want to spend time with her after everything that had happened today.

"All right, Karl," she began, her heart in her throat. "You may court me, if you wish. But I want you to understand that I'm not promising I'll marry you."

She held her breath, waiting for his response. She felt it when his arms closed more tightly around her.

"I won't rush you," he promised. "I'll give you time. And you'll see that I haven't lied. You don't need to fear me, or any man, ever again."

Alyssa could have wept, his words were so tender. Karl was so certain he could keep the devils from her doorstop. Oh, how she wished she could lay the burden of her past on his great shoulders and know they could bear it. Karl was very strong, but that was a weight too great for any man to carry.

Karl stepped back far enough that they could look each other in the eye. Alyssa managed a smile for him.

"Let's start over, shall we?" Karl said. "Hello. I'm Karl Eberhardt, the blacksmith. What's your name?"

"I'm Alyssa Moreland, Mr. Eberhardt."

"Karl, please."

Her smile broadened and became more natural, revealing the dimples that Karl liked so well. "Karl, please . . . kiss me," she whispered.

Never had Karl been so aware of his great size, his great strength, as he forced himself to gentleness with the woman in his arms. His lips sought hers tenderly, and he gloried in the taste of her berry red lips. But the passion that flared between them would not be denied. His mouth became more urgent.

Alyssa met his passion and demanded more. The feelings were so new, so exquisite, so exciting. It was as if she were a young girl again, fresh and innocent. And she was, for Karl. She clutched fistfuls of his shirt, striving to be closer to him.

This time it was Karl who put a halt to things. He pulled back his head and stared down at the woman in his arms. Her blue eyes sparkled, her lips glistened from the kisses they had shared, her cheeks were rosy with heat from the passion that flared between them. His body was hard as a rock and aching with need. But he had promised her that he would give her time. Alyssa trusted him to keep a leash on his passions, and he was determined not to frighten her again.

"Maybe it's time we headed back to town," he said.

Alyssa wanted to protest, but she realized the wisdom of Karl's suggestion. "Maybe we should," she agreed. "I'll go get Harmony."

Karl took her hand in his. "*We'll* go get Harmony."

"All right, Karl."

When they arrived at the bedroom door, they discovered complete chaos. It looked as though Harmony had played with every single toy in the box, on every single inch of the floor.

"My goodness, it looks like a tornado's whipped through here!" Alyssa exclaimed. She pulled herself free from Karl and began to collect toys and return them to the box. "I'm sorry, Karl."

"For what?"

"That she made such a mess."

Karl surveyed the room. It looked a lot like his own room when he was a child. It looked lived in. Like a home. Like his home.

Harmony tugged on Karl's trousers, and he reached down and lifted her and Marjorie Rose, whom she held clutched in a tight embrace, into his arms.

"Can I come back and play again, Karl?"

"Sure you can. But we'd better help your mother put everything away so we'll know where to find it next time." He bent down on one knee to set her down and began handing her toys, which she trotted over and dropped in the toy box.

When everything had been picked up and the room was neat, Karl turned to Alyssa and said, "I think maybe I'll give this place a coat of paint on the outside. What color would you like?''

Alyssa laughed nervously. "What would *I* like? It's your house, Karl. You should paint it whatever color *you* like."

"I like white," Harmony volunteered. "With red shutters."

"How does that sound to you, Alyssa?" Karl asked.

It sounded beautiful. "I think that would be lovely. White with red shutters. And a white picket fence out front."

Karl grinned. "How would you two like to come help me paint?"

"Really, Karl?" Harmony was jumping up and down in excitement. "Could we help you paint?"

"How about it, Alyssa?"

Alyssa already felt an affinity for the house. Helping Karl paint it was only going to make her wish even more for what she could never have. But it was a way to spend time with Karl that could be easily explained without admitting to everyone in town that he was courting her. "We'll be glad to help, Karl," Alyssa said. "When do you want to start?"

"Tomorrow. We can work early each morning, before the heat of the day. Then you can go on to your shop and I can go to work at mine. If that's all right with you?"

Alyssa's nose wrinkled. It meant getting up at the crack of dawn every day. How many dawns had she missed because she had worked into the middle of the night? Well, this was a new life. She might as well start seeing the sun rise. At least now she looked forward to each day, instead of dreading it.

She grinned and laughed. "All right, Karl. You've got yourself two painting partners."

If Alyssa thought the town would find nothing unusual about Karl Eberhardt finally painting his house white with red shutters—the house that had remained untouched and uninhabited for two years, while Karl mourned the tragic death of his wife and unborn child—then she was sadly mistaken.

Chapter Four

Alyssa surveyed her domain and was pleased with what she saw. There were mannequins in the window dressed in samples of the fashions she had for sale. The shop looked bright and airy. Bolts of silk, satin and velvet were arranged so they could easily be fingered by ladies desirous of buying. There were wooden cubicles on top of the cabinets Karl had built for her that held a variety of buttons and rolls of lace and ribbon to choose from. Alyssa's shop was full of women chattering to each other about fashions and babies and the latest gossip. The fact that some of their gossip concerned the proprietor of the very shop they were patronizing only made it that much better.

It had been a month since Karl Eberhardt painted his house white with red shutters. By now Alyssa knew the rumors that ran rampant about her relationship with the blacksmith. Because she had spent her life in a community of women, she understood, perhaps better than the women who talked about her, the nature of their curiosity.

"How do you think this brown velvet would look made up in that polonaise style you showed me in the latest *Harper's Bazar?*" Julie Andersen asked Alyssa. "Do you think Hank would like it?"

Alyssa smiled at the butcher's wife. Julie was newly married and still had the soft glow of love in her eyes. "I think he would love it—if you wore it in this peach silk."

"Peach? Silk?" Julie asked, eyeing the fabric doubtfully.

Alyssa laid a length of the fabric across Julie's shoulder and turned the young woman to face the full-length oval mirror standing in the corner. Alyssa draped the silk across Julie's bodice in a graceful swag and said, "The lighter color complements your dark hair, and the silk will wear better until the baby comes."

Julie flushed. "Does it show already?"

Alyssa hugged her new friend. "I measure ladies for a living. How could I not notice your waist growing larger? How does Hank feel about the baby?"

Julie chewed on her lower lip, looking like the eighteen-year-old bride she was. "He's worried what people will say when the baby comes early. I mean, we've been married such a short while, there's bound to be talk."

"If it's a healthy baby they'll slap Hank on the back and tell him what a lucky man he is," Alyssa said.

Julie's very young brow furrowed, and she let Alyssa see the worry in her dark brown eyes. "It just happened, you know. We didn't mean to let things go so far. But when Hank kissed me, when he touched me . . . it seemed so right. You don't despise me now that you know the truth, do you?"

Alyssa cupped Julie's chin in her hand, much as she might have done with her own child. "I think you and Hank are very lucky to be so much in love with each other. And I hope you'll let me hold a baby shower for you after the announcement is made."

"You're such a good friend! Of course I'll let you hold a party. I just hope people will come."

"Anyone who doesn't show up won't be allowed to shop here again," Alyssa said in a fierce voice.

Julie laughed. "Then I can be sure they'll all be there. Your shop is *the* place to find fashions in Fredericksburg."

Alyssa laughed. "I just hope it stays that way." She began refolding the fabric sample. "Shall I make up that dress in peach silk?"

"Yes, please. Just remember to add a few more gathers here and there so I can grow into it," Julie whispered.

When Alyssa had written down all the information she needed for Julie's new dress, she looked around to see who else might need her assistance. She saw two older women—Fredericksburg's reigning matriarchs—whispering together near the front window.

Alyssa approached them and asked, "May I help you, Mrs. Bowen, Mrs. Schmidt?"

Max's mother gave Alyssa a sharp look. "I want something special to wear to the Fourth of July picnic. Something elegant, but comfortable. What do you suggest?"

Alyssa pulled out her latest *Godey's Lady's Book.* "I think we might find something here you would like."

Mrs. Schmidt, whose husband owned the mercantile next door, pointed to a gown that was so full of bows it would have been laughable on someone of Mrs. Bowen's stout stature. "There it is, Louisa. That's the one."

"It is awfully pretty, Hazel," Mrs. Bowen agreed.

Alyssa hid a grimace behind her hand. The most difficult part of her business—and what made her such a success—was diplomacy. She ensured that the ladies who came into her shop didn't leave wearing fashions that didn't flatter their many and varied figures. The trick was talking them out of what they wanted and into what looked good on them.

Alyssa shook her head and clucked her tongue. "I was afraid you would choose that dress."

"Why, what's wrong with it?" Mrs. Bowen demanded, her elbows spreading like a hen with ruffled feathers.

"Nothing's wrong with it," Alyssa said. "Only, that was the dress worn by Madame...uh...Tattershell on the stage in New York last season. Her entire act, I understand, consisted of untying each one of those bows."

"Well. That would never do for me. Never do at all!" Mrs. Bowen assured Alyssa.

Alyssa was quick to offer an alternative. "Now, this dress, this would be comfortable and make a statement, as well."

"What statement?" Mrs. Bowen asked.

Alyssa said, with a perfectly straight face, "Why the statement that here is a lady of supreme good sense, a lady of consequence."

Mrs. Schmidt sniffed. "It looks awfully plain to me."

"This picture doesn't show the modifications I will make especially for Mrs. Bowen."

"Modifications?"

Alyssa nodded. "Every dress from this shop is unique. The only one of its kind. I may start with a fashion plate, but I take the personality of the lady into consideration when constructing the garment. For Mrs. Bowen, I must add...ribbon." Alyssa tapped her chin as she stalked in a circle around the rotund lady. "Only as trim, of course. And only at the neck and the hem. Yes, a camel silk with brown silk ribbon. What do you think?"

Mrs. Bowen's chin came up imperiously. "I told you, Hazel, the woman is a genius. I don't care what she's doing in her free time with Karl Eberhardt. We simply must come here for our—"

Mrs. Schmidt saw the darkening thunderclouds on Alyssa's face and interrupted the other woman to say, "Of course Louisa isn't suggesting that any-thing...untoward...is happening between you and Mr. Eberhardt. The blacksmith is a well-respected man in town, and a good, hard worker. But you must admit, Mrs. Moreland, that you have been spending an awful lot of time with a man who is not your so-cial equal."

Alyssa's jaw dropped. "Not my equal?"

"The man shoes horses, for heaven's sake," Mrs. Schmidt said disdainfully. "He's always covered with a layer of soot from head to toe." As a final insult

Mrs. Schmidt added confidentially, "Most of the time he isn't even wearing a shirt!"

"I know my son doesn't understand your apparent attraction to such a boorish man," Mrs. Bowen said.

"Boorish?" Alyssa gasped.

Mrs. Bowen and Mrs. Schmidt exchanged glances, then looked back at Alyssa's rapidly reddening face.

"We only meant to say that you could have your pick of men in this town for a husband," Mrs. Bowen said. "And a lady of your obviously impeccable background ought to—"

Mrs. Bowen was interrupted by Alyssa's hysterical laughter. "Oh, Mrs. Bowen! Oh! Oh!" She was laughing too hard to speak. It was too much! *She* had an obviously impeccable background, and *Karl* was not her social equal. If only they knew! If only they knew!

"Mrs. Bowen, Mrs. Schmidt," Alyssa said, tears squeezing from her eyes, she was laughing so hard, "you should know I think Karl Eberhardt is a wonderful, charming man. I am proud to call him my friend. And I would count myself even more fortunate if he were my husband."

"Do you mean that?"

Alyssa whirled. "Karl." Suddenly she didn't feel the least bit like laughing anymore.

Karl bowed slightly to the two matrons. "Ladies. I hope I'm not interrupting anything."

"Stay right where you are!" Mrs. Bowen ordered. "Otherwise you're going to get soot all over everything."

"Come in, Karl," Alyssa said in a firm voice.

Karl stepped inside and shot a grin at the two older women.

"Well!" Mrs. Bowen said.

"I never!" Mrs. Schmidt said.

Alyssa put a hand on Mrs. Bowen's shoulder and began ushering her out of the shop. "I'll have that dress ready for you in three days," she promised.

Where Mrs. Bowen led, Mrs. Schmidt followed. Moments later the two of them had exited, double chins held high.

Alyssa turned to face Karl, her hands on her hips. "Don't move. You'll get soot all over everything."

Karl grinned. "I didn't come to touch, I came to talk."

"I'm listening."

Karl's voice softened. "Did you mean what you just said?"

"What?"

"That you'd count yourself fortunate if I were your husband."

Alyssa flushed to the roots of her hair. "I was squashing pretensions when I said that."

Karl shook his head and *tsk*ed. "Then I suppose it's too soon to propose."

Alyssa's eyes narrowed. "Karl..."

He held up both hands, palms outward. The creases were lined with soot. Soot or no soot, Alyssa wanted those large, gentle hands all over her, caressing her. She forced herself to concentrate on what Karl was saying.

"—so I was wondering if you were planning to enter a picnic basket in the Fourth of July auction."

"I must have missed something. You want me to enter a basket of something in what auction?"

"Pay attention, *liebling*. The town fathers want to buy new desks for the school, and they've come up with the idea of auctioning baskets of food—and the company of the lady who prepared it—at the Fourth of July picnic."

"I never heard of anything so barbaric!" Alyssa protested.

Karl grinned. "It's a time-honored custom in the West. So what do you say? Will you enter a basket? It's practically your civic duty."

"I suppose you plan to bid on it."

"Of course."

"You know I'm a terrible cook," Alyssa said, a teasing smile on her face. "What do you suggest I make?"

"Sandwiches," Karl said promptly. "Sliced ham and cheese on some of Mrs. Cooperman's fresh brown bread. Boiled eggs. Pickles. German potato salad. I can manage to wash all that down with a few mugs of beer."

"All right," Alyssa conceded at last. "But only because it's my civic duty."

Karl started to reach for her, and she backed out of his way. She held a hand out to keep him at a distance. "You know they're already talking about us, Karl. About how much time we spend together. If you bid on my basket, it's going to give them even more ideas about our relationship."

Alyssa swallowed and continued, "And you know they'd be wrong, Karl." She searched his face, which had become remote. "Because I haven't made any kind of commitment to you."

"That might be argued."

"I haven't!" Alyssa insisted. *Because I can't!*

"You've allowed me to court you," Karl said in a harsh voice. "What are people supposed to think? What am I supposed to think?"

"That we're good friends."

"Friends, hell! I want you for my wife, Alyssa. I just heard you tell two of the town's matriarchs—and worst gossips—that you'd consider yourself lucky to be my wife! Don't think I'm going to let you back away from me, Alyssa. I don't know what secrets in your past are keeping us apart, but I've had about enough of wondering. Don't you think it's about time you told me the truth?"

Alyssa stared at Karl with stricken eyes. She should tell him now. Now. *Tell him now!* "I can't!" she cried. "I can't tell you, Karl. You'll hate me! You'll never want to see me again!"

Karl forgot about the soot, forgot about everything except comforting the woman he loved. He reached out and pulled her into his arms. "*Liebling,* dearling, you don't have to tell me. I don't care! I swear I don't! Just please don't push me away. I love you. I want to marry you."

"I can't marry you, Karl."

She wasn't hysterical when she said it, and that frightened Karl more than he would have cared to have her know. He put his hands on her shoulders and stood back from her, noticing with chagrin that he had left two sooty spots on her dress. He was going to have to get into the habit of washing every time he crossed the threshold of his shop. Especially if he planned to keep embracing Alyssa on the spur of the moment. Which he did.

"All right," he said. "I won't say anything more about marriage right now. But will you please enter a basket in the auction?"

Alyssa managed a small smile. "Yes, Karl. I can do that."

As the day of the picnic approached, Alyssa began to regret more and more her agreement to put her basket in the auction. Mrs. Bowen and Mrs. Schmidt had spread her foolish words about marriage to Karl far and wide. She was met with speculative looks wherever she went. There was no malice in the grins and whispers behind cupped hands, though there were many whose raised brows revealed that they wondered what a lady like Mrs. Moreland saw in a workingman like Karl Eberhardt.

She felt guilty for deceiving them all. But not guilty enough to tell them the truth. Because she had what she had come to Texas for. Her business was burgeoning. Most of the time, when she didn't think of Karl, she was happy. More importantly, Harmony was happy. Her daughter was thriving in the small-town atmosphere.

They attended church regularly, and Alyssa had the satisfaction of knowing her daughter was being raised to understand that there was a supreme being who wished all men to be brothers. Harmony was learning that He had made laws that must be obeyed for the good of all.

Alyssa was all too aware of how many of those laws she had broken. But she had found a peace and forgiveness in church that she hadn't imagined possible. Unfortunately, Alyssa didn't have the same confidence in Karl's ability to forgive and forget. Which was the same as saying she didn't trust Karl's love to be sufficient to deal with the huge secret she was keeping from him.

There was no getting around the fact that she had been enormously selfish where Karl was concerned. She had thought only of what she wanted from him, and not of what the consequences would be to him when he learned the truth.

Karl was going to be angry. And he was going to be hurt.

Nevertheless, Alyssa had decided to tell Karl the truth. She wasn't sure when the decision had been made. Perhaps that day when he had come into her shop covered with soot and grinned at Mrs. Bowen and Mrs. Schmidt. She had known then and there that she loved him with all her heart and soul and mind. Because she loved him, she had to tell him who—and what—she really was.

But not before she had made love with him.

Alyssa wanted to love Karl, and be loved by him, just once before he knew the truth. Because no matter how much he protested that it didn't matter, Alyssa knew it would. When she told Karl the truth, she would lose him.

Alyssa wouldn't have believed she could be so calculating. But she wanted the memory of one precious afternoon to savor for the rest of her life. She had never meant to love Karl, and she would never let herself be so foolish again. So it was now or never.

Alyssa had it all planned. Julie Andersen might not know how to prevent a pregnancy, but Alyssa did. She had learned from bitter experience the secrets of condoms and sponges and vinegar. She would make sure there was no child to suffer the consequences of their lovemaking.

Alyssa knew she was being unwise. Hundreds of times she had lain with a man above her. Lying with Karl could be no different from lying with all those others. He was just a man, nothing more.

But she wondered. His kisses had made her feel . . . things she had never felt before. And her emotions had never been engaged when she had lain beneath all those men in the brothel. She wasn't sure what she thought might happen with Karl, but deep inside her was a need she hadn't even known existed before she met him. A need to join herself with this one particular man, to merge both body and soul.

Alyssa was nervous as she sat beside Karl in the buggy as they rode to the Fourth of July picnic. She was dressed especially for the occasion in a soft pink cotton dress meant to entice the man she loved into making love to her. She had left her hair down, tied only with a pink ribbon at her nape. It would take no effort at all for Karl to release the ribbon and run his hands through her hair.

The dress had a square neck, cut just low enough to reveal the soft swells of her breasts, and short puffy sleeves that left her arms bare. It was fitted through the bodice, with large white buttons down the front, which could easily be undone even by Karl's big hands. The skirt had a swag meant to lead a man's eye down the length of her.

If the tension in Karl's big body during the short ride from town was any indication, the dress was a roaring success. In fact, with all the sexual sparks flying, it was a wonder Harmony, who was sitting between them, hadn't gotten singed.

When they arrived at the shady spot along the Pedernales River where the picnic was being held, Karl stepped down and lifted Harmony to the ground.

Since Alyssa would be having her picnic lunch with the gentleman who purchased her basket, she had arranged with Mrs. Cooperman to keep an eye on her daughter. "You be sure and look for Mrs. Cooperman," Alyssa said.

"I will, Momma." Harmony was gone an instant later, swallowed up in the nearby swarm of children playing a game of tag.

Alyssa started to get down on her own, but Karl stopped her. "Wait. Let me help you."

Alyssa saw the moment when Karl realized she wasn't wearing a corset under her dress, the moment when he realized that he could feel flesh beneath the single layer of cotton. His eyes darkened, and his nostrils flared.

Alyssa noticed the signs of passion and felt an answering curl of desire in her belly.

Karl couldn't resist the siren's lure. He leaned down far enough to kiss Alyssa's mouth. "You look beautiful, *liebling.*"

"Thank you, Karl." Her voice was hoarse as she tried to speak past a throat swollen with feeling.

"Hello, there."

Karl and Alyssa both turned, startled to discover they were no longer alone. Julie and Hank Andersen stood there, hand in hand.

"Do you mind if we join you?"

Alyssa's heart fell to her feet. She exchanged a glance with Karl. He didn't want to spend time with anyone else any more than she did. But Alyssa was reluctant to refuse. She couldn't tell Julie the truth, and she didn't want to make up an excuse that would hurt the young woman's feelings.

Alyssa smiled brightly. "We'd love to join you. Wouldn't we, Karl?"

Alyssa knew why she loved Karl when he smiled equally broadly and said, "As long as you trust a bachelor around that pretty wife of yours, Hank."

Hank's shoulders visibly squared with pride as he put an arm around his suddenly bashful wife's shoulders. "She is something to look at, isn't she?"

"Prettier than a newborn chestnut filly," Karl agreed.

They were several steps from the buggy when Alyssa remembered the basket she had brought. She had tied a pink ribbon that matched the one in her hair to the handle of the basket so Karl would know which one to bid on. She left him and raced back to the buggy, but Karl was right there with her, lifting it for her. He slipped it onto his arm, ignoring her protests that the other men would laugh at him if they saw him carrying a frilly basket.

"Hank is carrying Julie's basket. I'd be embarrassed not to do the same."

That silenced Alyssa's protest. She slipped her arm through Karl's, and they walked together with the other couple to the table where all the baskets were being collected.

Louisa Bowen and Hazel Schmidt were supervising things. A table had been created from wooden planks and sawhorses in the shade of an ancient live oak dripping with moss. The sounds of the Pedernales River slipping lazily by could be heard in the distance, along with children's shrieks of laughter.

"You're looking very well today, Mrs. Bowen," Karl said as he set the basket on the table.

Mrs. Bowen primped in the quite becoming dress Alyssa had created for her. "Why, thank you, Mr. Eberhardt. I don't suppose I need to ask which basket you'll be bidding on," she added with a sly smile.

Alyssa felt Karl's body tense under her hand, but his smile never wavered. "No, ma'am, you don't."

Once Julie had dropped off her basket, the two couples wandered off to mingle with others who were there to enjoy the fun. There was a speech by the mayor reminding everyone why the holiday was being celebrated, followed by sack races, a three-legged race and an egg toss—all enjoyed as much by the adults as by the children.

Alyssa didn't know when she had laughed so much or had so much fun. She was enjoying Julie and Hank's company a great deal. They were fun to be with because they were having fun together, just as she was enjoying the morning of games with Karl. But there was an edge to everything she said and did, because she knew about, and feared that Karl suspected, the seduction she had planned for the afternoon.

The auction was conducted by Rudy Schmidt, who surprised Alyssa by having a sense of humor. He wasn't a tall man, so he stood on a stump not far from the table with the baskets. He found something to say about each couple who ended up together that elicited raucous—but decidedly friendly—laughter from the crowd.

About midway through the auction, Rudy Schmidt picked up Alyssa's basket and held it high so the crowd could see it.

"What am I bid for this basket with the pretty pink bow? Who would like to start? *One dollar one dollar one dollar I have one dollar do I have two dollars two do I have three three dollars three dollars do I have—*"

"Ten dollars."

Karl's bid drew a gasp from the crowd, who suddenly seemed to realize which two men were bidding on Mrs. Moreland's basket.

"Fifteen dollars," Max Bowen countered.

Rudy Schmidt realized the bidding didn't need prompting from him, so he remained silent.

Karl and Max were both tall men. Their heads rose above the crowd, so everyone could see the smile on Max's face and the frown on Karl's.

There was a long enough pause that Rudy Schmidt said, "I have fifteen. Do I have another bid?"

Alyssa's heart was beating frantically. She felt like a butterfly trapped in a glass jar. Everything depended on Karl buying her basket. She might never have the courage to go through with something like this again. She was standing right beside Karl, quivering with fear—and excitement.

Please, please, Karl.

She kept her eyes lowered. It was too much money for Karl to pay, of course. Fifteen dollars! How many horses did he have to shoe to earn that much money? How many hours of work? The same amount would mean nothing to a banker like Max.

Karl squeezed her cold, shaking hand and said, "Fifty dollars."

Max Bowen sneered. That was the only word for the awful expression on his face. "I'm afraid that's more than I care to spend for my dinner. You win, Karl."

Karl merely nodded his head. He left Alyssa standing where she was while he headed up to the stump to pay Rudy Schmidt.

"If you don't have that much with you, Karl, I'll be glad to take your note," Schmidt said.

Karl pulled a huge roll of money from his pocket. He peeled off what was clearly only a very small portion of it and handed fifty dollars to the auctioneer.

Schmidt grinned and handed Alyssa's basket to Karl. "Well, son, I guess you weren't taking any chances. I suggest you take the lady somewhere cool and enjoy that very expensive dinner."

The crowd laughed and parted to make a path for Karl, straight back to Alyssa.

Alyssa's heart leapt to her throat when she saw the look in Karl's gray eyes. Love. And respect. And leashed—barely leashed—desire.

"I've got a spot all picked out," Karl murmured. He put an arm around Alyssa's shoulders and headed toward a copse of trees downstream. They had to pass Max Bowen to get where they were going.

"I hope you get everything you paid for," Max said to their backs.

Alyssa missed a step. Her face bleached white.

The muscles in Karl's jaw jumped. He stopped and handed Alyssa the picnic basket. "Hold this."

He whirled, and in the same motion his powerful fist, the same fist that hefted a flat peen hammer hundreds of times a day, drove straight for Max Bowen's face. Karl flattened the banker as surely as he had flattened any piece of iron.

A murmurous wave of sound broke across the crowd as folks speculated on what had happened and whether any interference was needed by persons in authority. Before anyone could call for the sheriff, Karl turned back to Alyssa, looped her arm in his, took the basket from her and proceeded on his way.

Since Max Bowen was out cold, there was no one to say him nay.

"Thank you, Karl. No one's ever stood up for me like that."

"You must have had one hell of a bastard for a husband," Karl said in a harsh voice.

"I didn't—" *Not yet. She couldn't tell the truth yet. But soon.*

Alyssa didn't defend her nonexistent husband, just tightened her hold on Karl's arm, telling him with her touch that she appreciated him, that she understood his anger, that she would not deny him the right to feel what he was feeling.

Karl still wasn't calm when they reached a secluded glade. He had searched out this quiet place once he found out for sure where the picnic was being held this year. They couldn't be seen amid the trees, and there was enough underbrush that if someone did approach they would hear them soon enough to avoid being caught in a compromising situation.

Karl felt a little guilty for the cold-blooded, calculating plans he had made. But he knew he was doing the right thing. Before he left this place, he intended to seduce Alyssa Moreland.

Chapter Five

It would have been difficult to say who was more nervous, Alyssa or Karl. Karl made a show of moving twigs and stones to make a space large enough for Alyssa to spread the small quilt she had packed in the basket as a tablecloth. They settled themselves on opposite sides of the picnic basket, which Karl placed in the center of the blue-and-white patterned quilt.

"Do you mind if I take off my shoes?" Alyssa asked. That was the one item of clothing she thought Karl might have trouble removing.

"Not at all," Karl said with a grin. "So long as you don't mind if I do the same." Karl had wondered what excuse he could find to remove his boots. Alyssa had made it easy. He pulled his socks off, too, and wiggled his toes.

"Why, Karl, what big feet you have!" Alyssa teased.

He grabbed one of hers and held it in his hands. "I can see where you might think that when yours are so tiny," he countered.

Alyssa froze. She had never realized how sensitive her arch was. Or her heel. Or her toes. She didn't think

Karl was even making an effort to arouse her. Nevertheless, a spiral of desire slowly uncoiled within her.

She tugged her foot out of his hand and hid it underneath her skirt. She suddenly felt shy and unsure, like a young girl out with her beau for the first time.

The first time. Fear. Pain. Blood.

Alyssa forced the nightmare memories from her mind. The past was over and done. She had spared her daughter that horror, at least. And she was about to steal an afternoon of wonderful memories for herself to replace the awful ones.

"Are you hungry?" she asked Karl. The sooner their dinner was finished, the sooner they could move on to other things.

"I'm starving," Karl answered. The sooner he finished off the contents of that basket, the sooner he would be able to find out if the rest of Alyssa Moreland was as soft as the arch of her foot.

Neither of them tasted a bite of the food they ate. When the last of it had been consumed Karl said, "That was a good meal," and Alyssa replied, "Thank you, Karl."

Alyssa reached for the basket at the same time as Karl. She let go of it, and he moved it off onto the grass, leaving an inviting space in the middle of the quilt. Both of them stared at it for a moment, mesmerized.

Alyssa broke the awkward silence. "It's beautiful here," she said. "So quiet."

Only it wasn't quiet, really. They could hear the wind rustling in the trees. In the distance, the river made rippling sounds as it rushed over rocks. Much fainter, they could hear the laughter of children playing. It was the only reminder that they weren't alone.

Karl leaned back on his elbows and crossed his bare feet at the ankles. It was as nonchalant a pose as he could muster with his stomach doing somersaults. He wasn't sure what Alyssa's husband had done to her, but he didn't want to make the same mistake. He only wanted to love her, to make love to her. He wanted to prove to her that she need never fear him. Then, maybe she would agree to marry him. His chest felt tight. He sat up, hoping that would make it easier to breathe.

"Karl, I—"

"Alyssa, I—"

They laughed.

"What were you going to say?" Alyssa asked.

"You go first," Karl insisted.

Alyssa reached out and plucked a dandelion. She blew on it and watched as each of its feathery petals was picked up and carried away by the breeze. "I never realized all I was missing, living in the city."

"So you're not sorry you came to Fredericksburg?"

Alyssa kept her eyes lowered. "Oh, no, Karl. I'm not sorry."

Somehow they weren't sitting so far apart anymore. Karl reached out and pulled one tail of the ribbon holding Alyssa's hair. The silky mass fell across her shoulders as the ribbon came free in his hand. "I've been wanting to do that all day."

"I've been wishing you would," Alyssa admitted.

"And I've been wanting to kiss you."

"I've been wishing you would," Alyssa murmured breathlessly.

Karl tunneled all ten fingers into her hair, turned her face up and kissed her. Karl felt her lips curve into a satisfied smile beneath his.

"Is there anything else you've been wanting to do?" Alyssa asked when he released her mouth at last.

Karl's chest felt so tight it was hard to breathe. One hand slid from her hair to her throat and then down across her chest to graze the flesh she had left exposed to entice just such a caress.

Alyssa's eyes closed and her head fell back, leaving her open to Karl's touch. She felt his lips on her throat. She shivered with pleasure as he kissed his way downward. She held her breath as he approached her breasts, waiting to see if he would dare . . .

He did.

"Oh, Karl," she murmured.

"Alyssa?"

Alyssa opened her eyes and found herself caught by Karl's piercing gray eyes. He was demanding to know if she was all right, Alyssa realized. Oh, she was more than all right. She felt quite, quite wonderful. "Don't stop, Karl."

She lifted a hand and brushed aside the curl that always seemed to fall onto his forehead. Her hand quite naturally slid into his hair, and she tugged his head down toward hers. "Oh, please don't stop," she whispered.

New. It all felt brand-new. The brush of his callused fingertips across her flesh raised goose bumps as big as eggs. Well, maybe not quite that big. She shivered and laughed.

"Alyssa?"

"It feels so good, Karl. Everything feels so good!"

His mouth found hers again, and Karl felt the wonder in Alyssa's response. It was impossible, of course, but she seemed as untried as a woman who had never lain with a man.

He took his time undressing her, thanking whatever gods had arranged to have such large buttons on the bodice of her dress. At last she sat naked on the quilt before him, her beautiful female curves exposed to his adoring eyes.

When Alyssa reached out to unbutton Karl's shirt, her hands shook.

"We don't have to do this," Karl said.

"But I want to, Karl. I want to touch you." She hesitated, then said, "And I want you to touch me." She reached for his hand and placed it on her breast. "Here, Karl. Touch me here."

Karl had never been so aware of his size and strength. His hands had to be rough against her soft skin. But he wanted to please her, so he did as she asked.

She was fire. And he wanted to burn along with her. Karl stripped himself in a tenth of the time it had taken him to undress her. Until he got to his long johns. He stopped there, afraid he might embarrass her with the sight of himself in such a state of arousal.

Alyssa laughed when he told her he thought he would keep his long johns on for a little while longer. "You're so funny, Karl."

"Funny?" he demanded, even more reluctant now to rid himself of the long johns, which were all that kept him decent.

"I never expected *you* to be shy."

"I'm not," he said gruffly.

"Then what are you waiting for?" she demanded.

Now she didn't look at all like a woman who had never seen a man. She was ogling him. The part of him that was hard and getting harder. Karl tumbled her onto her back and, while she was rolling back and forth with hysterical laughter, stripped himself down to the buff.

He grabbed her ankles and pulled her legs wide apart before mantling her body with his. Suddenly the laughter ceased. He could feel her quivering beneath him.

"Make love to me, Karl."

He revered her. He adored her. He desired her.

Karl tried to be gentle. He was, at first. But soon passion overtook them both.

He never felt the crescents her nails left in his back.

She never felt the love-bruise he left on her throat.

Alyssa cried out when he thrust inside her, and he froze.

"Did I hurt you?"

"No, Karl. No."

"What's wrong?" he demanded.

"Nothing. Nothing's wrong."

Karl wasn't satisfied with her answer. He remained inside her, but renewed his efforts to arouse her, until Alyssa went wild, bucking with need beneath him. She wrapped her legs around him, clutched his hair with her hands and arched her belly into his.

This time Karl finished what he had begun. He thrust as she parried. They were equal partners, both reaching for the ecstasy that comes when two lovers join not only their bodies but their souls, as well.

A harsh, guttural sound forced its way out of Karl's throat as he climaxed, spilling his seed inside her. Alyssa clung to him as her own body spasmed along with his.

They were both breathless, sweaty and exhausted.

Karl had never felt so wonderful.

Alyssa marveled at what had just happened between them.

Suddenly she burst into tears.

"Alyssa? I *did* hurt you! Dammit, woman. You should have said something!" Karl was furious and remorseful all at the same time. He hadn't meant to hurt her. He knew he was too big. He had been too rough! But the pleasure, the pleasure had sucked him down, and he hadn't thought of anything but driving them both to completion. Now he saw the bruise on her neck and realized there were bruises on her thighs, as well. Had he put them there?

He pulled her into his embrace as gently as he could. "I'm sorry, *liebling.*"

"You didn't hurt me!" Alyssa protested. "I swear it, Karl."

"Then why are you crying?" he demanded.

"Because it was so wonderful," she wailed.

"Women!" Karl muttered. What fragile creatures they were! So unpredictable! And he loved every hair, every muscle and bone of her. This looked like the perfect opportunity to speak.

"I love you, Alyssa. Will you marry me?"

"Oh, Karl!" She burst into a fresh spate of tears, and Karl rocked her in his arms.

"Was that a yes?" he asked with a chuckle.

"Oh, Karl! I told you, I can't marry you!"

Karl pushed her away so he could see into her eyes. "What's this all about, Alyssa?"

"There's something I have to tell you, Karl."

"Your deep, dark secret?"

"Yes."

"I don't want to know it."

"But, Karl—"

He let go of her and began dragging on his long johns. "Most people out west have secrets. They come here and change their names and their occupations and lead new and different lives. You just did what a hundred thousand other people have done. You left the past behind."

By the time he was done talking, Karl was practically dressed again. Alyssa was keeping pace with him. She had worn as few underclothes as she could, and it didn't take long to put everything back on. She had more trouble with the buttons on her dress, because her hands were shaking.

Karl shoved her trembling hands out of the way and did the buttons up himself. He handed her the ribbon for her hair and turned away to pull on his boots.

"But you don't really know me," Alyssa said as she pulled her hair back into its tail and tied it with the ribbon.

"I know everything I need to know," Karl insisted.

"But I tricked you!" she confessed. "I *planned* to make love to you this afternoon."

Karl grinned. "That's funny. I had the same plan. Now will you marry me, or not?"

"I love you, Karl."

"Will you marry me?"

Alyssa knew she was going to be sorry later. Someday, somehow, someone would show up who had known her in Philadelphia, and the truth would come out. She just knew it. But someday might never come. And she would have cheated herself of a wonderful husband and Harmony of a wonderful father. Besides, why would anyone from Philadelphia ever come all the way to Fredericksburg, Texas?

"Yes, Karl, I'll marry you," she blurted.

Karl wasted no time gathering up everything. He practically dragged Alyssa back to the picnic. More time had passed than either of them realized, and their disheveled appearance left little doubt about how they had spent the afternoon. A few eyebrows came up, but they relaxed when Karl made his announcement.

"Mrs. Moreland has kindly consented to become my wife," Karl said proudly.

Right then and there, the Fredericksburg Fourth of July celebration turned into an engagement party. The men dragged Karl off to share a beer. The women dragged Alyssa off to hear the details of Karl's proposal and to plan the wedding.

"When is the happy day going to be?" Julie asked. "I want to throw a party for you!"

"Soon, I trust," Mrs. Bowen said with a sharp eye aimed at the crumpled bow in Alyssa's hair.

"Soon," Karl said, appearing from nowhere and putting his arm around Alyssa's shoulder. Harmony was sitting on his shoulder.

"Is it true, Momma? Are you going to marry Karl? Is he going to be my poppa?" Harmony clutched a handful of Karl's hair in one hand and the sleeve of his shirt in the other as she clung to her precarious perch. Her smile was radiant.

"Yes, sweetheart, it's true," Alyssa said.

"Yippee!"

In her exuberance, Harmony yanked on Karl's hair, and he yelped, as well. He extricated himself from the little girl's grasp and settled her more comfortably against his hip. Then he pulled Alyssa tight against his other hip.

Karl wasn't going to take any chances that Alyssa might change her mind. There was always the possibility that there might have been consequences from their lovemaking. He had thought to bring the means to prevent conception, but Alyssa's teasing had made him forget all about it. "The folks are waiting to hear when we'll take our vows, *liebling*."

Alyssa blushed at Karl's use of the German endearment in public. "I don't know," she said, clearly flustered by all the interested eyes and ears surrounding her.

"All right, then," Karl said. "I'll decide." His brow furrowed as though he were thinking the matter over. "Two weeks," he announced at last.

"What's the rush?" Max Bowen asked, his implication clear from the way his glance jumped from Karl to Alyssa and back again.

"Alyssa and I want to be moved into our house before school starts in the fall," Karl said in a steady voice. "We want to be a family as soon as we possibly can." The threat was there for everyone to hear: *I will not tolerate any slight to my woman.*

Max Bowen tenderly touched a fingertip to his broken nose and bowed slightly. "My congratulations to you both."

Karl smiled. "Thank you. I'm a very lucky man."

Alyssa looked up at Karl and thought how much she loved him. She was the lucky one. Everything was going to be all right. She had never asked for the fairy tale, never even hoped for it, but she was going to have her happily-ever-after ending.

Nothing in the next thirteen days led her to think any differently. The whole town seemed determined to make sure their wedding was a wonderful occasion. She designed her own wedding gown, a lovely creation in pale blue silk with a white veil that she planned to crown with a wreath of wildflowers.

Karl looked happy. Harmony was ecstatic. Alyssa was euphoric—except at night, in bed, when she experienced an uneasy sense of dread. At night, alone with her thoughts, she couldn't shake the awful feeling that disaster lay somewhere down the road.

Julie was holding a party for the ladies the night before the wedding. Hank planned to entertain Karl and some gentleman friends at the local saloon. As her wedding day approached, Alyssa realized that the dread would always be hanging over her, a cloudy specter that threatened her happiness—unless she confessed the truth to Karl. He might think he didn't want to know about her past, but she had seen from the way he flattened Max Bowen that Karl wouldn't stand for an insult to his wife. She wanted him to know the truth. There was always the chance that someone from her past might show up in Fredericksburg and reveal to Karl's friends and neighbors that he had married a whore.

Alyssa had spent the day working on her wedding gown at her shop, in between waiting on customers. She set aside her sewing and sent Harmony to play at Ellie Cooperman's boardinghouse. She steeled herself for the confrontation to come. Her heart was beating fast, and so loudly she could actually hear it pounding in her ears.

The moment of truth had come at last.

Meanwhile, Karl was just putting away his tools. He wanted to bathe before the party Hank was throwing for him. It had been a long day. He had worked hard, but he felt good. Strong. His life had purpose. He was soon to be a husband. And a father. He hoped Alyssa would want to have at least one or two more children. She would be a wonderful mother—already was a wonderful mother, he corrected himself.

"Hey! You there!" a man shouted as he approached the open door of Karl's shop. "My horse threw a shoe. I was told you could fix it."

"Not today," Karl said.

"Dammit to hell! I've got to get down to Kerrville tonight. I've got a big business deal that's going to fall through if I'm not there. Are you sure you couldn't help me out? I'd be willing to pay extra for the service."

The man flashed a roll of money. Karl started to shake his head, then remembered that he had donated fifty dollars for school desks two weeks ago. Starting tomorrow, he had another two mouths to feed. "All right," he said, unbuttoning his shirt and reaching for his leather apron. "Bring your horse in here."

Karl watched the man handle his horse and wasn't impressed. The greenhorn sawed at the animal's mouth to get him moving and jerked on the reins when a tug would have done the job. The short man was dressed in a garish plaid ditto suit, a matching set of jacket and trousers no Westerner would be caught dead in. His brown hair was slicked down with some kind of oil, and he wore a mustache that was actually waxed into two stiff tips. It was clear the fellow enjoyed his supper, because his belly hung over the tops of his pants, which were held up by a pair of bright red suspenders.

Karl kept his opinions to himself and reminded himself why he needed the greenhorn's money. He tied the horse away from the heat of the forge, but close enough that he could get back and forth to the fire easily. Karl spoke to the horse in a low, steady tone, to reassure the animal. He saw at a glance that the right rear hoof was missing a shoe. He started at the hock and ran his hand down the horse's cannon, to give the animal warning that he planned to pick up his hoof.

Karl breathed an inward sigh of relief when the horse anticipated him and released the weight on his leg. He knew ways to shoe a kicking horse, or one who didn't like his feet handled, but it was a considerably more complicated operation. Karl picked up the hoof and rested it on his thigh as he checked the wall, the sole, the frog and the hoof itself for any aberration or injury. He breathed another sigh of relief. There was no repair work to be done. He slowly lowered the hoof, making sure the horse was steady on his feet before he let go.

"You can go have a drink at the saloon, if you like," Karl said. "I won't be long."

"In that case, I'll just wait," the man said.

Karl shrugged. "Whatever suits you."

Jack had already left for the day, so Karl worked the bellows himself and put another scoopful of wet coal on the fire. He heated the horseshoe at the toe first, and when it was hot, bent the heels together a little. He cooled the iron and punched the holes for the nails.

He had shod enough horses that he could have done it in his sleep. He wasn't even thinking about what he was doing, just worked by rote, doing what he had done many, many times. He only half noticed the greenhorn, who stood in the wide open doorway to the dark interior, his back against the wall, his patent-leather-shod feet crossed at the ankle, his straw derby tipped forward to keep the late afternoon sun from his eyes.

Karl trimmed the hoof slightly, then fitted the shoe and began tacking in the nails.

"That's a pretty little girl over here," the stranger said.

"Mmm . . ." Karl replied, pretty much ignoring the man.

"Looks like a kid I used to know in Philadelphia."

The word *Philadelphia* caught Karl's attention, because he knew it had been Alyssa's home. But he still wasn't really listening. He had only one more nail to go before he finished.

"Yep. That blond-headed girl sure does remind me of another little girl, daughter of a prostitute I knew back in Philadelphia. The mother sold the daughter to me when she was twelve. Promised she was a virgin." He grinned obscenely, showing pink gums. "She was. Let's see, what was her name?" He snapped his fingers. "Alyssa."

The greenhorn had all Karl's attention now. A dangerous amount of Karl's attention, if only he had realized it. Through a red haze, Karl hammered in the last nail. He dropped the hammer where he was, afraid of what he might do if he kept it in his hand.

The greenhorn went on staring at the little girl playing hopscotch in front of the boardinghouse across the street. "That Alyssa, she grew up in the brothel where her mother worked. Upper-class house, you know. Catered to the nobs. The ladies dressed real fine. But they were whores, all right!" He laughed. It was a raucous sound, like the bray of an ass.

"That Alyssa, I had her and her best friend together one night." He smacked his lips. "Ah, Marjorie Rose, you were some sweet thing!"

The greenhorn tipped his derby back and mopped his face with his handkerchief. His eyes once again sought out the girl playing hopscotch. "As I recall, that Alyssa, she had a little girl herself. Blond, just like her mother, with big blue eyes. Can't remember the girl's name. I would have had her, too, when the time came. Only—can you believe it?—the mother, she up and ran away and took the little girl with her!"

The skin was stretched tight across Karl's face. He felt a murderous rage, a dangerous killing urge he hadn't known since the war. His quiet voice could have cut steel. "Mister, if you want to live to see the sunset, I suggest you take your horse and get the hell out of town."

"How much do I owe you?"

"Nothing. Just get out of here."

"Say, you some kind of religious nut or something? Just because I had a little fun with some nestlecocking lift-skirt—"

The man didn't have a chance to say anything more. Karl's fist found his mouth and broke his front teeth.

"Sonofabitch!" the man screamed, spitting teeth and blood. "You sonofabitch! You're crazy!"

"Get out of Fredericksburg. Don't come back."

"Don't hit me again. I'm leaving!" Blood dripped down the man's face onto his plaid suit. He grabbed the reins and yanked his horse outside. He had to try twice to get his foot into the stirrup. "Goddamned crazy bastard!" he muttered.

Karl stepped forward and slapped the horse on the rump. The animal took off at a run, with the greenhorn hanging on for dear life.

"Karl! Karl!" Harmony ran toward him, her arms held wide, expecting him to pick her up. But Karl turned and stalked back toward his shop. Over his shoulder he growled, "I've got work to do. Leave me alone."

Harmony stared after him, wondering what had happened to make Karl so angry.

As Alyssa stared out the front window of the boardinghouse, her heart leapt to her throat. The bloodied man barreling lickety-split away from Karl's shop had looked alarmingly like someone she knew— a client named Ralph Croaty. Alyssa felt sick to her stomach. She watched with acid in her throat as Karl turned away from Harmony. When Alyssa saw that her daughter planned to go after Karl, she ran out and grabbed Harmony by the hand.

"I told you not to play in the street," she scolded in a shrill voice.

"Why is everybody so mad?" Harmony demanded.

"I'm not mad," Alyssa snapped, covering the fear rising within her. "But I didn't bring you all the way to Texas so you could get yourself run over by a wagon in the street."

"You are too mad," Harmony retorted. "And Karl is mad. Everybody's mad."

Alyssa took a deep breath and let it out. *Karl was angry.* Then, possibly the lone rider had been Ralph Croaty after all. Had Ralph somehow realized she was here and told Karl the truth about her? Alyssa felt dizzy. The ground seemed to drop out from under her, and she had the sensation of falling into a deep, dark hole, an endless pit that had no bottom.

Harmony's lips pouted. "Are you done being mad?"

Alyssa dropped to her knees and hugged her daughter close. "I love you, sweetheart. I could never stay mad at you. Go on upstairs now, and wash up for supper."

Harmony's lips slid into a charming smile. "All right. But would you talk to Karl? I don't like it when he's mad."

"All right, sweetheart. I'll talk to Karl. Go on now."

Alyssa stood and walked to the front door of the boardinghouse. She stared at the building across the street.

Almost. She had almost beaten the odds. She could imagine what Ralph Croaty would have told Karl. Ralph had been a regular customer at the brothel where she worked. He had asked for her—for "the Virgin"—often. "For sentimental reasons," he had always said. Because he had been the first.

Fear. Pain. Blood.

Alyssa shook her head, trying to rid herself of that awful memory. She thought, instead, of Karl. Of his tender touch, of his passionate need and her own marvelous, miraculous response to his loving. That was what the union of two people was supposed to be. Not the travesty she had endured at Ralph Croaty's pudgy, grasping hands.

She had to talk to Karl. She hoped against hope that she was wrong. That there was some other reason that the man who looked so much like Ralph Croaty had fled Karl's shop. But Ralph Croaty or not, it was past time to tell Karl the truth. She straightened her shoulders, lifted her chin and stepped down off the porch of the boardinghouse into the dusty street, heading for Karl's shop.

When she got there, Karl was gone.

Chapter Six

Karl wandered along the edge of the river, skipping stones across the rushing water, watching them sink, like his dreams of the future. He felt raw, stunned by the stranger's revelations. The clues had been there all along, but he had been too blinded by love to see them.

"Momma and Marjorie Rose were up late working at night so they slept in every morning."

"I never had a father."

"When you know the truth, you'll despise me."

No wonder she had known exactly how to arouse him when he kissed her. It was her job! What a fool he had been! He had suspected Alyssa's deep, dark secret was the fact that she hadn't been married to Harmony's father. It had never crossed his mind that she must have lain with so many men that she had no idea who the man was!

Alyssa Moreland was a tremendous actress, he would give her that. He had believed her when she acted like the sex was so special with him. The tears were a nice touch. He had wept inside for every glistening crystal that rolled down her flawless cheek.

Karl raised his face to the sky, opened his mouth and let the pain out in the hoarse, ululating cry of a wounded beast.

Oh, God! Her life had been too terrible even to contemplate! Alyssa, *his Alyssa*, sold to that awful man. And by her own mother! What kind of woman sold her own daughter into sexual slavery?

How had he missed seeing the ravages of the past in the eyes of the woman he loved? Somehow, Alyssa Moreland had fooled him into thinking she was a lady. But she was not. Oh, God! She was not!

By the next morning, Alyssa was frantic. No one had seen Karl for hours. He hadn't shown up for supper at the boardinghouse the previous evening. Nor had he shown up for the party being held in his honor. He seemed to have disappeared from the face of the earth.

"He's just having wedding jitters," Ellie Cooperman assured her as she and Julie helped dress Alyssa for the wedding ceremony. They were in Alyssa's bedroom at the boardinghouse. Jack was playing with Harmony downstairs and had promised his mother that he wouldn't let the little girl get her white dress dirty.

"Don't worry," Mrs. Cooperman said. "Karl will get over it and be waiting for you at the church. Why, I remember when George and I..."

Alyssa continued listening, but she no longer heard. *Karl knew.*

It was the only explanation that made sense. The stranger must have been Ralph Croaty, and Ralph must have told Karl what she was. Obviously, Karl could no longer bear to look at her. He would certainly never marry her.

She couldn't really blame him. She was a whore. No, that wasn't precisely true. She had been a whore.

It's all in the past, Karl. I would never, never touch another man. Please believe me, Karl. I love you. I want only you.

Her plea for forgiveness, for understanding, remained unspoken. Karl wasn't there to hear it.

"I have to see Karl!" Alyssa said suddenly.

"Why, darling, you can't see the groom before the wedding. It's bad luck!" Mrs. Cooperman protested.

"But I have to see him!"

Julie put a hand on Alyssa's shoulder to restrain her. "Ellie's right, Alyssa. Do you want to take the chance of jinxing your marriage? Why, your whole future could be in the balance!"

Alyssa sank onto the four-poster bed. "I have to talk to Karl."

"There'll be plenty of time to talk to him after the wedding," Mrs. Cooperman said with a smile and a wink.

If Alyssa had only known, Karl was having no better luck seeing her. He was stopped at the boardinghouse door by Hank.

"Where have you been? We've been looking everywhere for you. You're not even dressed yet! You'd better get moving. I've got all your things at my house. You can shave there."

"I have to see Alyssa first."

Hank shook his head. "Nope. I'm not going to let you do that. It's bad luck. Julie and I, we owe a lot to Alyssa. And I'm not going to let you start off with a run of bad luck because I didn't do my duty and keep you two separated before the wedding."

"I'm going to see Alyssa, Hank. Even if I have to go through you to do it."

Hank called to the two men lounging in the downstairs parlor of the boardinghouse. "Herr Schneider, Mr. Detmer, come here, please. I need some help."

Hank turned back to Karl with a grin on his face. "Now, you can probably get through the three of us if you try, Karl. But why bother? You'd end up at the altar with at least a black eye. Your bride won't like that, Karl. She won't like it at all. I tell you, it'll be better if you wait to talk to Alyssa until *after* the ceremony."

Karl's lips flattened. "Maybe you're right. Maybe it would be better to talk to her afterward."

Hank eyed Karl suspiciously for a moment, unsure whether he was really conceding the issue or planned to wait and take the three of them when they were off guard. When Karl whirled on his heel and began stalking toward Hank's house, Hank relaxed and did a hop-skip to catch up to him.

"Where were you, Karl?" Hank asked. "You missed your own party."

"I was thinking," Karl said in a tone that discouraged further questioning.

"You know, I experienced something very similar myself. Couldn't decide at the last minute whether I wanted to go through with it or not. Believe me, Karl, it'll be all right. Since I married Julie, I've been the happiest man on earth."

They had reached Hank's front door. Karl paused and turned, his features hard. "Even though she got pregnant and trapped you into marriage?"

The blow from the smaller man came without warning. Karl's reflexes were quick, though, and the knuckles that were meant to break his nose grazed his cheek instead.

"Get this straight, Karl," Hank said, his fists balled at his sides. "Julie wasn't the one with bad judgment, it was me. I was older. I knew better. My wife was a virgin when I took her, and if you ever suggest differently, I'll flatten you. I want an apology, and I want it now!"

Karl pressed the heels of his hands into the sunken sockets of his eyes. He hadn't slept, and he was heartsore and heartbroken. He had let his demons force him into behaving in a way he would have thought himself incapable of behaving twenty-four hours earlier. "I'm sorry, Hank. There was no call for what I said. I don't know what's wrong with me."

Hank slapped Karl on the shoulder. "Prewedding jitters. Happens to the best of us. Come on inside and get cleaned up. You'll feel better."

Karl followed Hank inside, feeling sick at heart for the cruel things he had said. But it rode him raw to think that he could never look at another stranger without wondering if the man had been one of Alyssa's customers.

Karl and Alyssa were scheduled to be married in the Fredericksburg Lutheran Church at eleven o'clock. Karl had chosen the time because he knew the sun would create a gorgeous rainbow of color through the stained glass windows at just that hour. As he stood at the pulpit, sweating beneath the unaccustomed suit and tie, he wished he had chosen to wed at night, when it was cooler.

The church pews were full, but even with the windows open along both walls there was only a slight breeze blowing through. In July the wind acted more like a bellows for heat than anything else.

Karl slipped a finger into his collar, which seemed to be getting smaller by the minute.

"Relax, Karl," Hank whispered from his side. "I've seen the bride, and I can assure you she's absolutely beautiful."

Ellie Cooperman was the church organist, and she beamed a reassuring smile at Karl as she took her place and began playing a familiar German march. Karl realized as soon as he saw Harmony at the far end of the church aisle that the music was intended for her.

The small child he had come to love along with her mother was dressed in a full-length white cotton dress. It had a ruffle at the hem and short, capped sleeves. Her hair had been left down, tied at the crown with a white grosgrain ribbon. She held a tiny basket in her hand, and she was scattering rose petals on the floor as she proceeded down the aisle. Harmony was concentrating so hard on what she was doing that her teeth held the tip of her tongue captive at one corner of her mouth.

Alyssa watched from the vestibule of the church as Harmony made her slow, steady way down the aisle. She had already been told that Karl was standing at the altar waiting for her. Yet she hadn't felt relieved at the news. She wished she knew where he had been the previous night, what second thoughts had sent him off alone.

There was still time to call the whole thing off.

But what if Julie and Mrs. Cooperman were right? What if Karl had just experienced a normal case of prewedding nerves? Was she willing to throw away her one chance for happiness?

Julie rearranged Alyssa's veil for the hundredth time. "You're so beautiful!" she whispered. "I wish I'd thought to wear a crown of wildflowers at my wedding. You look so pure and innocent. Like this is the first time you've ever walked down the aisle, and the perfect man is waiting there for you, loving you," Julie said.

Alyssa's throat constricted. "Please don't say any more, Julie."

Suddenly the wedding march began.

"That's our cue," Julie whispered. "I'll go first. You follow."

Alyssa watched Hank's face as his obviously pregnant wife began marching down the aisle. His eyes were soft, liquid with love. Her glance skipped to the big man standing beside Hank. There was nothing in Karl's face to tell her what he was thinking, what he was feeling. His features looked carved in stone.

If she wanted a chance at a future with Karl, she had to grasp her courage in both hands and walk down that aisle. Alyssa took a wooden step. Another. The music helped, and she kept moving to the cadence of the march. She glanced up once from beneath lowered lids and saw that Karl was watching her. She felt his gaze, intent, insistent.

Look at me. Look at me. Face me with the truth.

She knew that was her imagination talking. She had offered Karl the truth once, and he had turned it down.

At last she found herself standing in front of the altar with Karl beside her. He seemed like a stranger in that stiff white collar. The elegant, pin-striped suit made his shoulders seem at least another six inches broader.

They stood side by side before the preacher, but no part of them was touching. Alyssa felt the heat radiating from Karl—and a tension so dangerous that she feared any moment it might erupt into violence.

Karl answered the preacher's incantations in measured tones. His voice, at least, showed none of the leashed savagery she perceived in the man who was shortly to become her husband.

Alyssa tried looking into Karl's eyes, but he remained facing forward, so she could see no more than a stony profile. She only vaguely heard the words of the ceremony, until the preacher said, "If there be any man here who knows any reason why these two should not be joined together, let him speak now, or forever hold his peace."

There was an awesome silence behind them.

Karl said nothing. And Alyssa remained silent.

"If there is no—"

"Wait!" Alyssa cried. "Wait!" She turned to Karl and said, "I have to talk to you."

"Can't it wait?" Karl asked.

"No. It can't wait. We have to talk now."

The soft murmurs behind them became an excited buzzing, like bees, and then even more noisome, like mosquitoes.

"Please, Karl."

Karl clasped her hand in his and marched back down the entire length of the church, dragging her behind him. They left the church, and he didn't stop until they had reached a live oak far enough from the open windows that those inside couldn't hear them.

"All right, Alyssa. I'm ready to hear whatever it is you have to say."

For a moment, Alyssa considered leaving the veil down to cover her eyes. It wasn't going to be easy facing Karl with the truth. But he deserved a chance to look her in the eye when he told her he never wanted to see her again.

Slowly, carefully, she lifted the net away from her face. She looked up at Karl, her hands clasped so tight that her knuckles were white, her body braced for the pain to come. "I was never married," she said.

"I suspected that."

"And you still wanted to marry me?"

Karl shrugged. It felt like he was lifting stone. "Sometimes people make mistakes."

"I . . . That isn't the worst of it." Alyssa swallowed and forced herself to look Karl in the eye. "When I left Philadelphia, I was living in a brothel. I—I worked there. I was a whore. A prostitute."

Her eyes slid closed to shut out the agony she saw on Karl's face. In a dead voice she recited all the awful things she had heard herself called over the years. "I was . . . a harlot, a jade, a lewd woman, a—"

"Don't."

"—merry legs, a swallow-cock, a whore-bitch—"

"Please. Don't."

"—A trollop, a—" Alyssa's throat had swollen closed so she could no longer speak. She waited for Karl to say something.

"I know everything, Alyssa," he said at last. "I met a man from Philadelphia yesterday, and he told me everything. About your mother. About Marjorie Rose. About you."

Alyssa opened her eyes and stared at Karl.

There were tears in his eyes. One had slid down his blunt cheekbone.

She swallowed again, over a lump so big it hurt. "You knew I was a whore?" Alyssa's brow furrowed. "But you came to the church. You were going to marry me."

"Yes, I was. I am."

Alyssa bit her lip. Tears stung her eyes, and her chin quivered. "Karl." The word came out as a croak. She swallowed painfully and tried again. "Karl. Haven't you heard a word I said? I made my living—"

"I heard you, *liebling.*"

Alyssa's heart was pounding so hard it threatened to burst from her chest. "Karl?"

He opened his arms wide, and she threw herself into them. She clasped her arms around his neck, and he held her so tight she thought her ribs might crack. "I love you, Karl. I love you! Can you ever forgive me? Can you ever forget what went before and—"

Abruptly he shoved her away from him. His eyes were fierce as he stared down at her. She was sure he had no idea how tightly he was holding her arms. She would have bruises there tomorrow.

"I don't want to forget," Karl said.

When he saw the stark fear that rose in her eyes, he amended, "I don't need to forget. Do you realize what a courageous woman you are? You managed to rescue your daughter from a fate any other woman— your mother included—would have accepted as inevitable. But you didn't, Alyssa."

He shook her once to make sure she was listening, that she heard what he was saying. "You left your past behind in Philadelphia. You brought your spirit, the real you, here to Texas. That courageous woman is someone I would be proud to call my wife and be damned glad to have as the mother of my children!"

His face sobered as he drew her back into his arms. She could feel him trembling.

"I won't pretend I wasn't furious when I learned the truth. And hurt. And I won't deny there are things I learned about your life that will cause me nightmares for a long time to come."

"I'm sorry—"

Karl pressed his fingertips to Alyssa's lips. "No apologies. I haven't exactly lived like a saint. Nobody's perfect, Alyssa. In fact," he admitted with a grimace, "if you'd seen me last night, ranting and raving like a wounded bull, you might not have wanted to marry me."

"What if I hadn't stopped the ceremony, Karl?"

"I would have married you and never said a word about what I knew. But I'm glad you loved me enough to tell me the truth."

"Is that what I did?"

Karl nodded. He brushed a stray curl from her temple. "I love you, Alyssa. I think I have from the first moment I saw you. Now that I know who you *really* are, I love you even more.''

"Karl," Alyssa whispered. "What I was—"

"What you *are* is a woman who brought her daughter out of hell, who's left the past behind and made a new life for herself in the West, like so many others before her. You're a woman to be respected and admired—and desired.''

Karl followed thought with deed, sweeping Alyssa into his arms and kissing her with all the need he felt, sealing their union there and then, before God and nature and the wealth of witnesses peering out the church windows.

Karl might have gone on kissing her all day, except he felt a tug on his pant leg.

"Are you two getting married or not?" Harmony demanded. "I still get to have some cake, don't I?"

Alyssa exchanged a look with Karl, and they burst out laughing.

"We're getting married," Karl said. He scooped Harmony up in his arms, took Alyssa's hand and stalked back into the church. He set the little girl down beside Jack Cooperman in the front pew.

Max Bowen said just loud enough for Karl to hear, "Having second thoughts?"

Karl bent down so he was nose to broken nose with the banker. "None. And if you don't want your nose rearranged again, I suggest you guard your tongue around my wife in the future.''

Karl didn't wait to see the effect of his words on the banker. He just turned on his heel and joined Alyssa at the altar.

"Are you both certain now that you want to go through with this?" the preacher asked.

"Absolutely," Karl said.

"I do," Alyssa said.

"It isn't time yet for the I-do's," the preacher admonished. "I'll let you know when we get there."

Karl and Alyssa held hands through the ceremony. They exchanged rings. And secret looks.

"You may kiss the bride," the preacher announced at last.

They were married. Husband and wife. Karl took his time drawing Alyssa into his arms. No one in the congregation was left in doubt about whether Karl Eberhardt loved Alyssa Moreland. Mr. and Mrs. Eberhardt's first kiss revealed a tenderness that had the ladies weeping into their handkerchiefs and a passion that had the men running a nervous finger around their collars.

As Mr. and Mrs. Eberhardt stood in the vestibule greeting each of their friends and neighbors as they filed from the church, it was plain as a cow's face that Karl cherished Alyssa and she adored him. Whatever misgivings had sent them fleeing from the church had obviously been settled to their satisfaction.

"Have a wonderful life," Julie whispered in Alyssa's ear.

"I will," Alyssa assured her friend with a shy glance at Karl.

"You're a lucky man," Hank said, pumping Karl's hand.

"I certainly am," Karl agreed with a grin.

Harmony tugged on Alyssa's sleeve. "Momma, can I have some cake now?"

"Yes, sweetheart. You can have as much cake as you can eat."

"And can I have some ice cream on top?"

"As soon as it's ready," Alyssa assured her.

"Whoopee!" Harmony grabbed Karl's hand and began tugging him toward the buggy that would take them to their new home—the white house with the red shutters—where the reception was being held. "Come on, Poppa, let's go."

"Poppa. I like the sound of that." When they arrived, Karl allowed Harmony to lead him into the house, all the while keeping his arm around Alyssa's waist. He leaned over and whispered in his wife's ear, "I realize it's a little late to be asking this, but how do you feel about having more children?"

"You could talk me into another one. Or two."

"I had a little larger number in mind."

Alyssa arched a brow. "How large?"

Karl grinned. "I think this is a subject better discussed in bed."

Karl realized too late that the problem with having the wedding reception at home was that you couldn't go to bed until the last guest left. Finally Ellie Cooperman took pity on the newlywed couple and began suggesting that perhaps folks ought to leave the two of them alone to enjoy the married state. That elicited a round of hoorahs and friendly ribaldry, but it was well past midnight before the last guest departed.

"I'll be by to help you clean this up tomorrow," Mrs. Cooperman promised.

"Not too early," Alyssa whispered with a blush.

Mrs. Cooperman laughed. "Not too early."

Karl walked up behind Alyssa and slipped his arms around her. They stood on the front porch looking up at a sky full of stars and a hazy quarter moon.

"There's a shooting star," Alyssa said, pointing it out to Karl.

"Make a wish," Karl urged. When the star had burned itself out Karl asked, "Did you make a wish?"

Alyssa nodded and leaned her head back against Karl's shoulder. "It's a simple wish. Do you want to hear it?"

"Don't tell me, or it won't come true."

Alyssa turned in Karl's embrace and reached up to hold his face between her palms. "Oh, Karl, you foolish, adorable, wonderful man. It already has."

Karl lifted his wife into his arms and carried her inside. *Four children,* he decided. *I'll talk her into four. And they'll all have Alyssa's blue eyes.*

Five, Alyssa thought. *We'll have five more children, and they'll all have dark hair like Karl.*

The bedroom door closed with a soft click.

Six, Harmony thought. *I'll ask for three brothers and three sisters.* She clutched her rag doll close. Surely that wasn't too much to ask for. Harmony closed her eyes and made a wish. She snuggled down, confident that everything would turn out fine. She couldn't help remembering her mother's whispered words when she had tucked her into bed.

"Go to sleep, sweetheart. Dream wonderful dreams. Wish for the stars and the moon, if that's what you want. Because sometimes, when you least expect it, wishes really do come true."

* * * * *

A Note from Joan Johnston

I grew up in a family with seven children—six girls and one boy. My father was in the air force, and we moved around quite often. I've lived almost everywhere from North Africa to North Dakota and experienced a multitude of little adventures.

I've lived through a sirocco in Morocco and a Texas dust storm in El Paso, where tumbleweeds as big as cars rolled down the streets. I learned how to ride on an Arabian stallion not far from Casablanca and saw my first rodeo at Cheyenne's Frontier Days. I've survived a typhoon in the Philippines and a hurricane in Miami. I've had confrontations with cobras, scorpions and tarantulas. I've seen the desert, the plains, the mountains, the hill country and the oceans.

Moving frequently has allowed me the opportunity to make mistakes, and grow from them by leaving them behind and moving on. Perhaps that's why I've identified so well with the Americans who moved west seeking something newer and better in the nineteenth century. I've always been something of a nomad myself, amazed and amused as I move from place to place by how much things are different and how much they are the same. "One Simple Wish" is about a woman who leaves her dark past behind for a new life in the West. It's an experience I can relate to and understand. The past haunts Alyssa until a very special man helps her realize that the person she is inside is a very loveable and beloved human being. With his help, Alyssa learns, as I have learned, that the one thing you can never escape is yourself.

I hope as you travel through life you'll find what you're searching for—love, happiness and the greener pastures that always seem to be just on the other side of the hill.

Happy Trails,

Joan Johnston